Once Again

Ejaz Khan

Layout and Cover: Nadia Khan

From series Fantasy, Adventure, Fairytale

Font Cover: Excalibur SF

Font Interior:: Garamond
ISBN- 978-91-86173-04-3

Dedicated to my loved ones who fill me with joy.

iv

1

The king couldn't hide his joy from the court. He commanded three day festivities to celebrate the birth of another son. His admiration for his beloved queen knew no bounds. She was the centre of his attention, affection, and esteem for giving him three beautiful and healthy male children. Each member of his court was coming forward, bowing, and then cordially extending congratulations and best wishes on the occasion. Each of them was a master of flattery, knowing how to praise the king without appearing insincere. The king was aware of his courtiers' false and exaggerated way of behaving, but he never tried to stop them from doing so. Somehow this kind of behaviour was not only a tradition, but powerful, superior, and regal.

The king looked at his favourite minister and signed for him to come near. He too was playing two roles simultaneously, one towards the other members of the court, and one towards his master. "I feel extremely happy and want to show this by doing some great deed. Tell me, what shall I do?" The king asked for a counsel. "Let me think, milord. There are many ways for you to express your joy. You can abolish all the taxes for this year as the weather has been terrible, causing much damage to crops. The farmers would be very happy and shall always remember you and the little prince and the occasion of his birth." The clever minister spoke, looking discreetly at the king for his reaction. There were many hidden smiles as everybody knew that the minister was the biggest landowner in that country and the suggestion was to benefit him the most.

"No," said the king after some pondering. "It's not that I don't find the proposal interesting, but our treasury right now is not in a position to bear this burden." The king was blunt and realistic, remembering the years of drought when the royal treasuries had gone all empty, putting the entire country in unrest, despair, and chaos. This rejection disappointed the minister, but he carried on fearlessly, giving creative propositions that were advantageous to him. The wise king found flaws and discrepancies in all of the minister's suggestions. All the court members were now finding it more and more difficult to hide their amused faces, seeing the minister fail in every attempt to flatter the king. Unfortunately, the minister was so corrupt that he was incapable of suggesting something that would benefit the people.

The king looked at old Silos, who was asking permission to speak. The king had always admired this unmotivated character, who just sat and listened most of the time. Everyone knew that the old man's silence was not due to his lack of confidence or knowledge, but his indifference to the outer things. Why he had agreed to join the court in the very first place, was a riddle that everyone had failed to solve. Silos's readiness to talk had surprised the king, who signed him to speak. "I believe you should celebrate the birth of your son by by freeing the prisoners that are decaying in the jails of our country. Show mercy to those who have not done any harm to you, to others, or to the country." Silos spoke without flattery. There was no taint of disrespect or accusations in his flat voice, which was honest and unafraid. The whole court fell silent, marveling at the unwise person who had dared to raise the displeasure of the king. Many of the courtiers liked Silos but feared that his privileges with the king due to his old age were to come to an end; many were even pitied him. The king sat looking bewildered at the courageous fool. No one could tell what the king was thinking. The only person in the court who took the opportunity to react to that preposterous suggestion was the minister standing next to the king. Sakuri didn't want to let the occasion go, when he could prove his allegiance and loyalty to the crown and the king. "How dare you speak so disrespectfully to his royal highness?" Sakuri said in a contemptuous tone. "Surely your age is playing with your feeble mind. You should not advise the king, you senile old man. I would recommend his excellence to forgive you your thoughtless babble." Sakuri looked at the king, expecting some rewarding confirmation, but felt betrayed when the king laughed at last, making it clear to everyone that he had listened to the words of Silos. "Let all those prisoners free from all jails and dungeons who have not committed crimes against the king of the country. Let freedom be their gift from me, so they may be prudent, and not indulge in crimes again," declared the king. Everyone was jubilant, if not for the freeing of some innocent prisoners, then because the king was not outraged by the suggestion of humble Silos.

Three days of celebrations were attended by the vast majority of the population of that country, who were jubilant and thankful to the king for his generosity to relieve certain old debts that they had from years of drought and for waiving few minor taxes. These festivities were attracting people from far and near. One of those rare visitors to that the country was an old man who had been living in seclusion and destitution for innumerable years. Seeing him walk into the town, made everyone wonder, what he was doing there. People from all walks of life were curious and perplexed, fearing some unusual happening. They all knew that the hermit had been invited to the court many times, but had always declined the humble request of the king. The old loner went straight to the court of the king, where he was received with reverence and surprise. All minds were full of questions, but no one dared utter a word as it could put them in disgrace in the eyes of the ruler. With a respectful silence, they awaited the old man to proceed to the nearness of the king, who got raised from his high seat, to extend respect.

"Sit down. I'll not take much of your time," the hermit spoke. "I'm here to congratulate you on the birth of your third son. You have earned this right by pleasing the gods, who are ready to grant any of your genuine wishes," said the holy man. The king was still silent and overwhelmed by the presence of his immaculate guest, and struggled to think of a legitimate wish that he could present. "Make up your mind, I don't have eternity to wait for you," the old man said looking straight in the eyes of the king.

"I wish for all my children to become kings," said the king at last. The words of his strange wish echoed in his mind. "May it be so!" The holy man said and turned to go back, leaving the king and his court in utter shock and disbelief. How could a wise person like him wish such an unattainable thing? How could they all be kings without snatching the throne from each other? How could that silly goal be achieved without the striving of one brother against the other? Of course, the gods could grant the wish of the king, but surely he had given them a good laugh. The king was horrified by the possibility that his sons would lead short lives in competition for the throne. He wished to run after the holy man in order to withdraw his wish but realised that it was beyond his dignity, and the precious moment of the decision had already passed out of his reach.

Many were the people who were congratulating him on such wonderful tidings of having all the princes succeeding to the throne, but only the heart of the king knew the anguish he was suffering. He concluded all of the festivities and retired to his quarters to ponder the possible implications of his thoughtless desire that he had just disclosed to the holy man. His aides tried to console him, but soon realised that the anguish of the king was deeply genuine. There were different suggestions as to what to do, some advising him to seek the hermit and withdraw the wish, and others asking him to separate and place all the princes far away from each other, thereby diminishing the possibility of their fighting and claiming the throne one after another. There were even others, who taking advantage of king's anxiety suggested that the best thing to do in the given circumstances was to seek an expansion of the kingdom. "Perhaps the gods want you to conquer and expand your territory so that you can divide it into three parts when the princes come of age." The king didn't like the suggestion as he was a peaceful person with no ambitions to fight with their neighbours for some piece of land or some other bounty.

The king tried to search for the hermit but failed to find him. It seemed as if the holy man had disappeared from his country, moving away to some other isolated place. He was worried and that affected his taking care of the affairs of the state. His advisers tried to convince him that by worrying about some far-fetched problem, he could invite some larger problem to himself and to the country. They pleaded with him to actively take control over things and not to trust Sakuri as blindly as he was doing at the moment. None dared to be more explicit than merely hinting that Sakuri was not to be trusted fully. The king understood their distrust of the chief minister, but remained convinced that those fears were unwarranted. He knew that Sakuri was a greedy and power hungry man, but he was equally aware that such a person was not capable of any revolt. "Your highness, we are skeptical as to what that man is capable of or not. What really worries us is his loyalty; he doesn't seem to have any virtue," One of the king's friends said. "Sometimes I wonder about his loyalty, as well. The only thing he cares about is his own interests, but he has gotten this high position, not because of his own efforts, but due to the untiring services and sacrifices his forefathers have extended to my royal ancestors and those tie my hands. I don't want to do everyone an injustice and challenge his loyalty without any proof." The king was reasonable like he always had been. Just by looking at the worried faces of his attendants, he could feel their intense anxiety and wanted to release them from that. "I know the man and have a close eye on him," was his confident answer to all insinuations. "We are relieved. The king knows best." His advisers unanimously agreed, allowing the king to continue without their continual criticism.

The fears of the loyal advisers and counsellors came true when the news was struck that the neighbouring king had attacked their country. Their immediate suspicion fell on the chief minister, who had been found involved in some mysterious activities, but no one accused him of anything because it lacked the solid proof required for a full conviction. The king was furious and ordered an immediate response to the unexpected threat from the south. He decided to lead his army himself. He was a brave king, trained in the skills of warfare, and was confident that his army was not only capable of defending his country, but was even able to break any larger army. What he didn't know was the fact that most of his soldiers were unavailable. Many of them had been sent to their villages on leave. The soldiers who were still at hand suffered from some mysterious ailment that kept them from heeding the call for emergency. The wise ones around the king understood at once that the situation was dire and that the war had already been lost. They tried to make their king grasp that he and the country had become the victims of some hideous conspiracy and that they needed to seek some safe haven because they could not defend themselves.

"This kingdom was transferred to me after the death of my father, who had gotten it after his father. I can't run away from my legacy, without leaving it for my own children," was his confident answer. "Wisdom is not to stand firm for your principles and perish, but to adjust according to the presented circumstances." Silos tried to reason with him, but the king was unmoved. He had made his mind and was determined to give a severe fight, even to the last minute of his life. "All right, if that's the way you want to act, we'll be with you till the end and shall die protecting you," said his loyal friends. "But seeing the hopeless situation, we can sense that we are doomed. Show some prudence and at least send your wife and children away from these desperate circumstances." They were genuinely concerned about the security of their princes, who were hardly more than a few years of age.

The king reluctantly agreed to do as he was advised to do, seeing the hopelessness of the situation. But the queen refused to leave with her children. "It breaks my heart to separate from my children, especially from the youngest one, who is not even one year old," she lamented. "But no one can make me separate from my husband, milord. I've sworn to live, love and die with him," said the queen. They all understood that she too had made her choice, and there was nothing anybody could do other than to take all three young princes and place them in safety. There was no sign of Sakuri and the enemy could come any time, leaving but a very brief time for them to act and react. The soldiers available were not many, so it was deemed wise not to take the unnecessary risks. The enemy and his spies could have been lurking just around the corner, and thus the whole matter of shifting the princes became more problematic than it was first thought.

They finally agreed that there was no other safer choice than to split and separate the princes from each other and by doing so they could increase the probability of their survival. The anguish of the royal couple was heartbreaking as they couldn't tell whether any of them was to see the light of day or were ever to meet again. The queen looked the other way when her sweet little children were being separated from their royal ornaments and other emblems, so they wouldn't be recognized if they were to be stopped and checked on the way.

The king and queen took leave of their children, who looked

strange and unreal in their ordinary clothes. The both elder princes looked astonished and kept asking questions about, why were they to travel like that? Why couldn't they stay with their parents? Why were they concealing from others that they were the princes? No one had the heart to tell them the truth and looked the other way in despair and anxiety. All three princes had to flee to safety without the protection of guards, not because there weren't any, but because it certainly would attract the attention of the enemy. The only prince who was spared the trauma of separation and uncertainty was the youngest of them all, who kept smiling, making indistinct sounds or staring at others with his large innocent eyes.

After the princes had left the royal palace, a sudden tumult arose at the eastern entrance of the building, followed by the same clamour rising from the northern side. The enemy had arrived; they didn't have to search them out as the king had been eager to do. The palace was protected from the other two directions as it bordered a steep ditch from one side and a riverbank at the other. The few soldiers that the king had at his royal command fought fiercely and courageously, but they were hopelessly outnumbered. The end was not as dramatic as the king and his friends had hoped, but each one of them took his final stand and made their enemies admire their courage and fighting spirit in awe. Loyal friends heroically gave their precious lives defending their king and did that with a smile on their faces. The king was now alone, but capable of inflicting harm to the enemy. He was ready to die protecting his country, throne and his nobility. He was all surrounded by the enemy soldiers and had not the slightest chance of prolonging that hopeless struggle even few more minutes. He saw the worthy end approaching with an incredible speed and was ready to kiss the life good-bye. The swords were rising above his head, to befall any minute, when he heard someone shouting, ordering the soldiers to halt.

They froze in their actions and remained so, waiting for

further orders.

The king was exhausted, weak, and drenched in his own blood; he didn't want to prolong his misery any more. He awaited death and wished that his children were safe. He had no way of knowing what had happened to them. The king impatiently waited for the inevitable. He tried to raise his sword and attack his enemies, but was prevented by some strong soldiers who held him tight in their arms. He could still see the fear in their eyes; they were still scared of his might and fervour. He saw the king of a neighbouring country approach him with a broad cunning smile on his bearded face. He signed his soldiers to let him loose, they did as they were commanded, snatching away first the sword of the king.

"It has been some time, Tylon," said the king of the invading army. "You see, if you don't want to invade others, that doesn't necessarily mean that you shall not be attacked." He was reminding about some offer he had given to king Tylon a long time ago. "You know my principles, I couldn't agree to your despicable designs of oppressing innocent people by subjecting them to the evils of war." The king defended himself. "You and your stupidity see where it has led you!"

The conqueror laughed, scoffing the miserable state of the defeated king.

"To let you die is the greatest gift that I ever could give to you," taunted the conqueror with a vile laughter. "But I don't want you to die. You are such a great being, so I want you to live a very long life. What would you suggest my dear friend?" The invading king asked someone turning his gaze in one direction. King Tylon looked and saw the despicable face of the traitor Sakuri, who was shamelessly smiling at his miserable state. "I believe you should grant him very many miserable years, full of pain, tortured by the bitter memories."

Sakuri was despicable.

"That's a good idea!" The invader said liking the idea of prolonging Tylon's dejected state of being. The imprisoned king's face could not hide his despair; his solemnity stopped him from pleading for a quick death.

"Take his majesty to his new royal quarters," said the conqueror with a contemptuous laugh. He went on laughing as he found the situation, so entertaining, so very comic. Suddenly someone bowed before him and whispered into his ear.

"Wait!" he shouted to the soldiers, who were almost dragging king Tylon, away from the scene. "I agree with one of my counsellors that we have not been fair to our prisoner. He has the equal right to give us the counsel and advice," he said with a strange smile on his face.

"Tell me, how I should reward the man, without whose help I wouldn't be sitting over here?" he said holding the hand of Sakuri, which looked at Tylon as if mocking him.

"It's not for me to advise you, what to do or not to do, with those like him." Tylon answered without even looking at the traitor.

"I am disappointed to hear your answer, but then you are just a bitter man, defeated and humiliated." Said Razila, the conqueror and looked intensively at Sakuri, making him feel uneasy. "You and your forefathers have given him and his family before him, all they own today, but I have promised to bestow on him even more. I'll make him an exemplary figure, so that existing generation and those to come shall remember him." Razila said with a broad smile on his face. Tylon saw the beaming face of Sakuri and felt enraged but powerless. He was going with the soldiers, with bowed head, dragging him forward, and resisting the fall as he was getting weaker and weaker due to exhaustion and loss of blood. He wished he were dead instead of living with the humiliation of a defeat at the hands of a far inferior neighbouring king. But he was certain that his death was at the other end of the long tunnel of shame, suffering and physical and mental hells, which he had to live and endure for a long period of time.

The queen had just remembered that in the stress of the moment, she had sent her suckling child away, without feeding him in time. That remembrance made her terribly upset and anguished. How could she forget? She was angry with herself, but there was no time for any remorse; she had to run after the person, who was carrying her youngest child. She took a swift horse and followed the tracks of the rider, who had left just few minutes ago. She rode as fast as she could but came no closer to the man she was looking for. Her mind was working faster than her horse; she was waking up from one nightmare only to confront another. The meaning of the prevailing situation and all its horrors was dawning on her. She had lost all her children and was about to lose her royal status. What was to happen to her and her dear husband was something she refused to think of. She was a born optimist, but the situation was completely hopeless.

She kept riding and riding without coming in contact with any being that even resembled the man that she sought. Perhaps she had been following the wrong track, she thought with anguish. She decided to stop her pursue and turn back. There was no point in pressing ahead as it was impossible that any rider could have moved with her speed. She was torn by her worry for children, especially the youngest, and her anxiety for her husband, who needed her support in the hours of great distress. The awareness that she was fulfilling neither of her duties was tormenting her. With tears in her beautiful grey eyes, she was heading home - or at least the place that used to be her home - the royal palace. She tried hard to push the torturing thoughts away, but there was a strong possibility that there wouldn't be a home or even a husband waiting for her when she returned. She was coming nearer to the town when she almost froze with fear, hit by a sudden thought that she was wearing her royal clothes and could be easily recognised and arrested if the enemy had already captured her throne and palace and were looking for her and her children. She needed to change her royal dress, which was quite a difficult task in the given circumstances. She could seek help from many people and change into some ordinary clothes but wondered if she could trust anyone after the betrayal of Sakuri. She decided not to rush into some other possible trap and think more profoundly about the matter. There wasn't much time left either if she was to avoid being detected.

Finding everyday clothes proved to be a lesser problem, as she passed through some small village, where she saw some clothes hanging to get dry. She stole the clothes that were in reach and escaped before anyone caught sight of her. Disposing of her royal robes was on the other hand, a serious problem. She couldn't leave them there for fear of being discovered by some local peasant or the enemy soldiers. Suddenly an idea flashed in her mind, and she rode towards the side of the river, where she searched for some proper place to hide her expensive apparel. Far from the riverbank she saw some thick bushes, a perfect place to bury her clothes. Digging the soft sand was less difficult than she had anticipated. Even that simple job had taken its toll on her; she was not used to any kind of physical work and was pounding heavily. That reminded and indicated the tough times ahead if she was to survive. She was not ready for the sudden change of fortune that was to drag her down from the absolute heights of existence to humble living. She was unaware what degradation and downward mobility was to be like. The only thing she kept with her was her jewellery, which she hid in her shabby clothes, hoping that she might have some use of them one day.

When queen Haliba re-entered the town, its deserted streets and roaming enemy soldiers, she found no difficulty in recognising that all was already lost. She had left the horse and was on foot, covering her pretty face in the large cloak, she had stolen at the nearby village. She appeared to be some poor lady heading for home, unaware of the recent events. However, remaining outside could turn hazardous, as it exposed her to the lurking dangers. She needed a sanctuary where she could stay till the storm had passed and collect her strength, reassess the situation, and above all gather some information as to what had happened to her husband. The only person she could think of trusting was her youngest child's nanny, who lived somewhere nearby. Haliba had never visited her servant and didn't know how to find her, but decided to look for her in any case. By entering into the old city, she was breaking the ancient tradition of her royal family, which considered the whole older part like a pest. The small alleys and narrow streets were filthy and filled with an unbearable stench that made Haliba feel sick. She wondered how people could live in such conditions without going deeper in the causes that had been responsible for such terrible conditions. The deeper she went into the city the lesser the stench became. She was happy to notice that welcoming change, and she could breathe again. There were very few people on the streets, from which she could ask the whereabouts of Roxy as she used to call her, replacing the long difficult name she otherwise had. Roxy had suggested the shortened name, recognizing the queen's difficulty in pronouncing her real name.

There were many who failed to recognise the given name and went their way without being able to help her. Everyone seemed to be scared and in a great hurry to reach the security of their homes, very much aware that it was less of a protection and more of a sense of security.

"Are you out of your mind? Do you think that this is the time to search for some Roxy, or whatever you just called her?" an elderly lady shouted at her, pitying her naivety and stupidity. "I can see that you are young and beautiful, a valuable commodity in these terrible times. Please forget about this person you're looking for and hide yourself as far away as it is possible from those beasts that have just entered and conquered our country," the elderly woman pleaded before fleeing in the opposite direction. After a few steps, she turned to see if Haliba had heeded her sincere advice or was still there, challenging her fate. Seeing her still lingering there made her furious. The lady came back and screamed at her. "What's the matter with you? Are you too slow to perceive, or you want to be dragged into some tragic situation." Haliba was pale, unable to react or say anything. She was so nervous that even the insulting words of the elderly woman were unable to upset her. Surely the lady would have moved her way, considering her a hopeless case, but suddenly she peeped into her sad, disturbed eyes and saw rivers of anxiety and terror flowing in them. She could not remain angry or untouched. Her long life experience of life was telling her that the person before her very eyes was not some imbecile, or unthinking simpleton, but someone in serious trouble. "Tell me honestly, do you have any place to go to, except that whatever name you mentioned a few minutes ago?" the elderly lady asked getting softer and concerned. Haliba didn't speak but looked down and nodded negatively. The lady was quick to react to her expected gesture and almost dragged her to one direction. She wasted no further time in questioning her distressed queen, whom she had never even seen before. The highest priority of the elderly woman was to take her to the safety of her home if it was really going to be a safe place or not was to be seen, as yet.

2

The discovery that the queen and all the princes had succeeded in fleeing before the attack outraged Razila. He was surprised and wondered where the royal family could be hiding. His initial guess of some hidden place within the palace had proved to be wrong, and required new efforts to find the fugitive family in and around the city. Razila was furious for having lost much of his precious time in the early hours of his occupying the palace. The task to find the queen and princes had become tedious, if not impossible. There were no prisoner officials to press and torture in order to get the necessary information regarding the royal family. No one was more nervy and shattered than Sakuri, who feared for his life, knowing that the successors of the king were at large, and at some time could become a threat that he planned to avoid. All gates of the city were locked, stopping all entries or exits from the city. Sakuri blamed the soldiers loyal to him who had abandoned the gate once their task to open the gates for invading army had been accomplished. They in their turn, would point to the commanders of the newly arrived troops, who were to take charge of such matters from the time they entered the city. These commanders were quick to underline that there first and foremost duty was to secure the palace and the city, and to crush the remaining resistance, than to guard some unimportant gates. The finger of blame kept pointing in one direction or the other, making the impatient conqueror angrier. He agreed to Sakuri and put all the blame on the soldiers loyal to him and ordered their immediate arrest.

Searching teams were sent in all directions, to find the whereabouts of the royal family. People were threatened to be executed if they were found guilty of hiding the members of the royal family or even if they withheld some information regarding their whereabouts. These soldiers knew that it was not an easy task to perform but were confident that they would arrest those fugitives sooner or later. It was almost sure that the escapees did not have enough time to leave the city. Sakuri believed that it was going to be a simple matter to find and arrest the queen and her children. If they really were there in the city, he knew all the possible places and people who could provide that kind of sanctuary. A poisonous smile curled his lips. Sakuri was conscious that most of the king's men had perished fighting the invaders, but the royal family could be hiding in some of the places owned by those friends of the former king. He personally accompanied the soldiers, looking for the queen and her children, but there were no signs of them to be found. He was perplexed at that strange occurrence, "Look, the woman is carrying a little child, a very difficult thing to hide. Go and question people about suckling children, about feeding mothers and soon you shall have her on the hook" Razila made them spread far and near as he wanted his war trophy. His victory would lose all its glitter and glamour if he failed to capture the offspring of his enemy. "A victory is never complete as long as any of the doors leading to future revenge remains open," said Razila in irritation, withholding that those were the words that he had been taught to remember, when he was doing anything wrong.

Their search remained fruitless. No stone was left unturned, and no house in the country remained untouched, but the queen and her princes were never found, giving rise to the suspicion that they had escaped from the country and were no longer in the reach of their enemy. One could see the unhappy face of Razila, who was so very deprived of the initial sweetness of his astounding victory. "It's entirely your fault." He said angrily to Sakuri, reminding him of his promise to take care of all the details. "Your revered highness, you know that I am blameless as I didn't know that the Tylon was capable of taking any quick decision, regarding the safety of his family, and especially in the wake of his pride and dignity. I was sure that neither he nor his family could run away." Sakuri was explaining his innocence in a humble, scared manner He was avoiding to look at his new master, as it made him more nervous to see the rage in his eyes. He tried to please and soothe him by saying. "The queen is not a threat, she is too delicate to offer any resistance, especially when she is not even present in this country. The princes are too young. It would take years before they grow up into manhood, and what does a mighty king like you have to fear from some young, inexperienced and resourceless bunch of princes."

"At least there is some comfort that they had no chance to take any of the valuables with them." Razila said, getting some of his confidence back. "And the princes, without sufficient riches, are a useless heap of nothing." Sakuri could see that his new master was getting his old high spirit back, and that made him feel relieved. He wanted to remind him of his promises, but found it not an appropriate time to do so. There wasn't any hurry, and he could wait patiently for his reward.

What Sakuri didn't know was that the new king was not like the former one, who could take time in accomplishing his tasks, who needed cool, clear thinking before pressing ahead, if for no other reason than to eliminate the chances of error and mistakes. Razila was not only quick tempered and difficult to deal with, but too hasty in all affairs of the state. He was quick to respond to any given situation; even it meant a permanent regret. His wrath could come like an unprovoked thunderbolt, hitting whoever came his way. But that was just one side of that unpredictable ruler. The other side was darker, meaner, and more inclined to evil than he had first realised. At times, he would take sadistic pleasure in displaying an artful mastery of his inborn cruelty. This other side of the new master was to be revealed to Sakuri very soon. He was summoned to the court, a happening he had been waiting for since the arrival of the new king. Anticipating that this was the time when Razila was to reward his great deed before all the dignitaries and people of high esteem. He awaited a far greater reward than he was previously promised. He wore his best clothes with golden embroideries, put on the shoes made of golden threads and smiled in the mirror, admiring his own splendour and magnificence. Without a doubt, he was the richest person in the entire country. Even the new king couldn't match him in riches he thought to himself and smiled, perfectly knowing that it was the secret he couldn't boast about publicly.

Sakuri entered the court, smiling and nodding arrogantly to all those, his eyes met. He was there to receive the admiration of the king along with his unfailing reward. He couldn't hide his happiness. He came forward and bowed before the new king, praying for his long, healthy life. Everyone in the court could see the arrogant man forcing himself to his knees.

Razila smiled without granting him permission to rise. Sakuri felt the sting of embarrassment; he was remaining in prostration far too long. The new king wanted to exercise his authority and grandeur and was less attentive to the humiliation of Sakuri.

"You may rise," Razila said, looking pleased and amused with his own game. Everyone could see that Sakuri's confidence had vanished from his proud face, which had been replaced by astonishment. He dared not look directly at his master to assess what he meant by that humiliating treatment, but nothing stopped him from feeling that something was wrong. Roselle signed him to come to his side, which he did without knowing what awaited him. "By now you all must be aware of this man whose untiring efforts and loyalty has made our victory so painless, easy, and without much cost," said the new king and all attendants gave him a standing ovation. The pride, though a little dampened, was returning to Sakuri. "We have promised him riches, and that we are granting him today. He had asked for half of that land which lies in this country, and that means he would be the sole owner of the three fourths of the entire land available in this country as the esteemed noble already owns the other half," there were some exclamations from the audience, which died down, when the king raised his hand, demanding pin drop silence.

"The man will be given what he asked for, and we promised so graciously." Razila's words were a confirmation of all Sakuri had been hoping for and expecting from the new king. "We have decided to raise the reward even further, giving him all the available land, which lies in the country." Razila's words frustrated the courtiers, who looked fearfully at their king. Disbelief was apparent on their sullen faces. Even Sakuri looked puzzled and shocked as if he had not been expecting such incredible news. The king was deliberately silent, encouraging the whispers and argumentations taking place between his courtiers. He looked both amused and content. "By showing our kind gesture, we want to give a message that we reward our friends very generously."

Sakuri bowed down again and thanked the king for his great openhandedness and promised an everlasting obedience and loyalty. King Razila laughed and laughed, never stopping at his oath of allegiance. "No, no," he cried in his laughter. "Spare me your fidelity; I don't want any of that. Is there anyone in the court who needs this man's loyalty?" wiping his tears from the laughter, the king asked. They all soon understood what the king was implying and joined their king in nervous laughter, but they still were unable to grasp the wits of making Sakuri monstrously rich by granting him all the land of that vast country.

When the king calmed down, some of his advisers asked a private audience, but Razila was not in any mood to listen to anyone's advice. He had made an irrevocable decision to grant Sakuri the reward that he so earnestly deserved. His advisers looked pale and disheartened, knowing that there was little left for them to do. Sakuri was once again puffed up with pride and majesty, weaving the dreams of his further glory and splendour. Razila signed an old man who came forward and handed some documents to him. He carelessly glanced at them, put his royal seal on it and gave them to Sakuri with a spiteful smile. "Here is your reward and the fulfillment of our promise. Go and enjoy the fruits of your treachery." Razila's words were causing him great discomfort, and he was unable to determine whether he had reason to be joyous or a cause to dread. He kept standing there, having these serious thoughts, when he heard the king commanding his retreat and retirement. "I believe we are finished here," the king said. "I'd be more than happy to serve my king in any fashion," Sakuri said fearfully, not daring to speak openly about the promise Razila had earlier made to appoint him as his viceroy. "We believe you have accomplished all that you could; now it's the time for you to enjoy the fruits of your labour. We'll let you know about our other decisions regarding your well-being." Sakuri trembled at Razila's unjustified spite. The way he left the court was painful because no one even acknowledged his great service to their leader, nor did anybody congratulate him on the acquisition of the entire land of the country, a unique happening in itself. Despite the fact that it was the greatest day of his life, he felt miserable, defeated, and anguished. Apparently, there wasn't anything to be worried about; nevertheless, he did fear that some catastrophe was to befall him, not in some remote future, but rather very soon. If the weird feeling, he felt in his bone marrow was a genuine warning lamp, indicating some big trouble, or was just his unwarranted fears, it was too early to say. What he knew for sure was his mistrust for Razila. The more he thought about the man, the more certain he was that dealing with him was a mistake. But it was late for any regrets; what was done was done and nothing could avert the prevailing, uncertain situation. Sakuri was disappointed to learn that the king had no intentions of making him a high official as he had earlier promised, but on the other hand, he was really surprised that the promise to give him the land was doubled. There was no one to share his anxiety or great achievement; even his family was not at his side because he had sent them away as a precaution. He was a cunning person who knew that the game of treachery was not only dangerous for him but for the entire family, regardless of their innocence or guilt.

As soon as Sakuri had left the court, the advisers begged for an emergency meeting. One could see that they didn't want to discuss the sensitive subject in an open court. Seeing their worried faces, the king smiled and adjourned the court. All the attendants emptied the courtroom, leaving his closest friends and advisers.

"What makes you all so nervous?" Razila inquired in a light mood.

"We are all worried and confused, your highness. We don't trust the man; you just have made the most powerful and richest one in the entire country," one of his advisers said in anguish.

"What had you expected me to do instead? Doesn't the man deserve the reward we have promised him?" Razila asked politely. A silence fell as no one had ever seen the king caring anything about promises or words of honour. No one dared to ask when he had started caring the sanctity of those virtues that he always considered foolish vanities. The king was perfectly aware of their confusion, but kept enjoying the moment instead of clarifying himself.

"So, you agree that I have done the right thing?" the king asked dramatically.

"Yes, your majesty, we can never doubt your wisdom. You are without any doubt the kindest person, but…" started one adviser in a stammering voice.

"But what?" asked the king softly, making everyone around him look at each other in utter surprise. They had not expected a soft response from the person of his temperament.

"We know that your decision to reward the person in question is absolutely right, but it shall make him a bigger monster than he is today. We believe that such deceitful people should not be trusted with unlimited resources because they can be harmful in the long run." One after the other, they all were pleading their case, issuing the warnings about dire consequences if the man was not restricted immediately. The king listened patiently, sympathetically, and with concern apparent on his face.

"How absolutely right you are. A traitor is never to be rewarded and trusted simply because he has consumed his reliability. But I must say that I'm a bit disappointed in you. What do you take me for? Am I a fool, who'd grant a poisonous serpent like Sakuri, the entire country I have just conquered?" Razila asked, taunting them. Gone were the shadows of concern and worries from the faces of the king's advisers, who were more convinced than ever that their king was not just a man full of temperament but a person who was fully capable of developing and expanding conspiracies on his own. This confirmation was uplifting and soothing; relieving them from some of the tension and worries they had to go through on his behalf. They all looked content.

Queen Haliba was a remarkable lady; the way she was dealing with her sorrow, pain, and distress were beyond comprehension. To fall from her high position in itself was such traumatic happening, not many people would have survived, but her tragedy was manifold. In the twinkling of an eye, she had been deprived of her royalty, her loving husband, and separated from three wonderful children. She was unaware as to, what happened to the king and her princes, and there was no way to find out either. There were no survivors of the catastrophe who could tell her the story of her loved ones. There wasn't anyone with whom she could confide her true identity and ask more direct questions. The queen was suffering the pain, disgrace, and suffering in silence, without saying a word of complaint. She dearly hoped that her princes had survived the day of distress, and were in safety, but about her husband, the king, she was most worried and feared that he was no more in the world. She was a strong and resilient person, who could survive any disaster, regardless of their might and intensity. She was always taken as a soft person without a will of her own; a person enjoying a life in the shadows. Most probably her kind and loving heart and her wish to please others had contributed to that reputation. She never tried to clear the misunderstanding, for simply one reason: she herself had started believing the wrong notion of others.

Haliba had found refuge in the humble home of Aloha, an elderly lady, who despite age still was active and earned her living by working in a bakery. She lived there with her young daughter, who despite her young age had already become a widow twice. Aloha was a kind-hearted person, who had accepted Haliba as a guest and never pressed her for any details. Just by looking at Haliba, she could tell that the person was going through some crushing and painful processes, where her interference and pressures to reveal more about her would just make the things worse. She had decided to wait for the time her guest was to take the matter up. When she came home, Aloha would talk about everything including her work, the people she worked with, the customers she occasionally came in contact with, and the other happenings of the town. Her work was to bake bread, but sometimes she replaced the persons working at the counter, which allowed opportunity for her to meet people other than those that she worked with. She would bring some bread from the work and felt happy that she had that benefit from her kind employer. "You see, that explains the secret of our survival," Aloha would say with a grin.

Aloha's daughter Davreen was not so talkative and left Haliba in peace. She was always busy doing something, cleaning the house, making food, sewing the clothes, and many other activities kept her attention away from the depression of her tragic life. Her big, sad eyes betrayed her otherwise calm face. She was a pleasant woman, who never questioned the wisdom of her mother's decision to bring a stranger into their home, but she never strived to be extra kind to the newcomer, either. Davreen was indifferent to her as she had been for all other things in her life. In that short time Haliba had been living there, she never saw Davreen smile. Life had been not very kind to her, but that could not be the reason of her permanent unhappiness. Despite the worries and sorrows of her own, Haliba couldn't help but to feel sorry for the young woman who had the whole life before her, but there wasn't anything she could do other than to feel for her. She was left alone, so it was wise to do the same. One day, when Aloha came home she appeared to be very excited. She had just received some interesting news, and she wanted to share with her daughter. She was talking and talking, about irrelevant things as she used to do, without coming to the point.

"Mother, say it now. I'm getting sleepy." Davreen said, showing her irritation.

"You are such a bore!" Aloha was not happy to be interrupted in her lengthy description of the events and happenings.

"The great news I heard today is that our king is not dead as we all have been presuming!" Aloha said excitedly. Haliba was stunned by that unexpected news, which filled her with a renewed hope and happiness.

"And who gave you that information?" Davreen was not sharing her mother's enthusiasm.

"As I told you earlier, the prisoners in the jails have increased that much that t was practically impossible to provide them with bread from the prison bakery." The soldiers coming to buy bread talk to us sometimes. The one I had a chance to talk with today was outspoken, giving much of the information that we ordinary people would never hear otherwise." Aloha seemed to be proud of her access to some sensitive information. "He told that our old king is in the prison, having a miserable time, but what made me most happy was that, the good lady, our queen and all our princes have succeeded in getting out of hand from the new ruler." Aloha was eagerly telling.

"What it has to do with us and our own wretched lives, mother?" One could feel from her bitter tone that she cared less about the subject.

"Don't you have any interest in the affairs of the country? Don't you have any national pride?" Aloha was harsh on her.

"What pride mother? We are the commoners, who are in this world to suffer, regardless of who comes and goes." Davreen was quick to remind her mother of the truth.

"The poverty of the subjects is not the fault of the rulers," Aloha defended.

"Then whose fault is it?" Davreen was not in a mood to give

up either.

Haliba was dying to know more details about her husband and tried to ask questions about that, but the both women were busy arguing about the causes of their miserable lives and paid no attention to her and her questions.

Haliba gave up her attempts to seek a halt in their lively discussion, anchoring in the stormy waters of her own mind. The news, that Tylon was still alive was encouraging, giving her a reason to be hopeful and strive for continued living, though her heart bled from the knowledge that her husband was suffering at the hands of his adversaries. She was ready to pay any price - even her freedom - to come in contact with him. Sadly she realised that even if she did yield herself to the enemy, it was not to profit her as the new king would not reunite her with her husband. Aloha was glad to notice that her silent guest was changing slowly, taking interest in her conversation, in the gossip, she had heard and narrated further. She noticed that even the shine of her saddened eyes had returned, and she felt happy for that change. She wouldn't know what, and who had been responsible for such an occurrence, but she was happy that at last her guest came out of that state of being, which was holding her back from normal life and expressing the feelings she lived. "I can see that you like people and take an interest in the happenings of people around you. I don't know what bothers you, but you seem to be an integrated person. I'm sure you'll come out of your present state very soon." Aloha was praising her. Haliba looked at the old lady in surprise. Something was not fitting, something was wrong, she thought. The lady was not giving the impression of some uneducated, unthinking and unintelligent woman, but on the contrary she seemed to be a wise and sensitive person, who had the insight of a queen. But how could she ask such a delicate question from her, without disclosing her own intellectual superiority and status. She decided not to ask any questions as it was like opening the door to Aloha's questions, which she had been patiently refraining herself from.

"You should get out and meet people." Aloha advised.

"Please, don't throw me out. I'm not ready for that yet." Haliba begged her, getting scared.

"I'm not throwing you out in the street, though I believe I should." Aloha said with a smile.

"All I suggest is that you should get out of this stinking place and meet other people. I'm sure it'll do you good."

"I promise I will, just give me a little more time. I am so very thankful for the roof you have so kindly provided me, and for the food I consume. I'll always remember these compassionate gestures of yours. I wish I could repay your kindness in the same manner, if not more." Haliba was talking ceaselessly; she wanted to speak of her mind as she was genuinely touched by the gentleness and nobility of the lady. Aloha was listening to her with open mouth, not believing her ears. It was rather the first time; her guest had opened her mouth, to that extent. Until then, Aloha had heard only a few brief words from Haliba, which were not enough to determine, what type of person she was.

"Who are you?" Aloha asked in a surprised tone.

"I'm just an ordinary person," Haliba said trying to be credible.

"When I met you, I could say without a doubt that you were in deep trouble. With the same surety, I can say that you are not speaking the truth. But, I opened the doors of my home without asking a single question. In the same manner, I'll not press you to say something you don't want to." Aloha said calmly.

"Please forgive me for being not open to you. My situation doesn't allow me to speak the truth, but I swear that I haven't ever lied to you." Haliba was apologetic.

"Don't feel pressed. Take your time." Aloha said softly, caressing her.

"The difficulties in life are just tests and trials, to make you strong and to grow. So don't break up" She continued comforting Haliba while she was crying bitterly, sobbing and shaking violently in her whole body. The elderly lady was soothing her unknown, mysterious guest, which was finally dealing with her pain and sorrow, whatever that might have been due to.

Haliba had been thinking seriously and finally came to the conclusion that there was no wrong in confiding her secret to Aloha, who listened with awe and disbelief. "My revered lady, your highness, forgive me if I have been rude to you." Aloha was shaky, perplexed, and extremely humble.

"You have been, like a mother to me, and you know very well I'm not a queen any more. You don't have to address me with those titles; they remind me of my degraded state," Haliba said in a weak voice.

"I don't know why, but my heart has been telling me that there was something special about you, but not in my wildest dreams I could have imagined that the queen of my beloved country was staying at my humble quarters." Aloha was getting sentimental.

"O Aloha, You can never imagine the satisfaction and gratitude I felt the day you gave me a sanctuary, when I was dying of anxiety, standing there, without any friend, any belonging or any roof over my head." Haliba was describing her freighting condition that day, when the danger of getting caught was the biggest, she confessed that the offer from her was nothing less than a miracle; she had been hoping and praying for.

"Tell me, if you are still in the country, then where are the princes?" Aloha asked, remembering about her children.

"I really don't know, what became of them. We had given them to some trustworthy and loyal friends to protect and to put them in safety."

"At least they are together, poor souls." Aloha said with a sigh of relief.

"No, they aren't." Haliba sighed with grief.

"What!" Aloha looked shocked. "How could you separate them from each other?"

"I ask the same question myself every day." The disposed queen looked to the ground before continuing. "Sometimes fate is cruel and forces you to take actions that you once considered impossible. We had no other choice but to separate them to increase their chances of survival."

Aloha and Haliba sat talking for a long time. Aloha was relaxing and getting normal as she had been all the time before her disclosure of the secret.

"What do you intend to do now? Aloha asked.

"I want to be on the side of my husband, who needs me now more than ever," Haliba answered.

"What! Are you out of your mind?" Aloha exclaimed, but

then remembering that she talked to the queen, even though deposed, she apologised for her disrespectful outburst.

"I don't mind as I told you, I'm no longer queen. I understand the reason of your surprise, but what choices do I have? I'm already a mother without the nearness and love of my children. My husband, my king, is in captivity and is suffering. The least I can wish for in the current situation is to soothe him, by getting a chance to be near to him," Haliba explained.

"How could you even think of exposing yourself to such dangers? You know that Sakuri is still out there, looking for you," Aloha warned her.

"I am aware that the risks are high, but I am helpless. I have to follow my heart, rather than my head," Haliba said.

"Mother, are you aware that it is late, and you have to be early at work?" Davreen said with some irritation as it was the third time she had been reminding her about that particular matter. Perhaps she was curious to know what the strange woman had to impart, which had made her mother forget about her sleep, which was otherwise the most sacred thing.

"She is right. I believe you should try to get some sleep. We can talk some other day."

"For us ordinary people, there has been never enough time for anything." Aloha sighed, though she wasn't complaining. "And anyway, who can sleep after receiving such shocking revelations."

Before leaving the room, Aloha promised to Haliba that she was not to disclose her secret to anyone, not even to Davreen, not because Haliba didn't trust her, but for the simple reason that it would have caused Davreen anguish and unease. They all knew that there was a bounty on her, as well as a life threatening penalty was promised to all, which harboured her or her children

The whole country was now in the iron grip of the new king, who had given orders that no one was to be harmed unnecessarily, not because he was kind or cared about the opinion of the people. He wanted to give his new subjects a sense of calm and security, especially when they were not showing any resistance to his rule. He also wanted to concentrate on his preparations for further conquests. He hoped to raise an army from the citizens of the country that he had just conquered. Razila was pleased to find out that the treasury was full to the brink. But his closest advisors continuously reminded him about the need of dealing with the urgent problem of Sakuri. "Don't worry about the man; I'll be dealing with him soon," Razila would answer with a grin. He didn't want to act rashly, as was his custom. He was of the opinion that the delicate matter needed a clever solution, so as not to scare the future collaborators. He wanted to give the impression that he was generous in rewarding those who helped him achieve his goals. He had already succeeded in giving this impression. Everywhere people talked about the decree that had made Sakuri the absolute owner of the land in the country. There were many, which talked about his treachery with despise, but there were others who saw his act not so repulsing, especially considering its reward. "Look, the man gets in a single day, what his ancestors had collected in hundred years." Someone explained the whole miraculous phenomenon in few words. "May the curse of the gods inflict him forever for what he has done!"

Sakuri did not know that his time was quickly running out. After his initial fears did not come true, he had started getting relaxed as he could see no visible signs that would confirm his suspicions. He had accepted a non-political role on the condition that he was to be left in peace. With all the resources in possession, he could afford to wait for some golden opportunity, which was to knock his door sooner or later. He had wished rather sooner than later, but realised that it was not feasible. So confident had he gotten about the situation that he had sent the word, asking his family to return home. So he was astonished to receive a visit by king's messenger, he had been summoned to the royal court. Perhaps his luck was turning again, and the king had finally decided to redeem his promise and was to announce his appointment as his deputy, Sakuri thought. He tried to search for other possibilities but didn't come to any. He was relaxed and confident as he entered the court and was brought to the king.

"Your services we have already acknowledged, the reason to summon you today is a serious problem we are facing." Razila was looking serious. "You have proven your loyalty to us, and we deem you a valuable asset." The king was playing with the words and going nowhere. Perhaps it was deliberate, and he wanted Sakuri to be in confusion and thereby sweat.

"We can see that you are not very popular with your other countrymen, and that's the cause of our worry. Until now, our guards have been protecting your home and your properties, but it is neither our duty, nor is it feasible to provide you this protection indefinitely." Razila stopped to enjoy the sweaty face of Sakuri, who was a cunning person, capable to read between the lines. He was getting the message loud and clear, the king was withdrawing his protection and support, a thing without which he couldn't stay in that place even for a single day.

"Your highness!" Sakuri tried to plead his case. "I am perfectly conscious about the favours you have been bestowing on me, and am very thankful to your majesty's all kindnesses. But without your protection I'll not be able to live here. I need it to live and serve you," Sakuri said without hoping much as he could see that the king had made up his mind.

"Yes, we are aware of that fact, but our soldiers and guards are needed at other important tasks than to be sitting idle at your place. We believe that you have many enemies, but we also find these enemies not a major threat, as they lack the resources to stand against your economic power. We suggest that you employ some guards of your own, as from tomorrow, no royal guard would be attending you." Razila concluded, without giving him any further chance to beg, to plead, or to make some scene.

Sakuri left the court in a disgraced, defeated manner, with very few options at hand. He knew perfectly well that he had been outmanoeuvred and outwitted by the king and his cunning advisers. There was no way he could buy that required protection from his own people, who hated him and wouldn't even listen to his proposals, and to get it from outside the country was not permitted by law. What was he to do? Sakuri panicked. He was angry with himself, for having brought himself to that impossible, messy situation. He was completely aware what the king was driving at, but there wasn't anything he could do. All those loyal to him were already rotting in the jails for the crimes of negligence, and helping the enemy flee from the country. "Even if I had those loyal soldiers; the rascal would have found some other way to stop me." Sakuri thought getting anguished. His worst fears had come true, but the clever tactic had been beyond his imagination. There was no way he could stay in the country, without Razila's protection, which he was not to get. That fact left, but one option: he had to move away from that dangerous place, which in itself was not a simple task. The law of the country was quite complicated when it came to the property. He had been the driving force behind that lawmaking, which forbade the acquisition of any property by foreigners or non-residents. If he were to leave the country to seek personal security for himself and his family, it would disqualify him from the right to own anything in the country. After three months of his absence, all properties and lands were to fall in the possessions of the state or to whomever the king selected. The same heartless, blind law, which had helped him acquire most of his lands, was to be used in depriving him of them. Sakuri was sure that even if he was to stay, it would end up in his elimination, if not by the hands of some bitter countryman, then in the long evil arms of the king, who had nothing to fear from the consequences. Despite his desperation, he couldn't help admiring the ingenious scheme plotted against him. There was not much time for him to think. He had to decide and act as quickly as possible if he was to remain alive. He had to choose between his possessions or his precious life. He decided to choose the latter, and commanded his servants to prepare for his escape. The guards were still outside and didn't know what he had in mind. He gave the strictest orders that no one was to utter a single word about his intended departure. He was always generous to his servants and knew he could trust them with his mission. He behaved in his usual manner in order not to raise suspicion, waiting for the evening, when he used to invite the guards to supper. That day he had prepared a special meal for them, which they ate with great appetites and without knowing that it contained some elements, which were to put them in a deep sleep. Most of his servants had already left the town as he didn't want to travel in a large company, which would have alerted the guards at the gates. When Sakuri approached the gate in a disguised manner, he was casually looked at by the soldiers, which were busy talking to each other.

"Only a fool chooses to wait until dusk for his travelling!" said one soldier and the other looked at him curiously.

"Where are you heading to, old man?" inquired another

soldier, getting closer to him. Sakuri almost froze with fear of being recognised. He was hiding most of his face with a mantle. "I am a stranger, who was here looking for a doctor, but no one is ready to follow me to cure my family, which is in a dire condition and needs the immediate care that only a doctor can provide," Sakuri said apologetically. He was perfectly right in his assumption that the mentioning of some disease was a perfect way of scaring off the soldiers, who were curious to know why he was endangering his life by leaving after sunset.

"Go, get lost." Said the soldier fearfully and retreated his steps. He wouldn't take the risk of getting infected by some unknown disease. Seeing his cautious and nervous reaction, his companions laughed, but no one dared to come near to the old man, who could leave the gate without any further questioning.

Sakuri sighed of relief and drove his horse as fast as he could, to be away from that town before anyone was to discover his absence. He knew that the darkness of the night was the best cover for his escape from the place, he so desperately wanted to hold on to but which had turned life hazardous. His servants were waiting for him in a nearby village, from where they proceeded on fresh, strong horses. They were heading to the north of the country, where Sakuri had his family. He wanted to reach there before his family would leave for home. The way was long, tiresome and full of dangers, and he was carrying all the riches and possessions that he could carry. They had food, water, and arms to protect them, but they were still fearful because none of them were warriors. Sakuri was wishing that they would avoid any encounter with the lawless or any of the king's soldiers on the way. Sakuri was very upset about being forced to leave everything behind, which he and his forefathers had collected in the process of a long time, involving the hard efforts and cunning of many generations. But he was not to give up all that easily, he was just retreating temporarily and swore to come back and reclaim what was rightfully his.

3

After the loyal custodians of the three princes had left the royal palace, they took leave of each other, hoping for success in their sacred mission to take the minor princes to safe and secure places. They all were attentive to the fact that such places were quickly vanishing from their country. The separation of the princes was not the only measure they felt forced to take, but now even felt the need to head to all three directions still open to them. The south was out of the question as it was from there the enemy was approaching them. One rider carrying the eldest prince headed west. He was the most vocal, most daring, and least afraid. Once stopped and interrogated, he would reveal his identity without any hesitation. He was not only headstrong but conscious about his esteemed position, making him less inclined to be obedient. Shapario, the most trusted friend of the king was more nervous of his difficult task of dealing with the spoiled prince at one hand, and putting him in the safety on the other. He tried his level best to remain patient and respectful towards the prince, who lacked all manners and etiquettes. Shapario's biggest priority at that moment was to get out of that country in a quick way, without taking any risks, the problem of the bad manners was to be dealt with later on.

All day he pressed ahead, without caring for food, water, or fatigue. The little food and water that he was carrying with him, he spared for the prince, who was getting more and more difficult to deal with. It was sheer luck that they were travelling in the wilderness; otherwise, it was sure that someone would have stopped him, thinking that he was carrying the child against his wishes. Even a patient and most loyal person like Shapario was irritated by the insolent little prince. Had he not sworn the oath of loyalty and allegiance, he would surely have left the rude and arrogant prince there in the wild. He was so tired of his thankless job that he stopped the horse and placed the little prince on the ground and said firmly, "I can see that you don't intend to continue your journey with me, so I'm letting you go." Shapario said, looking deep in the eyes of the prince.

"I command you to take me immediately back to my parents." young prince said with a stern voice.

"Your highness can accomplish the task on your own; my orders are not matching your wish." Shapario said in a cool manner.

"I'll report this to the father," the prince threatened.

Shapario was getting impatient and decided to teach the prince a lesson. He turned and faced the prince. "I'll wait another minute; if you still wish to stay here I'll be gone, without caring what happened of you." The prince stood there, considering it a bare threat without any implication. But he was dreaded to watch that his attendant meant business and was riding away from him. He waited for a few minutes in disbelieve, hoping the person to turn back, but Shapario not even turned to look at him.

"Stop!" The prince shouted as loud as he could, but the rider didn't turn. He screamed louder, getting panicked and frantic. He was horrified to be left alone there, without food, water and protection from the wild beasts. Suddenly the rider turned back, pretending to listen. The prince shouted once again, seeing his last chance to get him back. Shapario knew that his bluff was successful. He had a triumphant grin on his face while he turned his horse to go back to the prince, when suddenly he was struck with a horrendous scene; some large animal was leaping towards the prince from the rear. Shapario screamed as loud as he could, trying to warn the unaware prince, but failed to call his attention to the lurking danger. He was desperate to reach the prince but found himself still at a distance. He made a strong alarming sound, this time forcing the little prince to turn back and see what made his custodian so very ardent. The discovery of the beast was too late. Shapario saw the beast fall on the boy's little body, collecting all his might he gave a heart piercing sound, which scared the beast away who looked at his prey indecisively for a few seconds before running in the opposite direction. With pounding heart, he bent over the prince to see if he was alive or not. He knew that the beast had had no time to hurt the little boy, but he could have been crushed under its weight. The lifeless body of the child was pushing him to unbearable grief His anxiety was so overwhelming that he wished he was dead. He had no time yet to be angry at his reckless decision of teaching the prince a lesson. He listened again, trying to find the heartbeat of the child, but once again he failed. With empty eyes, he watched the face of the prince, which was bloodstained, as were other parts of his body. These must have been from the sharp paws, which the beast had nailed in the body of the prince.

Shapario was sitting in a shock, unable to feel anything. He kept looking at the lifeless body before him, when he suddenly discovered the signs of life. First, he believed it to be his wishful thinking and ignored the signs, but then he almost threw himself forward, kneeling, bending and listening to the heartbeat. Yes, it was very much there, and so was the breathing of the child. Shapario almost cried of joy to find the miraculous survival of the prince, but he was not relieved as yet. He couldn't say for sure if the child was suffering from some inner or outer wounds or not, and if he did how severe they were going to be. There was no time to figure out that by just sitting and waiting. He jumped to his feet, placed the prince on the horse and rode as fast as he could, looking for help that seemed to be far, far away.

Shapario was dying of anguish. All he intended to do was make his prince a bit quiet and less troublesome. The happenings that had followed were not even in the remotest parts of his mind. He was now struggling with the guilt, which was invading from all directions, aiming at him with its poisonous arrows. His attempt to tame the wild prince had turned into a disastrous nightmare. His heart and mind were being occupied with worries about the king he had left behind. The king was not only his master but also even a dear friend, whom he had sworn to protect from all dangers and threats, but instead of doing that he was fleeing from the enemy, not for his own sake but to protect the prince. He knew that he was doing his duty, serving the wish and command of the master; nevertheless, he had left the man alone in the hour of his direst need. There was not even the slightest hope that Tylon could survive or win the impossible battle which awaited him. But all such thoughts had disappeared from his consciousness, replaced by his only concern: to save the prince on all costs. He was certain that had the prince died, he would be a dead man as well as he could never forgive himself for the negligence, which had caused such a devastating happening.

The person who carried the middle son, was heading west, with a hope of getting the prince out of the country without incident. He knew the way as he had travelled that path hundreds of times and knew every minor detail of it. The way was quite simple except for little pockets of difficult terrain, but he was confident of overcoming them without any major difficulty. He liked his charming companion who never stopped talking, inquiring about every detail that came to his keen attention. The prince was hardly three years old, but had an incredible curiosity to learn about things. He was less anxious about his separation from his parents or brothers. He seemed to be at ease with a complete stranger. His attendant was nervous about meeting other people on the way as it could disclose the identity of the prince, who was easy to communicate with. "Shall we play a game?" The attendant asked the prince.

"What game?" the prince asked, getting excited.

"A game where we pretend that I'm your father and that you are my son." The prince liked the idea and agreed to play that game. But just the mentioning of the word had reminded him that he was not with his family.

"I want to go home. I want to go to mother." The prince was getting impatient, making the attendant regret his game of pretension, he had suggested

"What is that you want most?" asked his attendant.

"I want to go home!" the prince cried.

That repetition of the words would not stop, and the attendant got weary after some time. He had no experience of dealing with children, especially those who were that young. All his efforts to calm down the child were bringing the opposite effects until he decided to ignore the child completely. "I'm hungry," said the prince, breaking the monotonous repetition of his words, he had been saying for hours. "I'll give you the food if you promise not to shout about your family and home. You see I'm your family and that's it." He noticed a surprise on the little face, and felt sorry that he said those harsh words.

"Play Game?" asked the prince with a smile.

"Yes, play game. Do you promise?"

The prince agreed and waited impatiently for his food, he must have been very hungry.

At nightfall, he waited until the prince had fallen asleep, before finding some place to sleep. He spent the night in a small village, where he even got fresh supplies of water and some food to carry with. At dawn, he left the village, before anybody woke up, he wanted to avoid all human contact with other people if he was to conceal his own mission and the true identity of the prince from others.

Before entering the desert, the stout fellow stopped his horse and waited before venturing into it. He wanted to be absolutely sure that not only that he was properly equipped, but even the prevailing conditions were favorable. He had the perfect knowledge of the place and had calculated the timings of entry and exit, so the best time to enter into the desert was before the sunrise, which would provide him the opportunity to cross that not so big but dangerous desert, before it became too hot. What this experienced man had not calculated was the sudden sandstorm, which took him by surprise at the halfway point leaving him no choice but to cover and protect the prince properly and wait for the storm to pass away. The prince was afraid of the complete darkness, which was engulfing them, and he felt suffocated by what his attendant was covering him with. They were forced to stay in the desert much longer than they had planned. The stormy sand and the unbearable heat had taken its toll on the man, who had spent all his energies in protecting the little, helpless prince, who was scared and needed comfort and reassurance that no harm was to befall him. When they came out of the desert, the man looked like a ghost.

The water he carried with him that was supposed to last until they came to some habitations was already consumed to the last drop. The prince was again whining, thirsty, and all the other things he didn't want him to be. He was dizzy and sick, but his sense of duty was pulling him ahead. He stopped at a place to rest, but kept resting, never to wake up. Was it too much inhaling of sand, or a heat-stroke, or some other inner failure, no one could tell. The little prince, unaware of the happening, kept shaking him, asking for some water, but got no answer. No one could tell how long he remained in that desolate place without food or water.

Surely he too would have perished in that wilderness, had not a party of some traders passed that way, coming from some unknown directions. They discovered the tragic scene and wondered what such a little child did in that hostile surrounding. They looked more surprised to learn that someone could be that foolish to not only travel alone, but even to take a little child with him.

"Is he dead?" asked one of the traders.

"It seems that way," answered the other one, without even checking.

"You should not guess. Look closely and find out the answer," said one of the men.

"It's amazing the child is alive; though I could swear that he looked completely dead."

"Give him some water!" shouted one trader.

"Be gentle, just few drops in a time." Cried the other one. They all were completely absorbed by the child and his enigmatic survival.

The traders felt for the little child, who was too young to be there in the first place. His unconsciousness persisted, refusing to give way, depriving them of getting any information, which could give them a hint, from where did he come, and where was he heading. There was a meeting among the traders, who wanted to discuss the issue of that child, who lay before their eyes, completely alone and without any future or a possibility to survive if they were not to find some quick answer to that pressing problem. Most of the traders were middle-aged themselves, not interested to take the responsibility of such a little child. They believed they had done their part of the duty of raising children, but Herzod was the only one who had not spoken as yet. "We can't simply walk away, leaving this child to die in this desolate place." He spoke at last, looking worried. "You're right, but what alternatives do we have? We're long away from our destination and can't imagine of carrying this miserable creature with us," the other trader said.

"Unless one of us takes the child and returns back." Said the third one, suggesting a possibility. They all agreed that that could be the best possible solution of the problem, except that no one was ready to turn back. "Alright I take the child and leave him to my wife while you continue your journey. I may come back and join you as quickly as possible, but you shouldn't wait for me," Herzod said without any hesitation.

"Are you sure he'll come out of his coma and survive?" someone asked shaking his head in disbelief.

"You know that no one can say that. But who can have the heart just to leave him here?" Herzod answered suppressing his anger.

"What about your goods?" asked one trader, pointing to the camels, which were loaded with merchandise.

"I entrust them to you. If I fail to come back, then you can sell the goods on my behalf." Herzod was casual. He sat on the horse and placed the little prince in front of him and turned to ride back to his town, when someone called him, and threw the dead man's purse towards him. "Take it with you, which is the heritage of this unfortunate fellow, whatever it contains."

It was Silos who had been entrusted with the youngest of the sons of the king, a responsibility he was horrified to have received. He tried to wriggle out of the task by arguing that he was an old and weak person unable to perform such an important task, but the king had been insistent. According to him, if anyone could be trusted with the task of carrying the infant in security and safety, it was Silos. Silos dared not ask why he thought so, but remained miserable. He was not discontent because he wanted to avoid getting involved in some risky enterprise on behalf of the king, but because he was aware of his natural tendency of staying away from the children, a reason for which he had never gotten married nor had children of his own. This new task was making him nervous. With great reluctance and fearful heart, he took the infant and looked helplessly at the king, hoping for a last minute change of orders. He kept turning and looking for any signs of the fulfillment of his wishful thinking, but no such change took place. He looked very miserable, but few had time to observe that.

Silos came out of the palace and looked at his great responsibility, looking at him with his big smiling eyes. He shivered, taking his gaze away from that helpless, little thing. He hated the situation and kept standing on the stairs leading to the palace. He knew that he simply couldn't afford to stand there, but had to move as quickly as possible, away from that place if he was to accomplish his duty truthfully. The time was running out of his hand, and there he stood, without any clear plan, strategy or even a destination. "These crises have turned the king into an unwise, stupid person. Look at it; he put an incompetent person like me in charge of the important task of protecting the prince." Silos was standing there, thinking angrily. He was feeling panicked, pulled between his uncertainty and the need to take a quick action. People were moving in all directions, unaware of the approaching enemy armies. Suddenly Silos face lit up and moved with the speed of a panther, he fetched his horse and drove towards his house. His housemaid looked very surprised to see him that early back in the house, but what astonished her even more was that he was nervously holding an infant in his arm. What had he done? Whose child was he taking? Why was he that nervous? So many questions were tormenting her, but she couldn't ask him anything. "Leave everything behind and follow me," Silos commanded, handing the infant to her. The maid did what she was told and without any questions sat behind him on the horse, holding the child, wondering where they headed. Old Silos was not a man of many words, he used them very carefully and sparsely, so there was not much point in asking him anything at that point. In the moments of great distress or anger, these words disappeared completely, and there were certainly moments when he seemed to be suffering of both kinds of feelings.

When they were coming out of the gates, they could see a dust storm approaching. Only Silos knew what type of storm was about to hit his country and the king. Without losing any more time, he turned his horse to the north, hoping that no one would have seen them from that far away, but even if someone did, no one would have cared about an old man. Silos was right in his assumption that they had been successful in escaping the disaster, if only by a slim margin. He waited quite long before entrusting his maid with the details of their journey. The maid became all pale and started shivering with fear. She was nothing but a simple working woman, who could never imagine getting involved in such a magnificent task. She was silent, but her mind was racing with questions. How were they to live and feed themselves in the new country? Even if they did succeed in reaching at their destination safely, how were they to manage their lives in the new place because Silos could not have arranged the needed money with him? She couldn't take up those issues and discuss them with Silos, who would just become more silent and anguished than he already was. She was crying silently because she didn't have the chance to meet and inform anyone about her leaving. She feared that such a strange happening was bound to grieve her old mother, who would be heartbroken, thinking of the worst possibilities. There was no way she could have helped her anyway. For a second, she felt angry with Silos, but listening to his anguished sighs, she could realise that the old man was sitting in the same boat.

The child was hungry and needed some milk, but where were they to find that rare commodity? For miles and miles there wasn't a sign of any human habitations. The infant was getting more and more desperate, crying at the top of his lungs. "What am I supposed to do?" shouted Silos in despair. "I knew that I'm not a suitable person to accomplish such a delicate matter. It'd be much easier to die fighting and protecting the king and kingdom." He sounded both unhappy and distressed. "Surely, we're to find someplace where we can get some milk to give to the infant," said Binti. "Where? Do you see any signs of any human beings around?" asked Silos sarcastically. "As a matter of fact I do, master," Binti said excitedly, holding the child with one hand and pointing in one direction with another. Silos was doubtful as to what lay in the direction, she pointed at. Even if they were looking at some human beings at a distance, they couldn't be sure if it was safe to contact them. "And what makes you think that they might have milk for the child?" Silos was as pessimistic as ever. "Yes, the chances are very slim, but we still have to check them out," Binti said without any hesitation.

They were met with astonished eyes, wondering what an infant was doing in the wilderness. Those people were camping for their night's rest. Silos told them that he was travelling with his grandson and daughter-in-law. He was accompanying them to the place, where his son had been stuck for some time. "We are looking for some milk or food for the child," said silos. They didn't have any, he was told politely, though he could watch their indignant faces. They were without any doubt judgmental, feeling pity for the poor, helpless infant, who seemed to be unable to deal with his hunger and thirst. "Give him at least some water to drink, or do you not carry even that?" said someone in an angry tone. "Don't be impolite to the stranger," some other person said sternly. They gave them something to eat and water to drink, but that was not going to solve their problem to feed the little prince. The prince was that hungry that he finally took the loaf of hard bread and started sucking at it, but all they could do was feel sorry for him. They were being offered to spend the night with that company as the night was approaching, they could not hope to reach the nearest village while there was still daylight. "We really hope that your grandson shall make it. A very tough path lies ahead, and you don't seem to be equipped with the provisions or even a road map." The leader of the company was a kind but straightforward man. "Take my advice and don't push ahead in a blind man's folly. Take your time, travel only small distances, if you are not weary yourself and your daughter in law is strong. Inquire about your road before setting your foot on it. You have the responsibility of that helpless being on your shoulders." The leader was talking sense, though he sounded harsh.

"Believe me, if you don't do as I suggest, you would be endangering the lives of everyone, especially the life of this innocent child."

They left early next morning, thanking the strangers for all their kindnesses and help. Silos was to seek the nearest village, where they were to find milk for the infant and food for themselves. Silos promised the leader of that party that he would be more careful from that time on.

The prince had been crying for the most of the night and was almost exhausted, dozing from time to time, too tired even to cry. Binti was scared to death, feeling empathy for the poor soul, regularly checking to see if he was still alive. Silos was trying his best to distance himself from that dire situation, taking the cover of anger. But that apparent anger towards his silly master, which in fact, remained responsible for the entire hopeless situation, had failed to release him from the concern and anguish he confronted. "He has not made a single sound from the last many minutes." Silos said with a trembling voice. She could feel his agony. "I believe he is exhausted, and can't find the strength to express his desperation." Binti told him. There was a silence until Silos spoke again. "Do you believe we shall make it?"

"You mean well if he'll make it?" Binti corrected him.

"Whatever!" Silos said with irritation.

"I really hope so," was her short but unconvincing answer. No one spoke after that. Both of them wanted to avoid discussing the possibilities that were them like bloodthirsty demons, making them pray to the gods above. Silos was not a very sensitive person, but at that moment all his heart was filled with one single wish that the prince would not die of hunger and thirst. Binti was putting drops of water in the dry mouth of the prince, who was showing signs of dehydration.

Looking at the early signs of approaching the village gave them a renewed fervour and energy, and Silos increased the speed of his horse, which was getting tired but relentless in his task to serve his master. The villagers were kind and hospitable and took good care of them. Seeing the condition of the infant, they shook their heads, not hiding the fact that there was a little hope of his surviving. However, they called for a person who was supposed to attend the child and do whatever stood in her power to save him from a sure death. "If she wouldn't be able to save him, then nobody can," one villager said, looking keenly at the infant. Silos had expected the woman in question to be some old lady and therefore, was astonished to see some young woman approaching them. She was hardly in her mid-twenties. Without entering in the formalities, she went straight to the dying prince, who was still breathing but had closed eyes and was looking all pale. Binti was sitting with bowed head, avoiding the piercing, judging eyes of her surroundings as if she was the cause of the trouble. The attending woman turned to her after she was through with her check up of the infant. " Are you the mother of this child?" she asked politely. Binti looked at Silos, seeking help. "Yes," she said in a weak voice. "Then why did you let the child starve? Why didn't you feed him, instead of searching for the milk?" The natural question had not crossed her mind earlier. She was certain that she would break down under pressure, but Silos was quick witted and came to her rescue. "That's a long story," he said, taking over. "Poor girl" has been unable to for the last several months." Everyone around Binti looked at her with pity; the man had solved their mystery.

"Is he going to survive?" Silos asked, hoping that it was to change the uncomfortable subject, which he knew so little about.

"It's difficult for me to say. All I can promise is, to do my best," the tall young woman said, before turning to some older lady, she was giving her some quick instructions. The elderly lady nodded and then went out of the room. After a few minutes, she returned and handed over some dark bottle to the young woman, who opened it carefully and started pouring the contents of it into the mouth of the infant. Drop by drop she went on giving that potion to the child. She was very observant of the child, after every few drops, she would stop and check his eye pupils, and then continuing with her slow treatment. She seemed to be not bothered by the presence of so many people in that little room. When finally done with her work, she looked to Silos and said calmly. "Now all we can do is to wait. If he doesn't come to consciousness after a couple of hours, you can consider him gone." She left the room without adding anything further; the other villagers did the same.

Against all odds, the little prince did survive, but his recovery was very slow and nerve breaking, forcing them to stay in that remote place. What worried Silos most was uncertainty as to where he was. Had they crossed over to the neighbouring country or were they still in their own land? The local villagers were unable to provide them the answers to any such questions. They were so often dragged from one side or the other that they simply had stopped caring to whom they belonged. "This king or that doesn't change our lives, which remains hard but independent." The villagers tried to assure them that there was no apparent danger to them as almost no one came that way, except the travellers, which frequently crossed that path. Silos was anxious to move from that friendly but unsure place, but he was forced to wait until the prince had fully recovered and was strong enough to resume the journey.

4

King Razila had grown bored and homesick. He had enough of his newly conquered country, which was vast and populace, requiring more resources to administer and govern than he had earlier anticipated. To recruit a strong fighting force from that vast land proved to be an impossible task, as the major portion of the former army never turned up to join the ranks of his new territorial army. So his own army was tied up with the task of keeping law and order instead of helping him accomplish his new missions, conquering new lands for him. Razila was disappointed, disillusioned and irritated, and wanted nothing less than to go to his own part of the country, which he loved most. Despite the strong recommendations made by his advisers, he decided to return home. He made his younger brother, his assistant ruler and gave him unlimited power. "Rule over these people any way you like. Consider them as a flock of sheep and treat them likewise." Razila was angry with the people, which had shattered his dreams of conquering the neighbouring countries. Razila knew that his younger brother was far worse than him in his cruelty and disregard for others, and therefore, was satisfied about his decision to appoint him as his successor. What worried him was the loyalty of his brother, which had never been tried. The best solution he could find for the problem was to disconnect him from the administration and control of the army. He was pleased to have gotten such an advice from his advisors. The army was to remain under his own command, and was to act only if he allowed it. The younger brother felt insulted and protested strongly, giving the valid argument that if implemented, it was to endanger not only his life but also the security of the kingdom. "How am I to rule over people if I can't even command my own troops?" the brother questioned, without offending him. "Sure you are going to command over administrating force, and that should be enough for your purpose." Razila made it clear that there was not any room for negotiations, the decision had been already made The only thing left to choose was to accept it or reject it. His brother had opted to bow before the will of the king, at least for the time being.

Now that the king was gone, leaving his brother to govern the country, life was getting a bit tougher for the people, who were levied new taxes, a clear punishment for not providing the king with the new soldiers. The new vice-king Pampicilos was not even trying to hide the fact that was a collective punishment. If the locals refused to serve in the army, it necessitated the bringing the required soldiers from somewhere else, which in their turn were more expensive, and justified increased taxes. Taxes were put on almost everything, unlike in the past, when most of the new taxes were placed only on agriculture. There was an outcry, which died down when they saw the great army of the king, determined to crush any resistance. Pampicilos knew what he was doing; he was cleverer and a more dangerous person than his brother. He was a born schemer but had kept that natural talent a secret from others. He was a patient man who could wait years to get a chance to accomplish something, a property completely lacking in Razila. He was a man who never forgot or forgave any thing. He was always remembering the most minor details, always learning new lessons from his experiences. Without a doubt, he was the most cunning man in that country. Had Razila known his brother's hidden qualities, he would never have made him his vice-king.

Now that the king had gone out from the country, the lives of people got worse than ever before. They remembered the good old days with sadness and wished if there was a way to go back to that period once again. But the wheel of time always moved forward, and it was beyond the power of any to turn it back. Sakuri's escape had enraged Razila very much. He had failed to capture the members of the king's family, and now Sakuri had fled the land, depriving him of a cunning plan to eliminate the greedy person. But now they both were absent from the political and physical scene of the country, the person, who was to get all the possible attention, was Pampicilos. He had already made his plan to move forward in the wake of given circumstances. His policies were clear; he was to accept the role of a trustee without full trust of the king and proceed accordingly. By raising the taxes substantially, he wanted not only to please Razila, but also retain some of that extra money to invest in his own future. He lavishly spent that money on the commanders of the army as a token of his gratitude on behalf of his majesty. The hesitation and surprise was significant among those army officers who became suspicious of his motives, but he succeeded in giving them an impression that his favours were without any cost. He never asked any counter-favours or gave the slightest hint that he had expected something in return. The commanders started relaxing, taking his kindnesses as a generous attitude of the vice king, but without even realising it their liking for the immediate ruler was growing fast. He never gave them any orders as what to do or not to do, as it was beyond the scope and power of his authority. But strangely, all his wishes and suggestions were heeded as commands.

Queen Haliba and Aloha had grown too close, invoking the jealousy of Davreen, who never uttered a word expressing her feelings but one could see that she was not very happy that a stranger had completely taken over the entire attention of her mother. Aloha was less mindful of her, hardly taking any notice of what she did or did not do. Davreen performed all the duties assigned to her in complete silence, without any complaint or a protest. The only thing reflective of her miserable state of mind was the permanent sadness on her face. "I believe you should give more attention to Davreen," Haliba suggested.

"Why?" Aloha looked surprised by the suggestion.

"I have a feeling that she is feeling neglected and unloved."

"Don't you worry about her. She was born with that miserable face." Aloha was bitter and pretended to have cared less. "I have given up all hope for her. She is full of negativity, and never wants to move one step closer to happiness. I really don't know what to do about her." Aloha sighed.

"Don't be that hard on her, she has had bad luck and deserves some understanding." Haliba tried to defend Davreen.

"Who could fight destiny and its cruel course? What does it help to be miserable and unhappy for the misfortunes that befall us?" Aloha said sadly. "Is she the only one to have suffered by the hands of fate? Look at you, look at me, aren't we all the helpless creatures in the clutches of that great, immense power?"

"What's your story?" Haliba asked curiously.

"Nothing particular about that, what I mean is that don't we all have some crushing burden to deal with?" Aloha tried to avoid the subject.

"Just by looking at you, and by listening to the words of wisdom, you so frequently utter, I can say with surety that you too are an outplaced person, degraded, and suffering from downward mobility." Haliba said looking at Aloha's face, which was turning cloudy. But she remained silent.

"I admire your enthusiasm, insight, and hopefulness. But everything in life can't be a product of those conditions and circumstances you live in." She was pressing Aloha.

Haliba left no choice for Aloha than to confide to her, the tragic story of hers. She was talking about her childhood, the most beautiful memories of the wonderful mansions and orchards that she enjoyed. She appeared both happy and sad from those memories.

These recollections were the treasures that time had been unable to deprive her of, and yet she was thankful for being able to retain those memories. She looked distressed when talking about her father, elder brothers, and other members of her family, who all lived happily, enjoying the fruits of abundance.

"I was hardly in my early teens when that perfect state of being came to an abrupt end. It was just before dawn when we were visited by the soldiers who arrested my father and both brothers. My mother begged and pleaded for her young children and her husband, but none listened to her cry for help, and the soldiers took all the male members, including our servants. My younger sister and I were shocked by the unbelievable incident." The old memories had brought back not only wonderful movements from the past but even also the pain and anguish of that era.

"Why were they arrested? What did they do?" Haliba inquired impatiently.

"We'd not know for quite some time. My mother was confident that everything was due to some misunderstanding. She tried to seek the help of influential people, but nothing was to help," Aloha said wiping her tears. She found it impossible to narrate the tragic story of her life. According to her story, her father and both brothers had been accused of some conspiracy against the king, which they strongly denied. No one listened to their pleadings, and swearing that they were innocent of all charges against them. There were no apparent proofs binding them to the crimes that they were accused of but that fact didn't prevent the king from sentencing her father and brothers to life imprisonments. Aloha and her family were thrown out of their estate in a helpless, degraded manner.

Queen Haliba listened to her story, feeling shame and sadness covering her whole being. She never had heard that particular story, which happened a long time before, but knew that such tragic incidents occurred during their own reign, as well. Until then, she had never questioned the decrees of the king or even tried to look at the hidden motives and games behind such accusations, and the dire consequences of such tragic incidents. So ashamed she felt that she dared not look in the sad eyes of her wonderful host. She had no difficulty in guessing who could be behind all those accusations as the benefactor had been only one family in all those years.

"I'm really sorry to have heard all of this," said Haliba.

"I'm still sorry, though it happened many years ago. My mother couldn't bear the tragedy and died almost within a year after." Aloha's eyes were wet.

"So only you and your sister survived the tragedy."

"No, only I did. My younger sister got sick right after the death of my mother and died without any fair chance to survive. We had no money to call for a doctor or buy medicines for her." Aloha was filling her with more and more shame.

"All these terrible things and you're still so kind to give refuge to a person like me, whose family had been responsible for those terrible things." Haliba couldn't help but to appreciate the generosity of Aloha.

"It wasn't the fault of you, or even your husband, the king, who might not be even born at the time all these things happened." She said soothing Haliba.

"Does Davreen know about these sad truths?"

"Heavens no!" Aloha exclaimed. "Without knowing anything she is so very full of negativity, what would become out of her, if she knew?"

Three years had passed since queen Haliba moved into that little house of Aloha. Hardly a day went by when she didn't miss her children and husband. She could have given anything to have been able to see them, even a brief glimpse, even for a fraction of a second. But she knew that there wasn't any such possibility. Her heart bled to think of the suffering that her husband might have been going through, but she could do nothing but to cry. At such moments, she wished to have the power to penetrate the thick walls of the dungeon where her husband was kept. How she wished to be a gust of fresh air, which could fill the lungs of Tylon with renewed hope. Aloha told her that the jail administrators were looking for some new workers who could help them with minor assignments. Haliba's eyes shone with the mere possibility of getting a chance.

Aloha looked horrified as she watched her face. "No!" she rejected the idea, without even considering it.

"Why not?" questioned the excited queen.

"You are the queen! You are not supposed to be working, and surely, not in a jail!" Aloha argued, but the queen was not deterred by her strong argumentations. She was not afraid to perform the most simple and degrading duties, as long as it offered a remote possibility of getting an inch closer to her beloved husband. She was ready to take the chance of being recognised and arrested, for whom she was. "It's worth taking a chance." Haliba said. "Please, help me get that job." she pleaded.

"Your highness…." Aloha tried desperately to make her refrain.

"You know that I'm not a queen any more. I am a burden on your elderly shoulders. You have been so kind and generous to me. Help me and I'll be even more grateful."

"As you wish and command milady!" Aloha gave up her resistance and promised to inquire the possibility and do whatever stood in her power.

"I'll always remember your kindnesses, the list of which is long," Haliba said embracing Aloha, who had stopped her insistence on keeping the formalities intact.

A few days later, Aloha gave her the news that her job at the jail had been arranged. She was still hoping to convince the queen of changing her mind.

"I guarantee you that this is not a job for you, neither is the environment in which you'll be performing your terrible duties," were the last words she used to deter her from pursuing the job.

"You are an angel!" Haliba kissed Aloha on her cheeks.

"You are a strange person; nevertheless, you are my queen." Aloha was amused, though still looking worried.

"Come I want to show you something." Haliba took her to the little box she had gotten from Aloha, to keep her things in. She opened it and started digging in the few clothes she had there.

She unwrapped something and stretched her hand towards Aloha.

"What's this?" Aloha asked surprised.

"It's a humble present to you." Haliba said with a smile. Aloha looked shocked, holding the most beautiful necklace that she had ever set her eyes on. The diamonds of that wonderful necklace were without any doubt the most precious stones she had ever dreamed of. She was not a jeweller, but knew that the necklace only could be worth of a queen.

"Your highness!" Aloha almost cried. "I'm deeply touched, by your generous gesture, but there is no way I can accept this valuable gift from you."

"And why not? Haliba asked

"Where am I to use it? To who am I to show it off?" Aloha went on. Haliba smiled, getting her point.

"You may sell it and use the money for something you have a better use of, buy a better house, for example," Haliba purposed.

"Yes I could, but I would not."

"Why not?"

"Selling and buying such precious items is a privilege and a right of the wealthy. For poor people like me, it is just trouble." Aloha was explaining herself in a sad but realistic way. Haliba agreed that no jewellers in that country or any other was going to buy that necklace from a poor person, without asking a million questions, and even if he did, there was no way of obtaining even one tenth of the original price.

"If you like me as you so often declare, then don't ask me to accept something, what'll cause just sorrow and inflict pain." Aloha begged in earnest.

"Alright, I'll not insist as I agree with your logic. Even I myself wouldn't dare to go and try to sell my own jewellery, without risking the dangers of being recognised by someone or taken as a thief." Haliba gave up. "But is it possible for you to keep all my jewels, as a deposit?

"Your highness, don't misunderstand and misinterpret my reluctance into anything other than what it is. Of course, I feel honoured by the trust that you intend to put in me, but how am I to safeguard these valuable jewels of yours?" Aloha was giving a clear message that she should forget about entrusting her with greater responsibility.

"You believe these would be safer with me at the prison?" Haliba was not to let her go that easily.

"I never claimed such a thing," Aloha said getting cornered. After some discussion, she finally agreed to become a trustee of Haliba's valuables. Both women knew that they needed to be careful if they were not to endanger each other's lives. Any mistake or negligence on one part was to lead the suspicion to the other.

"Good luck, your highness. I am sad to say good-bye. It was the most giving time of my life; it was a real pleasure to know you."

"How am I to make you less formal and more like a family? In such a short time, you have gotten that close to me." Haliba said holding Aloha in her arms. Suddenly, she turned and saw Davreen standing and looking at her from a distance.

Haliba went forward to her and looked deep in her dark brown eyes and smiled. "Thank you Davreen for everything."

"Thanks for what?" Davreen wondered, looking astounded.

"Thank you for opening the doors of your home for me, for giving food and shelter, for being kind to a stranger, for…"

"I was not always kind and gentle to you." Davreen confessed, cutting her words

"That's true." Haliba smiled. "But I don't blame you for that. You had reasons and problems of your own. I wish for you to find some happiness in the world, but for that reason, you have to change yourself, as well. Happiness may knock your door, but you have to let her in."

Davreen avoided looking at Haliba, she felt ashamed for having ignored the woman for such a long time.

"You just asked me for what I'm thanking you for. Honestly, I thanked you for all you did or didn't do for me. I thank you for having patience with me, for tolerating my presence in your home, and most of all, for sharing your mother with me. Believe me, I would not have survived without her help and love." Haliba went forward and kissed her on her forehead and took leave. Davreen was standing like a statue, unaffected; but that was just outwardly; inside she was in the grip of stormy winds, shaking and affecting all her being.

Haliba covered her whole body with a large shawl and walked in the most insecure manner. It was the very first time since her coming to the old town that she was heading towards that part of town, which was once her home. She felt as if all her confidence had been drawn out of her from the hard circumstances, but somehow or other she still stood intact and complete, as if untouched by those crushing conditions, she had gone through. Not even for a single day had she regretted her decision to separate herself from her children. She was convinced that they still were alive, and this hope kept her going. She had been few times out on the street, but it was only in the neighbourhood of the house where she lived. No one was paying any attention to her and yet she walked with staggering steps as if intoxicated or sick. "Don't be afraid. You are a strong woman, who can make it." Aloha said in a whisper.

"You think so?" asked Haliba timidly.

"We can always turn back if you feel unsure." Aloha said looking at her.

"No, no, keep going. It'll be alright with me."

"Are you sure?" Aloha seemed to be equally nervous.

"Absolutely." Haliba tried to make a confident sound, and went a few steps ahead of Aloha in her fervour, without even noticing it, making Aloha smile. She was admiring the courage and steadfastness of Haliba; she was the only person who recognised her as her real queen. Aloha couldn't stop worrying, questioning again and again if they were doing the right thing in letting her enter the dangerous den. But perhaps the time for thinking had long passed, and the only thing left was to pray for the safety of that kind person.

5

Shapario was absolutely sure that he had left the boundaries of his country long behind, and needed not to worry about the enemy soldiers anymore. What he was still lacked, was the knowledge, as to how long more he had to travel, before coming to some human habitations. The boiling sun was making his move ahead a torturous act, but worry about the dying prince was even worst. As far as his eyes could reach, there wasn't any sign of the wilderness's end. His hope was fading with each moment ticking away, and he was getting sure that he had already lost the child. With trembling hands, he searched for the heartbeat of the child and sighed, still clinging to the hope as it was very much there, though it was getting weaker. He was fully covered in order to protect himself from the heat, making his body drenched in sticking sweat. He was riding as fast as he could, without caring that the horse already gave the signs of fatigue. He was certain that if he didn't come to some habitations soon all hope for them was lost. The prince was already getting beyond hopes; even he and the horse were to collapse if they didn't cross that barren place very soon as they were running out of the water. Shapario tried to halt the horse as he could feel that the large beast was giving way and was about to fall. The intense labour, lack of water and the burning grounds were too many factors against his race against time. Shapario noticed how the faithful animal took his last staggering steps before halting completely. He was panting and shaking in his large body, giving the chance to his master to get off before he would collapse. Shapario jumped down and took the body of the prince off the horse, as well. The horse didn't fall immediately. He stood there, struggling against the fatigue, thirst and the incredible force, which was drying him out of all energies. He looked at Shapario with regretful eyes, it seems he was sorry to have let him down in the moments he needed him most. Shapario was extremely anxious, mostly with the realisation that his trusted friend was leaving him for good. He went forward and caressed and patted his friend, taking the risk of his falling over him. There was a brief eye contact between them, a non-verbal communication, and an exchange of thoughts took place before the horse fell down and died shortly after. Shapario stood there with tearful eyes, not knowing what to do next.

He was getting weaker by the minute and felt dizzy and exhausted. He tried to reach the body of the prince to check if he was still alive, but couldn't reach him. The distance of just few meters seemed to be spread for miles. If he a strong man was dying of those unbearable conditions, then there was no reason to believe that the injured prince was still alive, he thought pessimistically, before passing out.

When Shapario opened his eyes, he looked around to check where he was. It was relatively cool place. He could not tell what time of the day it was as the place was not very bright. His memory of the events just before his getting fainted was returning, giving him a renewed anxiety. He got up from the place he was lying and got astonished to notice that he wasn't sleeping on the hard ground as he had earlier thought. It was some kind of clothing, which gave little protection against the rocky ground. His eyes searched the surrounding and finally rested on the opening. It was a cave without any doubt, but how did he come there? He wondered. He didn't have to think for a long while, he saw one man entering the cave. Shapario was both happy and surprised to find him there. It was the same ascetic, who had visited the king some time earlier, and whom they had been desperately trying to locate. After the greetings, the older man explained to him about the things that were puzzling Shapario. The old man lived there and had found him unconscious in the wilderness. Shapario looked amazed as it was impossible for an old man to transport a well-built person like him on his own. Suddenly, he remembered about the prince but dared not ask a question about him. He was afraid of getting bad news. The old man offered him something to eat, but he felt too sad to do so. He seemed to have lost all appetite. "You have to eat if you're to regain your lost energy," the old man said politely. Shapario thanked the man for his kindness, but told that he wasn't hungry for the moment. "How are we to proceed without a horse?" the man asked "It's no problem. I'll manage, as the need to hurry seems to be gone." Shapario answered looking down at the rocky floor. The old man remained attentive without speaking any further. "I'm thankful to all your kindnesses. I owe my life to you; perhaps one day I'll be able to repay."

"What's bothering you? You seem to be quite depressed. If it's the horse, you'll get another very soon." The old man said carelessly. Shapario looked in astonishment at the man, how more insensitive a person can get, he wondered. The man had mentioned so many times about his dead horse, and not a single time had he inquired anything about the little prince. "Look, I'm going out to attend some other matters, there are water and fruits over there, in case you feel hungry or thirsty." The old man said turning to the entrance of the cave.

"May I ask you something?" Shapario asked full of anguish.

"Sure you can."

"What have you done with the body of the child? Shapario asked

"You tell me first, what your relation to him is. I can tell that he is not your son."

"You are right that I'm not his father, but he was more than a son to me. He was a great trust put in my hands and I have completely failed in honouring that confidence. I have disgraced myself, and nothing can ever wash the stain away."

Shapario spoke in gloomy, defeated tone.

"Why you keep talking in the past tense? What made you believe that the child is dead?"

"So the prince is still alive?" Shapario exclaimed, forgetting that in his excitement, he had just disclosed the secret and the identity of the little child. He looked more ghastly than before.

"Relax. You haven't revealed anything that I didn't already know. He is alright, well taken care of, and sleeping peacefully. The injuries on his body and brain shall heal soon, but he'll not remember his previous life. Raise him like your own son and prepare him for the task awaiting him in the future," the old man said with a smile.

"Where is he??" Shapario asked.

"Don't worry about him, he is doing well and will soon be returned to you."

"Is it just a coincidence or there lies some mystery behind my meeting you like that?"

"It's not important to know the answer to your questions, concentrate instead on the task assigned to you by the gods." The old man avoided the question.

"How am I to proceed with the upbringing of the child? He is headstrong, lacks respect for all and is without a doubt an arrogant child. I'm afraid to...."

"Loss of memory will not wash all these things away from his personality, except the knowledge that he is superior to others, so take the opportunity and re-form him." The old man suggested. "He is all yours, so raise him the way you see

71

fit. Don't betray the trust invested in you," The old man said before going out.

Shapario sat there perplexed, joyous and worried, all at one time. He could not understand the logical explanations, which could explain the survival of the prince, except that it was really due to the favour and mercy of the gods, who had some purpose hidden in their consciousness. What made him worried was the great burden he felt on his weak shoulders. He was a strong man, who had taken the assignment of taking the prince to the safety, without going in a further depth, the real meanings of which were just dawning at him. So it was not just a commitment to bring the prince from one place to another. He was stuck with the child for a long time, perhaps even for a lifetime. He had no previous knowledge of raising the children, and the mission seemed to be scarier than any other thing he ever had accomplished in life. He would have run away from this strange task if he could, but he knew he was doing it, whether he did it happily or with a troubled heart. "Why me?" he asked looking above as if he was addressing the gods in their high abode. He was sure that he was not to get any answer as gods never communicated with the mortals, or at least not for the types like his. Just by peeping outside he could tell that it was hot and dry and that it was much better to stay inside the cool cave.

The first thing that Herzod did after reaching his town was to rush the child to a doctor, who became astonished to see him that quickly back to town. Herzod explained about the unfortunate child they had discovered in the way and who was still unconscious. "I'm not sure if you can do anything for him. I have brought him with a hope to be able to save him."

"Without a doubt you are a kind soul. I'll try to see if we can save him or if he has gone beyond human power." The doctor was doing the checkup, taking a deep breath. "The child is still breathing but gives no other indications of life. I'm not sure if he'll be able to win the battle against the inevitable." The doctor was pessimistic. "But on the other hand, the body is full of vital energy, totally capable of fighting back. All we can do is to wait and see." The doctor said without giving him much hope. "The symptoms aren't that clear and visible. I can't say for sure if the child is suffering from starvation and thirst or has eaten some poisonous thing or some other ailment is tormenting him." Herzod left the child at the doctor's, promising to come back later to see how he was doing. He was dead tired and needed rest as he had been riding all day. "I'll put him in observation. There's little you can do anyway, so go and rest." Doctor said, looking at his tired and worried face.

"Are you sure?" Herzod asked politely.

"I wouldn't have told you otherwise. Believe me; you have done your part."

"I'll be back in the morning to get the news. I really hope he'll make it." Herzod sounded concerned.

The doctor and his wife had a very tough night before them. They were treating the child for all the possible ailments, hoping to save him by taking all the measures simultaneously, just to be sure. They had nothing to lose as the child already seemed to be beyond all hope. His pretty face was changing the colour like a chameleon, giving the committed couple hope and despair alternatively. The child had not moved a muscle since he came to them and that was alarming. If there was any mental activity going on, there was an expectation to register it on the body. But the mind was failing to evoke a corresponding reaction from the body, a very bad sign from the point of view of the doctor. The young wife was assisting her husband, doing whatever she was asked to. She went on wetting the towel and wiping the sweat away from his face, which was getting cold or hot without any apparent reason. The child wasn't suffering from the fever, but that was all they could be certain about. "If he doesn't come out of coma very soon, he is gone."

"What a pity!" the wife said without looking at her husband. She wanted to hide her tears from him. She remembered the loss of her own little daughter, who had passed away two years ago.

"It's not for us to decide who lives and who doesn't." the doctor said, realising her pain and anguish.

They both kept silent and concentrated on the boy who lay in front of them in a helpless and hopeless state. By the morning hours, they both were exhausted without being able to bring any visible change in his condition. "I'm afraid there is nothing more we can do for him," the doctor said, giving up.

"As long as he breathes we can fight his battle as well."

"Not quite so. We have just won little more time for him," the doctor said.

"You can go and get some sleep, and I can attend him," the wife said.

"My mind is too much active, too preoccupied with this little being, and it'd be impossible for me to get a nap. On the other hand, you can get some rest."

She agreed to go and rest, asking her husband not to be too anxious.

"Don't worry!" the doctor said with a tired smile. "The nature has equipped us beings with a very efficient defence system.

We don't get over sensitive to everyone who comes our way."

What he meant to convey was simple. Despite his wish to save the poor child, he was not emotionally bound to him, which could give him extra pain and anxiety. He was determined to stay detached and intact, even if something bad was going to happen to the kid.

When Herzod came to visit the doctor, he looked terribly tired and not so hopeful. "I believe the kid's beyond any help. We can count on that he'll not survive."

"Do you think the end will be soon?" Herzod asked.

"It's not possible for me to determine. All I can say is that he doesn't react to all treatments I have given him." The doctor was honest. He was explaining the case from a medical point of view, making Herzod look in the other direction. It was not easy for him to confess that he knew almost nothing about the body and its functions. He was a frequent traveler, who knew much about people, countries and things lying so far away, but the thing closest of them all, he was completely ignorant of. "We have given him medicines that are potent enough to have brought back the dead, but this child has refused to respond. And herein lies the reason of my hopelessness." The doctor concluded.

"I'm really grateful for all your efforts. I'll compensate you for all your hard work. "Herzod said, looking into the doctor's blood-red eyes.

"Don't worry about my fee. It is the kid's condition, which worries me most."

"Can I look at the child before I leave you to rest a little? I can see your sleepless red eyes."

"Of course, come and look at him. He is in the other room."

Both Herzod and the doctor were looking at the child, feeling pity for him, and wondering whether he was to live or die. None spoke about the sensitive issue any more. Herzod and the doctor looked content and satisfied. They both had done whatever stood in their power to drag the child back from the valley of death if he was to quit the world anyhow; no blame was to be placed on them. Herzod turned his gaze from the child and looked at the doctor. "Do all what is in your power and save him. I'll be thankful to you for eternity. This child has given my wife and me a hope. You know how desperately we have been missing the presence of a child in our otherwise rich lives. Last night, when I told her about a remote possibility of getting a kid, she became so very excited. All night she prayed, for the safety of the poor kid, even if driven by her own egoistic reasons." Herzod said in a sentimental way.

"I wouldn't give her much to expect if I were you."

"Yes, looking at the child's condition."

They both reacted simultaneously to the minor movement in the body of the child. They were both unsure of what they just had witnessed. Was there really a slight movement in the body or they were suffering from some collective illusion?

"Did you notice any peculiar thing around?" the doctor asked, without mentioning the actual occurrence, which he believed took place.

Herzod didn't react to his question but kept staring at the motionless child. It looked like he wasn't even there. His gaze was fixed on the boy when he made another slight movement, leaving no doubt that his body had started communicating with the brain. They were both so excited by the happening that their faces glowed with happiness. So not all was lost. The young fighter had not given up his hopeless struggle to survive.

The change in the condition of the young prince was remarkable, though gradual. They had to wait another day before he came out of his coma. He finally opened the eyes and smiled at the people around his bed. His movements were weak, and he struggled hard to recognise their faces. He seemed to be confused but unfazed by the presence of strangers. Herzod smiled back and tried to communicate with the child, but the doctor signed him to take it easy and come out of the room, leaving his wife to remain with the kid. "I believe he doesn't remember anything, and it's wise not straining him." the doctor said. "With time shall he tell us the sad story of his and conditions, which had caused the death of his father. I still wonder why his mother wasn't accompanying them." Herzod said to himself, "I doubt if he has retained any memory of that." After discussing the subject for a while, they went in and watched the doctor's wife give the child some liquid from time to time, giving him support to sit leaning on pillows, holding his head before inserting drops of liquid in his dry mouth. The child wasn't fully in his senses, but they had all the reasons to believe that the danger was over.

All the princes had succeeded in escaping the brutal hands of the enemy. Their journeys to the safety and security were long, perilous, and crossed the valleys of fatality and perdition, where they had experienced the cold hands of death. But they had proven to be more resilient and stronger than anyone could have expected. All three of them had shown an incredible capacity to overcome the hardships they had been exposed to. All three of the princes had won the race against the time, but not without paying a price. All of them had lost the previous memories of their names, status, and parents. On the other hand, they were spared the agony of losing parents, a kingdom, and the tragic plight. Two of the princes did so, due to prolonged unconsciousness while the third did so for other reasons. Their return to life was not due to an inherent fighting spirit that was a part of their bloodstream. The hand of fate was playing a major role in enacting of that drama. Only few people knew about the true identities of these three kids. Not even they themselves had retained that knowledge, except in the bottom of murky water of their memories. What nature had in store for them was as yet unclear to all characters involved.

Queen Haliba had not been fully aware of the terrible duties and conditions waiting for her at her work. She was wrong in assuming that the work she was about to take resembled the life she had at Aloha's. She would have surely broken down under the crushing pressure of her harsh job, had she not been equipped with an unwavering will power, and a strong wish to come in contact with her husband. She knew that the attempt could lead to her own death, but she was ready to take her chances. She was assigned to the kitchen, where she was to wash all the dirty dishes and big saucepans, which were impossible to clean. All those iron plates and pots had thick layers of dirt and grease on them, which refused to give way. She tried to ignore the stench coming out of the kitchen. It seemed like no one had ever washed and cleaned the place. Everything was rotten: the food, the dirty floors, and even the fatty walls. The first few days she felt nauseated and couldn't help but vomit. Her co-workers laughed. Most of them were prisoners themselves and looked aghast when they learned that she took the job voluntarily.

"But why?" was their first reaction. "Couldn't you find anything better than to come to this rat hole?" they would wonder. Most of them were women as no man would enter that filthy place, even at the threat of losing his life.

"Many times have we gotten male prisoners to work here, but

none has survived more than a week, and yet they are the stronger sex!" boosted a skinny woman with a giggle.

"Why don't they do something about the dirt and stench?" Haliba asked. No one answered. They just looked at her as if she was from some other world. Haliba knew that if nobody changed the terrible situation, she was going to die.

"You have only two choices. Get adjusted to your new realities, or run away from this stinking place, and do it quick," some woman suggested.

"Yes, do as she recommended. You are a free worker. There are more like you, but they are older ones, forced to take this job because they couldn't find work anywhere else." another woman said. "Only a fool would come and live in this hell by choice." another younger woman added, looking at Haliba as if she were out of her mind.

Each morning Haliba would come to work in the kitchen, only to get nauseated and throw up. The penetrating stench was becoming an integral part of her being and was haunting her even in her sleep. The overwhelming smell was giving her nightmares. She was sure that soon she was going to give up, unable to bear the unbearable. The only things that kept her going were the adjustments that the other women had succeeded in making. If they had succeeded so could she. But she was ignoring the fact that they had not been queens while she had been. She noticed that even she had become a part of that terrible smell as the guards trying to get her attention in the beginning were drifting away from her, giving her a sigh of relief. There was some good in every evil she remembered in some old saying. Her duties in the kitchen were never going to bring her any closer to her husband, who was not even present at that prison, but she was gaining the trust of the administrators of the prison, who saw steadfastness and recognised the inherent stupidity, a thing they seldom found in their own environment. Queen Haliba had little time left to talk with other women who had lost all interest in her. She was too kind, too strange a woman, to have ever entered into their discussions of vanity and vulgarity. She was not one of them and therefore, eligible to complete ignoring. The only woman who remained sympathetically inclined towards her reminded her of an old friend of hers. Bisoona was almost of her own age, a silent type who neither complained nor tried to claim her innocence to the crime for which she was imprisoned. She would jump in to help Haliba each time the workload became too much or the stench became unbearable.

Haliba felt very much touched by her kind gestures, but Bisoona would just brush away her words of appreciation.

"No, it's nothing. We all are the victims of misfortune, who can only gain satisfaction by helping each other."

"You are a nice being, who thinks that way." Haliba would say, admiring her, but she would just smile away. "You are a free worker, so why don't you go and get some fresh air." She would suggest, almost forcing her to go and enjoy that freedom, none else in the kitchen could ever enjoy, as long as they were there in that prison.

"Tell me, why you are in prison?" Haliba asked one day.

"There's no point in discussing my story. We are meant to be here, whether we deserved it or not is inconsequential," Bisoona said with a bitter smile. "Look at you; you didn't do any wrong, but not only that you were brought here but even did so with a free will."

"That's true, but it's also true that you didn't come here of your free will, like me." Haliba was not to give up.

"I'm here for a crime I'm really proud of."

"And what's that?"

"My husband is a trader, and he was out on a long journey. While he was away, the new vice-king decreed a new tax on all goods that entered from anywhere in the country. I was worried that all the hardships and labours of my husband were to come to no avail if all the profit was to fall in the hands of the greedy vice king and his administrators." Bisoona was telling her the story of hers. "My husband had a tradition of announcing his coming in advance. He did as he used to do, by sending his trusted servant to give me the happy tidings of his safe return, with the only difference that I sent the servant back, asking him to warn my husband and his other companions about the new tax. My husband took the message and turned back to selling his goods somewhere else while his other companions ignored the warning and did come back, as they had argued that saving of a little tax wasn't worth all the trouble of going back."

"But that doesn't explain your arrest and sentence to the prison." Haliba wondered.

"You would understand, if you gave me a chance to finish my narration. "No-one was more wrong than the returning traders, who had anticipated a minor tax waiting for them. They were greeted by the hard-hearted administrators of the vice king, who evaluated the whole merchandise, they had brought with them and put so heavy taxes that even the most cowards of them couldn't help crying of indignation. But none of the protests were cared for, and they were forced to surrender all the goods till they paid the taxes." Bisoona smiled, looking at Haliba, expecting her to fill in the blanks.

"I still don't understand." Haliba was honest to confess.

"Don't you know anything about your fellow beings and the way they function?" Bisoona seemed to be disappointed at her naïve co-worker. "Try to imagine the wrath and pain of those traders, who had been robbed of all the hard labours and even the invested capital. Visualise the anxiety and the regret and jealousy of those people who had been given the equal chance of avoiding economic devastation but who had chosen to ignore it. This envy was opening the gates of hell for me. The administrators were informed about my role in issuing the warning. They were told that they had been deprived of great merchandise by the unpatriotic act of mine. And the result of all that is before your very eyes." Bisoona didn't appear to be sad or remorseful.

"Do you think it was worth the price?" Haliba asked, looking sadly at her.

"You mean my imprisonment? Absolutely!" she answered with a big smile on her face. "Not that I care for money more than my own freedom, but one must resist the evil of the vice-king. I'm happy to have taken some money out of their greedy reach." Bisoona was defiant.

"Who would be taking care of your children?"

"They are taken care of my mother, I hope," she said, getting anxious for the first time.

Haliba was deep in her own thoughts, remembering her children. She was cleaning the plates and other pots with all her energy, wishing to get rid of all the oily substance, which had refused to give way during all the time she had been there.
She was approached by a guard who told her that the jailor was pleased with her work, but her services at the prison kitchen were no more required. Haliba became disturbed by the news as it meant her going away from that place, which

was keeping her possibility and hope to see her husband, alive. She was too proud to show her dismay to the guard. Silently she turned to him and asked if she was supposed to quit at once, or could go on till her duty hours came to an end.

"We have a newcomer to take over." He pointed out an angry lady, who was fainting of the terrible stench. She comforted her. "You'll get used to it, believe me." The middle aged woman looked at Haliba in disbelief and disgust if that was due to the smell, arising from her whole being or had some other reasons she couldn't tell.

Haliba left her working place, making room for the frightened lady to take over the disgusting job assigned to her. With defeated short steps, she went towards her own quarter to get her things and leave the place, when another guard contacted her.

"Where do you think you are going?" He looked astonished.

"Going away from here, I'm told that there's no need of me any more." Haliba told him.

"You misunderstood. It's true that your services at the kitchen are no more required, but you are still on the payroll. You'll be assigned new duties very soon. So go and rest for the day."

She felt relieved that her work at the prison had not come to an end. She could go on nurturing the hope of seeing her husband. No one at the prison had ever heard of the presence of some important prisoner there. "What do you mean by an important prisoner? Aren't we all just prisoners?" Bisoona had laughed away her question. She was aware that getting access to the quarters where her husband was kept couldn't be an easy task. But she was waiting for a miracle.

That wonder did happen a few days after she was relieved from her duties at the kitchen. The old lady who usually took food to the imprisoned king got sick, unable to perform her duties. There were strict orders that no one was to approach the king but the most trusted ones. The jailor believed that Haliba qualified for the job, not only because he considered her a hard working and quiet person, who avoided company, but also for her quality of not being nosey.

She was shaky when she was brought before the jailor, who asked her to stop at a distance, a clear indication that she still stank. The tall, strong built man kept looking at her with his searching eyes. He wanted to be absolutely sure that he was making the right decision about her new duties. The hesitance in his face was to wither away after he watched the calm, empty face of Haliba.

"I've called for you to inform that from now on you'll be given some new duties to perform. You shall be bringing food to the most dangerous prisoners. You are not supposed to communicate with them, because they all are doomed to complete isolation."

"These duties are of a temporary nature, and will be withdrawn the moment the person performing them until now returns." Haliba's heartbeat was getting stronger and stronger, and her face flushed. Just the mere thought of seeing her beloved husband was filling her whole being with an incredible sense of achievement and bliss.

"As you command, sir," Haliba said bowing her head, not of respect and humbleness as the jailor understood it, but to hide the glow of her bright face.

Queen Haliba was very excited, more than any other time in her life. Even more than when she married the king, more than giving birth to male children, and yet this happiness was enveloped by a serene realisation that the sorrowful state of her husband was bound to break her heart. She was prepared to live that pain, but only if she was to get the equivalent pleasure from that great happening. The jailor dismissed her, and she came out. She was then led to her new quarters, which were much better than her previous place of living.

"You can live here as long as you work with the newly assigned task," the guard said in a rough tone, and left.

Haliba's whole body shook from excitement as she was led to the special part of the prison, which lay quite apart from the main building. She had never visited the prisons before. She had always felt sorry for the prisoners, but now she was heading to the detested, wretched place, where her husband was kept captive. Her eyes were fixed in the building at a distance, and her heart was already by her husband's side. She was hardly aware of the weight of the heavy buckets she was carrying. Her fervour dragged her forward, and she moved forward willingly and eagerly. The guard walking in front turned to see if she was lagging behind or was close to his footsteps. He hesitated as if indecisive about something, but then he came to her and took one heavy bucket away from her hand. She smiled, seeing a gentle side of that brute.

Every day she was brought to that part of the prison, which was not in the awareness of many. Not even all guards had knowledge about the place, and even if they did, they had no access to it. It was built differently. A narrow, tunnel-like, dark corridor led her to the dungeons, which lay at the other end of the tunnel. The guards never entered in that dark, gloomy place, as if they were afraid of some hidden ghosts in there. She felt the same horror and negativity creeping in her body and made it shiver as the others must have felt, when they had tried at some time. She was repulsed, but had to fight back her fright, which wasn't an easy task.

She had returned from the halfway point all sweaty as if she had seen some phantom. The guard laughed hysterically as he watched her fearful eyes. "Go yourself and give it a try," Haliba said without getting angry. The grin immediately disappeared from his face, which was turning black just by the very thought. But now she had grown accustomed to terrible feelings. She was certain that the creepy feelings had less to do with the unfortunate prisoners and more to the general atmosphere, which prevailed in that gloomy, dark, suppressed place. The absence of fresh air and light had contributed to the hellish environment. The shrieks and groaning was not making the place any better.

"Why do some groan and scream?" Haliba asked the guard, one day.

"Wouldn't you, if you were to go behind the bars over there, all alone, without anyone to attend to you if you were sick?" Haliba could tell he was scared and didn't want to discuss the subject any more.

"I would get insane," she confessed.

"And so they have done, or at least the majority of them." The guard said, pointing in the direction of the horrible portion of the prison.

Haliba stopped before each dungeon, thinking if it belonged to her loving husband or not. She was not supposed to speak to any of the prisoners, making it an impossible task to search for the king. She always placed the food before the iron bars of the prison cells, collecting the empty plates more often than she was supposed to do, invoking an outcry from the kitchen because of the workload had enhanced. Some officer demanded angrily why she did that. It was for the best of all, she tried to explain as it would have caused some serious epidemics. Just the mentioning of the word had taken away all the opposition she had feared. No disciplinary actions were to be taken against her for breaking the clear-cut rules.

The people behind the bars were as different as she could have expected. Most of them never even tried to communicate with her, while others did try occasionally, but she ignored their attempts to do so, some had gone beyond all human touch and just stared at the walls, she could feel while there were even others, who were the border liners, living on the edge. "I'm innocent. Please take my message to the king." Someone cried from his cell.

"Shut up, you weakling!" someone screamed from the far end of the corridor. "Don't you ever understand that it's better to talk to the rocky walls of our cells?"

Haliba was getting more and more disappointed and was losing all hope of ever meeting her husband. She didn't care if the sick lady returned to her job, making her go back to some other duty. She had lost all the enthusiasm that she once possessed, and wanted to leave the prison. Not that her love for Tylon was thinning away, but because she had realised the impossibility of the undertaking.

"I feel tired and depressed and want to quit my job," Haliba told her employer.

"Certainly, you are a free person who can decide herself what to do or not do. But is it possible for you to go on working just a little while more? The lady you replaced may come back to work soon, but even if she doesn't, I'll have a little more time to search for an appropriate substitute." The jailor was not that stupid as his reputation. He was correct in his dealing with her. The old lady was not to recover that quickly, and that matter was not pursued by her or by the jail authorities. Haliba performed her duties, though with less eagerness. She went into that scary place, gave food to the prisoners, and came back as quickly as it was possible for her. She had given up with her earlier attempts of searching for her husband. She stopped even peeping in those dark cells as there was hardly any point. Her eyes were unable to penetrate into the complete darkness.

"Excuse me!" Haliba heard someone say in a soft voice. She almost froze in her blood, without any doubt it was the voice of King Tylon. She felt like screaming of joy, but couldn't utter a single word. "I have no intention of being pushy, or seeking a contact, but you remind me of a very good friend of mine." King Tylon said in a soft, low voice. She was losing all control, but knew her work needed all her time. "Can you see me?" she asked in a whisper. "Of course I do as my eyes have gotten used to see in the darkness. I believe the daylight, on the other hand, will be blinding."

"It's me, my king!" Haliba whispered.

There was a complete silence in the cell. She could not see anything, but her heart was giving her the vision, in which she could watch the shock, the helplessness, and piercing sorrow that was paralysing her husband. She cried silently, before moving to the next cell and the next. Her entire body was trembling like a dry leaf in the stormy autumn wind. She had to be strong if she was to take the fruits of her labours if she was to establish a contact with her king, who needed her much more than she had realised.

She came out of the dark prison defeated. The guard ignored the distress that was, apparent in her eyes. They all knew the strain associated with their job, and considered it better not to inquire much about the feelings of others. The queen felt terribly sad. She couldn't sleep all night. Her mind was torturing her in ways that she had never anticipated. Even though she was aware of the conditions all the prisoners went through, the encounter came as a shock to her. She had dearly wished to sit and talk with him, listen to his sad story, to give him comfort and a bit of hope, to embrace him, to reassure him of her everlasting love, but she knew that none of those things were in her power. He was a prisoner by necessity while she was a captive by choice.

The next day she went and told to the jailor that she had changed her mind and wished to continue with her job as long as it was possible. He looked a bit surprised by her change of mind but didn't ask too many questions as she had feared. She had great difficulty in hiding her fervour from the guard, who was accompanying her that day. "What a strange person you are. I've never met anyone in such a hurry to reach that horrible place," said the young guard who was holding buckets full of food. "I hate this carrying the food for the prisoners. If it were up to me, I would just let them starve. It'd be good for them, good for the country, and I wouldn't have to carry all this weight."

"You are a naughty, cruel young man!" The queen said without offending guard, who laughingly agreed to her diagnosis. "My mother is of the same opinion," he said still amused by her words.

"Look, don't get impatient if I take some time. I'm not young like you and need to work in my own tempo. The other guards are aware of this fact." Haliba wanted to mentally prepare the guard.

"It's no problem for me. No one wants to stay there more than it's needed, anyway." He laughed. Haliba was working feverishly, giving food to the prisoners, collecting the empty dishes, and hardly paying attention to anything else. Finally, she came to the cell of her husband and stood there waiting for the king to take a contact, but there was a complete silence on the other side of the iron bars. "Are you there?" she whispered but got no response.

"Talk to me my love; I have so little time and so much to say." Haliba said in a whisper like tone, being certain that he was standing there, watching her. "My heart bleeds to find you in these horrible conditions." She was trying hard to suppress her cry. Still there was no response from Tylon. "The silence will not take away our pains" She tried again.

"I'm shocked…." Haliba finally heard Tylon. She tried once again to refrain from sobbing.

"I'm all right, No harm has come to me. But I would have preferred death, rather than seeing you in this degraded state." Tylon's voice was trembling; she could imagine his face getting red with rage.

"You shouldn't get upset; all we're going through is nothing but fate."

"Is it supposed to be a comfort?" Tylon sounded sour.

"No, but certainly a bitter reminder that we all are just toys in the hand of fate." She was silently crying, talking in a whisper so that no one would listen to what they said to each other. She was aware that there was not enough time to talk. She told him that they could get the chance to speak with each other but briefly, as long as it was possible. She promised to come again the next day.

"Don't ever come back. I command you to run away from this gloomy hell and never turn back." Tylon was telling her, he was begging, pleading, with a trembling voice. He couldn't bear the thought of her getting into some serious trouble because of him. Haliba didn't answer to any of his requests or commands as he called them. She was sure that despite all his worries and fears, Tylon would impatiently wait for her next visit.

6

Shapario had moved to the western kingdom and was leading a simple life there. He had taken a work at a blacksmith's workshop, an ancestral occupation, which he hated more than anything else in the world. He had been trying his best to do something else but found no opportunities available. The king and the people of that country were very suspicious of foreigners and seldom encouraged them to live there. The best way of doing so was to close all doors of any employment for them. The law didn't permit the ownership of a business, either. Shapario had no means of sustaining himself without income, so he started looking for it right away, but realised soon that was impossible. He knocked on many doors, but none was opened to him. He had some money, but that was to end soon as the country was very expensive. Shapario was an immovable character, which wouldn't give up even in the face of impossibilities. He went on with his untiring efforts, with a clear understanding that it was a matter of life and death.

He would have surely failed in his hopeless strife, had he not been told of the dim possibility of getting a job if he knew the skills of a blacksmith. Shapario looked horrified at the very mentioning of the word as he had hated it from the time of his childhood. He had sworn never to adopt the ancestral profession.

"No, I'm not interested in that kind of work," he said angrily to the person who had suggested it.

"I just wanted to be helpful." The man was really surprised.

"I'm sorry, it's not you, but me," Shapario apologised to the stranger.

"I've hinted to a remote possibility, not that you may get the job," the stranger said with a smile.

"What makes you that sarcastic?"

"The man I mention is not easy to work with. He is harsh, abusive and above all violent, making him an impossible person to work with," the stranger explained.

"Most of the blacksmiths are of that temper," Shapario said remembering his own father and uncles, who were responsible of his hating the profession. With dread he remembered the hard, crushing job, the burning furnaces, the unbearable, scorching heat and above all the presence of unsympathetic, ill tempered and intolerant grown-ups, and the most despicable things that had consumed the best years of his childhood. Some strange sadness was creeping in his whole being, a weird feeling, he always had feared as far as he remembered. He was not paying any attention to the stranger, who was watching him with a keen interest.

"You seem to be really absorbed by the topic."

"Yes, it has brought back some memories," Shapario confessed.

"I can give you the address in case you change your mind and want to try your luck." The stranger offered once again.

"No, thanks" was the brief answer.

Shapario was quite sure that sooner or later he was to get work, if not with the king, then at some noble's. The need for bodyguards and soldiers was a never-ending thing. People like him were always needed, both in peace times and in times of war and chaos. They were the fear invoking machines, which made the masses calm and passive, despite the poor conditions they lived in. Strong well-trained people like him were always in demand as they could provide the kings, rulers and the elite with a sense of security and a tool to control and expand. Shapario was sure of himself and knowledge, but what he didn't know was that the kingdom was swarming with the valiant young men, who were well equipped, well trained and without any other possibility to sustain them than to join the army. If the king could find the courageous people in his own home, why would he hire some stranger from a far away country - a stranger that he didn't even trust? Prince Hidas had fully recovered before he ventured to the western kingdom. His previous memory had been erased, and he had been behaving strangely as if he was mourning a great loss. Somewhere in his consciousness he had kept the knowledge that he had been bereaved of his glory and true identity. The indication of that likelihood never ceased coming to the prince. His temper had not become better by the disappearance of royal status. He was an arrogant person that he had always been. Shapario didn't have the heart to treat him harshly as he hated the method of roughly dealing with the kids. He had decided to take the path of patience and kindness in tackling the insolent prince. The poor child had already suffered the loss of his mother, father, brothers, and a throne, so he didn't want to add despair to his already miserable life by coming down hard on him.

"What made you take that long? Didn't you know that I was hungry?" The prince Hidas was angry. Shapario didn't like the tone but remained silent. He had no intention of confronting him as yet.

"I have been looking for some work," he told him politely.

"Sure you can do that, but first you have to arrange some food because I'm starving." Hidas showed no respect, hurting the feelings of Shapario.

"I have brought some food. You can eat it." Shapario pointed to the bag, he had placed on the wooden table. Hidas went to the table and eagerly started looking for food. He looked pleased to find his favourite food there. Without paying any attention to Shapario, he started eating. One could see that he was really hungry. Shapario was watching Hidas with sad eyes, wondering how was he to proceed with a self-absorbed person like him. He had not eaten anything during the whole day because he was thinking of the child sitting hungry at home, and there sat the same child consuming all the food that was supposed to be for both of them. He watched so intensely that he failed to notice that his sadness and disappointment was turning into anger. He had had enough. There was no way; he could let that disrespectful child go on behaving that way. Prince or a beggar, a person most blessed or a miserable orphan, he was to teach that boy some manners and mend his intolerable and rude ways. But he was a clever person, who knew that he could do the job better if he waited for the right moment and found a proper tool to accomplish his task. He had no lust to get out and buy food for himself, so he went to sleep with an empty stomach. On the other hand, his mind was not so empty, which kept searching and searching for the best possible way of dealing with Hidas. He was getting more and more convinced that some solution to his difficult problem was imminent, and all he needed to do was to keep thinking. The solution was the need of the hour, for his own peace of mind, and even in the best interest of the prince, if he was to adjust to his new humble status. He was terribly hungry, which was keeping him all. His thoughts were getting more and more entangled with each other. His past was getting mixed up with his present and the future remained hidden behind the foggy curtain of uncertainty. He got up, sitting erect on his bed, almost afraid of being drowned. All of a sudden, he saw the solution emerging from his own past, almost like a gift from high above. The golden idea was to give him the hope that he had been so desperately looking for in those hopeless times. He knew how to proceed from that point on. With a big smile, he was resting on the bed, without caring for the hunger till he finally slept.

The first thing Shapario did the next morning after waking up was to have a big breakfast. He was getting ready to leave the house. He was in a good mood, smiling, singing, and changing his clothes in an active, cheerful manner. Hidas had not seen him that happy before, so he was watching him intensively, wondering what had changed his mood. "When would you be back?" he asked Shapario. "It doesn't matter, it may take the whole day, and I don't care." He said in a careless tone.

"I may get hungry." Hidas reminded him why he asked about his absence in the first place.

"You are going with me." Shapario informed him.

"What shall I do while you'd be looking for a job?"

"No, I wouldn't be looking for a work only for myself; we both would be looking jobs for both of us."

"What!" Hidas exclaimed, looking at him in disbelief and with a panic-stricken face.

"You are a big boy now, and need to help your old father." Shapario pressed him further.

"But I am just a little boy." Hidas gave an argument.

"You are absolutely right, and I'll have this fact in mind while I look for an appropriate work for you." Shapario was not giving in as Hidas had hoped. Without much further questioning, he got dressed and went out of the house. Just by looking at his distressed face Shapario could guess what was bothering the little prince.

Shapario was not in a hurry, he was inquiring about the blacksmiths around, and it didn't take long before he could pinpoint the one he was looking for. Kestarius was worse than he had gathered from others. He was tall, powerfully built and had a furious face, with a large cut mark on his right cheek. The curly hair man was busy at his work, standing near a burning furnace. Shapario waited patiently for him at the entrance. "Yes!" Kestarius finally came to him and asked what he wanted. He told the strong man that he was looking for a job. "Go away; I don't have a work for you." The blacksmith was in a bad mood.

"I believe I am the person that you are looking for," Shapario insisted.

"Who told you that I need a helping hand?" The blacksmith asked rudely.

"Everyone in the town knows that you are ill tempered and thus the persisting need to find new workers," Shapario said fearlessly. The blacksmith got red in his face; he looked astonished at the courage of that stranger, who had dared to speak that way with him. He controlled his anger and asked Shapario to go away before he was to throw him away.

"I don't mind leaving you in peace, if only you can convince me that you don't have a need for a skilled worker." Shapario was unmoved. "Even if I did need a worker, it is never going to be you," the blacksmith was spiteful.

"Why not? Is it because of my big mouth, or do you believe I'm incompetent? Shapario was determined to test the man and the limit of his anger. "Look, don't you try my patience. I'm busy and don't have a time to stand and argue with you."

The blacksmith went back to his work, without turning back. Shapario watched him walk, and noticed that he was limping.

You're all mine, sooner or later, Shapario thought with a smile. He was right in his assessment that the blacksmith had much work in pending while he worked all alone. The untenable situation was to make him crumble under the increasing pressure and burden or to force him seek a helping hand. Which of those alternatives he was to opt was not a difficult guesswork?

All he had to do was to sit idle in the corner and wait for the right moment. Hidas was happy to notice that his search for the job had come to an end, except for his visit to the blacksmith from time to time.

Kestarius was conscious that he was being watched by Shapario, a fact that made him both angry and curious about the person. But he decided to ignore him, avoiding all confrontations. He had had enough of those and sought no new troubles. Shapario was sitting just few meters away from the workshop when he saw a brigade of the army approaching the blacksmith. There were about a dozen of them, riding on the horses. They were discussing something with the blacksmith; he couldn't tell the topic from the distance. The only thing he could see was the angry hand gestures of that large blacksmith. It looked as if he was arguing with the soldiers, protesting about something or perhaps even threatening them. He waited until the soldiers had gone back to the direction they had earlier come from. He decided to approach the blacksmith, smelling that it was a proper moment to give the last blow, a feeling which could have cost him life. He heard the angry growl of the blacksmith as he approached the place. The man seemed completely ferocious as if he was at war with someone. He was screaming, cursing, and throwing the metal pieces in the oven, when he caught sight of Shapario. His eyes were red of the both the inner and the outer heat. He looked at him with his murderous eyes and rushed towards him, without giving him any chance to take any precautions or defend himself. In a mad rush, he came near and held Shapario in his strong arms, and lifted him in the air as if he was going to throw him in the air. Shapario, unexpected of that frenetic behaviour, was struggling to get out of that powerful grip. Suddenly the blacksmith's eyes met the terrified eyes of Hidas, who was also taken by surprise. Perhaps it was the reason, which had brought Kestarius back to his senses. Gone was the fury, after a few moments of thinking about the whole situation. Shapario was still hanging in the air, almost certain that the danger was over.

"Whatever has caused you this rage, believe me, it's not me," Shapario reminded him, hoping to come back to the earth.

"I'm sorry. I don't know what possess me sometimes" Kestarius said regretfully.

"Certainly you have reasons to get mad." Shapario tried to cheer him up.

"I'm not in a mood to talk to anyone, so please leave me alone." Kestarius said looking down at the ground. Shapario could see his strong body being pressed by some unseen crushing weight.

"I can see that you are a lonely man." Shapario stopped, anticipating a new frenetic attack. "You see, all the great people in this world are lonely," he added quickly to appease his anger. He had succeeded in realising the blacksmith that he wasn't referring to any shortcoming but was talking about something, which indicated the inherent defects in other people's behaviours.

"What do you want this time? Why don't you leave me in

Once Again

peace? I've problems of my own, so please go your way."
Kestarius demanded him to leave, waving his hand in the air.

"I was coming here only in a hope to get some work. But I can see that you really don't need a working hand. I promise not to bother you again." Shapario said patting the blacksmith's powerful shoulders, which angrily brushed away his hand. He hated all physical contact, a fact Shapario had known from his earlier experience of other likewise people he had come across.

He knew perfectly well that behind all hard nut shells, hid softer surfaces; all one needed to do was to crack those. The force one needed to apply was not necessarily the physical one. He was trying to find some crack, which would allow him a penetration, and soon he was to find it. The man was almost of his own age, which indicated that he had time to get married and have children of his own. The profession was always sought by the successive generations, what made him work alone, he thought quickly and didn't hesitate to place it before turning to go back.

"Don't you have any children to assist you in your hard work?"

The angry looks confirmed that he had pinched at the right spot; the large bodied man opened his mouth to say something unpleasant, but refrained doing so, finding it hard to fight a person, who seemed to be friendly and sympathetic. But he was still reluctant to speak of his heart, and about the troubles that bothered him. "I'm sorry to have asked you a personal question. I was just struck by the spontaneous thought." Shapario turned to go his way. Without looking back, he could swear that the giant looking blacksmith was watching him. If that contemplation was not for his sake, then it did concern the young person he accompanied at the time. The way he looked at the prince with sad, remorseful

99

eyes, made it almost sure that he saw someone else in Hidas.

"Wait!" He finally heard the voice of Kestarius. He had been expecting it. He hid his grin before turning to the blacksmith.

"I don't know why I'm even asking you, but what do you know about the trade?" The blacksmith asked.

"All a good blacksmith needs to know." Shapario was confident.

"You look strong, but can you deliver that you claim?" Kestarius was reluctant to take his answer at its face value.

"You can first see my work, before offering a job or coming to the terms and conditions. If I boast and tell lies to get the job, then I would be standing without." Shapario said with a smile.

"It's fair enough." Spoke the blacksmith, still without a smile. "You can come tomorrow, but do come alone."

"Why?" Shapario asked." He is my son, and I intend to teach him the trade. He'll be my help as I had been to my father."

"He is too young and our profession too dangerous. There is no room for him here." Kestarius made it clear that the child was not allowed there.

"I'm a widower, and there is no one to take care of him, leaving me no choice but to keep him near." Shapario was not to give way.

"That's your headache; as far as the work is concerned you shall not bring him with you."

"Even though this work is very important for our survival,

I'm afraid that I have to turn your offer down." Shapario was taking a stand, fearing that he was pushing his employer too far.

"You mean the deal is off?" The blacksmith seemed little surprised.

"I'm afraid that's the case. You see, he is all I have left, and I don't want to lose him," Shapario said in a decisive manner, hoping that the blacksmith would buy his bluff. He was absolutely right in his judgement that the man would agree, if only at the end.

"I must confess that you are a stubborn person like me. You may bring him with you, but the responsibility would be all yours." Kestarius gave up.

"You'll not regret your decision, I promise. And this little helper shall not cost you a straw." Shapario said, hiding his joy.

The person least happy with this change in Kestarius's mind was Hidas, who was bitter and didn't try to hide his anger. All the way he kept to himself, not saying a word. He was not surrendering his childhood without giving some resistance. Shapario was ignoring the rage of his young master, quite confident that the prince was to give in ultimately. All was for his own good, he thought with a happy face. To convince Hidas was a harder task than he had assumed; the prince refused to follow him the next day to his work. There wasn't any threat or incentive strong enough to make him change his mind. He seemed even ready to be abandoned by Shapario. There wasn't anything more he could do; he had used all the arguments and warnings he could think of. He was getting late, a thing he hated to do and beside that he knew that it wasn't going to be a good start, especially with people like Kestarius. He saw a golden opportunity to get meaningful work and a possibility to sustain them, slipping out of hand. Of course, he could go to work alone, leaving the stubborn prince at home, but that would have meant a clear failure of his plan to make a real man of Hidas. "Look, I don't have any time to waste on you, I'll give few more minutes to you and then I'll go my way."

"I don't care." Hidas was equally tough.

"And I'm not coming back." Shapario threatened. The prince didn't react verbally and just shrugged his shoulders. He wasn't giving the impression of being scared.

"All right, as you wish!" Shapario seemed to be surrendering. "If you have decided to remain a skinny, little boy, it's okay with me." He was right about the effect of his words on Hidas, who looked scared the very first time. He had finally succeeded in breaking his hard shell and found the weak point. He smiled to himself for that breakthrough he desperately needed.

"What do you mean?" Hidas asked.

"You see, work makes a man strong in the body. The earlier you start, the more probable it becomes that you grow up like Kestarius." Shapario deliberately mentioned the name, as he was certain that Hidas was impressed by that giant like a person. There was a silence. Hidas was weighing his choices; finally, he left his place to follow Shapario to his work as he had decided to grow into a strong big man.

Kestarius was busy with his work when Shapario appeared along with Hidas. He pretended not to be caring that they were late, but Shapario was sure that the big man was in great agitation. He refrained from taking up the matter as it would have made things worse. "What do you want me to start with?" he asked. Kestarius pointed to the side where he kept the iron ore. "Go make these horse shoes, which we have to deliver soon." Kestarius could see, the unpleasantness appearing on the face of Shapario, he didn't like that expression but chose to ignore it, and that he did with a great effort. "Go and sit there." Shapario told the prince.

"Am I not supposed to work?"

"No, not today. Just sit and watch" He said with a broad smile, before going to his work. All day long Hidas watched both men working hard with different objects. They were putting the pieces of metal in the furnace, melting them down, putting them in the forms, to get a bit cold, before taking them out, holding them with tongs, watching them carefully, before hammering them, to give the desired shapes. It was without any doubt the most amazing thing to watch for the little prince. He looked fascinated and impressed at the work of those craftsmen. But he was even scared by that demonstration of skill, wondering if he was ever to be able to master that art. Kestarius was busy, pretending not to notice the work of Shapario, but he kept observing the new comer from side-glances. He looked pleased with his work; just looking at the way he dealt with the tools convinced him that the person knew his trade very well. He had given him the simplest tasks, but knew that he could be entrusted with the most complicated and difficult jobs, as well.

"Shall I come tomorrow as well?" Shapario asked rhetorically.

"If you want to." Kestarius answered carelessly. If Shapario was expecting a word of appreciation, he wasn't going to get that for a long time to come. Shapario looked terribly tired. The hard work had taken all his energies. He wasn't used to that rigid work any longer and besides that he had been consuming extra energy to give a good impression to the blacksmith.

Hidas was happy to come and work with Shapario. If that was called work, he didn't mind doing it. What he did all day long was to watch those two sound men struggle with their painstaking job, all drenched in sweat, glowing with the incredible heat and hardly taking a rest. They looked like two obsessed persons, who were without any other interests or obligations in life. Their days were long and filled with rigorous work, but they seemed not to mind that. What Hidas didn't know, was that he was being entrapped into that work. Slowly, slowly he was getting tamed, without even knowing it. The words of appreciation coming from Shapario were like ropes, ensnaring his independent thinking, likings and disliking. All day long he would sit and watch them work, play around or watch the people passing on the road. Occasionally he was asked to bring some coal for the burning furnaces, or do some other light work, and felt happy and proud, when Shapario rewarded him with big appreciations. "You are some crazy man." Kestarius would mumble.

"Why do you think so?" Shapario would ask with laughter.

"You treat your son as if he were royalty."

"Aren't all children princes and princesses to their parents?"

"Maybe! But you are the only one who treats him like he is one."

"You know I'm both a father and a mother to him, and then he is too young to work. All I want to do is to make him mentally ready." Shapario was convincing his employer that his methods were not that wrong either.

"Think about when he doesn't get this appreciation in real life. Who would be responsible for his disappointment and bitterness?" Kestarius said, looking at the glowing object in his hand.

Shapario didn't say anything but he was thinking deeply, realising that there was some logic in what Kestarius said. He had hated his father for being pushy, for never saying a word of praise and for always criticising him, but he was doing the opposite, which could be equally harmful for the growth of the child. He had to deal with the kid in a more careful and balanced manner if he wanted to achieve his goal of turning him into physically strong and mentally tough man. He had to tone down his appreciations in a successive way if he was not to cause some astonishment and disappointment to Hidas.

Kestarius was happy to have gotten a co-worker who was skillful, hardworking, and trustworthy, the qualities he had been looking at his employees ever since he had started working. The biggest cause of his anger and bad temper had been those incompetent workers who brought nothing but shame and complaints from customers. He wasn't very verbal and open-hearted person so Shapario could not expect him to come and confess that he was pleased with his work. The workload was growing more and more as the news spread that Kestarius was not only taking the new assignments once again, but was even delivering the goods within the promised time. His biggest customer was no one else but the king, who demanded but the best of the best, something only Kestarius was able to provide.

7

Silos and Binti had been living in the eastern kingdom of Kildia. It was a calm, nice place to live if one wanted to enjoy the inner, softer side of life. The king there was a great patron of art, music, and other aesthetic arts. There was a sound of wonderful music coming from all directions and beautiful girls dancing to the rhythmic tunes, giving the whole atmosphere a magic touch. There were philosophers, intellectuals, and learned all gathered in that country, and Silos was like a fish in water. Despite the fact that he was without any money or influence, he was extremely happy to be at that place. He was quick to seek work at the king's court. The relatively young king was kind and cordial, giving him the full chance to plead his request.

"What are you best at?" The king asked him.

"Nothing," Silos confessed helplessly.

"How can I help you then?"

"Though I'm not good at anything, I'm good at many things," said Silos. "I can teach astrology, astronomy, I'm good at languages and can even a little bit of philosophy."

"I believe we can have a use for your talents and give you a suitable job. What have you done previously?" The king inquired. He was about to disclose his attachment to the court of Tylon, but refrained from doing so.

"Tell me a little about the unfortunate happening of your country." The king was curious.

"I'm afraid I wouldn't be able to contribute much as the terrible things occurred after we had left the land." Silo excused himself for not being able to provide much information. He couldn't find any trace of anxiety in the face of the king. The king gave him some money calling it an advance payment for the services he was to render to him in the days to come. With little reluctance and thankfulness, he received the money, showing his gratitude by bowing down. The king smiled because he knew that his gestures were genuine. "Go, enjoy yourself and get accustomed to our country. I'll be calling you when I have found a reasonable work for you."

The country was green, peaceful and rich. A most rare combination, Silos had seen in his entire life. The people of that country were polite, refined, soft speakers, and most of all not interested at all in the martial arts. The later mentioned quality did worry him most as he could feel that the situation was unsustainable, and was to ultimately invite an invasion. There was an abundance in everything, making the whole kingdom flourish like a beautiful garden. There was a unique kind of peace in the air, exciting people to turn inside, find beauties there and then to reflect them in their immediate surroundings. That the atmosphere was good for the soul, but by no means made the country a perfect place to live, or a harmonious place, where no problems existed. There were difficulties like any other place on the face of the earth; the only difference that made the kingdom better place than others was its mature approach to the problems it faced. All efforts were made to turn the attention to those problems and find some amiable solutions to them. A stress was laid on the inherent weaknesses in the human heart. Silos was impressed but saw that not all those qualities were as positive as they had appeared to be. He was astonished to learn about the prevailing laws in the country and was horrified by the penalties, which existed for the offenders. There was something, which scared him, and he wished to take it up with the king if the circumstances permitted.

The king of Kildia, Afshar, was not as naïve and stupid as he might have looked at first sight. Despite his great interest and love of the fine arts, he had remained fully awake to the dangers lurking around his kingdom that made it vulnerable to outside aggression. Silos had learned those new things by having a serious discussion with Afshar. The king had smiled when Silos took up the subject by saying.

"The most revered king knows that my intentions are noble. I'm compelled to talk about something that bothers me."

"You can feel free to speak about any subject."

"I love the atmosphere of your peaceful kingdom, but peace in the world is a commodity that one has to safeguard." Silos spoke. The king agreed.

"I can see that the people of your country aren't prepared for the unforeseen circumstances and dangers. Their love for peace and tranquility has deprived them of the knowledge that peace is not all a product of one's own actions and wishes." Silos said.

"How very beautifully you have presented this truth," King Afshar said admiringly.

"I'm pleased to notice that your majesty is well aware of these bitter truths," Silos continued.

"The world is full of greedy, aggressive, and violent people who are constantly searching for the weak points to make their attempts to possess and occupy what is not theirs."

"I understand what you mean, but what are you implying?" King Afshar asked with a smile.

"Your majesty, I'm just showing my concern about the need

to be even prepared for the worst."

"And you think that we are not?" the king asked politely. Silos's silence made him smile.

"Silos, I'm impressed from your wisdom. There aren't many in my kingdom who would even think of such terrible possibilities. They just think in terms of their own little lives, a life of abundance, and an existence uncomplicated and without any threat. But no one is ready to defend that freedom and peace if it were attacked. Isn't it a most preposterous equation?" the king asked dramatically, without even sounding sad. Silos was surprised and confused if the king was conscious about all those things, then why didn't he do anything to change that situation The king must have read his face, as he said this with a smile.

"The kings and rulers are the brains of their subjects, which are supposed to do all thinking.

I'm aware that my subjects don't want to take the arms; instead they love the inner side more. What am I supposed to do? Force them to attend to the needs of a strong viable defence, or close my eyes to a danger like them." King Afshar was putting the dilemma in a powerful manner, making Silos speechless.

"Tell me, what would you do if you were in my shoes?" Silos was still silent, not finding a quick answer to the question. "You see, a king's job is not always a dance on the roses. I'm a king, mindful of the needs of my people. But I am also attentive to the requirements of the time." Silos felt confused, not understanding what king Afshar was imparting.

The king smiled and told him that he was very well prepared for all eventualities. He had a small but very well-disciplined and effective army, which was ready to defend his country if the need was to arise. Most of his soldiers were trained not only in the art of warfare but even were equipped with moral strength. That defensive force was never exposed to the general public for two reasons. Firstly, because it would have been seen as depletion of resources as people were too simple to feel any imminent danger approaching them, and secondly because they were to be spared any anxiety.

"I believe it's good to demonstrate latent power, so the enemy is cautioned. Sometimes, a show of power can avert the dangers without the spilling of a single drop of blood." Silos gave his opinion.

"The element of surprise is the best of weapons, don't you agree?"

"Yes, your excellency, that is very true," Silos agreed. "But why expose yourself to the threat, when all you have to do is to expose wisely that you have at your disposal." He continued.

"Perhaps you are right, Silos. But don't you know the truth, that gathering of all power in one place and one hand is dangerous and can turn evil?" the king said with a smile.

King Afshar was capable not only to see that the power and glory entrusted in him by some unseen forces but also recognised his limitations. He was aware that there lay a pressing need for strong defences, but he also was conscious that that force couldn't exceed a set limit as most of his subjects were unwilling to join the defence force. His limitations had forced him to find some innovative solutions; without a doubt he was an improvising king. He had taken the best trainers from outside the country, which had trained and equipped those soldiers. These soldiers were given not only a hard training in the use of weaponry, but were also provided with the strong convictions and believe in their unwavering cause to defend their motherland. Despite all those highly elevated principles, high morals, and conducts of behaviour, king Afshar had remained skeptical about the army's incorruptibility. He was afraid to bring it in the vicinity of his cities, both distrusting that robust force and his own capacity to handle that power.

Binti had been very much disturbed and depressed but was slowly coming out of her miserable state. She was rather forced to as the entire responsibility of prince Beran had fallen on her tiny shoulders. Silos had done his part of duty, by bringing the prince and her to their new place of living. He had even found a paying job, so what more could be expected of him? Binti was too worried about her mother as she had never gotten a chance to inform her about her leaving the country. She felt cross but dared not take up the issue with Silos. She was a very efficient maid, but had no experience of bringing up an infant. She had never been near to any baby in her life, and didn't know what to do with her newly emerged duties and responsibilities. No wonder she was nervous, and there wasn't anyone to spill that nervousness on, either. Even though the youngest prince was a sweet little person; nevertheless he was an infant, with certain natural needs to attend to and a certain stubbornness to deal with. At times, she cried as it was taking all her time. The boy needed all her attention, leaving no time to cook or take care of other household tasks. She was getting more and more aggressive, irritated, and desperate as there was no outlet for her frustration. What really made her even more disturbed was the fact that there was no understanding on the part of Silos, who despite his wisdom and knowledge behaved worse than the baby. He would become sour if the food wasn't ready when he came home, or if the kitchen wasn't as clean as he was used to during all those years. All her patience was taking a toll on her health; she was feeling like a wreck, suffering from a constant headache. The worst of all were the nights when Beran would keep her awake all night, and she just would cry, not knowing what to do about the unbearable situation. She wasn't the mother of the child, nor had she the experience of raising others children, and yet she was attached to that unlucky fellow, who was not even aware of his misery. In the hours of her despair, she sat and thought about her situation, questioning her plight. What made her responsible for the kid? Why was she obliged to go on taking that great responsibility? She had a strong urge to go back to her country, where she had spent all her life, where she intended to spend the last days of her life. She wanted to go and live at the place, where all her friends and relatives lived. She was a free person and in full control of her own life and decisions about it. She had almost made up her mind and wanted to inform Silos about it. She was sure that Silos could easily afford to hire the services of someone, who would take care of the little prince. She was resolute not to revoke from her decision. All night the little child had been crying, none of them could sleep, but she was quite calm, well aware that such torturous nights were coming to an end. Silos kept sleeping as it was none of his problems. When he woke up and was getting ready to leave from home, she informed him about her decision to quit. "You wouldn't dare to!" was his first reaction. She didn't say a word and just looked at him firmly, giving him a clear message that not only that she had all the rights to do as it pleased her but even had the will and determination to exercise those rights.

Silos didn't pursue the subject, considering it her empty threat. She was without any doubt under an immense stress, and didn't know how to handle that. All he could do was to make her realise the importance of her sacrifice, which was being demanded of her by her loyalty to the king and by the gods. He was to take up the matter at some other point in time as that moment wasn't a good time to discuss the serious matter. Binti saw him going out of the house and felt even more offended. Before that minute she had thought of giving Silos enough time to find a substitute, but now she decided to quit immediately. She started packing the few belongings that she had. Beran was still sleeping, unaware of the fact that even Binti was about to abandon him. He had no memory of his real mother and had gotten attached to her as if she was his mother. She was doing everything in a robot-like manner, without showing any signs of the inner struggle, which was raging in her heart. For the last twenty years, she had been working with Silos, in whom she had found a nice and sympathetic person, a complete gentleman who never interfered with her work and had given her the full liberty to run the affairs as it pleased her. He was a man of integrity who always gave her the respect and honour that she found so rewarding. These were the factors that had made her stay with her employer for such a long time. She had been so satisfied with her work that she could ignore the shortcomings of Silos. Silos had never married as he considered the institution a very tough task, especially for those, who rated their freedom highest. Most probably he was afraid of taking on more responsibilities.

Her decision to quit her job was more complicated than she had earlier thought. On one, hand, she wanted to do so because she felt insufficient and incompetent to raise a child on her own, but she didn't want to give up on Silos. For many years, she had fostered the hope of his asking her to marry him, which never even crossed the mind of Silos, who had other things in his head. She was disappointed and wished that she hadn't lost so many years in waiting for a man who had no interest for her. She was worried about her journey back to the homeland, dreading the torturous, arid wastelands lying in between. She was even worried about the little prince, whom she had also grown attached. With which heart was she to leave him; she shivered by the mere thought. Her resolve was getting weak, and that gave her more anxiety than even before. When Silos did come home, he looked more tired and worried than before. Without saying a word, he went to his room and stayed there for the rest of the day.

That wasn't a normal happening, a thing sufficient enough to make Binti get worried. He had not come and demanded a meal, as was his custom. He had a habit of eating his dinner at home. No party or a feast could make him break that rule. Most of his acquaintances knew and respected his tenet. Binti waited a long time for him to come and have his meal. When he failed to do so, she decided to go herself and see if he was all right.

"I'm not hungry. You can go and take rest." Silos informed her, without inviting her in the room as he used to do.

"Is all well?" Binti asked in a worried tone

"I'm completely alright. I just want to be alone." Silos answered without looking at her, and she turned back from the doorway. She knew without the slightest doubt that her master was in a serious pensive mood, trying to solve the mysteries of existence. But doing so had never prevented him from taking a dinner before.

When she woke up in the morning, she was surprised to see Silos already sitting in the living room. He looked pale and tired. His red, sleepless eyes were indicating that he had not slept all night. He greeted her with a smile and asked if she had a good night's sleep. She was surprised as it was not only the first time she was seeing him that early but even the fact that he never spoke a word when he got up. It seemed as if he was mute and dumb and incapable of talking.

"So, you are serious about your quitting?" Silos said with a smile, pointing to her packed bag. She kept silent.

"I have been pondering the matter." He was looking at her sad face, trying to detect what was crossing her mind at that minute, but there were no clues, except a dark, gloomy shade, which betrayed that she wasn't very proud of her decision to leave.

"I have come to the conclusion that you have an absolute right to make your own choices. The responsibility of Beran is all mine as it's my mission to raise and protect him and not yours."

Binti tried to speak, but he stopped her by raising his right hand, indicating that he was not finished as yet.

"You have been a great help, not only now in the distressed hours of mine, but even during all those years. I don't know how I would have managed without you taking care of my household and me. I want to thank you for all these years, which you have devoted to me, and without a doubt you served me well."

"Master!" Binti tried to speak with a trembling voice. "I am sorry to have caused you distress, which was never the intent. I have never done anything for you, which I didn't do with a conviction and a sense of duty, but I don't find myself strong enough to meet the demands of motherhood."

"I agree with you that it is a tough task; even I'm dragged into this role of parenthood involuntarily," Silos said.

"But there is a difference between our roles." Binti said without any tint of bitterness. Your role of a father is more of a bread provider while I have to do the rest." Silos agreed with her without confessing it openly. They both sat and discussed the subject in a cool, clear manner, without any division of master and servant, without any hesitation of Silos to face the problem. Binti couldn't describe her astonishment at that sudden change in the behaviour of Silos. He was talking about the arrangements he would make to ensure her safe journey to their homeland. He was ready to give all the money he had in his former country as a compensation and appreciation to her long and untiring services. She was listening without saying a word, just sitting head bent, hiding the tears, which were streaming down at her cheeks. How she wished to tell him that she didn't want that money, she even had no real wish of returning to the country, where a bleak future waited for her, but she was too proud to speak of all those things. Her dignity wouldn't allow her to withdraw her decision to leave. When Silos begged her to stay a little longer to give him more time to find a replacement for her, she nodded in agreement, without saying a word, but inside she became unhappier than ever.

For many days, Silos avoided her. He was leaving in the early morning and returning late, taking his supper in his room, instead of eating at the kitchen table. All these things made Binti feel more sad and disturbed. She couldn't translate his strange behaviour in any other way than that he hated her that much that he had decided to freeze her completely. She was so troubled by his ignoring her that she had a renewed urge to leave that place immediately, but she had given her word, a thing more important than even her miserable state. She was waiting in patience for the moment, when her employer was to announce that he had found the person he looked for. When Silos approached her, she was certain that he was to inform that he finally had succeeded in finding someone. She looked in anticipation at the serious face. She was right Silos was talking about some woman, who was ready to work for him and take care of the prince.

"Is she an experienced person" Binti inquired.

"She has two kids of her own; both of them are quite young." Silos told her.

"What about her husband?" Binti put another question.

"I never asked. What he has to do with her job?" Silos asked in astonishment.

"Wouldn't she be coming and living at your house?" Binti asked, making Silos a bit confused. He agreed that he had not thought about the practical things. "Why don't you meet and discuss the details with her, as you know I'm so bad in such matters." Silos was suddenly not happy about the prospects of having a family of four moving into his house. Binti declined his request in a polite way. "I'm sure you shall find some amicable solution to your problems. I would have helped you if I could, but find no energies to do so at this very moment." Silos didn't insist on her getting more involved than she already was. He had great difficulty in dealing with his own weird thoughts, which were getting stronger and stronger, like the water currents. The decision of Binti to quit the job had brought the realisation that his relationship with her had grown deeper and of more complicated nature than he had realised till then. He was terrified to notice that she had become an integral part of his otherwise lonely life, and a life without her around was unthinkable. He had difficulty in accepting that reality, which had struck his consciousness with a surprise. What had caused such an immense change was not easy to identify. The realisation was shocking and yet difficult to deal with. It was impossible for him to confront his own feelings or to face Binti and confess his feelings for her. The only way, which could spare him the difficult task, was to avoid her, and that he had been doing since the last many days or perhaps weeks. The stronger he felt the desire to tell her about his feelings, the more distanced he became giving her the wrong signals.

"I believe I can't go on waiting indefinitely." Binti confronted him one night, when he was on his way to his room. "I feel bad and want to finish my job as quickly as it's possible." She looked miserable but collected.

"I understand. Just give me a little more time."

"How long?" Binti stood firmly to make him bind himself.

"I really wish, if I could tell you that." Silos said avoiding looking at her.

"What prevents you from that" she was not retreating. Silos kept silent as if he was trying to find some excuse or proper words to express his thoughts. The pressure on him was mounting, a thing which he always hated.

"You see Binti; I have been struggling with certain things from sometimes, but come nowhere." He said still not looking at her. "When you told me about your decision to leave, I hardly took it seriously, as I was sure that you shall never leave me." He said staring at the floor. "But seeing that you meant each and every word, has made me realise that you have become a part of my life, and I have great difficulty in letting you go. I'm sorry for my selfish behaviour as I have been holding you here, with my lies, pretending to be searching some substitute for you. The truth is that I never searched for anyone, who could take care of the prince. I promise not to hold you another second, you may leave whenever you wish to do so." Silos looked the very first time in her eyes. He was terribly sad and regretful. He didn't wait for her reaction and went into his room, leaving Binti to stand there in a stunned state.

All her disappointment and anger to his weird behaviour was gone instead a feeling of disbelief and strong emotions were taking over her touched heart. The reasons for which, Silos had been avoiding her made her like him even more.

"I wouldn't leave if you don't want me to." Binti told him, going after in the room. Silos raised his gloomy face and watched her in disbelief.

"Really!" he exclaimed.

"Yes, master." Binti said with a smile, making Silos joyous.

8

Herzod and his wife were not very young any longer, but had already given up the hope of ever getting the fruits of a marriage. Herzod had constantly rejected the suggestions of remarrying, which was a general tradition in that part of the world. He told his wife that he wouldn't do that even if there were a guarantee of conceiving dozens of children by his new bride. He was deeply in love with his wife and would never do anything to hurt her. "You wouldn't be hurting me. Get married, and bring that great gift of nature and I'll be pleased" his wife would join others in putting pressure on him. "No, " was his answer to all requests and suggestions on that matter. The unexpected return of her husband, along with a little child had excited her a lot. Despite the words of caution, she went on believing that the discovery of that little child in the wilderness couldn't be translated in any other way than that it was an answer to her prayers, a gift most precious from above. Herzod was regretting to have told her the truth, fearing a major setback for his wife if the poor child wouldn't make it. Herzod hoped and prayed but knew that there was a little chance of the child's survival. His wife, Nori on the other hand, was already taking the arrival of the child as a given fact. She was preparing a big feast to celebrate the occasion. Had Herzod known about that he would have horrified by that, but luckily he was at the doctor's when his wife was getting herself braced to meet the new challenges of her life. She had already sent the news to all her friends and relatives that the gods had granted her long awaited wish and request. She was to become an honourable mother of a child.

When Herzod came back from the doctors, he was astonished to find so many of his friends and relatives waiting impatiently for him. "Where is the child?" they all asked in unison.

"Which boy?" Herzod asked in a surprise. It didn't take long before he understood what went on there. He asked everyone to go back, promising to let them know if there was to be any major change in his life.

"You shouldn't have done this." he said, looking disappointed. "I know that your special circumstance has made you obsessed with the word child, but there is no excuse in your acting this irresponsible way." Nori looked regretful as she clearly could see that some of her actions had disturbed her husband, a very unusual happening in it. She told him that she was sorry if she did something wrong.

"The child is in a most critical state and is not even fully conscious, and here you are celebrating his coming into our lives. The whole idea is appalling." Herzod was really hurt.

"It was stupid of me. Please forgive me" Nori looked aghast by the mere possibility of losing the child, a great gift from the heavens above. "How is he doing?" She inquired with a strange calm, which had returned to her.

"I don't know." Herzod said. "The doctor believes that he is giving signals of his continued struggle with the death. Maybe he'll live or maybe he wouldn't." Herzod told her still being unsure.

"Don't you worry he'll live and have a long happy life." Nori said cheerfully.

"What makes you that confidant?" Her husband asked in surprise.

"I don't know how, but my heart says that all I say is true." Nori was not worried a bit, making her husband shaking his head in pity.

The waking of the little child came very successively, and even he was fully conscious, it took some weeks before he could be allowed to go and live with his new family, which were dying to have him. Herzod and Nori spent most of their time in the home of the doctor so that the child would get accustomed to the faces of his new parents, before he moved into them. As the child couldn't tell his name or any other detail, which could indicate anything regarding his past, so they had decided to give him a new name. Nori was to choose some suitable name, and she could not think of any other suitable name than the one she had always wished if she was ever to give birth to a male child. She had not given birth to that child , but nevertheless he was to be named as Shamon. They were aware that the child had been deprived of not only his father but also his entire family and identity, but they didn't see it as any negativity as they intended to provide him with even a better than he could have thought of. They were rich and lived in a big house, which was the largest in the whole surrounding. He was to be offered a life full of luxury and abundance, and a very bright future. Nori had already decided that her son was to get the best education, not that they had wished him to go and seek a job, when he grew up, but because she wanted him to understand all that happened around in life. Herzod was of a different opinion, he thought that a general know how, and a minor mathematical knowledge was enough for Shamon to learn. "The profound knowledge is neither required nor very advisable as it serves only to make one more confused than to help in everyday life." But he was unable to put an impression on her. "My son shall learn all the arts one can learn. We shall turn him into the most smart and successful person on earth. Even the kings shall come and seek his advice." Nori was obsessed, making him tremble in his heart

"There's nothing wrong in dreaming but don't fly that high, there is safety in remaining on earth." She would just laugh at his fears. "I know you consider me crazy, but you'll see that this child of ours shall make us shine like stars." Herzod knew that there was no medicine in the word, which could cure her of that conviction. He saw her getting unrealistic, but considered that there was no harm to anyone else but to her, but she wouldn't even think of herself. She had merged her own self in the little being of Shamon, who was the king of their home, a monarch without a crown.

Herzod had accepted the unnatural tendencies of Nori in upbringing of Shamon, and had many times tried to convince her that she wasn't contributing anything positive by spoiling him. The child needed love and care but even more important than that was to have some insight and perspective about life, something which he was not to learn as long as she went on providing him whatever he asked for. Nori believed that the child had enough of troubles and tragedies and needed full attention, at least for the time being. "Life is not always fair or even kind. I want him to be physically and mentally fit if ever he falls in some serious trouble."

"What do you suggest?" Nori asked

"I want him to become whatever you think he is capable of, but…"

"But what?" Nori became scared.

"We have to be careful and not spoil him. You have to promise that you'll help me in teaching him the balance." Herzod put the emphases on his words.

"I promise." Knowing that there wasn't anything to worry relieved Nori.

The situation in Elbon was getting worse by every day. Pampicilos had the entire kingdom in his iron grip. The army was still under the direct control of his brother, king Razila, but by the time it had gone ineffective and out of focus. There wasn't any practical purpose for it to fill as all administrative work had been taken away from them by the passage of time. All was done in a successive manner, not to raise any suspicion by the commanders and the king. The officers and the commanders were getting used to the luxurious lifestyle, and saw no reason to prepare themselves for any emergencies as there loomed no danger from anywhere. From time to time, King Razila did visit Elbon but only to see that everything was in order and to remind his subjects that still he was the ruler of that country. He was still suspicious of Pampicilos but found no proof of any wrongdoing. His army commanders spoke well of his brother and attested his loyalty, suppressing his unwarranted suspicion and calming him down. Razila didn't like the fact that there were now more administrators in the country than there were the soldiers. Pampicilos had ready-made answers to all his questions.

"In war times it's best to have a large army, for both defensive and offensive purposes," was his doctrine. "But once there was peace and no imminent danger, it was best to use the civilian forces, to control, to squeeze and to rein the masses." King Razila hated to think about such matters, which had always remained beyond his comprehension. He decided to watch his brother even more closely than before, in order to guard his interests jealously. He could change Pampicilos with someone else, but where was he to find someone he could trust blindly.

What king Razila didn't have any idea about, was the fact that Pampicilos wasn't increasing the administrators from the civilian populations but was systematically recruiting the ex-soldiers. Most of these soldiers had no other mean of sustaining their lives and the conditions were worsening, leaving them no choice but to seek the jobs, which were being offered. So in secret Pampicilos had a large potent army working for him in a civilian disguise, a force, which could be converted into a fighting force in a twinkling of an eye. He was changing the whole structure of that land, building new roads so that his capital city could be connected to all other towns and villages. He was giving his people a possibility to travel easily within the country, but what he wanted in reality was a perfect road system, which would give him and his army, a quick communication possibility. He knew that more easy and rapid communication was to result in more mobility, which in its turn could mean more income for the state. On each road were his administrators to collect the toll from those, who were to use those pathways. These taxes were for the security provided by the state. At each entrance, stood his men demanding a toll for visiting the towns. The goods brought into these towns were taxed, as well. These unfair and immense taxes were crushing people, but there was nothing anyone could do but to live under those unbearable conditions.

"Your highness, the people of this country are getting more and more miserable, the situation is not sustainable." One friend of Pampicilos tried to warn him.

"I know that." Pampicilos answered calmly.

"Then are you thinking to ease up the situation, before people revolt?" The friend asked.

"No, not at all. Instead, I am to increase this burden twofold." Pampicilos wasn't joking.

The friend remained silent, not questioning the wisdom of his master. Pampicilos was studying his face and saw his confusion and smiled. "Don't you know that there is a meaning behind all our deeds?"

"That's an absolute truth" The adviser said without any

hesitation.

"Then with time shall you know what we had wanted to achieve by exposing people to such hardships"

Pampicilos had been waiting for the proper time, and was convinced that that moment was approaching very rapidly. All he had to do was to go on mounting the pressure, squeezing the people more and more, in order to drive them to the breaking point. He was perfectly aware that there was a drought in the country for the last two years it had not rained, and the crops were insufficient to support the population, but he had not eased up the taxes put on the agricultural products. That little food which was there to consume, was not taken to the towns for fear of heavy taxes, creating a famine like situation in the country. People were growing angry, but the mood was still of resignation rather than of revolt. There were abundant food stocks in the royal treasures, but no measures were announced as yet to use them. Pampicilos had replaced his civilian administrators with the army units, declaring it an emergency. The king's orders were to deal with the mob and the situation without any hesitation if any emergency was to arise. Razila's doubts about his younger brother were giving way. He was not exploiting the situation for his own benefit but instead had given full control to the forces loyal to him. Pampicilos had gathered all his administrators and was to give them the shocking news that their services were no more required. He looked at their anxious faces and informed them with regret that he was forced to let them go. He appreciated their great services, but found no means to continue giving them jobs and salaries. "Why not? The treasuries must be filled up to the edge, so why can't you give us a chance to feed us and our families?" demanded someone in anger.

"You all know it's not for me to decide. I'm also a servant like you, without any power to change anything." Pampicilos told them. Without speaking openly against his brother, the king, he was poisoning their minds. Indirectly putting all the blame on the army, which was preventing him from helping the needy people. If it was up to him, he would have opened up all the treasuries of the country, to provide them a relief, he assured them. There was an outcry, but he let them go empty-handed. After the army of those civil servants left he could envisage the first seeds of revolt being sown in the fertile land of Elbon.

"Dear brother, your days in this part of your kingdom are numbered." Pampicilos thought with a smile on his face.

He didn't have to wait for long. The army units were daily coming under attack by the armed groups, who were looting the food stores reserved for the army. The situation was very alarming as the regular army was caught up between their military and civil duties. For such a long time, they had been sitting idle, doing nothing and had grown used to of easygoing lives. The sudden change had taken them with the surprise. They weren't accustomed to the administrative work, and they weren't ready for their tasks for which they got salaries. The unprecedented situation was making them nervous as they were not ready for that. The army requested Pampicilos to relieve them of their civil duties, but he refused, saying that the emergency required a strong presence on the roads, and not some unarmed civilians, which anyhow had been relieved from their duties. The situation was worsened by every day, forcing the army to leave their civilian duties and concentrating only on guarding the official buildings and the treasuries. The retreat of the army units was sending strong signals to all rebels, they could see that the royal army wasn't that strong as they had earlier thought. But nevertheless there wasn't anything that could worry Pampicilos or disturb his plans. There was no reason for him to be alarmed as he knew that the sporadic attacks were just the results of special circumstances and not due to some organised rebellion. The people of Elbon were his, once the army of the Razila was to leave the arena. He was adding to the anxiety of the commanders, by asking them to deal with people more heavy-handedly. "How can we fight an enemy, which is not there? We are attacked only when we are off guard. No one can be alert all the time." The commanders were showing their frustration. "That's not an excuse. The king expects from you better performance than that." He was making them even more fearful than they already were. The situation of law and order was getting worsened by every day as the absence of soldiers from the streets was turning even ordinary people more brave and daring.

"Your majesty, I am unable to understand that, what goes on in the country." His adviser said with a concern.

"It's not difficult to see that. The things get worse by every minute."

"Why doesn't your highness take an action?"

"Why should I? Am I the king of Elbon? Is there any power put in me? I have always done my job without having any real authority. The king trusted his army more than he did trust me, his own brother. It's high time that they defended his honour and kingdom." Pampicilos said with a cruel smile.

"But your majesty, you are the vice king. Any harm to the kingdom is a direct harm to you as well." The advisor reminded him

"Maybe!" Pampicilos said with calm.

"I am lost to understand why the army is incapable to deal with the threat. Weren't they trained to deal with all situations?" The advisor asked, changing the subject.

"The armies are like waters." He said with a broad smile. "You have to keep them on the move if their vitality and the latent force are to keep intact. May that be a movement guided and driven by the circumstances or a simulated activity, it'll fill the purpose, as long as it moves. A static army is like dead waters; which will ultimately stink, and lose its strength."

"Why did the king do it." the advisor asked.

"He didn't. But I did." Pampicilos said with laughter. He looked amused to have tricked Razila. "That's my revenge, for being robbed of the throne. Everyone knows that he had sworn in as a king though it was me, who was the crown prince. Razila took advantage of my being minor, and my inability to stand before his staunch resolve to get the power." He was bitter to his brother one could see. "Razila has been ever since demanding a gratitude for his not harming me, what a great king we have." Pampicilos smelt a final episode of the ongoing drama, and didn't feel the need to hide his true feelings about the king.

How the downfall of the king was to benefit the vice king, was the question still bothering the advisor, but Pampicilos was not a trusting type either and didn't want to reveal too much of his plan to anyone.

Pampicilos was accusing the army commanders of being incompetent, cowardice and disloyalty. He couldn't trust at their ability to provide with the needed security for him and his family. He wasn't hiding the fact that he had a genuine need to hire his own guards and that he did without consulting the king or the commanders. He had not expected any opposition from anyone as everyone was busy dealing with the severe situation. "I believe the king is needed to come himself and suppress the rebellion" was the message sent by the vice king. Pampicilos was sure that Razila was not to come to Elbon, not only because he hated to lead the demoralised army but even because he was also facing drought at home and was afraid to have a similar situation there. He even refused to send some fresh strengthening units; to boost the morale's of his men. The commanders felt disappointed, bitter and abandoned. A moment, Pampicilos had been waiting so long and so patiently was finally there. He knew that he could easily get the loyalties of the demoralised army, but he had no intention of keeping that force, which had fulfilled its function, which was devastated and of no practical use to him. He speeded his quick process of rehiring his former civil servants, with a difference that he was recruiting them as soldiers and not as administrators. He had a sense of emergency as there existed an unpleasant chaos in the absence of the army, a vacuum was taking shape, which he had to fill with his own force and power before someone else did it. The new army was formed with such an amazing speed that it surprised everyone. He ordered his army units to distribute the food to everyone in the country. He relaxed all taxes for the rest of the year, promising to reconsider all policies and to review the need of all those taxes, imposed on them by the authority of the former king. The use of the word was deliberate as he wanted to avoid any formal declaration of independence. The people were happy with his new policies and blamed the former tyrant for all their ills. He had succeeded in achieving his goal to grab the power. The army could now clearly see his cunning scheme, but it was too late for anyone to do anything about it. They wished to join the new army, but Pampicilos declined their request, saying that the interests of his new kingdom were better served by the indigenous population. He thanked them for all the help they had provided in the past and ordered them to leave his kingdom.

"You are from us. We are no strangers to you. Who can serve you better than us?" The commanders tried to make him change his mind, but Pampicilos knew what he was doing. He was to give them a free passage to retreat to their former homelands, without any riches, without any arms.

"But this is our home as well." They argued, but saw no point in hoping that he would change his decision to banish them.

The army of king Razila was retreating filled with shame and ignominy. There wasn't any trace of that confidence and arrogance, which had made their faces shine at the time of their ingress in the country a few years back. None of them wanted to look back at the crowds, which were making fun of them, and were laughing at their humiliating exodus. They were wearing old rags instead of their clean and colourful uniforms. They were experiencing the bitter taste of disgrace They had not been defeated by an enemy, but were the victims of some internal strife, but nevertheless they were the display of an emerging reality and an exhibit of a power that was waning, so quickly if only from that part of the kingdom, where they had been stationed. They had entered that country, with dreams of getting a big booty, and they were leaving that place now, filled with disgrace and empty handed. They walked in disarray, without the show of discipline or self pride, fearful of their long journey to the homes, which had ceased to exist for a long time, without the certainty of any bright future. The division of the officers and the soldiers had disappeared as they weren't a ranked army any longer. Pampicilos was standing on the top of the tower in his palace and watched the retreat of the king's disbanded army. His emotionless face wouldn't reflect his thoughts, even in the moments of his loneliness. Was he happy, sad or indifference? His true feelings couldn't be seen by the expressions on his face. All one could say for sure was the fact that he didn't regret his decision to disgrace his former countrymen. They were first and foremost loyal to Razila, something he found hard to forgive them for. He was the king now, and there was nothing his brother could do to change that fact. "I'll make such a strong and loyal army that you'll never dare to look at this direction, and if you did I'll make it a memorable lesson, the one you'll not forget as long as you lived." Pampicilos spoke those words, without ever letting them leave his mind. "I'll haunt you like a nightmare." The first time his face lit up by imagining the rage of the king, when he was to see his tattered army.

Pampicilos was rejoicing his successful maneuvering of the events and circumstances. He had not only emerged as a victor without shooting a single arrow, without any need to raise a little finger, and without the need to engage his newly formed army in any battle. He was proud of his mental powers, but also for having inborn cunning. He had held the grudge against Razila for such a long time, but had never got a chance to prove that he was a much better alternative. He was content and happy to have finally become a full king. He had hated the word vice as it indicated the imperfection, which he never considered himself to be suffering from. In the stressful days of chaos and unrest, Pampicilos had been too much busy in his planning for detailed and foolproof schemes, finding little time to give thoughts to the other important matters. Now that the former king's army had been routed, another period of euphoria took over his activities and celebrations. But there wasn't a moment when he didn't feel the pressing need to attend to something, which had disturbed him ever since he was appointed as the vice king, and that was the former king of Elbon, Tylon. According to his philosophy, the kings were dangerous as enemies, but they grew even more dangerous, if they were allowed to go on living. The best way of eliminating the future revenge thirst was to kill the enemy king on the spot. He was against his brother's decision to imprison Tylon, instead of beheading him, as was the rule. Many times he had taken up the issue but without succeeding in changing his brother's mind. "No, we are the best judge." Razila had always asserted

Pampicilos was finally in opposition to exercise his own will, regarding the matter. He wasn't happy about the escape of the queen and princes but had decided to do that which remained within his power that was to finish the life of Tylon, removing a potential threat once for all.

He had planned to do the job, without making a big issue of that. Except a few people, none knew the fact that the king was still alive and was getting rotten in the prison. He was a patient man, who never acted in a hurry, so he decided to wait for another few days to implement his plan. "Your highness, your days of endless misery are numbered, soon shall I release you from the bitter memories" he thought as he was to give Tylon some favour.

Suddenly he was struck with an awful thought and almost jumped from his seat. He was angry with himself, for not having thought about the subject. He had completely forgotten about the prison, and that place was still run by the authorities loyal to the former king, who surely had been aware about the political changes that had occurred in that country. He had to act as quickly as possible and change the officials in there. He called for the guards and ordered them to arrest all guards and officials from the prison, which belonged to the former king.

"Be careful and don't let anyone leave the place, not even the free staff" he was very explicit in his orders. He couldn't believe that he a minute planner could make such a blunder. He wasn't worried as few of the prison guards were not any significant threat to him.

He waited for news about the prison and the guards there, but he had to wait for a very long time. When finally the news came, it wasn't that, which he had been hoping and waiting for. He wouldn't believe his ears that the prison stood all empty, without signs of the prisoners or the staff working there. No-one could tell him, as to when that entire dreadful thing happened, and who were the responsible for that. He was pale, looking like as if he was drained of all blood, silently cursing himself for that great misfortune. He felt the rage, but that was not directed to anyone else than himself. "There is another portion of the prison, where the most dangerous prisoners are kept. Have anyone been there to check the prisoners?"

No, there wasn't a single soul in that place, from whom they could get any information, he was told.

It was through Aloha's visit that Haliba had gotten the knowledge that something was going on out there. She was told about the breakdown of law and order, and about the rising attacks on the army quarters. She was sad to learn that people of her country were suffering from the famine like situation, but what worried her most was the question as to what was to follow that unrest. She couldn't tell, if she had reasons to wait something good or had the grounds to get nervous. She was sure that the people were not even aware that their king still lived, so no change was to benefit them. Aloha's visit had made many things clear, now she could better understand the general nervous atmosphere at the prison. The guards had been jumpy and resigned, doing their duties in a less efficient way. They weren't sure about their future anymore. She had continued working at the part of the prison, reserved for the most dangerous prisoners, as the lady, to whom she replaced never recovered from her ailment. Haliba heard that the lady was suffering from some incurable disease and was dying. There were rumours that she had gotten the disease from some prisoner, which scared away many possible candidates for the job, making it easier to retain her job. King Tylon had come out of his initial shock, and refusal to face the reality and was happy about the possibility of spending a few moments with his wife Haliba. She was careful not to raise any suspicion, only spending fleeting moments at the side of Tylon, giving him courage and reason to endure those horrible conditions. He wouldn't know how? But he believed and trusted her soothing words, which she whispered in his ears. "Have patience my love, soon this tormenting shall come to an end" There was no reason to base that assertion upon, but strangely he always trusted in that, without thinking, ignoring all logic. He had never complained about the most miserable conditions or the suffering he went through every minute of the day. He could bear his pain and afflictions as long as he continued having a glimpse of his beloved wife. He preferred to listen than to speak as it was her sweet little whispers of comfort and hopefulness that filled his heart with a desire to live and gave him new energies to face his otherwise intolerable life.

Haliba was called into the prison warden, who was in a terrible mood. She became alarmed and feared that she had been disclosed. The anger in the eyes of Prison keeper was so persistent that she couldn't think of anything else. "How long have you been working here?"

The warden asked.

"I don't know sir, maybe two years, maybe three, I don't have the record." Haliba told him honestly.

"For whom do you work for? Do you have any family?" Why he asked such questions, she wondered but didn't dare to ask. She was reluctant to answer his question, not knowing how much he knew about her. "I have some relatives." She spoke without giving him exact details.

The warden told her that the reason of his wondering was the astonishing discovery he had just made that she hadn't had gotten her salary from the time she started the work. "There must have been some mix-up, and you were considered a prisoner, not eligible of having any salary. Don't you need a salary?" He asked, without easing his tense face.

"It's so meagre pay that it really doesn't matter if one gets it or not. I have been thinking that I'll get that all in one time, when I'll be quitting my work here." Haliba answered confidently, once she was sure that she had not been busted. What continued making her astonished was the fact that the warden was still looking terribly angry.

"May I ask you something sir? Haliba asked. The prison in charge kept silent, signaling her to speak. "You look agitated sir; if I have caused any trouble I'm sorry for that." Haliba excused.

"No, it's not you." He said waving his hand in the air. He gave her permission to leave without explaining any further the cause of his anger. It took another two days before she was paid all her dues and came to know at the same time that the jailer and the other prison staff were scared to death about the changes that were taking place around them. They had learned that Pampicilos rapidly distanced himself from the king and the forces loyal to him. The news was causing alarm that he was replacing the guards with the locals, a very bad omen if true. They were receiving the messages that something big was to happen them all, so all their attention was to the news, and when it did come, it sent shock waves. They were baffled to know that Pampicilos was banishing the entire army out of the country in a disgraced manner. If there were any doubts before about the vice-king and his intentions, they were all gone now. They all felt sad and outrageous but powerless to do anything.

9

The prison warden called an emergency meeting of the staff to discuss the terrible situation. He made no secret that he was very much disturbed by the happenings. "I can guarantee you that it's just a matter of time before it would be our turn. Learning of the news, we can tell that Pampicilos has made his choice. He has preferred the locals on us. Our friends and brothers are not allowed to take even the simplest of their belongings with them. They are given two days to leave the country. So we have to be quick in deciding what we really want to do." These words of warden were to open a hot debate, in which the anger was to flow, the bitterness to be expressed, fears were to be tossed in the air and anxieties were to be wrestled with. They all were busy looking at the grave situation from the point of view of their own tiny, miserable lives. The only person, who was not thinking of herself, was Haliba, who was deeply disturbed by the meeting. She was trembling to think of the consequences, which were to follow if some drastic change took place. The hot discussion was getting even hotter while her heart kept sinking to some unknown levels. The staff was unanimously in favour of getting out of that place and country before the trouble was to find them. "We should move away, as fast as it is possible" suggested someone. They all agreed, especially if they didn't want to be robbed of all their assets and savings.

"What are we going to do with the prisoners?" asked one guard. Haliba had been desperately waiting for the question to be raised.

"Yes, what about them?" The warden asked, as waiting for some magical suggestions from his staff. "Who cares? Let them be here, all locked up. If someone discover them or if they die of starvation, who'll mind it?" His words made everyone laugh. Haliba almost died of fright, imagining the prospects of such dreadful happening. Most of the prison guards were indifferent to the fate of their unfortunate captives, but there were few, which believed that even the prisoners deserved another chance, and therefore, should have been freed.

"Do you know what it'll mean?" screamed one of the guards.

"No, I don't know, please refresh my memory." the guard, which had given the proposition, said in a sarcastic tone. The other guards understood that there was no point in considering the best of that society, which had become unlivable for them.

"I agree that our responsibility to keep all these prisoners will end with our quitting the job. I favour their release, though it should not occur simultaneously as it can jeopardise our escape from this larger prison, we called our country." The warden gave his final words.

"What about the dangerous prisoners, sir." One guard asked.

"What about them? The jailer asked. "They are more dead than they are alive. I don't see any point in freeing them as they would not survive the freedom. Most of them haven't seen the sunlight or felt the fresh air on their faces for years; they are surely going mad if they are not already insane." The warden was saying pessimistically, looking not happy to leave them behind. "These prisoners are the doomed ones if we made them free or leave them behind, matters not much" he concluded.

"If that's the case, then give them a fair chance. Set them free, as well. Even if a single innocent would be able to make it, it will wash away many of your sins." Haliba said in an unafraid manner.

The warden looked perplexed at the request of her but more so, on her daring insinuation that he had a sinful job. Everyone could see a rage passing like flash on his face, but he remained calm. "All my life I have been a soldier, serving my duties in as honest manner as it was possible for me. I have no bad conscience of doing any injustice to anyone. If the prisoners brought to me, were guilty ones or innocents have never þeen my task to judge and condemn, but to execute the given sentences." The jailor seemed hurt by her words. "But I agree with you that a fair chance should be given to them"

"I am sorry for having used the wrong kind of words. I intended no disrespect, or accusation, but only a request to do something which may please the gods." Haliba explained her point of view. The warden smiled and accepted her explanation. He was instructing them how to proceed from that point on. The warden and the guards were to leave the prison the very next day, with all their possessions, taking the cover of night. The old system had collapsed, and the new system had not been evolved, so no one was to notice or to question their moving in or out of town. The little resources, which were available, were used to guard and watch the movements of the army garrisons. The lower local staffs were to wait for the daybreak, to do the rest of the job. They were supposed to free the prisoners, asking them to go their way. Haliba had taken the responsibility of opening and freeing the most dangerous prisoners as no one else would even think of going near to that horrifying part of the prison. "Don't let those creeps touch you," said a guard, which had grown close to her.

"Don't worry about me. I'll be all right." Haliba assured the young lad. His calling those unfortunate prisoners creeps seriously hurt her. How could she ever explain that those were the prisoners, which she felt most for as they were prisoners of conscience and not the ordinary criminals and therefore, needed more sympathy than others, but there was no time for her to waste on such trivial matters. She was impatiently waiting for the sunrise as it would give her the golden opportunity of freeing her husband and the other prisoners. She had hid the great news from Tylon as she wouldn't risk the disappointment if the attempt were to fail, because of any reason. She was far away from the sleep. Each minute was ticking in such a slow speed that she became certain that that night was special long. She was excited, but that was just half of the truth, the other half of the truth was making her very nervous. She had no idea as what to do after attaining freedom for her husband, or where they were to go, Which direction were they to proceed. How healthy or sick was her husband, she wondered. There were so many questions bothering her, but she kept pushing them away. She was confident that there was going to be some way open for them, and that was all she had a need for.

She was supposed to wait until the sunrise, but she couldn't wait for the sun, which was taking longer than usual to appear. Already at dawn she jumped from her seat and rushed to that part of the prison, where Tylon and the other prisoners were held. She was so obsessed with the thoughts of freedom that she could not think of anybody else than her own husband. The word freedom and Tylon had become synonymous, and of course she didn't mind the mix up.

The other prisoners were of secondary importance, and that was the most natural thing for her. There was a pin drop silence in the cells as most of the prisoners were either sleeping or were exhausted by their moaning and crying. No-one had expected such an early visit. Even Tylon sounded alarmed by her untimely visit

"What are you doing here at this hour?" Tylon whispered.

"I have brought wonderful news." She told him excitedly trying to search the key of his cell.

"What news? Tell me immediately. I can't wait any longer. Please give me the good news "Tylon was impatient like a child.

"The good news is that you are going to be free, my love." Haliba almost screamed with joy.

The sound of her carefree loud words was reverberating in the stinking atmosphere of the prison. When her sound died down, it was filled with a silence as if none had listened to those strange words, or had rejected them as an impossibility. In so many years, they had seen newcomers coming and occupying the cells, which were still empty, or that they were being emptied by the death of their inhabitants, but never had they heard that someone was getting free, alive.

"What say you? Are you out of your mind? Why speak you that loud? I'm scared to death." Tylon's voice was trembling. Haliba had succeeded in searching the key and opening the iron gate of the prison and was looking desperately for her husband. Soon she was holding him tight, embracing, kissing and crying. He was unmoved, still not believing that the happening was true and not just some dream.

"I don't have time to explain everything. We have to free others and then to find some safe corner for us to hide." Haliba told him, wiping her tears of joy. Haliba opened the next cell and instructed him to free the others by giving him the keys.

"Where shall I go?" The wretched man asked, trying to look at her.

"I can't tell you, but please free all, so those of you, who both can and want, may seek the freedom" She said quickly, dragging Tylon out of prison. She had shifted the responsibility of saving others on someone else's shoulders and wanted to get out of that place as quickly as possible. She didn't wait to see if others were ready or not for the task of escaping the prison, she was. It was still dark, when she silently came out of the prison holding the shaky hand of Tylon and walked towards the older city. She was taking quick paces, without caring that the king was not in the best shape.

"I'm out of breath," The king complained.

"I know my love, but you have to make the strife. We have to rush if we are to succeed.

"But I am weak; I'll fall if we didn't stop." Tylon was giving up.

""Just a few more meters and we'll be within the old city, we'll be safer there. You may rest a few minutes over there." Haliba wasn't ready to risk standing there in that early hour. Even after entering into the old city she would not stop, begging him to go just a few steps more and another few steps and then another. She was leading him to Aloha's house and wanted to achieve that goal before sunrise and without the detection by others.

Aloha was on the way out to go to her work. She was astonished to see Haliba standing near to her door, with a complete stranger. Without asking any question, she opened the door for them to enter into the house.

"Is all well?" She asked impatiently.

"Aloha, we need your help." Haliba spoke without losing any time.

"I'm your humble servant milady."

"Here is my husband, the king. We have succeeded in escaping the prison and would need a shelter for a while before we'll be searching some long-term solution to our refuge problem.

Aloha wasn't ready for such shocking news. She went all pale, looking at the thin bearded face of the king with tearful eyes before she bowed her head in respect

"No, please Aloha don't do that. We are no more your king and queen. Look at us, all we need is a shelter and help to flee from this country."

"You know that my home is open for you and his highness. I'll not hesitate to sacrifice my life for you." Aloha said with a bowed head. She woke up Davreen and sent her to inform her employer that she wasn't feeling well and needed some rest to recover, Davreen was happy to see Haliba, but again and again she glanced at the dirty looking man, she had brought with her. Haliba had no intention of introducing her husband to her or at least not at that particular moment, when Tylon was deprived of all his honour and glory. Haliba had been so preoccupied with the security of her husband that she had hardly taken notice that he looked more like a skeleton than a living being. She was shocked to see his poor condition, and sobbed silently, trying to hide her emotions from Tylon.

"What have you in mind, your majesty?" Aloha asked her. Haliba smiled sadly, knowing that for Aloha she was a royalty and was to remain so forever and ever, regardless of what she told her.

"I believe that we should hide in your home until my

husband gets stronger." Haliba suggested.

"I don't think it's safer or even wiser," Aloha said. She believed that the timings were perfect for their escape as the law and order of the country had broken down and there were no controls of going in or out at that particular time.

"But Tylon is not in good health, he needs time to recover."

"It might be too late then." Aloha insisted. Haliba and Tylon were both silent, not knowing what to do. "I have a nephew, who can help me to transport you out of the city." Aloha offered after some thinking.

"Getting help to be out of town is indeed a great help, but we need fresh horses and some other preparations, but most of all, can we trust the man?" Haliba inquired.

"Yes, he is trustworthy." Aloha said with a conviction. "If you agree, I'll talk to him right away so that you may leave the town after sundown."

"Can we manage that quickly?" Tylon asked with anxiety, those were his first words since they came there.

"We got to be swift if we are to succeed. Go; take some rest and sleep, so that you're braced for your tough journey." Aloha was nervous, seeing a great task ahead. She was afraid that the roaming bands of bandits on the road could turn dangerous for the royal couple and her nephew, especially in the darkness of night. Her nephew was a cart driver, and transported goods from one village to the other, who knew all the ways in and out from the town. Haliba was still skeptical about the physical condition of her husband, but found the advice of Aloha to leave as quickly as possible, a wise recommendation.

At the time of their departure, Aloha and Davreen were both standing with anxious faces, both were extremely nervous about the outcome of the royal escape attempt. Davreen still looked shocked, unable to absorb the news that Haliba was the former queen and the man she had brought with her, was none else than the king himself. She wouldn't even dare to imagine what was to happen to them if they were caught hiding the fugitive couple. From time to time she was glancing at Aloha in a wounded manner, she had hard believing that her own mother had had held a secret of that magnitude, hidden from her. King Tylon was sitting in a resigned mode, not showing any excitement, concern or nervousness. The outcome of their crucial attempt to flee the country was not bothering him. If he was to succeed or fail in his effort, was less important than the fear of taking a long, hard journey, which was certainly going to kill him.

"Here is your deposit you left to me long ago, please check that everything is there." Aloha handed over Haliba's cloth bag, which contained all her jewellery and ornaments, she wore at the time of her distressed search for her youngest son.

"These are for you, my humble gift, just keep them." Haliba refused to hold them.

"But they are of no use to me; I'm content with my life while they may provide you with a new start." Aloha insisted, leaving her no choice but to get hold of the bag.

"Oh Aloha, how I am going to get a chance to repay your kindnesses?" Haliba cried full of emotions, embracing the lady.

"You don't have to. My satisfaction is a reward enough." Aloha said with a smile. Aloha and Davreen were standing and sadly waving their hands, wishing them both a really good luck and a safe journey. Looking at the king they could tell that it had more likelihood of ending in a disaster, but they hoped that he was to succeed, if not by physical strength, then through his mental capacities and the will power.

10

Kestarius was very happy to have hired Shapario that day. He was the man; he had been looking for in all those years, a reliable person, who not only knew the trade into perfection but also a man, who understood the importance of the undertaken tasks and the priorities attached to them. Not a single day he had the need to tell him, how he was supposed to do his duties. Shapario had given him the fame he always deserved, bringing customers from far and near. It had been long since they had stopped doing the petty jobs; instead they were known for the manufacture of the weaponry. The swords they produced, the arrows they made and the spears they manufactured had the strengths unmatched. So high was the quality of their products that they could demand any price for them. Shapario had succeeded in making a skilled blacksmith of Hidas, who had grown into a strong, young man. Hidas could work all day long, without feeling tired. The burning fires of the furnace, the melting metals and the scorching heat had done their needed work. He had been initiated into a world of blacksmiths, with all the knowledge about that art and the secrets un- revealed to him Hidas was not even aware that the cunning guardian, to whom he still considered his father, had tricked him into a profession, unworthy of his royal heritage. Kestarius had moved his workshop in the near hood of the royal palace, on the insistence of the king. He had so many times offered Shapario a partnership, but he always rejected the given opportunity, telling him that he had other plans for his life than to get stuck with the workshop. The long days of labour were not the only hardship in his life. Shapario would send him to the teachers, who taught him the martial arts, where he had learned the use of sword and other weapons. His strong and muscular body could handle any weight or weapon, without any exertion. He learned everything in a most natural manner. Without a doubt, he was the most talented and promising young kid of that town. His skills were fast getting the renown, and even the offers were frequent to join the ranks of the army, but Shapario politely declined these offers, telling that the services of Hidas were needed in the workshop, where he still had much to learn and accomplish before he could serve the king.

Shapario was too clever to let Hidas join the army and get hooked with a salaried job, or to offend the king by refusing his offer to honour his son with a prestigious job, with a bright future. Kestarius remained suspicious about his hidden motives.

"Tell me, what drives you Shapario? You are but a strange man. I can never understand you."

"What is there, which made you talk like that?" Shapario asked in a light mood.

"I know now that you are an equally skilled blacksmith, if not better. What has brought you to work for me than to take a partnership?"

"Maybe simply because of my reluctance to take more responsibility. Perhaps I feel more secure with a guaranteed salary than a profit, which sounds more uncertain." Shapario gave his usual answer. Kestarius looked at him as if he was not convinced of his answer.

"Ok, now give me the logic of Hidas working free of cost?"

"Wasn't it a part of our deal?" Shapario reminded him

"Don't make a fool of me Shapario, you know that was your offer and was about a little kid, which was good for nothing while we talk now about a strong person, who is capable to work more efficiently and vigorously than us." Kestarius confronted him.

"You are right, maybe I am too hard on him and perhaps you should start giving him some minor salary." Shapario said, hoping to have him off his back. But Kestarius wasn't in a mood to leave him alone that day.

"I won't let you sneak out this time. I know that you are hiding something from me, and I have known it all those years. Tell me what it is? Tell me what your relation to Hidas is?"

Shapario was taken aback by his words. "What do you mean?" He demanded angrily. This time it was the turn of Kestarius to smile, seeing that Shapario did have some secret.

His silent smile was saying more than Shapario could bear. The colour of his face kept changing as he struggled to guess, what and how much Kestarius had figured out. He didn't answer to the question, placed by Kestarius but worked all day without entering into any further discussion with him. Kestarius didn't take up the matter either. "You know that you can trust me with whatever secret you have, concerning Hidas." Kestarius said to him before leaving the workshop and going to his home.

Shapario and Kestarius never discussed the issue after that day, but Kestarius's piercing looks with strange smiles were too much for him, he could not work in peace, with knowledge that he was constantly being watched in silent anticipation of revealing some secret. He had started liking the big man and knew that he was a gentle person behind that fierce outer shell; he had created to keep people at a distance. He was absolutely sure that his secret was to remain safe with Kestarius, so he decided to tell him about the story of Hidas. Kestarius looked in amazement, listened to him with a great interest and then burst into laughter.

"What's that for?" Shapario asked confused.

"For your remarkable performance." Kestarius was still amused. "Not in my wildest fantasies I could have imagined that"

They both sat and discussed the matter, leaving their work aside. Kestarius told Shapario that he did a great job in bringing up the prince in the way he did and that he could entrust the secret, without any anxiety of getting it leaked.

"It's not that it can harm the prince any longer, but I want him to know about the truth, when he is ready." Shapario explained.

"Tell me, why did you expose the child to such hardships, knowing that he was a prince, used to of an easy life?" Kestarius asked

"I wanted him to be a strong and resolute person if he was ever to strive for his throne and the country. So we two had been providing him that opportunity, I, in a conscious manner and you in some unaware fashion. Kestarius liked his way of explaining things.

"How long do you think his training period shall continue?"

"I don't know, but we shall know, when the time comes."

"How shall we know?" Kestarius was amazed by his assertion

"The day Hidas get conscious that you are exploiting his labour, without giving him any salary that is going to be the last day of his training period." Shapario made a joke, and they both laughed.

"The day he shall be fighting for his throne and country said Kestarius.

"Or carved by yours," said Shapario. Hidas was busy heating up the furnace and didn't know what the talk was keeping them from fulfilling their tasks of the day. He had enough work of his own to accomplish and so little time for any other things to pay attention to. Both men were watching him poure the melted metal in the form. They looked content as the young kid was paying all his attention to work, a concentration, which was the key to his future success.

All three princes had been growing into manhood, without any knowledge of their true identities and knowledge about the other members of their family. Their upbringing was diverse and the conditions being offered to them were completely different one from the other. They lived in different countries, spoke different languages and had developed dissimilar trades and skills. Even their features and figures bore no similarities if they were to place beside each other. The reasons for which Hidas and Beran were not told about their background were not the same. Shapario had wished that Hidas knew about the truth, when he had overcome his pride, uncontrolled anger and his superiority complex, the vices, which were still haunting in his unconsciousness. While for Silos, it was rather a favour, which he had given to the youngest prince. He knew that there was no way of Beran's attaining the throne of his former country. The land of Elbon had been long lost, and the memory of that glorious past served no purpose than the melancholy, and he wanted to save the prince from that pain. He was sure that the truth was going to be too overwhelming for the feeble mind of Beran. But if he thought that the young meant weak and frail, he couldn't be more wrong. He had given him all the care, love and attention, he found possible. But he couldn't have done the job on his own, without the help of Binti, to whom he had married long ago, after the realisation that he, loved her. Binti had been his rock, his devoted wife, ready to serve, eager to implement all his wishes. She had happily taken over the duties of motherhood, mindful of all the needs of her husband and a child to whom she loved as if he were hers. Beran was very intelligent child, who had shown keen interest in all subjects and arts, which existed in that country. He had learned many languages and even could help Silos in his work of translating different books in the local language. He was good at solving mathematical equations, finding geometrical solutions and taking part in riddle solving exercises. He was more inclined to the music, poetry and philosophy than the wrestling and other such like sports.

He was quick witted, brilliant at problem solving and had a bright future before him. King Afshar was very fond of him and always praised his sharpened intelligence.

"You are a lucky man to have such a brilliant youngster by your side. I wish if one of my princes had those interests and talents." King Afshar never hid his disappointment in his own princes, which were just interested in vanities and luxuries given to them by nature as a birthright. "They get the best of the tutors, but to what help, if their minds remain closed to the learning process. Sometimes I worry about the future of my kingdom." King Afshar seemed gloomy.

"They are young, inexperienced and carefree. With time shall they learn to behave in a responsible way." Silos used to cheer him up. The king wouldn't say anything more, but sighed, not believing a word, he said.

"I'm proud to notice that Beran has not only learned those subjects, which you command but can even those, which you have no idea about." The king was showing his delight. "Look at the perfection with which he works on the stones while carving the shapes out of them. Watch the way he plays on the instruments, creating such a beautiful music, the things so alien to you and your talents." King Afshar went on

That day he felt extremely happy and proud. He had accomplished his task and mission of bringing up Beran. He had succeeded achieving the goal, which had seemed not only far-fetched but also even impossible to attain. The praising words of king Afshar were humming in his ears like sweet music, coming down from the heavens. He wanted to share his joy with his wife Binti, with whom he met already in the hallway.

"Your shining face betrays that you're very happy today." She greeted him with a smile.

"You'll be glowing as well if you knew why I do so." Silos exclaimed, before sitting down by her side and telling her about the discussion he had with the king.

"I'm really pleased with the knowledge that we have succeeded in our hard task. Though I must confess that neither of us had been ready for the assignment as it was laid on our shoulders," Silos agreed with her. "Look, we can proudly say that we have turned him into a sensible, art-lover, and a young man. Even his father king Tylon would have been proud of him." Binti said.

"Yeah!" Silos sighed remembering his king. "We never can tell, what became of them, certainly they must have perished with the fall of the country." Binti kept silent, she was unable to find any words, which could convince him of the opposite.

Even Silos was a bit sad and distracted by the thought of the king and queen. He kept thinking for a while before he asked, looking unsure. "Do you really think that we have done to the prince, what the king had had expected from us?"

"I don't know, what you mean. But as far as I'm concerned no one could have done the job better. He is sensitive, caring to the needs and feelings of others, he is creative, always coming forward with novel things, he is courageous, not fearing anything and speak only truth. What more anyone could have demanded. Not even the king himself could have given him a better upbringing than that" Binti was not shy to defend his hard work.

"You know what I mean. I haven't raised him the way the princes are raised. He is too sensitive, too soft and too tolerant to be a king in the future, remember the prophecy." Silos was still unsure.

"I don't think that he is ever to become a king, but if his destiny did attract his feet to his goal, I'm sure he shall be a good king with those qualities you have implanted in him" Binti wasn't letting him worry for anything. "You have done an excellent job. Be proud of yourself." She was supportive like she always had been.

"Soon it's his seventeenth birthday, what present shall we give him?" Binti asked

"I have had a word with the king; he is ready to give him a job, as my assistant. I believe it's going to be a wonderful present." Silos told her.

"You are stingy like always. Why can't you think of giving him something he might have a need for?" Binti was unforgiving. She laughed and laughed, making fun of his reluctance to spend the money. Silos was laughing along with her, but only half heartedly, as he didn't consider the matter that funny. "What you know about the worth and importance of money? One has to be careful about it, not knowing what is about to happen." Silos defended his approach.

"And what does it help, the piling of money, when you can't make a use of it, when some emergency was to hit you?" Binti was reminding him about all the riches and possessions he had been forced to leave behind before coming and settling in Kildia.

"You are right." Silos confessed, giving up. "Never mind, a fool like me. Do what you think is a proper thing to do. I wouldn't stand in your way." Silos concluded with a smile.

"I knew that I had your blessings, so I have already bought a present for him, from both of us." Binti disclosed

"May I know what that is?" Silos asked getting curious.

"I had thought to keep it a secret even from you, but now I can't withhold. The present from us is nothing else than a beautiful horse." Binti said with a pride in her voice.

"Hmm, a horse, that's a good present, remembering that a thing more common in our previous country is worth gold here. What need does Beran have of this luxury animal? I hardly can imagine him sitting on his horse to go to his work at the library." Silos kept wondering about the benefits associated with the horse keeping.

"You're such a bore." Binti finally said, giving up all her hopes on him.

"No, no, don't misunderstand me; I believe that is the most beautiful present, all I wondered was the practical part of it." Silos tried to justify his behaviour, but failed to impress Binti, who remained smiling, and taunting at his carefulness with the money.

"You know that we don't have expensive habits and can afford a luxury every now and then."

When Beran got his birthday present he couldn't believe his eyes. He kept looking at his father and mother, who were enjoying each and every twitch of happiness on his glowing face. "So you liked the present?" Binti asked. "Like! Exclaimed Beran. "I love it. How did you know that I was fostering a strong wish to own one?" Beran was almost dancing around the strong animal. He had difficulty in hiding his emotions from his parents.

"You should thank your father; it was he who thought that the present would fill you with joy." Binti told him, patting the horse. Beran rushed to embrace Silos, who felt embarrassed, and looked in a complaining manner at his wife, who was giggling, making him more uncomfortable.

"What's so very special about a horse?" Silos asked Beran.

"Everything" was the short answer of Beran. "It's an animal I love; I have always loved riding it…" Silos cut Beran in the middle of his sentence.

"And where was I, when you learned to ride a horse."

"You were busy teaching the princes" Beran replied calmly, reminding about the years, when he accompanied Silos to the royal palace, where he was left to play with other kids of the guards and other royal staff. "But why didn't you ever tell me that you rode on the horse there?" Silos asked

"You never asked what I did there and I never thought it was some remarkable activity."

"Didn't you say you loved it?"

"Yes, I did. Without a doubt, it gave me very beautiful feelings, but it was not something to boast about." Beran defended his apparent contradiction. Binti was standing aside, smilingly; she didn't want to interfere in their meaningless discussion. She was enjoying the moment fully, seeing her present making such an impact on the two people she loved most.

"Why don't you tell him about the other present, Silos?" Binti said, in a try to change the ongoing debate between, Silos and Beran.

"What other present?" Beran asked, getting excited

"That's a present from your father alone." Binti stressed, teasing Silos.

Silos was excitedly telling him about his long discussion with the king and his consent to grant an assistant's job to Beran. From the unconcentrated looks of Beran, he could judge that he was not very enthusiastic about the prospects of getting a work.

"I can see that you aren't very excited, I thought that you liked the work." Silos looked a bit disturbed, and that made Binti get sober.

"Yes I do like the job, it is fun to work with you, to learn new things, but there isn't anything more I can learn from there." Beran was honest in confessing that the purpose of his was already achieved. Silos didn't say a word but looked unhappy.

"Father, don't take it personal. I have no intention of belittling your great work, but that is not the work I want to do for the rest of my life." Beran was apologetic but firm. Binti was sorry to have brought up the subject. Had she known that Beran would reject the job offer, she would have done everything in her power to make that difference less hurting. But it was too late to do anything, so she went in the house, leaving them alone to solve their differences like men. She knew that if Beran didn't want to take the job, there was little anyone in the world could do to make him change his mind. She was mostly worried about Silos, who despite his old age had a tendency of behaving like a teenager, getting hurt for unimportant and insignificant things. It was best to leave him alone, to work on his emotions, unaided, unattended and without any pressure of any kind. He wasn't a difficult person to deal with, only if one had the patience and knowledge of right timing. Beran was still looking and appreciating the beauty of his horse, ignoring Silos's sad face. He was a sensitive young lad, but he had learned that he was not responsible for the happiness or the miseries of others, and even if he did cause some apprehension to someone, that was of a temporary duration, disappearing with time.

That night Silos was very upset, not because Beran had made it clear to him that all his efforts to raise him into a scholar had not succeeded at all, but what really bothered him was the fact that Binti had been not very kind that particular day or at least he took it that way. He was hardly participating in any discussion, giving clear signals to her that he was unhappy.

"Are you angry Silos?" Binti asked looking in his eyes.

"No, I am not." Was the typical answer he gave.

"Why have you always denied the truth? We both know that something is bothering you. I think it is better to talk about it." Binti said. Silos didn't respond to her invitation to express the feelings.

"If you are still crossed for my taking up the question of Beran's employment, I repeat my apology once again. It wasn't my meaning to compete you or arty to degrade you in the eyes of Beran. You should be aware that I could never do that on purpose."

"I know that you had no intention of doing so, but in reality it did turn that way. He loved your present while he turned down the opportunity of getting a job, without even considering it." Silos said in a sad, upset manner.

"Now you are unfair. Didn't I tell Beran that the horse idea was yours?" Binti protested.

"Yes, you did so, but why was I hurt anyhow?"

"You aren't hurt because of that. You are troubled for Beran's sake. Somewhere you foster the fear of failing your mission." Binti told him. Silos kept silent, pondering on her words.

"I think you did a wonderful job, and should stop torturing yourself. We have never been negligent about our duties. We have given him the love, care and devotion, more than that no one can demand of us."

"You are right Binti. I'm sorry for being upset, but I can't help thinking, wondering if I have done my task, as it was required of me." Silos was pensive.

"There is no one to judge that, except your own conscience, and I see nothing, which could make it feel bad." Binti was supportive.

"I wonder if Beran's coming into our lives was a blessing or a trail of character as I had earlier thought that it to be." Silos said with a sigh.

"As far as I'm concerned, it was, it is, and hopefully it's going to remain a blessing. What would be our lives, if we didn't have him?" Binti tried to be vocal about her feelings.

"Do you think I have succeeded in my role, as a father?" Silos asked.

"Maybe even more than his own father may have succeeded." Binti reassured him.

Both of them were talking in a low voice, just sitting outside in the little garden, unaware of the presence of Beran, who had a really bad conscience for having hurt the feelings of Silos and was approaching to tell him that he was sorry for his thoughtless behaviour. He had just heard the last words of his mother and was shocked by them. Binti and Silos were still busy in appreciating each other for their incredible sacrifices and hard work. They were thanking each other for the help and support, without which they couldn't have achieved their success. Perhaps they would have continued their discussion for another part of the night, had Binti not felt that they were no longer alone there. To discover that Beran was standing a few metres away from them in the dark made her shiver. She was not sure as to how much Beran had heard of their conversion She tried to stop Silos from saying anything further, but he was too unconcentrated, to pay attention to her signal that they had a company.

"Come my child, I thought you were asleep." Binti said loudly, almost announcing to Silos that Beran was there.

"I had difficulty in getting asleep and thought to have a chat with you instead." Beran said dryly. Binti could notice from his shaking voice that he was upset.

"Come and join us." She signed him to sit down, but he stood staring at them in sad confusion.

"No, I have changed my mind. I feel suddenly tired and need to rest." Beran said before turning to go back.

"He's behaving little odd today." Silos mumbled. Binti was silent and extremely anxious.

"I really don't understand the logic, how can he get so tired all of a sudden." Silos repeated his astonishment.

"Don't you realise that he has heard us talking?" Binti said restlessly.

"Heard what?" Silos said a little irritated. Binti kept silent, just looking in the thin air.

"O heavens no! You don't mean that he has..." Silos exclaimed, getting her point and cause of alarm. They both were sitting in complete silence, trying to figure out, how were they to handle the situation.

"I believe we have to disclose the truth to him, there is no other way left open." Binti said.

"But it would be so hard for him." Silos opposed her idea.

"He is a young man, who can deal with his sorrow. Better expose him to the bitter truth than to turn him bitter against us."

"All right then you inform." Silos said.

"No, you do it, it's your call. Though I would be there to give you a moral support." Binti concluded. "By tomorrow shall he know the truth about us and his own identity and origins."

"Oh, what I hate these terrible duties!" Silos didn't like the task of informing Beran about his past.

Beran was looking like a sleepwalker, very much disturbed, in the middle of some troubling thoughts and above all crossed. He couldn't help but to feel betrayed by his parents, who had kept it secret that they were not his real parents. Who was he? Who were his real parents? Did they live, or were they no longer in the world? How had he ended up there? There were more questions than he could handle on his own. He needed a serious talk with Silos and Binti, the only people he had ever known and considered as his family. He felt agitated, without getting hateful towards them. He was sure that there was to come some logical illumination, some reasonable explanation about the matter and the rational motivations, which had kept them from disclosing the truth to him. Many times that night he had felt the compelling urge to go and seek the answers, but each time he had refrained from doing so. He didn't want to act in haste, fearing some terrible disclosure. No-one could understand his pain and agony. He felt all alone in the world. Even those he had considered his own, had turned out to be just strangers, a fact which was strong enough to kill him. He left the house before Silos and Binti came out of their room in the morning. He had no forces to face them at that particular time. He didn't come home for many hours, but when he did; he had not expected to find Silos in the house. It seemed that Silos had stayed home that day, a very unusual happening indeed.

"Come and have your meal, you didn't even take your breakfast today." Binti said, putting the meal before Beran.

"I'm not hungry, I have eaten from outside." Beran shovelled the tray aside.

"I believe your father, and I need a serious talk with you."

"I don't see any need." Beran said sourly.

"I know you have heard us talking last night. You need to listen to our story before you judge us." Binti was not to give up. Beran looked back at her in anger, but calmed down, meeting the same loving eyes, he had been observing from the times he could start remembering. He knew that even if she was not his real mother, she had always given him the impression that she was. Her love to him was as real as any other real thing could be, without any adulteration, without any falsehood involved in it.

"Look at me. Do you ever remember a day when we didn't care you? Can you point out any moment, when we hesitated in loving you?" Binti was forceful in her arguments and appeal.

Beran sat with a bent head, listening to Silos, who was narrating the entire story, without hiding anything from him; even he had no shame in confessing his reluctance to undertake the responsibility the king had wished him to do. Beran was listening in disbelief, searching their faces minutely, to see if they were telling him the truth or not. He looked sad but composed, just listening, without any questions or other interruptions.

"What happened to my parents?" He asked finally, when Silos had finished his story.

"No-one could tell as we were not there to witness the happening. By looking at the circumstances, I can presume them dead, both of them." Silos told him undramatically.

"And what became of my other two brothers?" Beran inquired.

"I'm not even sure if the guardians succeeded in taking them to safety or not. All came in such haste that we could not plan the things better. But I really hope and wish them to be alive." Silos admitted to having no knowledge about the subject.

"Who were the people they were entrusted to? Where were they supposed to take them?" Beran asked in an impatient voice.

"I wish I knew the places they were heading to. There were no particular instructions. We were to use our common sense and improvise as the situation demanded. As far as the names are concerned, I have not so good memory; as a matter of fact I never had, when it comes to the names and places." Silos said helplessly.

"How did my brothers look like? How old were they, when those terrible things befell my unfortunate family?"

"How can I describe the faces of those young children, to whom I had a chance to see but few times? You see, they were just small kids at that time. The faces do change with the growth of the body. They would not have remembered anything from that time, except the eldest of the princes, who might have retained those terrible moments of agony and distress." Silos couldn't give him much hope. Beran sat there, deep in his disturbing thoughts, without paying any attention to Silos and Binti. He was completely absorbed by his own tragedy and distress. He had never believed in the fate, and supposed that one could carve one's own destiny, but the disclosure of his own life and its secrets had made him re-evaluate his beliefs.

Binti signed Silos to leave Beran alone. Both of them left the room in a discrete way as to leave him alone to work on his sorrow of losing the family in a tragic manner, years ago. Beran was a strong young man, who was capable to wrestle with the problems and difficulties, both from the past and of the present time.

"It's going to give him strength." Binti said, coming out of the room.

"How possibly it can do that?" Silos wondered.

"It always does. The truth is always strengthening, always freeing, I've been told of a wise man." Binti said, reminding him of his own words.

"I don't know Binti, I don't know any more. I always feel confused, when it comes to personal problems." Silos confessed that his philosophical talks were one thing, and the real life another. She didn't say anything to comfort him as she used to do.

"He is going to hate us." Silos worried.

"He can't if we have raised him the way we believe we did." Binti was confident.

For a few days, Beran refused to come out of his room, refusing to eat anything, anguishing and worrying both of them. It seemed as if he really hated them for all that had happened years back. His refusal to talk to them could not be translated in any other terms than that he blamed them for his misery. They were unable to comprehend that Beran neither hated them nor could he blame them for anything. He was not a thankless person, who would ignore all their efforts, sufferings and sacrifices in all those years. All he wanted was to go through his pain and sorrow. He needed some time, to mourn the tragic past, to ponder upon, what he had been missing during that long period, and most of all to contemplate, what could he do in the days to come. He needed to think, where lay his destination? Where was he to search for those members of his family, who could be still alive? He didn't agree to Silos that the circumstantial evidence was enough for presuming that both his parents were dead. He needed concrete evidence, a confirmation, but the question was where he was to get that verification? Both Binti and Silos were waiting patiently for him, not stressing him any more. They were sure that he would finally find a way to accept his fate and wouldn't make a big issue of that. They both believed in the healing power of the time. One day Beran did emerge from his self- imposed isolation. The calmness on his face was giving them the comfort that Beran had finally made compromises to his fresh knowledge about the things concerning himself. He was a sensible young man from whom they couldn't have expected anything different.

"How glad we are to see you again. You can't imagine our anguish, seeing you suffer like that?" Binti told him, without getting all over, as was her normal routine. Beran tried to smile, but she could only see a thin, sad, grin appearing and fading all in the same moment.

"I hope you aren't very mad at us. We meant no harm, when we kept the knowledge of your glorious past, your royal birth and…"

"Mother please," said Beran gently, making Binti looked perplexed. She had not waited for him to call her mother. She looked in astonishment at Silos and then at Beran before she could bring the trembling words out of her throat.

"You know now that I am not your mother but a humble servant"

"Even this disturbing knowledge can't make me forget that you two are the only parents I have ever known. And so is it going to be for the rest of my life." Beran said giving them a hug. The hand of Silos was shaking violently, when he patted him on his back. Binti couldn't control her emotions and cried of happiness.

"And we thought that you hated us." She said holding

Beran's hand.

"How could I ever hate the people, to whom I owe my life?" Beran was getting sentimental.

"We can't tell how much we are relieved to know that you are taking the truth like a man. We are sure that a bright future awaits you." Silos tried to express himself.

"I'm what I am, all thanks to you two." Beran was describing his admiration for their loyalty, sense of duty and good hearts. He was thanking them for their love, care and devotion.

"I'll always remember you two with great warmth and gratitude." Beran was crying.

"What do you mean by all this nonsense?" Binti asked pulling herself away from his kind embrace.

"He is just expressing his love, and nothing else." Silos tried to defend.

"Don't talk like that to me. My heart trembles." Binti addressed him, still holding his hand

"I'm sorry mother, but I have to leave and search for my brothers and find them if they still live." Beran spoke in a weak voice.

"Shall you leave us, to whom you call your parents? How intend you to find them, when you don't even know their names, faces and addresses? You can't even know with the surety that they live." Binti tried to stop him in his quest, but remained skeptical about the effect of her words. She should have known better that the emergence of Beran from that seclusion could not have been without some resultant resolve on his part. Silos didn't utter a single sound, he was sure that if Binti was to fail in her pursue Beran to change his mind, then he couldn't add anything better. Binti begged him to reconsider his decision, but knew that was not to help in preventing him from leaving. Beran was not to listen to the arguments about his young age, inexperience or the dangers lying ahead. He was busy preparing his journey, by collecting important information. He had learned all that he needed to about the way, the people and the other necessary details. He could press ahead to Elbon, the land of his ancestors, as quickly as possible, before the hot summer with scorching heat started, or he had to wait until autumn.

"Why Elbon?" Binti was horrified to learn his plans.

"Isn't it there everything started? A place of my birth, a place I never learned to know and love. A place, where I lost my parents and my brothers." Beran said

"But there's nothing left for you to collect in that country." Silos tried to reason with him.

"If I am to collect any information about the fate of my family, I have to start from that place." Beran insisted.

"At least promise to be more careful." Binti begged.

"That I can promise, without any hesitation." Beran said with a smile.

"Take this with you." Silos handed him a clothed bag.

"What's in there?" Beran asked.

"I don't know. But I presume there are some royal ornaments, some medallions that could confirm your royal heritage." Silos told.

"And you want me to carry them with me in Elbon, father? Where is your logic you used to teach me?" Beran asked in a light, joking way. Binti smiled at his intelligent approach and felt that there was less reason for her to worry about Beran; he was a sensible person, who could take care of him.

"May gods be with you and protect you from all evils." Binti bade him farewell.

"They did protect me till now." Beran said with laughter, trying to make her relax. "But more than the protection of the gods, I need best wishes of you two."

"Those wishes shall always accompany you, regardless of where you are." Binti said, kissing him goodbye.

11

Herzod and his companions were heading to their destination. They were all fresh, well equipped and well-guarded by the young members of their group. They had been already on the way for some time and had the pre knowledge that the way stood all clear of hindrances and difficulties. The early spring air was still cool, and the arid grounds still bearable to travel. They had just crossed the desert, where Herzod had found Shamon many years back. He could not have ignored the place, which had dreaded many, but to him it was a blissful place to look at. He looked at the exact place, and then turning his gaze to the heavens above, he smiled. The smile was his gratitude for getting a son; he never could get of his wife. Few of the traders, who knew about his story, observed his actions and gazed and smiled, praising the unseen forces, which guided their steps and hearts. Herzod had grown not only very rich in all those years but even also old. He wished to quit his journeys, but before doing that he wanted to train and teach his trade to his son Shamon. It was from the last few years that he was taking the young man on all journeys he made. It was supposed to be his last journey before he could retire from his tiresome and long journeys. He was convinced that Shamon was ready to manage on his own. Herzod had equipped him with not only the secrets of trade but even with so many other subjects and knowledge about various things. His task had been not easy, considering the negative influence of his beloved wife, Nori, who did everything thing, to spoil their son. Had he not been equally stubborn and vigilant, Shamon would have turned into good for nothing. Herzod's work was extra difficult as he loved his wife more than anything else in the world. Taking Shamon away from her wasn't an easy thing to do, but he succeeded doing so only by convincing her that was a necessary step if she wanted Shamon to be a learned and successful person. That conviction had apparently saved the young kid. Herzod placed him in the countryside, where the best private tutors taught him. Where he was disciplined and could learn to live a simple but a meaningful life. He was a brilliant student, learning everything in a quick manner, using his intellect and other inborn qualities. The astounding speed, with which he mastered the art of trade and his sense of economic matters, surprised even Herzod, who considered himself as a clever trader. He was a natural talent in his choice of goods, price bargains and selling techniques. He had an eye for those things, which were in demand and people were ready to pay any price for them. Everyone knew that he would never pay over prices; therefore his margins of profit were more than others. While other traders went around in search of the goods, he stayed relaxed, hardly taking an interest in anything; he was not even searching for any particular goods. He always would wait until the last moment, before buying his wares if for no other reason, then for the sake of hiding his choice from others. He believed that if all copied him then there was going to be more competition, which would without any doubt press down the prices, and as a consequence the margins of profit, which of course he didn't want. The other traders couldn't afford to wait for him, before buying their own stuff as it was not only difficult but also almost impossible to search those items in that short time left before they were to return to their home tracts. Despite their inability to copy Shamon in the purchase of the merchandise, the other businessmen couldn't help in recognising his talents as a sharp merchant. Herzod watched him with a satisfactory smile on his face and knew that Shamon was a far cunning trader than he himself ever had been Shamon was ambitious, generous and courageous young man, who had a sense of humour, openness towards people in general and a friendly attitude even towards the strangers. Nori had wanted to keep the fact of his being found in the wilderness a secret, but Herzod never tried to hide the fact that Shamon wasn't his own child. This knowledge had not imprinted all those negative effects on him as were feared by others around him. On the contrary, it had helped Shamon in remembering the fact that people could be kind and helpful without any apparent reason. He had been wondering every now and then about his father, who was found dead beside his unconscious body, his mother, whom no one knew anything about and other relatives if there were any. But there were so many unfilled blanks, so there wasn't much to ponder upon. He was grateful that Herzod and Nori had adopted him. He loved those wonderful people, who treated him as if he would be some very special person. Shamon never called them mother or father, but they were much more than that, they were his hope and ladder to the bright future.

Herzod had informed him that he kept some bag, which they had found by his father's side and which he could get when he grew old enough. Shamon had never inquired as to what that the bag contained. Nori had shown the wish that it was high time for Shamon to get married. Each time she brought up the subject, he would just laugh, telling her that there were so many other things he wanted to accomplish before settling down. "What things?" Nori always asked in surprise.

"I want to see the world." Shamon would answer while trying hard to find some reasonable excuse.

"Don't worry; you don't have to confine yourself to the home. You may still be able to travel." Nori would argue.

"Why do you think, he wants to travel around?" Herzod would come to rescue. "Let him find his own wife. We have done our part, by providing the best of everything to him."

Shamon had grown into a handsome young man, who was as soft speaker and a charmer as he was bold and skilled in the use of weapons, the qualities, which were considered necessary, if one was a trader and travelled to far away places. The most amazing thing about the way Shamon handled his weapons was his casual way, never taking it in a serious manner, to him it was more like a sport, a fun-giving activity. Herzod had many times tried to have a serious talk about the subject, but he would not pay any attention to his words.

"Despite the fact that you are good in the use of your weapons, you need to be sober about their importance. Never take your enemies in a light way. Deal them fiercely, show them no pity," Herzod's warning words never reached his heart. What enemies? He would think and found none as far as he could look.

Now that he was passing through Kildia, they were more relaxed as the situation of law and order was that perfect that they all could sleep, without worrying about their security. That was the only part of their journey when they relaxed the need of guarding their camp in the nights. They all slept, when they woke up by a scream. It was little before dawn, and there was confusion in the camp. The members of the group were not sure as to what had happened; they all had drawn their swords and looked at each other with inquiring eyes to find out the cause of that distress. The realisation was quick that the emergency had its roots not in some sudden attack as they had earlier feared, but one member, who had had snakebite, caused the urgent situation. They all stood around the young man, who looked aghast, looking at his leg, which was swelling. There were so many questions about the size, kind and dangerousness of the snake, but the young man couldn't provide them with any answer as he had not seen the snake. "How you know then that it was a snake?" asked another young man. No one answered to his question and attended the young man, who was suffering from the pain, anguish and fear of dying. No one was more anguished than the father of that young man, who was all pale and shivering as if he had already lost his son. "Who can help the kid?"

Cried Herzod and met with a silence. "There must be someone in our group, who can cure such ills?" Herzod repeated his question with a surprise.

"How very typical?" murmured someone.

"What do you mean?" Herzod asked. He was told that the physician, who used to accompany them on each travel, was not with them that time. "Do you mean we are travelling without any experienced person, who has the knowhow of facing the emergencies" Herzod asked surprised.

"These emergencies never occur, when we do have such a person among us, and now..." the person tried to explain away the fatal mistake of ignoring a vital rule. There wasn't any time for them to sit and find the causes of negligence and put the finger of blame on somebody but a pushing need to do something and to do it quickly. The knowledge that they were without any wise and knowledgeable person made them all panicky and alarmed. Do this, do that, were the several advises, but they all lacked the surety of conviction and knowledge.

The time was slipping from out of their hands, and they all stood powerless to do anything for the young man, who was about to die a slow death. The anxious faces were avoiding the looks of each other, well conscious that the responsibility of that unnecessary tragedy lay on them all. The father of the young man was holding his son and was praying silently, shedding tears and not communicating to his companions. Perhaps he too was dying of anguish, bad conscious and regret, as he was the fiercest opposition to the proposition that they could spend the night in some inn as they were travelling so near to the human habitations. He was trying to save a little money, but was that money worth the life of his only son if he were to die. Many of his companions wanted to give him comfort and assurance that everything was to turn all right, but couldn't give a false hope to him. The silence was killing and nerve breaking than the actual tragic scene before their eyes. The sound of a galloping horse made them look at each other in surprise. They were not ready for any more unpleasant surprise, and few of them went out to see who was approaching them that early in the morning.

"Who was it?" asked Herzod.

"Just a young rider, who saw us camping and came to say that the town was not far, in case we wished to stay little longer" told one young member of the group.

"Where is he now?" Herzod asked.

"We told him that we were to move our way, but thanked him anyway." The same person told.

"Did anyone tell him about the terrible accident?" Herzod asked.

"What would he do? He was hardly a teenager."

"Go and ride after him, bring him back by telling him that we are desperate and need an immediate help." Herzod said to Shamon, without turning and showing his anger to the young man he had been addressing before.

"Okay!" said he, before rushing out. The leg was swelling more and more, and the colour of the face was getting darker, a clear sign that the venom was spreading in the bloodstream. After a few minutes, Shamon entered the tent with a stranger and pointed to the direction of dying youth. The stranger looked in the eyes of the young man, checked his heartbeat before he turned the company.

"Who is in charge?" He asked without losing a moment.

175

"You may speak as we all are equally in charge." Herzod spoke.

"I can see that you are aware of the gravity of the situation. One of your companions is bitten by a poisonous snake and is bound to die if we don't do something quickly." The stranger youth declared.

"What can be done to save him?" Herzod asked.

"Not much, by seeing how badly he has been dealt with."

"Please tell if there is anything which can be done, he is my only son." The father of the young man almost cried.

"I know a man, who may be able to cure this man; the only problem is to find him in time. It seems to be already late for him."

He told them that there was not much time for him to go, search and bring the person back to their camp. He proposed instead if someone accompanied him to the witch doctor, along with the inflicted, young man, who was dying.

"I go with you," said the father of the young man, who saw his son drifting away from him.

"Not you, you are too weak right now and emotionally a wreck. I shall accompany the young man." Herzod declared, and jumped on his horse, without wasting any time. The young stranger was galloping his horse and Herzod was tailing him, holding the reigns with one hand and the dying man with the other. The whole group was seeing them getting disappeared from their sight. They had very little hope of seeing their young companion ever again; they had already lost him and were silently mourning him.

The uncertainty was the worst of all possible ills, they had been always taught, but never knew the truthfulness of the assertion more clearly than at that time. Each minute that ticked away was as piercing as a sharp spear, making them turn and move in agony. They had accepted the death of their companion in a more natural way, had they known that he had not survived, but to sit idle for hours and hours, without the knowledge as to what became of the young man was a far worse thing. The sun was going down and still there wasn't any sign of them. Shamon remained calm and relaxed.

"Their prolonged disappearance is a good omen and not a bad sign as told by some of us." Shamon said, refusing to worry.

"Why is that? What's the cause of your optimism?" Asked the young fellow, who had first met the approaching youth and had let him go.

"It's logical, had our companion not been able to survive, then what's the reason for father and the stranger to linger on?" Shamon spoke with a calm voice, making most of them to agree with him.

"To tell you the truth I am worried." one middle-aged trader confessed.

"What for? Shamon asked a bit surprised.

"I don't know. The whole situation is scary. A young man having snakebite, a stranger appearing out of nowhere, Herzod's foolishly accompanying him and not coming back even after so many hours." He was making all of them more fretful than they already were.

It was getting chilly, but they were still standing outside, waiting in expectancy, when they saw someone approaching from a distance. It was dusk with poor visibility, so they couldn't be sure if it was one or more people coming to them. Their hearts were pounding full of anxiety and in anticipation. It was three of them, Herzod, the stranger and the young man, their companion. They hurried to greet them and to check if the young man had survived or not as he was still lying on the horse, without making any movements. The anxious father didn't dare to come near as if he was afraid to get some terrible news.

"He is going to make it. The worst part is over." Herzod announced in a tired way. He turned to the stranger and invited him in the camp.

"It's early spring, but still it's chilly in your country. Come in so that we can have a supper."

They all sat and ate silently, they looked relieved and wanted to ask many questions but saw that both men were looking exhausted and terribly hungry and that made them refrain from asking questions. After food Herzod was talking to his companions, leaving the stranger in the company of younger members, who were encircling him, asking millions of questions. He told them about his own and Herzod's race against the clock, to save the young man, who was already in the clutches of death.

"I can't call it anything else than a mere luck, a miracle that we found the witch doctor in his home outside the town. He had just returned after a long absence and didn't see much point in even trying as the young man was more dead than alive."

"Why did he change his mind?" asked someone.

"What I know! Perhaps his compassion and empathy for

other beings" the stranger told them

"Who are you? And what brought you our way?" Shamon asked.

"My name is Beran, and it was just a coincidence that I discovered your camp as I passed that way. I was sure that you people didn't know about my town, which lies not so far from here; otherwise you would certainly have spent the night there as most of the passing by groups do.

I just wanted to inform you that, but how could I ever know that a dying person desperately needed my help, in order to survive. The ways of the gods are mysterious. Aren't they?" Beran asked with a smile. He told them about the efforts of the witch doctor, about their nerve-breaking wait while the frenetic efforts went on. According to him the main cause of the desperation wasn't the poisonous snake, but the spread of the venom, which had broken down the nervous system completely and had taken the young man beyond the healing process of antidote. The recovery was to be not only slow but could even leave permanent damages on the person, he told his listeners. "I wasn't there when the witch doctor had a talk with your leader, but I am sure he must have informed him about all possibilities and precautions required." Beran concluded

"We have already lost a vital day, sitting not doing anything, just waiting; I really hope that we shall proceed early morning. No one spoke in response to that insensitive statement, but there were a few exchanges of angry gazes. But everyone chose to ignore the young man and his thoughtless words.

"Where were you heading to?" Shamon asked

"I'm going to Elbon." Beran told.

179

"Isn't it a wrong way, you have adopted?" said someone.

"Maybe it looks that way, but all I am trying is to avoid certain wastelands, which aren't hospitable." They all smiled, seeing what he meant by that.

"Why do you want to go to that country?" Shamon asked once again "Are you from there? If not, then what errands force you go to place all strangers are advised to avoid?" Shamon was curious.

"I didn't know that the country has that bad reputation. Please tell me all you know about that land." Beran asked with a smile.

"Not before you tell me the purpose of your visit to that oppressed kingdom." Shamon said

"I have some unfinished business there; my parents once fled that part of the world, so you see I have some roots over there. Some properties to check about, some information to collect…" Beran was not secretive about his visit to Elbon.

"Take my suggestion and turn back. There was a reason for your parents to leave that place, believe me; it's wiser to stay away. The country is long enveloped in the dark clouds of tyranny, repression and economic misery. All traders, both indigenous and outsiders avoid that route, in order not to become the victims and prey of the greedy king." Shamon said.

"You speak as you know, though I can see that you are as young and inexperienced as I am."

"Sometimes it's better to learn from the bitter experiences of others than to try getting your own." Beran could see that Shamon was not very happy about his comments about his young age.

"How old are you?" Beran asked. He could see that Shamon was uneasy with the topic.

"It really doesn't matter." He said with a little irritation. "What's important on the other hand, is the necessity, which drags you to Elbon. Yes, that is true that I never have been to that country, but we are traders as you can see and getting the relevant information about the countries around is our business. So the advice I gave to you is based on that information.

How you use this piece of advice, is up to you."

"Which country you are heading to?" Beran asked.

"We are coming from Parnvan and we are going to the land of Furzomia," Shamon told him.

"I have heard so much about that great place and wish to visit it one day." Beran said.

"Which of the two you mean, Parnvan or Furzomia?" Someone asked in a light way.

"I'm curious about both places, but right now I meant Furzomia" Beran told undiplomatically.

"When shall you take up your journey?" asked someone.

"I believe the next morning" was his answer.

When Herzod learned about his plans, he came immediately to have a serious discussion with Beran. He felt as if it was his moral duty to persuade him to give up his intention of travelling to Elbon. He was putting all the weight of his lifetime experiences; his knowledge, understanding and wisdom achieved in the process of time, and did his best to stop him. "We have just saved one precious young life, from getting extinguished. I can't sit still, seeing another youth heading to a sure disaster." Herzod pressed him.

"I really appreciate your deep concern, but the matters I seek can't wait for the times to become better." Beran was determined.

"I really don't know what these matters are? But I heard that your parents are from that land. Is it true? Herzod asked looking into his eyes. He nodded.

"Then how did they agree to your going to that land? Take my advice and go back. You are too young to enter in that hell." He was carefully reading his face. "If you have to go somewhere then come and join us, accompany us to Furzomia. You'll like the country." Herzod was trying to convince him by telling that they needed an extra hand and companion, especially when the young man, bitten by the snake and his father were to drop. The young man was going to take a long recovery time and none could take care of him better than his father.

Herzod could see that despite all his efforts, the youth remained unmoved.

"It's clever not to enter Elbon with a sword as it would just provoke some stupid response from the local authorities." Herzod admired his prudence.

"No, sir, you misunderstood. I'm not carrying a sword because I don't own one, and if I am to be honest, I don't even know how to use it." Beran told him.

Herzod looked at him in disbelief and couldn't utter a word.

For a long time, he kept silent as if not knowing how to react to the given information. He was constantly staring at Beran, trying to determine if the person in front was as naïve, inexperienced and unaware of the dangers lying ahead or some confident, stubborn youth as he gave the impression of. "You have really surprised me but more than that I'm stunned to learn that there are parents, who would allow a youth like you take such a dangerous journey, without any experience and weapon." Herzod said. "It's not that I can stop you from pursuing your goal, but I beg you to reconsider your plan, wait at least for some group, which wants to head that way." He suggested. It was the first time that he saw the clouds of uncertainty appearing in Beran's eyes, a moment he had been waiting for. It didn't take long for Herzod to convince him to change his mind about going to Elbon. His argument that if his errand wasn't of a pressing nature, then it was best for him to wait until the right time, had worked.

Beran had agreed to join the traders in their journey to Furzomia. "What would he do there?" protested one man. "It's for him to decide, all we can provide him is a safe passage." Herzod said with a determined tone.

It didn't take long before Beran became friendly with other young men of that group, who had stopped jesting about his inability to handle weapons. He had remained in good humour, not minding their jokes and laughter. He tried to explain that he was from Kildia, a kingdom, where weapons were less important. It was a place, where the attention was concentrated instead on subjects closer to the inner side, where the beauty and sharpness of the intellect were more valuable than the brutal force. They all laughed and refused to understand his logic. "No wonder we never meet traders from Kildia." one young man said in a joke. "They all would be robbed and killed by the bandits in the way, defending with their sharp edged intellects." The other completed the sentence. They all laughed, and Beran felt a bit hurt at those comments.

"Don't make fun of him. He is just telling you, how the things function in his country. I don't find it a very healthy approach but that country has been surviving for a long time, with all their peculiar philosophy." Shamon came to his defence. Beran noticed that his companions didn't mean any insult or harm but were simply not convinced that they had a healthy and realistic attitude towards life. Beran was curious in their weapons but was too shy to confess. Shamon's hawkish eye had been observing that enhancing interest and decided to exploit it while the chance remained. He had already taught Beran the basics before they reached Furzomia. He had understood that the youth lacked the natural talent in the use of the weapons, but still he could learn to handle the sword, without losing grip on it.

"You are never going to be a warrior." Herzod said with a smile, looking at Beran's poor performance.

"Why should I be a warrior?" Beran asked getting little embarrassed.

"Warrior is not only who fights wars, even those are the warriors, who can defend their honour, dignity and freedoms." Herzod explained.

Beran didn't say anything, but he was busy thinking about his father, mother and country, which were lost because of the use of armies and weapons. No one could help him in achieving his goals to search for his lost brothers and then to seek revenge and recapturing of their lost kingdom if he was to remain an amateur in the use of weapons. For the first time in his life, he felt remorse and bitterness creeping in his heart. Silos had not been very prudent, when he had kept him away from learning the martial arts. He was a prince, who had the need to be a warrior, not only for his own sake, but also for the sake of his kingdom and subjects if there were to be any in the future. That realisation wasn't something he could discuss or share with Herzod or any other person on earth. Silently he withdrew from the place, deeply disturbed, extremely unhappy. Beran knew that the time to learn and master those arts had long gone, but he felt the pressing need to catch up as much as was possible in the given circumstances. "Where are your thoughts?" Beran turned at looked at Shamon, instead of answering him.

"I was wondering if I could ever learn the use of the sword." Beran came to the point.

"Why not? You are still very young and can learn anything you really want to. What makes you doubt?" Shamon asked sitting beside him.

"I know that I am very clumsy and a slow student." Beran confessed.

"Aren't we all like that in the beginning?" Shamon tried to cheer him up. "Of course there are those who learn without putting too many efforts as it's a natural thing for them to do. But then there are others who have to give sweat and blood to achieve the same results." Beran was pondering on his words.

"Can you teach me to use the sword, knowing that I am inapt?" Beran asked.

"I can't, even I would have liked to." Shamon was straightforward.

"Why not?" Beran wasn't giving up without any valid and acceptable excuse.

"You know we are the traders. That's our livelihood. I'll be giving all my energies to the task I have come for. I'll simply not have any time to be your teacher." Shamon excused himself.

"But on the other hand, if you have money, you can get the best teachers in Furzomia. I have heard that they are the best in these tracts." He concluded. Beran kept silent and thinking.

Shamon was trying to find out what crossed Beran's mind, but the expressions of his face didn't lead him anywhere.

"If you are out of money I can arrange some for you." Shamon offered.

"No, it's not money; I have enough of my own." Beran told.

"Then why this reluctance?"

"I was thinking about the embarrassment and ridicule of coming to some person and confess that I didn't know a thing about weapons." Beran said. Shamon couldn't stop his laughter.

"Don't worry about that, you are not the only person, who lacks this art and besides no one shall laugh at you as long as you pay the person adequately." Shamon assured him that his fears were baseless.

Beran was relaxed and waited impatiently for their arrival in Furzomia, where awaited for him a tough task of learning something he had to have learned years back.

12

In Furzomia, all the traders disappeared in the labyrinth of the town, searching for the commodities they had come there for, finding the addresses of the merchants, which could provide the needed supplies, hunting the bargains which lay open. Even Shamon and Herzod had been too busy and hardly found any time for him. Beran was busy in his own quest. He went around, asking about the best available teachers, who could give him lessons. The place was brimful of teachers, who were experts of their professions, but none seemed to be interested in a completely raw hand beginner. "You are at least ten years too late." Said someone. Most of the teachers had the similar opinions. Beran was losing his hope of finding any good teacher, who was ready to give him private lessons as he was considered too old to join a class.

"Are you looking for a teacher?" one young man asked, seeing him coming back after a discussion with a teacher.

"Yes, but it seems to be an impossible task in your country." Beran said in a disappointed tone.

"They all have up to here, and wouldn't take a newcomer." The youth said

"Why not?" asked Beran.

"They have to work hard, and why should they when they can earn their living without putting too much effort?" The stranger explained with a smile

"You mean there isn't any hope to get a willing teacher in this big country?" Beran was disgusted by such a prospect.

"I didn't say that." The stranger corrected him and then added. "There are still left those, who believe in the noble profession and who are ready to serve without demanding huge payments in return."

"Who are they and where can I find them?" Beran joked, not taking his words seriously.

"I can give you the address of at least one such teacher, without any guarantee that he'll accept you." The stranger offered. Beran was desperate to find any teacher at all, so he took the address without any hesitation, thanked the youth and went in search of the given person.

The address was either a hoax, or he had completely misunderstood the directions. Beran had come out of the town and was heading to some desolate place. What the teacher did in those remote and hostile tracts was a question that constantly bothered him. How the teacher was able to attract students and if he didn't, how was he sustaining himself? Beran had difficulty in finding the man at the given address and place. He was certain that the youth had made fun of him. Strangely he didn't feel offended or angry, but instead a smile came on his face as he imagined the amused face of the stranger at his folly of seeking, that which didn't exist. He decided to turn back to his horse, which he had tied to a tree as he looked for the person, when he caught sight of a boar, standing and staring at him. He became stunned by that unexpected situation as there wasn't any time to flee from the boar, which was ready to attack. Beran saw no point in running away and stood waiting for the animal. Strangely he had remained staring into the eyes of a certain death, without panicking, without getting too scared.
The beast looked back into his eyes and stood motionless, without charging an attack. The reluctance in those eyes was somewhat weird thing, but what hindered the beast from attacking was no phenomenon, he had time to understand. If

the animal was scared, then there wasn't any reason for him to worry. His fearlessness had startled the beast, which was now retreating in the bush. He was wrong in his assumption that he wasn't scared at all; he stood all drenched in sweat as the beast retreated. His legs were shaking, reminding that he had just escaped a dreadful incident. Beran was walking towards his horse, when he saw a bearded man coming towards him. The short man was to the older edge, with dirty looks. He looked surprised to find Beran there.

"Who are you young man?" The short stout man asked.

"I'm looking for a person, who is supposed to live somewhere around." Beran told him

"What want you of him?" The man asked in a rough tone.

"I'm told that he is a great teacher, who can teach me the use of the sword."

"What makes you believe that he may be interested in the task?"

"He may be interested, or he may be dismissive, I can't say before I have a chance of asking him." Beran told the man in a polite manner.

"Go back to your world, I am not interested in any contact with that the world anymore . I'm happy to live in the wilderness and seek no human presence around me." The old looking man said in anger, waving his left hand in the air, and it was that moment Beran noticed and got shocked to realise that the right arm of the man was missing. The man was asking him to go away while heading to the direction he had recently emerged from.

"Wait!" Beran shouted, going after him. "I understand if you refuse to take the assignment." Beran told him. "Is it due to your inability to do so?"

"What inability?" the dirty looking man asked in surprise. Beran found it awkward to mention about the person's missing arm, but he couldn't help staring at that direction

"Oh I see" the man finally understood his insinuation and laughed hysterically.

"You people never stop amazing me." He was shaking his head in disbelief. "This inability has never bothered me from taking a service in the army, from taking part in the battles and from always surviving against all odds." Beran felt embarrassed.

"Please forgive me for my stupidity." Beran was quick to apologise. The stout man didn't react to his expressed regret but stood staring at him in a confused manner.

"Your towns are full of competent teachers of all kinds, what forced you to look for a crippled in the wilderness?" He asked with a bitter smile. Beran felt even more embarrassed from his choice of words, but there was little he could do to get rid of his wondering about the man's handicap. Beran told him about his problem to find a suitable teacher, who was ready to accept him as a pupil. The man listened to everything Beran had to say, starting from the prevalent traditions of Kildia to teach and train the children of other subjects and matters than were usual in the other parts of the world. The word Kildia had made one armed person smile, if that was due to some good memory or some bad one, he couldn't judge as the smile disappeared as quickly as it had appeared.

"Not all of us tread the same path. Perhaps you were not meant to learn these arts. Maybe your destiny requires another type of skills from you" reminded the man But despite all attempts of the man to discourage him from spending precious time on learning something, which he had found no inclinations to up till then, he failed to convince Beran.

"Have you gotten a sword?" the man inquired. Beran went forward to the horse and showed him his sword. He checked it from all angles before returning it to him.

"This is not the best sword I have come across, but it'll do for learning purpose." His words were clear signal that the man was taking him as a pupil.

"What's the catch for me?" He asked Beran.

"I've money, so I can pay for your services. You just mention the fee, and I shall happily pay it." Beran told him without any concern.

"What shall I do with the money in this wilderness? You see there isn't any need for that."

"If not money, then what else can I do for you?" Beran was confused.

"You can give me back a favour." Trindras bargained.

"Anything, you just name it." Beran said eagerly.

"One should never promise in haste, without learning the errand first." Trindras warned. Beran felt ashamed and waited impatiently for his elaboration.

"If you promise to travel to the land of Senklour and bring me back my lost arm, I can teach you not only the use of the sword but even other weapons." Trindras offered him the rare opportunity.

"Is it possible to get back your arm?" Beran asked with wide eyes.

"No, not the arm I possessed once, but an alternative arm, which can make me whole, once again." Trindras said with shine in his eyes.

"What makes you believe that I can accomplish what a warrior like you could not achieve on his own?" Beran asked frankly.

"Not all of us are gifted with the same talents, not everyone bears the stamp of Senklour on his forehead." Despite the request of Beran, Trindras refused to expand on the subject any further. "Your promise is enough for me. Just remember your promise, when you reach there."

Trindras had no intention of talking about the strange country, he had never heard of or about the possibility of bringing an arm for him. He watched Beran playing with his sword and knew that he had a tough task ahead, and there wasn't any time to lose if he was to succeed. He was a very demanding teacher, who wouldn't let him rest, sit idle or relax even for a moment. He was forced to be on his feet all the time, running, rushing and doing strange errands, which had nothing to do with the sword. Trindras wouldn't care his protest and complaints, always reminding him the conditions that he could quit his training whenever he wanted to, but still remained bound by his promise to bring him an arm from Senklour. A week had already passed and he felt completely exhausted, drained of all energies, and yet not a single time had he even held the sword in his hand. It seemed that Trindras was exploiting him for his own petty jobs, instead of teaching him the art of mastering the sword. Beran felt cheated by the contract he had entered without much pondering. The contract neither mentioned about the duration of his apprenticeship nor defined any responsibility on the part of the teacher. He was to accept all orders and instructions, without any question. He regretted his entering into an unequal agreement. But it was too late for any renegotiations.

Beran had the feeling that he had entered in some sort of bondage, from which there was no escape. All he could do was to obey and do that blindly. He was depressed and resigned, having only few hours' sleep before his master would wake him up and give him a long list to accomplish before the sundown. He had stopped counting the days. It was hardly few weeks but already seemed as eternity had passed since he came there. He was not anxious of wild animals, nor cared what happened to him, if some beast was to attack, he had gone beyond such worries. Even he had stopped caring his hunger as Trindras always had little food to offer. Beran was surprised when he was told to bring his sword one day.

"Hold it high in front of your face, close your eyes and walk straight" he was instructed.

He couldn't do as he was told to and fell on the ground. If he was finally seeing the training period to start, certainly his hopes dashed to the ground when by the fall came in the end of training, or at least for that particular day. Beran was toiling and saw no end to his miseries. But without even getting conscious about it he was making progress. His hard duties were now curtailed a bit to give space to his other training exercises. He could walk long distances with closed eyes and without falling down. His fear to fall on the sharp edge was disappearing as well, instead was coming the confidence and reliance and ability to make the given tasks.

"From tomorrow shall we start with the sword" Trindras gave him the happy tidings. He took the news without expecting too much.

"You don't appear to be happy about it." Trindras said staring at him.

"Do I have a reason to?" Beran questioned sarcastically.

"Without any doubt, it's going to be the most important day of your life. Didn't you desperately want to learn the use of the sword?" Trindras reminded him of his quest.

"I had lost all hope of ever achieving that goal." Beran was still sour.

"I don't know what you had in mind. But for me nothing comes easy. You needed all the training period before you were fit to proceed."

"What do you mean? Which training are you talking about?" Beran asked still crossed.

Trindras didn't speak but looked at him with a smile on his face. Beran wasn't looking happy, he had expected some justification for the meaningless labours he had been exposed to for the last few weeks.

"You are not supposed to challenge any of my judgements, and here you stand doing exactly the same." Trindras reminded him of the contract. Beran bowed his head and refrained from further questioning.

"You'll do all the activities as you used to do every day. Come and seek me when you are through. Remember the quicker you shall accomplish the given tasks, the more time we shall have to give to the sword." Trindras concluded, before leaving the place. Beran was still agitated and knew that his sword lessons were to be just a minor activity, as his slave like activities consumed the lion's share of the time. But what choices did he have than to make a compromise with his teacher, who was more like a slave driver than a teacher. He wanted to think about the prospects of ever coming somewhere, but was too tired to do so. He was dragged in the valley of sleep, where there were not even dreams any longer.

Trindras was giving more and more time to the teaching as he had originally promised to do. Beran was not any more skeptical about his hidden motives and was whole-heartedly concentrating on the task of learning to use the sword. Despite the fact that he lacked the natural inclination to sword and other weapons, he was doing well. He noticed that his movements were less clumsy, and hold on the sword was firmer. Just within the short period of a few months, he had learned the use of the sword. He could handle the weapon with ease and with mediocre skill. He was ready, he was told by his teacher.

"You have come to the height of your learning and can't improve your skills any more." Beran was happy even with that. He was not perfect in the use of the sword, but that it wasn't what he sought either. He was aware of his limitations and knew that he had a whole life to better his skills. His teacher looked also content as he was the worst student he ever had.

"Tell me why were you torturing me to death with all the pointless labours?" Beran asked before he was taking the leave. Trindras watched him with a piercing look before he opened his mouth in a smile, exhibiting his yellowish teeth.

"There isn't anything, which is meaningless in this world. The secret lies in perception and understanding." Trindras said.

"What was the meaning then?" Beran asked.

"When you came to me, you were in complete physical disarray. Everyone could see that you were never exposed to the realities of the physical world. Your all attention had been focused on the mental body, and it was there one could see the strength."

"It's ridiculous to declare that I was weak in my body." Beran protested.

"Not only weak but even imbalanced. Good for nothing." Trindras said without caring what Beran would say. "Your body needed to be trimmed, to be reigned by some severe exercises, all I did was to make you as fit for your task as it was possible in that short time."

"You might be right as you are the teacher." Beran gave up.

"Not always a teacher is right, and not necessarily the pupils are wrong in their judgements, it all depends. And I am not even your teacher anymore. Don't focus on what lay behind but look forward, it's there your energies are best needed." Trindras gave him a piece of advice.

"Tell me master, what can I do for you?" Beran asked before going away.

"Nothing for the moment, but do remember our deal, when you finally confront Senklour." Trindras said with a smile.

"What's this strange land, where lies it? Why shall I be visiting it?" Beran asked.

"Only time shall provide you with the answers of your questions."

"Any last minute advice?" asked Beran.

"Buy some good sword. A sword is compensating the handicaps of its user" Beran saw him laugh for the first time and felt good.

"What about the horse? Shall I keep him?" Beran joked.

"He'll do for the time being" Trindras said with a smile and disappeared into the bush, without waiting for him to go his way.

Herzod, his son Shamon and other traders had long left the country, he was told. Shamon had left his address, and a standing invitation to come and visit him in his country. He left even a promise that Beran could count on his help in learning the use of the sword if he still needed that. Beran smiled to himself, feeling the pleasure of achievement. "Did he leave anything for me?" Beran asked the inn owner. "No," was his answer. Beran had been promised by Shamon to get him a beautiful bag, made of sheep leather, a souvenir from his country. Certainly it has slipped from his mind, he thought. The first thing he wanted to do was to buy a new sword as was advised by his teacher.

"Where can I buy a good sword in this country?" Beran asked his host.

"The shops are full of such merchandise. Enter into any of these shops and you shall find thousands of beautifully designed swords of all kinds." The inn owner told him.

"But if you are looking for something unique and are ready to pay a price then you should seek the place, where you shall come across rare beauties." One stranger, who sat and listened to their conversation, said in a friendly tone. Beran showed the interest and started talking to the stranger instead, who was very talkative and well versed. He was talking about his encounter with the best craftsmanship of not only his own country, but even of other far away places, but nowhere had he seen the likes of swords he had come across at a place, which lay not so far from, where they were at that moment. The man was praising the sharpness, the mouldings and engravings and most of all the strength of those swords. "I must confess that those swords are very expensive, but they are worth weight in gold. One must see them as the beauty is beyond the words or descriptions." The man was as obsessed or a spokesman of that shop. Beran smiled, almost losing interest in the subject. The person must have noticed his change of mood and smiled, realising that his words were counterproductive, he kept silent before concluding.

"Perhaps you don't believe my words but it's worth investigating. Why don't you visit the place before buying? No one can force you to buy something if you don't like, or if the price is too much." His argument was strong enough, and Beran promised to visit the place before he bought the sword.

Beran went to the Kestarius's workshop, which didn't look any different from the many others he had visited several times before in his life. It was lunchtime, but all three men were busy working, just glancing at him, without any hurry to approach him. He wasn't in a hurry, so he tied his horse in one corner and waited patiently for the blacksmith.

"What can we do for you?" Shapario approached and asked in a friendly tone.

"I'm told that you have the best swords in this country." Beran said.

"Maybe we do, but they are very expensive to buy. How much money do you have?" Shapario asked politely, without showing much enthusiasm

"Money shouldn't be a problem, only if I liked the sword, would you show me some?" Beran asked.

"Some!" Shapario exclaimed. "I can't show you any as we have sold all we had in store. Some traders visited us a while ago and bought all we had."

"Too bad. Then I have to look somewhere else. As you can well understand, I can't buy a pig in a poke."

"It's a very clever thing not to do so. Do come back in a couple of weeks' time. We may have something to offer you." Shapario said before returning to his work.

"You mind if I look around?" Beran asked.

"No, be our guest." Shapario said with a smile. Beran went around looking at the few things which lay there half or semi-finished. He was struck by the beauty and craftsmanship of those products, which were not even processed as yet. He became convinced that the reputation of the place wasn't false. Without a doubt, he had come to the right place. He couldn't wait for several weeks to get his sword delivered, so he decided to look at the other shops in the town. He was about to turn and go his way, when his sight was struck by something he couldn't ignore. It was a sword in sheathe, which was hanging on a wall, the handle of the sword was decorated with ivory and attracted all his attention. He went forward and looked at the decorated sheathe, which in itself was a real beauty. He could not resist touching it and praising the incredible craftsmanship of the object. Without giving any thought, he got hold of the sword's handle and drew it slowly out of its wrap. If he had felt struck by the beauty of the sheathe, he stood perplexed by the sword, which was shining in his hands. It looked like as if he was holding a glittering star. He felt a strong wish to own that wonderful sword, he turned to look for the man he had a conversation with but instead his gaze met a pair of agitated eyes, as fierce and as ablaze as the naked sword in his hand. Beran tried to smile but found no softening signs.

"Who allowed you to touch this sword?" The person asked angrily. Beran told him that he had no intentions of intruding but had found the sword irresistible. But the face of the young man he confronted was not getting gentler.

"I don't understand your anger? Aren't the customer allowed to inspect the goods before they buy them?" Beran said unafraid.

"If the goods are for sale, yes! But who told you that my sword is for sale." The tall young man with a strong muscled body said, stretching his hand. Beran felt embarrassed as he knew well that he had been clearly told that there were no swords for sale at the moment. Without saying anything further, he handed the sword back to its owner and that with an apology.

"I would pay any price for the sword." Beran said while going to the exit.

"And you'll still not get it." Hidas said without any smile.

"You aren't a good businessman. You could sell it and make a new one for you." Beran tried to tempt him.

"Not everything is replaceable." Hidas was determined

"Is there no way I can make you change your mind?" He got no response from Hidas, who just stared at him without a smile.

"Did you make it yourself?" Beran inquired. Hidas's got relaxed a bit and a broad smile spread on his face.

"Not in a million years I can do a thing like that. It's a present, created by a combined work of two masters" Hidas said looking in the direction of Kestarius and Shapario. Beran could see that the young man was proud of his sword.

"By the way, who bought all the swords?" Beran asked. Hidas shrugged his shoulders, without making it clear to him as to what he meant by that gesture. Was that he didn't know or didn't care.

"I couldn't help, overhearing your question" said Shapario coming near to them. "As I earlier told you, they were some foreign traders, very polite but shrewd businessmen. They were ready to pay any price, but did bargain in the end. I was rather impressed by the younger man, he was a tough negotiator." Shapario was laughing. It didn't take long for Beran to guess that who could be those traders.

"I happen to know those people. Perhaps I should rush after them to get one of those swords they bought from you." Beran said in a joke. Shapario looked for a long time at that youth and smiled at his light and friendly way of communication.

"It seems you wouldn't leave until you get that, what you came here for." He saw both, Shapario and the young man smiling and saw an opportunity. He kept silent and waited in anticipation.

"You can buy my sword. I don't have any use of it right now." Shapario offered.

"I wouldn't hesitate a minute if it is even half as beautiful as this one." Beran said still looking at the sword of Hidas.

"You have to travel around the world and cross seven

seas before you can even think of acquiring a masterpiece like that." Shapario said with a big grin.

"I would rather settle down on your sword than to make the trouble" Beran was quick to answer. They all laughed. Shapario disappeared in the interior part of the large workshop and came smiling after some time. He was holding a sword with a simple sheathe. Beran had a quick glance at the sword and felt a bit disappointed by its simple, unimpressive looks. He could hear a big laughter of Hidas and felt odd for revealing his disillusioned mind.

"One should not be allured by the appearance," Shapario said with a smile on his face. Beran could swear that the both men were pulling his leg. He received the sword and weighed it in his hand as he had learned from Trindras. A sword was not a piece of metal, but a piece of art; he was told and should never be too light or too heavy in the hand of its user. He noticed that both men were looking at him with a big interest. He wasn't in a hurry to go further as the real weighing was a lengthy process and not something like putting in the scales and knowing.

"What do you think?" asked Hidas.

"A perfect weighing" Beran confessed, before taking the sword out of its wrapping in a slow manner. He was looking at its shape, curve and checking its sharpness with a broad smile and satisfaction on his face.

"I'll take it." Beran told them without any hesitation.

"Without even asking the price?" Shapario said.

"Whatever price you may be demanding, it would be justice to it." Beran answered waving the sword in the air.

"Be careful, it may cut the air." Hidas warned, and they all laughed.

"You aren't a good buyer," Shapario said with a disappointment. "You can be easily cheated by some crooked trader, but luckily you have come to us, the guardians of honesty and champions of high morals." Beran knew that the man was trying to be funny but felt that there was some truth hidden in his friendly words.

"I may be looking young and inexperienced, but I am from a country, where we are taught to look deep in the eyes of the people you deal with and see if one can trust them or not. Believe me, I have the feeling that I can trust you people blindly." Beran told Shapario, who laughed at his words.

"I like you young man, you can take my sword. Consider it a present."

"Never deprive a man the recompense of his blood and sweat, I am taught by my father. So there is no way I can take this sword, without paying for it." Beran insisted.

"A very noble approach, I must say." Shapario said amused, and agreed to take whatever Beran saw a right price.

"I offer three golden coins, what do you say?" Beran gave a bid.

"It's quite close to the real price, I accept it." Shapario looked amazed. He had much to accomplish but stood talking to the youth even after he received the payment of the sword. He was asking him about his country and how it was like to live there and what had made him come to Furzomia and many more questions. Beran told him, how he was on his way to Elbon and met the traders, who bought all his swords. "Those were the people, who made me change my mind by telling that it was a dangerous place to be." Beran told him. The naming of Elbon had made Shapario look distracted; he was no longer listening to him but was somewhere far away.

"Have you ever been to Elbon?" Beran asked curiously.

"Yes." Shapario's answer was short and dry. "What errand was driving you to that country?"

Shapario asked in an unfocussed way.

"My parents are from that country, I have some unfinished business there." Beran told him as he had told to the traders before.

"So you aren't really from Kildia."

"Of course I 'm. There is no other country I know other than Kildia, where I have lived all my life." Beran said with a smile.

"What's the name of your father?" Shapario asked in by the way, tone.

"Silos." Beran said. He saw some strange smile spreading on the face of Shapario.

"I know your old man, a very refined man. Now I know from where you got all the charming ways and a sharp intellect." Shapario looked really happy to find some connection. "Come at closing time, we'll go out and have a meal together. It would be fun to talk about things from old times." Shapario said before going to his work, which he had completely forgotten about. Beran was happy for having come to that place, where he met a person, who could give him all the information he needed about Elbon, who knew Silos and most of all, where he had gotten a beautiful sword in a bargain price.

13

The traders were already approaching the borders of Parnvan, their fatherland, the country of the wealthy people. A place, where riches were cultivated without putting much labour and where the task to defend those treasures was a state religion. The country had no king and no regular army and therefore, had been exempted by types of taxes. Each and every member of the society was taught to grow into a responsible citizen of the country, where he took all the obligations attached to his living there. They all were not only the traders, the farmers and artisans but were also the soldiers and workers, whenever the need arose. They loved their freedoms, even more than their wealth, which they were confident of reproducing, even if they were lost. Their easy going and luxurious way of living had not made them careless of the dangers, which always loomed in those tracts. The abundance of wealth was causing envy and a strong temptation to subdue these people, but none dared, looking at their preparedness and zeal to defend them. The women in that country were exempted from the direct involvement in the defence of the country but in no way were they excluded from the vital role of defending the country from outside aggression, if there were a need. The women were trained to make the traps, prepare the needed weapons and different ways of distracting the enemy if it did dare to come that way. They all were happy to live the lives in a complete absence of state authority.

Even though they were coming back in the security of their fatherland, they hadn't completely forgotten the lesson of almost losing a companion few months earlier. When Herzod gave the proposition of spending the night at some nearby inn, no one opposed his idea. They all were weary and needed some good cooked meals and a possibility to fresh up before they resumed the remaining part of their journey.

"I know an inn, which lies not so far from here." One trader told them. "And it's not so expensive either." The same trader informed them.

"You should be least worried about the price, considering your piles of money." Herzod joked.

"Don't get jealous of my money, Herzod. Soon you'll surpass my riches, the way Shamon is generating that for you" the man was quick to counter his joke. Despite their enormous resources they had remained stingy in certain circumstances, and it was that fact they so open heartedly joked about, making fun of each other, without getting hurt.

"How come that I haven't heard of the place before?" asked Herzod.

"Because you have not come this way from a long time" answered someone. He was told that the place had been a farm until sometime before, when some couple bought it and converted it into an inn.

"But not many people pass this way, how do they manage?" Herzod asked.

"Perhaps they don't have significant expenditures and can run the place with that little they earn."

"I wouldn't live in this faraway place with so few customers." Herzod said.

"We are not people, who can live the isolated lives, we are used to of living among other beings, neighbours, relatives and all the other comforts of collective living," someone said agreeing with him.

"What do you think Shamon?" Herzod tried to raise the interest of him and to drag him in the conversation.

Shamon smiled and kept silent as if thinking, what to answer. He was never in a hurry to answer a thing if he had not pondered upon it earlier.

"I believe it's not possible for me to declare my opinion about the subject, without first knowing what we are talking about." He finally spoke.

"That's a clever approach." Herzod said proudly.

"No one is asking about some particular place but your general opinion about the subject." One middle-aged man asked looking directly at Shamon.

"Well then." Shamon said with a smile. "I can live anywhere and everywhere, as long as there remains a possibility to earn good money." They all laughed, enjoying his honest answer, any other answer would have been wrong as they all knew his obsession with making money. They had often joked that Shamon was more a Parnvanian than they had been. They used to tease Herzod that Shamon had been born in some wrong place, but he had forced his poor parents to seek his real home. He had succeeded in reaching his goal; even it meant the death of poor parents. Herzod disliked those jokes but knew that was their nationalistic character.

They were not greeted by the inn owner as was the custom in most of the places they had been, but had to knock at the door, announcing their arrival. They were welcomed and shown to their rooms, which were Spartan but cosy and tidy, something which they had not expected at all.

"Who is the owner of this inn?" Herzod asked.

"An old couple, which are resting at the moment," he was told by the youth that showed them in the rooms.

"Do you have any relation to them?"

"No, I am a simple employee."

"When shall they be available?"

"Soon it's evening, they should be through with their siesta" the youth said before disappearing to arrange some drinks for them.

"Imagine that the place is extremely expensive," said someone anguished

"So what? We all are well off or rather very rich people, so it shouldn't make us worried." Said the other.

"It's easy for you to say as you still have a lot of money left with you. I have spent each and every penny in buying the goods." The man protested.

"Who asked you to do so? You know that is not our custom. We are supposed to have some reserves for unforeseeable situations and happenings." The same person continued.

"Don't waste your energies on vain talk. Money is our least problem at this juncture; when we are at a stone's throw away from our homes. Whoever is in a need of money can borrow it from me, as I have much to spare." Herzod offered. All discussion died out as they all knew that no one was to ask the favour of borrowing money. It was considered a shame and disgrace to ask for money from one's neighbours and friends, the only transaction, which was not considered shameful, was that which took place between family members.

"You know that none shall borrow from you." one of them pointed out.

"Why not, aren't we one big family?" Herzod joked, nobody spoke but laughed seeing the man, who had initiated the discussion, searching his pockets and pretending to have found a substantial amount of money there.

"That proves the proverb that where there is a will, there is a way." Shamon joked

"Or that, where there are Parnvanians there is money." Added another and they all laughed.

"I'm terribly thirsty and hungry." Said one of them reminding the fact that they all were hungry as they had not eaten anything the whole day in expectancy of a good meal at the inn.

They were sitting in the large hall, when their host and hostess emerged from the rear. Both of them had a smile on their faces as they came near to them. After general greetings, the couple asked from where did they come, how long were they stay in that inn and other relative questions. They asked if their baggage and lodging had been taken care of. The traders were polite as were their hosts, hiding the fact that they were terribly hungry and thirsty.

"Fresh up you, soon can we serve the food." The lady of the house said with a smile on her face. No one spoke but looked at each other in disbelief.

"Excuse me Madame, but do you really mean that the food is already cooked, ready to be served?" Herzod couldn't keep silent

"Yes, that is exactly, what I have just announced." The lady replied.

"How? We are coming unannounced, and we don't see the signs of other guests in here. For whom did you make so much food for?" Herzod was really surprised.

"We shall have a lot of time to talk to each other and surely your surprise would be removed by logical explanations." The lady said before turning to go away from there. "Excuse me but I have to go and see that all is well in the kitchen."

The tall host remained there asking different questions. He was strong built but looked as if he had been afflicted by some fatal disease but had overcome, though not completely recovered.

"Why have you chosen to live in this out of the way place? How many people use to come and stay here? How do you meet your expenditures?" Now was the turn of the traders to ask him questions.

"I'm not so good at explaining, I have transferred such tasks to my dear wife" the host said with a pleasant smile. "Soon shall she be here and you can ask whatever comes to your heads."

"These are clever people, believe me, that we are to pay dearly for our naïve approach. This couple is talking about everything but the cost. I am not stupid to believe that they were unaware of our visit. They knew and were well prepared." Said the man, who had been worried about the cost the whole time, when the host left, excusing him.

"What's the matter with you? Why can't you relax for a moment and forget about the whispering of your suspicious mind." Herzod said forcefully. His choice of the words was deliberate; as it was the polite way of saying that he was paranoid. The man didn't like his words as he could see all of them turning away and smiling. After that nobody heard him say anything about the expense anymore.

The food was delicious and as rich as they could have expected from the best of the feasts. The food was served in very simple but clean plates, the people serving them were also simple dressed but without a stain or dust on their clothes. They all were more and more surprised by all those weird things but had no courage to ask anything from the host couple, who were busy taking care of their guests.

"I must confess that the food is superb, something, which we couldn't even imagine in our wildest fantasies." Herzod verbalised the thoughts of his stunned companions.

"We are really pleased to know that you liked our food." The host was pleased to receive compliments.

"Who make these wonderful dishes? One feels like blessing those hands that create such delicacies." Herzod praised once again.

"We have been lucky to find such a talented cook." the hostess said with a smile.

"Can we have the pleasure of meeting him?" Herzod asked.

"It's a female cook and not a male as you presumed" corrected the hostess with a broad smile.

"That's amazing, not that I doubt about the talents of female but isn't it a male speciality to cook meals for larger groups." Herzod tried to explain about his surprise.

"I am rather surprised too, seeing so many servants working at this inn. How can you sustain an army of workers, keeping in mind that very few travelers frequent the place?" one of the guests asked. "No, no, they aren't workers at all," said the host little amused. "These are our friends, who came here to celebrate the occasion, which is the most important day for us."

"And what's that?" Herzod asked.

"It was ten years ago, we first came to this country, an occasion we use to celebrate." the host told. "Many of our friends have joined us ever since, and we all gather here to thank and appreciate the freedom we enjoy."

"So the food we are consuming was prepared for guests, who have turned into the role of hosts." Herzod asked with a surprise.

"You are right in your conclusion, but believe me there is nothing in the world, which is more pleasurable for us and our friends than to serve you strangers, who needed that food more than we did." The hostess said in a soft voice.

There was a pin drop silence. All of a sudden the actions were frozen and none took another loaf of bread, anymore. They were looking at each other in confusion.

"How very stupid of us?" said Herzod very much embarrassed. "Please forgive us our insensitivity."

"Please keep having your meals. I'm sorry that we have had the stupidity of mentioning our friends in the middle of the meal." The hostess said in a regretful manner.

"It's out of the question; we can't take another bite unless you all come and join us in our meal." Herzod insisted.

"Alright," said the host, giving up and signing his friends to join the company and eat with them. They all sat and ate their meal, having a small chat about every possible topic. Herzod sat beside the hostess, who seemed to be a very refined lady. He was stunned to find a person like her in the middle of nowhere. Many times he was so close to ask such a question but refrained from doing so. "Which one of you is the cook?" asked Herzod.

"I am," said someone weakly.

"So you made the food?" Herzod couldn't hide the surprise and confusion from his voice, when he looked at the little old man. They all laughed. The hostess stood up and raised her hands to draw their attention. She introduced the man, who worked at the place as a cook and then looked around in search of someone. The person responsible for the tonight's successful dinner is none else than my dearest friend and mother like figure, Aloha. They all clapped their hands, but the old lady was getting too uncomfortable from that attention. She didn't seem to be a shy type but still a person, not comfortable with the crowd.

"She is the person, to whom, me and my husband owe our lives to" The hostess encouraged them to applaud once again.

"May I ask from where did you come to this country?" Herzod asked her.

"From a neighboring country." The hostess gave a short answer.

"Why this desolated place? Why don't you come and live in our town, which is only at a few days' distance."

"We are happy with the place, we all live around here and are happy to receive groups of traders like you, travelling individually or in groups. This crossroad is a perfect place for us." The hostess said.

"What's so strange about this place?" Herzod asked.

"Nothing is peculiar about this place, except that it lies in the area, which connects three kingdoms." She tried to explain.

"So what?"

"We are looking for some news and some people, who might one day cross these areas." Herzod could see that the hostess didn't want to talk more about the subject and was feeling uncomfortable.

She gave a few names and asked if he knew those people. Herzod politely told that he had never heard of them. "Please let me know if you hear anything about these people. We can give a big reward." The hostess sounded desperate for a minute. Herzod never asked but presumed that those men must have hurt the couple at some point, and perhaps they were after some vengeance. After the meal, they went to sleep, leaving the host and his friends to celebrate the occasion. They had a long, tiresome journey ahead and needed a good sleep to gather the energies. Herzod had wanted to pay their dues already in the night but found it rude to discuss the matter while the host was busy, so he decided to wait till the morning. They could hear the voices till late in the night, but were surprised to find both the host and the hostess, sitting and waiting for them in the morning.

"Your breakfast is ready." The hostess announced.

"Didn't you people sleep?" Herzod asked.

"We did, but apparently there are some who didn't" said the host pointing to Shamon and other young members, who were not looking so happy.

"Perhaps it's better we settle down our account before we take the breakfast." Herzod offered.

"It's no hurry; just have your breakfast in peace." The host insisted.

They all were busy taking the morning meal and had no anxiety regarding the rest of their journey. They felt properly rested and energised to endure the remaining distance. They were already feeling the smells of their home tracts and looked happy and content. "Soon is coming the moment of truth, which I have in vain tried to warn you about." the trader, who had been so suspicious about the host and hostess said. No one paid any attention to his babble and continued eating, but that didn't stop him from proceeding with his hypothesis. "It's without any doubt the cleverest policy, to ignore the talk about the money, until the last minute, when it's too late to negotiate. And one has to pay the demanded price." The man sounded bitter to his companions, which had been ignoring his warning signals. They chose to disregard him.

They all were ready to leave and were waiting for Herzod to make the payment and join them, but he kept lingering. He was standing near the couple and busy discussing with them in a forceful way. They couldn't hear what they talked about, but watching from their gestures and faces, they all could understand that a there was some problem. Few of the members tried to ride that way, but the middle-aged members stopped them from doing so. "There is no need to interfere, we have full trust in Herzod's ability to handle the situation." one of the merchants said. The dispute seemed to be taking much longer time than they had hoped for. No one was happier than the trader, which had been suspicious; one could see a despicable smile on his face as if he were demanding recognition for his farsightedness.

"We are getting late. We have to interfere and pay whatever they demand. It's not worth a debate." Shamon suggested, the others agreed to him. As Shamon was about to ride in the direction of Herzod, when he saw him coming back from the direction of the host and hostess.

What really astonished him was that Herzod had not even shook hands with his hosts, a very peculiar and rude thing, which he couldn't have imagined from him.

"Have you settled the things?" Shamon asked. Herzod was too upset to answer his question, but gave a sign that all was well. The strangest thing was that the host couple was looking as untouched by the conflict as if it never had existed, and were coming to their side to bid them goodbye, to give them the best wishes for their journey. For half of the day, Herzod would not even discuss what had made him so upset, but when finally he did tell them, they all looked shocked and ashamed, cursing their poor judgments. It was not at all, what they had presumed. On the contrary, the quarrel was about the money, which the hosts refused to accept as they considered them as guests sent by the gods rather than the ordinary traders. They could not allow them to pay for something, which was there for the guests to eat and drink. Regarding their accommodation, he was told that the rooms were there regardless of if some customers came or didn't come, they were to get the compensation, one-way or another, he was told.

"Why did you let them? Why didn't you tell us on the spot, so that we all could force them to accept the money as gratitude?" one of them said.

"That was the problem we had so hot discussion about; they made me swear not to tell any of you until we were far away." Herzod told, making them all silent, sad and regretful. Presumption about some unpleasant discussion had made them all behave a little reserved in their taking leave from the hosts, to whom they had taken as some greedy cheats. The truth was giving them a very bitter taste, and all wanted to avoid looking at their companion, who had poisoned their thoughts. They were very much impressed from those strangers, who had treated them as if they were their own and had given them the best possible comfortable stay, without demanding anything in return. They were wondering and searching in their hearts the true meaning of riches. Which were richer, those who had the bigger resources or those with generous hearts? Right then, they were quite convinced that the latter was truer than the former suggestion.

Shapario had invited Beran to his home, where he quickly made some food for them all to eat, despite Beran's insistence that they all could go out and eat their dinner there. Shapario wanted to show him that he wasn't just good at his work as a blacksmith but was even an excellent cook. Those two arts were not matched in any way. If one required a strong, powerful muscular body, the other had a prerequisite of a mental inclination and balance in the soul. He seemed to have mastered both. He was as soft to the delicate ingredients and foodstuff, as could be any sensitive person. None could demonstrate the raw but focused power as he did. Beran was smiling to watch the unhappy face of Hidas, who was reluctantly helping his father Shapario. One could see that he didn't like the job, and just did it with a force, which unmatched the need.

"Certain people never learn to use the force proportionately." Shapario joked. Hidas ignored his comment, but he tried not to hide the fact that he didn't want to be criticized, at least not before some stranger. Shapario was pretending not to have noticed his silent protest

"You were telling that your parents live now in Kildia, Were you born there?" Shapario asked.

"No, I was also born in Elbon." Beran told him.

"Hmm," Shapario said tasting the salt. "But that's strange! I never heard that he had some child, rather he was not even married, and he was a known bachelor." Shapario looked puzzled. "How old are you?" he asked.

"I don't know, maybe seventeen, perhaps eighteen." Beran said as if he cared less.

"Either the man had kept everyone in complete darkness about his marriage and child or he has lied to you." Shapario said with laughter.

"About what?"

"It could be your age, or your being born in Elbon, or it could even be his claims of parenthood. I like the man but know that he has difficulty in taking responsibilities. I wonder what made him marry and then make a child." Shapario was amused.

Beran didn't say anything but got convinced that Shapario really knew Silos and did that well, but there was no way he could reveal the truth about his own background. Instead, he decided to press Shapario for more information about the things he was interested in, namely his parents and their fate.

"My father claims to have worked with the king of Elbon, Were you also in the royal services?"

"Yes, I did work for the king."

"What really happened to the king and queen?" Beran asked.

"Didn't your father tell you? I thought he was there and knew about the fate of them."

"No, they had also left the country before that occupation." Beran told.

"I wish I knew, but I too had left the country before the enemy army moved into the town" Shapario told. "But presumably both of them are long dead."

"What makes you think that way and why such certainty?"

"If you knew the king, you would also think in the same manner. He was a courageous man, who would face his fate by confronting it in a manly way and would not adopt an escaping route." Shapario told him with a sigh.

"What's so manly about it? Isn't it better to retreat, gather one's forces, reorganise and face the enemy anew, especially an enemy that had chosen a deceitful way to overcome and occupy the territory?" Beran questioned. Shapario didn't speak for a moment but just looked in the eyes of Beran and smiled.

"We all are different in our approach and strategies. Personally I agree with you, but for certain people it's not considered to be honourable to flee, whatever the reason might be."

"Is there anyone who could tell for sure about the fate of the king?" Beran asked.

"Why do you have that burning interest in their fate?"

"I've got a passion for history," Shapario smiled at his answer.

"I believe in history as well, not to read it, but to make it." Hidas said. It was the first time he was taking part in their conversation. Beran smiled, looking at that big bodied young man.

"What history you have made until now?" Beran joked.

"I will, when the time comes." Hidas didn't like his smile.

"I am certain you will do great things, but right now you are required to go on with your given tasks." Shapario intervened, trying to appease Hidas anger, which he feared could turn ugly. There was no way he wanted his guest to witness that.

The all three were busy eating, when someone knocked at the door. Hidas tried to get up, but Shapario signed him to remain sitting. He got up from his seat and went to open the door, and looked surprised to see Kestarius standing there. It was very seldom the man came to visit him if he did come to say hello, then it meant some big news. He requested him to come inside and invited him on the food table. He told that he had just taken his meal.

"Is everything all right?" Shapario asked.

"You can finish your meal, we can talk later." Kestarius said trying to suppress his anxiety, but they all could guess that he was worried.

"These young men can go on eating while we can have a chat." Shapario said and took him to the other room.

"What could be so important, which forced him to come running to this house?" Hidas wondered.

"Perhaps some business problems," Beran said, chewing his mouthful

"You don't know the person. He is not very social and hates even to go and visit his closest friends. So if he has chosen to come, there must be something larger than his reluctance to socialise." Hidas wouldn't let go.

When the both men reappeared, one could see that Shapario was looking as much worried and anxious as Kestarius, who was on his way out from the house. Shapario didn't resume his eating but sat aside in deep thoughts.

"I can see that he brought some bad news, what's that?" Hidas asked, leaving his handful of food. Shapario didn't say anything for a while.

"Why didn't you tell that you were joining the royal army?" Shapario asked looking at Hidas's face.

" Before I informed you ," Hidas said in a casual manner. "Was that all? Did he come all the way to tell you that?" Hidas was getting relaxed.

"As a matter of fact, no, he was here to tell me that you have offended his excellence and are in a danger." Shapario said looking a bit angry. Beran could watch Hidas turning pale.

"So it wasn't just the matter of joining the army, which you have kept secret but even your friendship with the princess Danor. What's going on? Why the anger of the king? What have you done?" Shapario was angry and confused.

"I haven't done anything wrong." Hidas answered anguished.

221

"The anger of the king is incomprehensible."

"There must be a valid reason. The king is not unjust, who would just turn against you and order your arrest." Shapario said little irritated.

"It's no crime to love a princess." Hidas said angrily. Beran and Shapario looked at him with a surprise in their eyes.

"How? When you had time to look for that love? Why didn't you realise the status of a king and a blacksmith?" Shapario asked in frustration, but without any anger in his tone.

Hidas kept avoiding the eyes of Shapario but looked unafraid. He was explaining how and where he had met the princess Danor, and how he had fallen in love, without even realising it. They both shared the same teacher, who taught them archery.

"Why didn't you tell me?" Shapario asked, still worried.

"I knew that you were going to be angry. The reason that I wanted to join the army was also to get a chance to get closer to the princess" Hidas confessed.

"What were you thinking? Did you hope that the king would place you at his royal guards?" Shapario asked sarcastically.

"Why not? I am one of the most well trained people in the country. Who can match my skills and power?" His question had offended Hidas.

"You should know by this time that these qualities can entitle you to get in his highness's services but not enough to make you part of his personal guards." Shapario corrected him.

"What did Kestarius tell you exactly? " Hidas asked.

"That you are in danger. The king is angry and is considering putting you behind the bars." Shapario told.

"For what crime?" Hidas was defiant.

"For the crime of defaming his royal name, for the crime of forgetting your humble position and background, do you want more details?" Shapario was asking gently, without any anger.

Hidas looked agitated but couldn't express his desperation other than to clench his hand.

"You have put me in a difficult position, but I'll try to solve the issue in some amiable fashion. But you have to be away from our home for a while so that no harm shall come to you." Shapario looked suddenly very confident.

"There is no way I can give up the princess if that's what you are thinking" Hidas made it clear, so that there shouldn't be a misunderstanding.

"What? Do you intend to fight back?" Shapario taunted.

"I don't have the power to do so, but if I was in a position, I wouldn't hesitate." Hidas answered fearlessly.

"You are some character!" Shapario said with laughter.

Shapario was of the opinion that Hidas needed to be at some safe place while he sorted out the problem. How was he to approach the king and with which arguments were he to convince him to relinquish from seeking an arrest and sentence of Hidas, was something he had to think and find out later on. He wasn't at all anxious anymore; on the contrary, he seemed to be amused and happy at the prospects of Hidas getting married to the princess at some stage. How that impossibility was to occur was nothing less than a riddle, but he was not interested to discuss that matter at that very moment. He believed that it was better for Hidas to leave immediately, but the question was where to? He rejected the possibility of staying at the Kestarius, right away as it was the most obvious place, where the king's men were to look for Hidas.

"We can go and live in some town, where no one knows him," Beran suggested.

"The smaller towns are even harder places to assimilate and hide. All eyes watch the strangers, and report to the centre, as quickly as they receive an inquiry." Shapario talked like a wise and experienced person.

"Perhaps he can follow me to my country. He can stay at my home until we get all clear signal from you," Beran suggested.

"That could work. The knowledge that he is in safety would give me less anxiety." Shapario agreed to his suggestion. "But are you sure that your parents wouldn't mind, you bringing some stranger into the house?" Shapario wanted him to reconsider his offer.

"Don't worry about my folks, they would be delighted to receive anyone I chose to bring home," Beran assured him.

"No one is asking what I think of the whole affair. I refuse to flee, I am not going anywhere," Hidas announced.

"Don't be a fool. Be prudent! There is no shame in making a strategic retreat sometimes,"

Beran said, fully aware that Hidas was to be flared up by any words coming from some stranger like him.

"Who has asked your opinion?" he asked angrily.

"Don't be a stubborn fool like your father," Shapario said angrily. He looked aghast at his own words and made some strange sound as if he was trying to laugh. Both Beran and Hidas were watching him with surprise on their faces, trying to figure out what he meant by those words. "I think you're stubborn and foolish like me. But I believe you should have a better performance." Shapario was trying hard to erase the impact of his earlier uttering. Hidas continued making the resistance as he didn't want to leave the country, but finally was convinced to do so if only just temporarily.

"Just a few months and no more am I to be away." Hidas made a compromise, making it clear that he was to return to Furzomia after a couple of months' time and face the consequences, whatever that might have been. Shapario promised that he would do all in his power to calm down the king and make him agree to give the princess's hand to Hidas in marriage.

"I know that the king likes you and Kestarius, but how do you plan to make him agree to such a thing?" Hidas remained suspicious that Shapario was ready to promise anything to have him off his back.

"Believe me I have my ways of convincing people." Shapario told him confidently. "Even if I failed to persuade the king, I promise to help you get married to princess Danor."

"How?" Hidas asked in disbelief.

"Even I have to raise the mighty armies to accomplish my mission, I shall not hesitate. Now don't waste your time and leave the country as quickly as possible. Avoid all contacts with small towns and don't leave any clue or information about your destination, if you have to get in touch with the people on the way." Shapario gave them the final instructions before they left his home.

They were moving fast to get out of the country, not because there was any imminent danger to their lives, but in order to do it as painless as possible. They had to rely on food and water they carried with them if they were to avoid any human contact. Hidas seemed to be impressed by Beran's confidence with which he led him on the way, being unaware that he was just treading on the footsteps of his own and the traders he had accompanied few months earlier. Beran was trying his best to make Hidas relaxed and be more open than he was. To travel in the company of a person like Hidas was worse than to travel alone, at least one had none to blame for the boredom.

"I have heard that you are very good at the use of weapons." Beran started the discussion.

"That's all I have learned in my life," Hidas answered shortly.

"I myself have recently learned the use of the sword. My teacher had a really hard task of making me understand even the basics." Beran said with laughter. And before Hidas would ask the reason of his not learning the military arts, he started briefing him about his country and the way things functioned there.

"That's some strange country of yours!" Hidas looked surprised.

"The world is a strange place to live in, with so many varying ways of life," Beran said.

"You really know a lot more about the world than I do." Hidas confessed, making Beran look very content. "But the knowledge of the world will not help you if you were to counter some trouble one day, while my acquaintance with the weapons shall." Beran was amazed to see how his companion was working hard to disregard his own lack of knowledge.

"You are absolutely right about this assertion of yours. That's the reason, why I wanted to learn the arts of war." Beran tried to remain polite and friendly.

"How good are you in the use of the sword?"

"I don't know, but indubitably not even half as good as you are."

"I would like to put your skills on test one day," Hidas said with a keen side look.

"And I'll do my best not to disappoint you," Beran said with laughter.

14

They were completely unaware of the fact that while they were pressing ahead to Kildia, the messengers of the King Pampicilos were heading to the eastern country of Parnvan, bringing a message for those traders, asking them to surrender their sovereignty for a continued peaceful existence. The king had reminded those traders that the peace of human living required a strong hand, which could not only protect them but even gave them glory and purpose. He was quick to remind them the dangers, which could arise if the advice wasn't heeded. He had stressed at the need of protecting their riches, which they had collected during the process of generations. He was ready to provide that protection if they were to accept him as a patron and a king. King Pampicilos was absolutely sure that his offer was to be rejected immediately by those traders, which had the tradition of fighting back with all the might they had. But he had not offered them that protection without carefully studying their strengths and weaknesses. For years, he had been planning his scheme for expansion, and felt that the time was ripe for that. He had calculated that the traders were his weakest neighbours, not because they were going to give him the least of resistance but because he was aware of their inadequacy in numbers. All previous attempts to subdue them had failed because the defence of the country was not properly studied before the attacks were made King Pampicilos was certain that he could break down the defences of Parnvan.

The traders were not hesitant in their refusal to accept his proposal of concord and peace, which in reality meant nothing but subjugation and slavery. The decision to turn down the offer was unanimous, though the fears of the consequences varied from person to person.

Most of the traders were confident that they could face any

threat while the others knew the reputation of Pampicilos better and feared him.

Herzod was most anxious about that serious situation. He had called for an extra meeting to discuss the solemn state of affairs. None, but few understood his alarm about the issue, but everybody did come to the meeting. Herzod was quick to underline that his entire life was public, and none could accuse him of cowardice. Nevertheless, he had the feeling that the problem they faced was much more dire than they could anticipate. He was talking about the possibility of some huge attack coming, much bigger than they imagine, much faster than they could withstand and capable of wiping out their entire existence.

"Come on Herzod, be reasonable, from where do you think such attack can be made. If you see the attack coming from the west, then it would be the first time in our long history that we shall experience that as no one can bring a large army from that direction without endangering its destruction. Even if the army of Elbon succeeded crossing the arid wastelands, they shall not have the forces to withstand our fresh and well prepared force." One of the traders tried to brush the baseless fears of Herzod aside.

"If it were the normal circumstances and if we faced an ordinary enemy, I would agree with you without any problem. But here we are talking about an enemy, which is cunning, which is brutal and having enormous populations, which are forced to serve his ambitions in order to survive." Herzod's words were strong enough to ignite a serious debate, in which they were forced to see that some terrible clouds of destruction were looming over their heads. Half of them were determined to take their stand, even if it meant the end of their lives while the other half wanted to act according to the situation.

"No, we shall not compromise. We'll not wave from our resolve to defend our properties and our freedoms. We'll rather die defending our land than to think of any other possibility." The trader leading the militant group declared.

"I think that we still have the time to act. Let us remove all our valuables and women and children and place them in safety while the able men stay and wait for the enemy's next move, which I don't see coming before the end of the summer," Herzod suggested. It triggered another hot debate among the participants. This time, most of the traders agreed to the suggestion, and decided to get braced with the given tasks. The remaining opposition had no choice but to stop arguing as the majority had spoken.

They had decided to move in the direction of Kildia, but in a discrete manner, travelling only in small numbers, in order not to raise the suspicion of the enemy, which might have her spies spread around. The families were to be transported out of the country before they think of the valuables. They were aware that it was a painstaking process but had no alternatives but to follow the path. To leave the comforts of the home was a shocking experience for women and children. The women had been confident that they could face any enemy, but their men were not as convinced of their women folk's ability to do so, especially not against the brutal armies of Pampicilos. They were moving Northwest into Kildia, but they had their spies placed in the bordering areas of both Elbon and southern Kildia and that for only one reason that few of them suspected that Pampicilos could use Kildian territory to avoid hardships of his arid landscape and to get the element of surprise at his disposal. Within a few months' time they were to complete all their preparations, but right then a hard summer lay ahead. Shamon had been assigned to that group of young men, who were tirelessly transporting the women and children away from Parnvan. They had many times stayed in the inn on their way back to the country. They had strict orders not to discuss the nature of their duties and tasks with anyone, as it could jeopardise the whole enterprise, but it wasn't an easy thing to pretend and lie especially to people like Tylon and Haliba, which looked at their frequent comings and goings, without understanding what went on.

"When shall you come again? We ask so that we can prepare food for you people," Haliba would ask.

"We come and go as the need arise." Shamon tried to answer in a light manner.

"We know it is none of our business, but what goes on. You young men are certainly not on some trade mission as we can see," she said in a curious manner.

"How you can be sure about that?" Shamon asked.

"Isn't that obvious? Your elders would never allow you to travel alone on some long journey. You never bring any goods with you and the frequency…" He laughed at the observation and analysing capacity of the hostess.

"You are absolutely right, but my lips are sealed by my orders not to talk about our mission." Shamon was apologetic.

"Why didn't you say so, I would never have raised the question," the hostess said with a smile and never asked any questions regarding their mysterious journeys after that, till one day Herzod came along those young men. He was as polite and friendly towards the host couple as ever.

"I hope you all are prepared to leave!" Herzod said.

"Leave? Where to?" Tylon and Haliba asked in astonishment.

"So, you are not informed about the happenings, which is a

strange thing." It was Herzod's turn to be surprised. Haliba asked impatiently what it was all about, and Herzod explained to them about the message they had received from King Pampicilos and their own refusal to do as they were asked to and about their decision to evacuate the women, children and elderly. Tylon and Haliba looked extremely disturbed by the news and kept listening to his theories and the precautions they intended to take. Herzod was not sounding very optimistic about their prospects of winning over the army of Pampicilos, which he had heard was consisted of young, aggressive, and hungry people, a very dangerous combination, according to him. Tylon sadly agreed but could not come up with any suggestion.

"I don't know what we'll choose to do. But thanks for informing us about the danger." Haliba said to him.

"I am really astonished to see how the young men have handled the whole issue. Of course, they were instructed not to disclose the information to the strangers, but I had no idea that they hadn't even informed you about the danger that loomed over our heads." Herzod was apologetic.

"It's no blame to them. We understand that they were just following the instructions, without using the common sense. Isn't that a common characteristic of the youth?" Haliba was defending the young men.

"And beside that, we are but strangers to you," Tylon added. Herzod assured them that they no longer were some strangers to him. He deliberately talked about his personal feelings as he couldn't talk about his whole community, which had remained skeptical about all strangers coming to their land.

"You people must get ready and leave this country as soon as possible."

"How your preparations are moving?" Haliba asked.

"We are almost done. Now the time to move our possessions is underway."

"How long do you think we have?" Haliba asked.

"No one can say for sure, but my guess is that we have from one to two months time," Herzod told her.

Tylon and Haliba looked pale but showed no signs of fear as Herzod had expected. He was even more impressed with those people than before. He had often thought about that couple and wondered why there were no young people in that household. He had never raised the question but suspected that they too were barren like him and his wife Nori.

"Why Shamon is not with this party this time?" Tylon asked.

"He wasn't feeling well. Perhaps it is the fatigue as you know these young ones have been doing an incredible job, which dries them out of energy," Herzod said.

"He is a very refined young man. Both of us believe that you have succeeded in raising him into a gentleman." Haliba gave him the compliment, and he just smiled with a slight bowing.

"You are a very nice person, who sees goodness in everything," Herzod said with a smile. They all laughed knowing that they could go on giving compliments to each other for the rest of the day, but it was time for Herzod and his company to leave.

"I know that there are no young men to leave behind, so you must brace yourselves for the movement. In a couple of weeks' time, I shall send some youngsters to escort you to safety." Herzod told them.

"We are old people and have nothing to be afraid of or protect from the army if it came this way, so maybe we wouldn't be going anywhere and just stay where we are," Tylon said in a resigned manner and Haliba looked aghast, staring at her husband in disbelief.

"Certainly we are moving away from this place. There is no way that we wait for the armies to come, and do us some terrible things." Haliba was decisive. "With thanks shall we accept all help which you can provide us."

"In that case, I'll instruct Shamon to take care of you folks."

"Where do you intend to move? Is Kildia a safe place?" Tylon inquired.

"It all depends, but right now we are making that land as our destination. We'll have little respite to think and plan about our future plans. I wish and hope that our misgivings about the designs of Pampicilos are wrong." Herzod still had a hope that they were to return to their homes as soon the danger was over. He prayed that the theories of others were truer than his own fears about the future developments.

The first thing Beran and Hidas came to know when they entered Kildia was that something terrible was going on in Parnvan. No one could tell exactly what all was about, but there were rumours about that land of the east, the most peaceful neighbouring country, with which they had very cordial and friendly relations, was in some kind of turmoil. Some strange and mysterious activities were going on from that direction, making Kildians very nervous. They had traded with each other for centuries, but had never seen those traders bringing their wives, children, and elderly with them. They were not coming and living in their big towns as they had expected those luxury loving people to do in normal circumstances, but were choosing to stay far from the Kildian towns. The population of these traders was rapidly growing without any apparent reason. The traditional liberty to move freely between the two countries was preventing the officials from asking any questions about the subject. Beran was alarmed, knowing that his friends in Parnvan were in some serious trouble, as there could not be any other explanation to that exodus.

"I must travel to Parnvan and find out what goes on there. In the meantime you can stay with my parents, I'll not take long," Beran suggested. But Hidas rejected his offer without giving it a thought.

"I am already unhappy to be with a stranger and you want me to be with someone I never have met. It's out of the question."

"Give a suggestion then, as you might know that I like my new friends and wouldn't leave them in trouble if there was any. I have to proceed in the direction of Parnvan." Beran was determined.

"Alright then, I follow you."

"You don't have to, they aren't your friends, and it's not an easy journey"

"I have also made up my mind, there is no way I can sit at your parents' home and get miserable," Hidas told him. "We will arrange some water, food, and a night's good sleep, and we'll be ready for the journey."

Hidas looked in amazement at the barren land, which spread as far as his sight could reach. For miles and miles they couldn't find any sign of vegetation or animal life. They travelled as fast as their horses could make it, in order to not get entrapped in that hostile landscape. Beran had difficulty in confessing that he had chosen the wrong path and consequently had the possibility of getting it rougher than they had calculated. He feared that if they were forced to spend the night in that inhospitable place, then they were going to be more tired the day after. He had no idea how far that desolate stretched and that uncertainty made him press ahead like a mad man.

"Take it easy, you are stressing the animals too much. I don't know the reason for your doing so, but believe me I don't think it is a good idea." Hidas tried to warn him. But Beran's mind was moving faster than the speed of his horse.

"I believe we have taken a wrong path." Beran finally decided to confide his companion.

"When did you notice that?" asked Hidas in a cool manner.

"I had my suspicions from some time."

"Why didn't you disclose it immediately? Why wait until it's too late to turn back?" Hidas's question was genuine, but he had no satisfactory answer. He was silent avoiding the angry gaze of Hidas.

"O, how I hate the situations where I have to follow others blindly." Beran could see Hidas getting more and more excited.

"There is no time to get upset; we should really hope that the way shall not turn uglier than it is already." Beran tried to cool him down.

"How difficult it is to resist the temptation of killing you" Hidas was furious.

They were riding with the same rapid speed, without talking to each other. Only the angry side glances of Hidas reminded him that they were not only moving in some hostile place but even faced the challenge of holding their nerves intact.

It was the horse belonging to Beran, which collapsed first, forcing Hidas to stop, as well. He still looked angry and didn't say a word. Beran turned his gaze in a hope to find signs of some greenery, but there were none.

"Take these bottles of water and go on riding. I hope you'll succeed in getting out of this strange place," Beran told him.

"And let you die here?" Hidas was sarcastic. "No, I wasn't brought up to be a selfish person," Hidas told him. "Of course it would be a different thing if you were dead like your horse."

"We have no other choice but to save whatever it's possible to save." Beran tried to reason.

"You mean I go my way, leaving you here? I can't do that even if I wanted to," Hidas said, getting off his horse.

They both knew that their chances to survive were diminishing with the fall of darkness. The horse wasn't in good shape, and they were running out of water for the horse, even though they could still have that for their own use, at least for a time being.

"You know that you are some stubborn person," Beran told him.

"It's no revelation."

"You could save your life. Your horse is still alive," Beran reminded him.

"For how long? Sooner or later it's bound to follow the fate of your horse." Hidas was right in his analysis.

They sat in a dejected mood, without knowing what to do about their hopeless situation. Hidas was no longer angry or accused him of the situation but tried to be friendlier than he had been ever since they came across each other. What had caused him to change his attitude was nothing less than a mystery. He appreciated his none finger-pointing approach as that was the last thing he could bear at that point. He was full of guilt, which was killing him.

The night was falling, and their hopes of getting out of that place alive were fading. They both knew that the heat was diminishing their chances of survival drastically. Their bodies needed liquids to maintain the balances, and it was a commodity that they were running out of. The place had the appearance of being void of life, but the impression was different in the darkness of the night, as they could clearly hear the sounds of different animals coming from some unknown distance.

"These sounds are the guarantee that we are not so far from life and water, but which directions we have to seek?" Beran said.

"The sounds are coming from all around, even from the direction; we have been treading from so many hours. I haven't seen any life there, did you?" Hidas said in a calm manner.

"You are right. I think we are losing our minds. There is no hope for us, we are lost." Beran was pessimistic. Hidas kept silent.

"The biggest mistake we made was not to change our tired horses, if only we had the fresh horses." Hidas said with a sigh.

"Or we had a sense of the right direction." Hidas said with only difference that he didn't sound unhappy or bitter.

"Tell me Hidas what has made you calm? Only a moment ago you were so aggressive and annoyed."

"I don't know, that is something, which makes me wonder, as well. In the face of emergencies, I grow sober, strong and more patient. Perhaps it is knowledge that we share the same fate, and there is no point in making you more miserable than you already are," Hidas explained.

"If we are to perish here, can you forgive me my mistake of choosing the wrong direction?"

"I don't think you need to worry about that. Perhaps we shall do it anyway, or perhaps we shall not have time for regrets or forgiveness," Hidas said in a careless tone and then laughed.

"What makes you laugh in such a terrible situation?"

"Nothing special. I just remembered what my father used to remind me."

"And what's that?"

"When I was very young, I am told that I almost died but was brought back to life by some miracle. I just wondered what was the purpose of that return, if I am to die in this barren place." Hidas seemed amused by the comic-tragic situation.

"Don't we all have such stories in our past? I was told a similar story from my childhood." Beran was more depressed than his companion.

"I'm too young to be wasted like that," Beran said.

"And I'm eighty years of age, ready to say good-bye to the tiring world," Hidas was unforgiving and showed that he intended to embrace his death with courage and a smile on his face rather than dying a miserable death.

They both were sweaty and far away from sleep. Suddenly they heard some sounds coming from some distance. Despite the complete darkness, they looked at each other as if they wanted to confirm that they were not suffering from some hallucination.

"Did you hear that?" Beran asked first.

"Without a doubt these are the sounds of some people, wait here and don't move, I shall try to locate them and see who they are, how many, and if it's safe to contact them," Hidas volunteered.

"No, let me go instead," Beran said.

"Why, isn't it better that I go, I can deal with them if they were not good people." Hidas whispered and silently moved to the direction the sound was coming from. Beran sat and impatiently waited for his companion to come back with some good news. He was happy to hear something, which reminded the human beings sounds, but strangely he remained jumpy, fearing some terrible thing to happen.

Almost half an hour had passed, but Hidas had failed to come back and report about the source of those voices, which kept growing and receding with intervals. It was impossible to tell if they came from east or west. It seemed as they were carried by the winds from afar, but the strange thing was that there was hardly any wind in the atmosphere. That sudden realisation made the whole thing more terrifying and suffocating than it was. He could no longer sit there and get dragged into some mysterious fear, so he decided to go and search for Hidas. It was completely dark, and he had no idea, as to which direction Hidas had headed to. Suddenly he knew which direction he had to head as the murmur started getting clearer and clearer. Despite the obscurity, he moved swiftly and came closer, but still couldn't see the faces of those people who were lamenting in some strange language. He tried to figure out but failed to recognise the language, certainly that was some minor tongue, which was completely unknown to him. He was moving stealthily, without making a sound. He wanted to come closer to those people, to see who they were and what had kept Hidas from coming back. His eyes were unable to penetrate the blackness, but then some strange thing happened. The whole place was lit with tiny lights, which were held by beings. He desperately tried to hide, but there wasn't any place to hide. He stood exposed and yet no one took notice of him. They all were busy watching something. In the dim light of those lamps, he saw Hidas standing encircled by those strange beings. The whole scene was incredible as Hidas had his hand raised in the air, holding his shining sword, but something hindered him from moving. Beran tried to find some explanation to Hidas immobility, but could find no logical reason for his inability to do so. It looked like as if he walked in a dream like state, deprived of all self-consciousness, or a will of his own. He looked more like a drugged person than in his normal state of being.

These short beings, which reminded him of children rather than full grownups, were moving with their gazes fixed at Hidas, chanting strange words, making weird sounds from time to time. Their circular movements were remarkable, forcing Beran to watch in bewitched way. He would deem such a movement impossible, especially with regard to the speed. It didn't take very long for him to figure out that Hidas was being controlled by those beings and was moving forward as a puppet. Beran could see the terror stricken eyes of Hidas and knew that his companion was not all unconscious. His first thoughts were to rush to aid his companion, but his head warned him to refrain as he couldn't help Hidas in any way. The only thing he could add to the hopeless situation was to become a part of it. He decided to wait and see what those strange beings intended to do. If they were not blind, then all their attention was kept locked up with the task of controlling Hidas and neutralising him.

In a sense, he was happy that he was not in any immediate danger himself and could follow these beings without the danger of getting exposed. In this way, he could help Hidas whenever those beings came to their destination. So horrified was he, so very absorbed had he been by the incomprehensible event that he hardly paid any attention to anything else than the actual happening. The procession of those beings was moving as fast as one could think of, making Beran to move with a rapid pace, soon he was out of breath while the short people were moving or rather gliding as comfortably as they had been doing from the time he first observed them. Who were those beings? Were they some primitive human beings or some other species? By looking at their half clear faces, as the tiny lights were insufficient to reveal much, one could swear that they belonged to the human family, but not their hands and feet, which were more like paws with long nails. They were wearing some strange type of clothes, which had no apparent openings to enter into them or to come out of them. It looked like as if they all wore one piece of cloth without any stitches. Perhaps it just appeared that way, and worked differently, If one saw it closely, maybe one could find the logical explanation or understood the secret in a better way.

Beran was following a group of strange creatures as if he was enthralled, without noticing that he no longer walked on the surface of the earth. They all were moving through some wide, tunnel like passages. Beran wouldn't have detected that fact, had he not run into a hard rocky wall of the tunnel. The realisation was quite shocking; as it meant that he was getting into something he had no idea about. He had completely forgotten that they only a while ago faced a danger of dying of thirst they were still endangered, but the danger was of an entirely different kind. He felt a bizarre feeling creeping into his being, a creepy feeling of getting into some unknown sphere. The sounds of those creatures were getting louder and louder. These sounds were reverberating in the confines of those hollow rocky pathways, making the whole atmosphere very mysterious. Beran had not been mentally prepared to that peculiar encounter, and found it scarier than he had first realised. The frozen state of Hidas was most alarming. Why was he unable to move and defend himself against those apparently unarmed creatures?

With which force had they bound him so effectively? There were many questions but no answers. Beran couldn't tell how long he had been moving along with those beings; he had no sense of fatigue or thirst, the only thing preoccupying him was his own fate and that of Hidas. He couldn't understand the cause of that strange sound, which resembled more as lamentation than a triumphant war cry. He felt puzzled and deprived of all contact with reality. All of a sudden, the circular procession, came to an end. Beran could see that they stood in a hall-like place, facing a throne, which glittered with the colours of all kinds, spreading the beams of incredible beauty to all directions. No one sat on it, but the creatures were standing with their eyes fixed on it in respectful anticipation. Their cries became subdued and slowly came to complete cessation, forcing him to look around to find out what had caused them to do so. He found no apparent reason for that absolute silence. But then he turned his gaze to the seat and felt frozen. He could swear that he had not seen anyone coming from any direction to ascend that throne. How and when that figure did occupy that seat? Or was that person there all the time? He could equally vow that that was not the case.

All eyes were fixed on Hidas as he was the cause of their unwavering attention. Beran felt unthreatened and undetected, but the words coming from the person sitting on the throne made him feel frozen

"Welcome to our world." The figure which had its face hidden in a hood spoke. Just by hearing the soft voice he could tell that it was some female. To whom the figure spoke to was confusing for Beran as he could say with certainty that she didn't address Hidas, who was standing there with his hand up above his head, holding the shinning sword of his. If it wasn't Hidas, then to whom did she speak to? The same creepy sensation was making him fear that he was the addressee. So the person sitting on the throne had discovered him, he panicked.

"Come nearer, and don't fear us," the person said softly. Beran looked around in nervousness and was struck by the fact that those creatures still stood focusing on Hidas as if they were still unaware of his presence. Reluctantly he took few steps towards the seat, and felt as if he had come into some spotlight; a warm air was licking his face, making him uncomfortable.

He tried to retreat his footsteps but failed to do so. The person sitting in the throne laughed and assured him that there was no reason to be afraid.

"Who are you and why is my friend's bereft his ability to move?" Beran asked getting the courage to speak.

"Don't worry about him. There is no danger either to him or

to you." The same person said in a light manner. Beran looked at the feet of that person and could see small, human-like feet.

"I can see that you are a human being but what are these creatures? Surely they belong to some other species," Beran inquired. The person ignored his question and said.

"You and your friend are in the land of Senklour, we have been expecting your visit for some time. Though you are to cause us pain and separation, we say welcome to you." The person was friendly.

"I don't think my companion can feel welcome here." Beran sounded unhappy.

"He is not in any pain as it might be looking like to you. He is simply put in some controlled state of being for the good of his own and the others, considering his temperament." The person explained about the necessity of keeping Hidas pacified. She was telling about them about their expectant arrival that his taking the wrong turn was not any mistake but a conscious manoeuvre by forces at her disposal. Beran was relieved but alarmed by that disclosure, wondering what she meant by that statement. She was explaining that his visit to her land was predestined and preordained by the gods, who had given that right as a favour and blessing. There was little she could do to deny them the visit, so she thought it better to cooperate instead.

"I have heard the name of your land before but what is this?" Beran wondered.

"How and where did you learn the name?" The female figure asked curiously. Beran told her about his teacher Trindras and the strange condition he had attached to his promise to teach him sword fighting.

"How very sad, how bad that you made such a promise?" The figure said in a concerned manner.

"Why is it bad?" Beran asked. The female figure kept silent for a while. But then she started telling him about things he was so curious to know. She was telling him about the land of Senklour, which had existed from the beginning of the times. The land existed everywhere and had its existence in the underground world. There were all kinds of creatures that constituted its citizens. There were those with the most advance consciousness and those with the most primitive and base instincts. They all lived there in harmony and without the dangers that faced other worlds. There were no conflicts to be found there, no strife for domination and no cessation of existence as he knew from his world.

"You mean you people are immortal? Isn't that a quality attributed only to the gods?" Beran interrupted her.

"There is no need to explain and expand the subject, except the fact that we live differently than your world," the figure said casually. She took up the subject once again and started telling him what her world was all about. They were the people, who were the builders of the worlds both solid and intangible. They were entrusted with forces immense and potent; in order to create or destroy as was required by the will of gods. They were the custodians of mysterious deep and the source of all types of knowledge. It was they, who could unleash the truths or withhold them from the worlds. The construction of the world wasn't a mere accident but a result of a conscious act and the will of those who knew. These builders could be blind forces as he was witnessing right then. Those were the primitive forces, which were highly developed at the same time.

"What do you mean by this assertion?" Beran was confused

at that contradictory statement.

"It's not easy to understand, especially for a being like you, but let me try," the figure said

"These creatures are highly developed in the use of the powers entailed to them, though they are just created and trained to accomplish the tiny, insignificant tasks. They are blind to all other things than what they are focused at in any given time."

After explaining her world, she came to the point.

"I don't know how, but you and your friend have earned the right to visit our world and share some of the secrets we guard here, and here lies the clue to your unwise promise to that old fox."

"Do you claim that no secret is concealed from your eyes?" Beran asked in disbelief.

"Mysteries exist only where there is no knowledge, and you have come to the very home of the knowledge." the female answered.

"Why was it unwise to promise Trindras an arm from here?" Beran asked.

"You have the right to take a suitable gift from our world, but now you are forced to make a choice, either to take something for yourself or for your crippled friend, or whatever you may choose to call him." The female figure was getting amused. Beran was not happy to learn that he had made some stupid choices.

"Why was it so important to learn the use of the sword? You had lived without that for seventeen years; you could afford to live another few years as well." She was doing everything to make him miserable.

"Can he also choose some gift for himself?" Beran asked, pointing to Hidas.

"Of course, isn't that the reason of his arrival in Senklour?" She was quick to add, "Though there remains a difference between you two. Contrary to you he shall never really know and remember his visit here or that he had borrowed some magical gift. His gift of choice shall remain unconscious act as long as he beholds it, and so it functions for the majority of people who have earned the right to come here."

"Why I am allowed to retain this knowledge?" Beran asked with a surprise.

"I am not to tell you about that secret. Perhaps you shall know by the passage of time or perhaps you too shall remember the whole thing just as a dream, a diffuse, faint but temperate memory, lurking in your consciousness." Beran could swear that he saw her smile, though her face remained concealed from his sight.

"What made these creatures lament before and why are they so silent now? Are they still awake?" Beran asked.

"The reason for their lamentation was the knowledge that they were going to be separated from some of knowledge or things they highly evaluate. My presence is always soothing them and thus lays the secret of their calm" She explained.

"How long are we to stay here?" Beran asked.

"The question needs re-addressing; it's not me but you yourself who hold the answer."

"What about him? How he is to make his choice?"

"As I earlier told you, don't worry about him. We are already in a process of communicating and offering him the possibility to make a choice." Beran could not understand in which way a contact had been established between Hidas and the world of Senklour. But the female was not in a mood to discuss the matter with him.

"I give you a day or two to decide what you want to accomplish. Be my guest and feel free to roam about in our world and observe whatever you may come in contact with, but remember nothing of knowledge of this world shall you be able to retain in your physical memory, once you leave the place, though it shall remain with you for the rest of your life in the shape of a dim reminiscence of some mysterious feeling."

15

Beran was too excited at the prospect of learning entirely new things, observing the things he could not have dreamt before. He went around freely and unhindered and saw amazing things, saw deep secrets and felt happiness, by seeing the simple explanations behind them. The mantras and magical formulas were nothing but mathematical calculations, so simple to comprehend. He saw the sun, stars, and the movements of revolving planets and understood the meaning behind all bodies rotating in the space. He could see the whole and couldn't make the distinctions and separations existing between those segments. It felt like as new doors had been unlocked for his perception to grasp and comprehend. He was so busy with his observations of the world he had come to that he hardly noticed that time was already up. The feelings of awe had made him perplexed, and he wished to stay there forever and ever. The place had bewitched him, and he felt the whole universe as an open book, without any unsolved mysteries, without any wish to achieve something, without any need to strive or without any fears for the unforeseeable. He was content and wanted to remain there, enjoying the fruits of perfect knowledge. But the time was up, he had to go and reappear before his mysterious hostess, who was waiting for him in her high place of the throne. He was looking at the throne with completely new eyes. He saw it no longer a seat of some precious stones or metals but saw the rays of energies flowing through those metals and stones. The powerful, vivid rays reminded him of nothing he had seen in his earthly life. He was fascinated and watched with great interest at the hostess, who was emanating the rays of her own, some very bright and colourful emissions were intermingling with the rays coming from her throne, making it all a spectacular scene. He could even see the brilliant face behind that veil like dark hood. She smiled at Beran and asked if he had enjoyed his stay in her wonderful land. He told her that he had not only enjoyed each and every moment of that time but also showed his wish and desire to stay there, for a little while longer if it was not possible to stay forever.

She laughed reminding him that his visit there was only for a short while. He didn't belong to her world and there was no point in discussing the possibility.

"But you shall make me so very happy," Beran requested.

"You have your destiny to follow, and should concentrate on that. Have you made up your mind about what you want to carry with you from here?" The figure asked.

"Oh, there are millions of things to choose from, which in itself is not an easy task, but there are few things I could ..." Beran brusquely stopped.

"What has made you silent from your enthusiastic expression?" she asked.

"Nothing, I just remembered that I can't take any of these wonderful gifts with me." Beran said sadly.

"Why not?" the female asked. He couldn't have any doubt that she had the answer but wanted him to verbalise it.

"I can't take anything for myself I have already given my words to Trindras. I'll take an arm for him, whatever it may mean." Beran told her in a low tone.

"But you don't have to if you don't want to. There is nothing which binds your words. The crippled have already taught you the use of sword and can't take it back. Take your gift and don't tread the direction in which he lives," she suggested. For a moment, he felt the strong temptation to

251

follow her advice, but the realisation was swift that that stood beyond his moral convictions. There was no way he could betray the trust laid in his solemn words. All he could do was to follow his own conscience, a stern master that he could never ignore.

"I can see your reluctance; believe me, it is nothing to care about. It's just a guilt producing mechanism, which you can easily deal with. I can give you some knowledge that can help you overcome its powerful influence." She offered him a helping hand.

"No, thank you. I have made my choice. I'm taking an arm for Trindras." Beran was relentless.

"The final word is with you. All I could do was to give you the possibility of revoking from your commitment. But as you have chosen not to utilise it, so I'll grant an arm for your former teacher. Did you know what he was asking for?"

No, was the answer Beran gave her. She told Beran that his teacher had not been asking for a physical hand as he had translated it wrongly, but he was asking for a position of power and glory. He wanted a conquest and a vast kingdom, a natural result of the arm; he was to take for him.

"The man is neither better nor worse than the others in your world, when it comes to handling the power of the arm, but it may change the course of history. There are certain people who would consequently lose the right to ascend to the thrones they are otherwise destined to. But of course you are the judge." She was making it clear to him that it was not a clever decision to provide a tool to someone else while he needed that better. Beran was conscious about the dire consequences and saw his own wish to seek revenge on the people, who had destroyed his family, disappearing but even then he remained unyielding.

"What about my friend? I haven't seen him ever since we came here. Has he made up his mind regarding his choice?" Beran asked.

"Not only that he has verbalised his desire, but he has carved the present into a physical shape as well." The female answered with a smile.

"So can we proceed now? What about the present for Trindras? Who is going to deliver it?

"You can leave whenever you wish to and don't worry about the present to your teacher, by time due it would be sent to him." She was shining behind her dark hood.

"May I ask something that puzzles me?" Beran asked and then continued without waiting for her permission.

"I have seen and understood the meaning of each and everything in your realm and beyond. All the secrets of the universe have been laid naked before my eyes and yet I couldn't comprehend the mystery behind you." Beran heard her laughter, which was sweet and incomprehensible.

"You have failed to penetrate through my mystery for only one reason. I am the mother of all mysteries, which can be revealed to no one. That is the nearest that one can get near to me." She told Beran not to exhaust his energies on such things he could never solve, but to concentrate on their journey ahead. She warned that his task ahead wasn't an easy one, especially Hidas was to be a big problem, and he needed to be patient and understanding towards his companion.

"The problem you face is double-edged. It is not going to be easy to convince him about that what happened to his immediate memory. He wouldn't let go and will ask millions of questions regarding the things, which have been erased from his memory."

"Why should he ask about something which is not in his mind?"

"For the single reason that the removed memories are always leaving unfilled gaps behind, and thus follow the questions," she told him.

"And what's the other part that you mentioned?"

"Your friend has chosen the gift of a sword. He was allowed to carve his own sword in the furnaces of eternal fires, and herewith comes the difficulty and caution," the female said.

"Please do explain, as I can't grasp the significance of what you just revealed." Beran didn't hide the fact that he was unaware of the significance of the sword. The mysterious lady told him that there were no other weapons in his world, which originated so directly from her world. The eternal flames of the furnaces there had made that sword the mightiest sword in the world, which none could withstand. It wasn't only the materials but even the intense and dreadful energies of the fires themselves, which made the weapon invincible. The power and splendour of that the weapon was not an easy thing to handle for a person. Even those who had taken the needed initiations could tremble to handle that immense power. "Be mindful of him. Be always a friend who has the duty to protect and conceal. He can be the biggest enemy of himself, as the power corrupts and destroys the unready and unworthy. That's true of even the ordinary power, but remember, I talk about the power emanating from the sources most potent."

"How long can he keep the sword?" Beran asked.

"As long as he lives. And then he shall die with the power of the same sword. He would be too weak to handle that huge force." She gave the word of warning. "This is not the last time that we will meet. Once again shall you come to my world and get some further warnings and revelations. Wait patiently for the day and seek knowledge, because that'll furnish you with the understanding, which in its turn shall give you wisdom." She concluded.

She receded without making the slightest movement. Beran opened his mouth to ask a question, but she vanished from her throne as if she had never been there.

They were riding their horses, and Beran was avoiding all kinds of communication with Hidas as it would open the door of unending questions from him. He could understand the surprise and frustration of his companion who found himself at lost. He had lost all track of the events and was curious to know why he didn't remember. He had difficulty in believing the words of Beran, who blamed everything on Hidas's high fever and dehydration. As far as he remembered, Beran had lost his horse in the desert, and they had only one or two bottles left of water, which was insufficient to cross the desolate tracts. Why didn't he remember meeting strangers in the wilderness, which had helped them survive the terrible conditions? There were so many questions, which Beran either refused to answer or had no logical answers for. His curiosity was not letting go.

"How long have we been on our way, since we left the strange rescuers?" Hidas asked.

"I really don't remember, except that you still weren't feeling perfectly well." Beran told him, knowing what could be the next question if he answered straight.

"Alright, maybe I have forgotten all the events because of my high fever, but who gave us the right directions? And from whom did you get the horse and bottles of water?" Hidas asked looking at him with suspicion.

"It was the last thing on earth I wanted to confess, but I see no other way than to tell you that I found the horse and bottles of water in the desolate place, beside an old man, who lay dead there. The man didn't have any need of these things anymore." Hidas looked at Beran and knew that the youth was not telling him the truth, but there was little he could do to make him speak the truth.

"If the man had a fresh horse and enough water, what did he die of?" Hidas was sarcastic.

"What I know?" Beran was casual, "Perhaps sunstroke." None spoke after that as their conversation was not leading anywhere. Beran was absorbed by the green hills before his sight; he was still thinking about the recent happenings and wondered what the real significance of those mysterious events was. He was told that Hidas had chosen to carve his own sword in some strange burning fires, but all he could see was the same old sword with beautiful engraved shield, hanging by his waist. Perhaps it was also not some solid sword as the female talked about, but was expressing some truth in a symbolic manner. Many times he thought that all was just a dream, but the panting horse, water and hills before his eyes were enough proofs to reaffirm the fact that he had been to some strange place.

The small green hills were not difficult to cross without any difficulty. Beyond them was the area, where ended the territory of Kildia. There were no regular borders or any demarcations, except a vague sense that the authority of Kildia didn't affect beyond the hilly tract.

How far from there lived Shamon and his people, they had

no idea of. The landscape was rather tricky and needed extra vigilance.

"I think we should halt and carefully decide which way to take. Any wrong turn can be fatal and will either bring us nearer to our destination, or would take us long away from it." Hidas warned Beran who immediately agreed with him, remembering the fatal mistake he had earlier made, which could have cost them their lives. It was dusk and Beran was uncertain of the direction in which they were to proceed. He thought it better to spend the night at some suitable place.

"I have a strange feeling about spending the night over here, but there is little choice we have right now other than to stay until the dawn, if we want to be absolutely sure that we are following the right path." Beran had started regretting his decision to stay in the open.

"I don't know about the feeling, but I am dead tired and want to sleep. We can sleep in turns if you want to be secure. Wake me up after the midnight." Hidas said and lost no time to go to sleep after they had eaten something. He was quick to fall asleep, unlike Beran, who always found it difficult to relax and bundle off all the thoughts. He was sitting beside Hidas and feeling the pleasant presence of some entity, which kept entangling, enticing him like some seductive force, to yield and surrender. He was dozing and was about also to fall asleep, when he suddenly sat erect, shook his head as if trying to get rid of the sleep. He had returned from the brink, a thing he was proud of, because had he also fallen asleep, then he wouldn't have forgiven himself as it would have meant irresponsible behaviour on his part. He got up from his seat and started strolling, back and forth in the night. Was that the effect of the hilly area or was summer giving way, he couldn't tell, but he felt that the night had grown chilly in just a couple of days' time. They were travelling very light clothed. He put his head cover on Hidas's body and smiled seeing him straightening his legs after some time. His companion had fallen into deeper sleep, once his body got the needed heat. It was getting midnight, and it was his turn to sleep but he refrained from waking Hidas up. What it matters if I don't sleep tonight, he thought to himself? "Hidas seemed to be a person who can't function without proper sleep." Beran kept waking all night, fighting with his sleep, which was attacked again and again, but always found him at guard, ready to fight back. Hidas was surprised to find him guarding alone, when he woke up.

"Why didn't you wake me up?"

"It looked as if you needed to sleep properly."

"But it's you who need this sleep more than me. I've been just sleeping, when I fell sick, didn't I?"

"Yes you did, but that was different. The body gets weaker by the attack of any disease and requires time to recover." Beran was not easy to beat with words.

"It's not that I mind the full night's sleep. I just pitied you for staying awake, but you seem to like being tortured." Hidas said with a smile, teasing him.

They waited till sunrise and then Beran went this way or that, trying to find some clues, finding the traces and marks, which could point to the right direction. Hidas was sitting idle, enjoying Beran's stressed movements. He could understand the sense of responsibility, which was burdening his companion, but he didn't even try to relieve him from that crushing burden. Finding the ways wasn't his speciality and he decided to stay apart and just get amused.

"Have you found a clue?" Hidas asked.

"The place is as unknown to me as it is to you? Why did I make it my headache alone?" Beran looked unhappy.

"Perhaps because you are the natural guide, a wayfarer, a confident adventurer." Hidas laughed despite the seriousness of the situation. Beran gave up.

"I believe that's enough with my responsibility. This time you chose the direction." Beran said sitting down beside him.

"What! Me? I don't know anything about the ways." Hidas was nervous.

"So what? What possibly can happen? That we'll get lost? At least you'll not be blaming me for that."

"Alright I get your point; I'll not make any fuss if you chose the wrong way." Hidas said seriously.

"That is kind of you, but still you'll choose the way this time." Beran was determined.

Hidas miserably pointed in one direction, and they both set off that way. Beran was happy to watch the anguish of Hidas, which was so apparent that one could see that by just looking at him. He tried to comfort his companion by telling him that he himself would have chosen the same direction. They heard the sounds of a galloping horse and turned to see whom that could be. The rider was some distance away, but they had detected the sounds because the wind blew in their direction. They slowed down their own pace so that the rider could catch up with them. They were happy to have seen the first human being ever since they left the human habitations behind, regardless of what he had told Hidas. The rider was some young man, who wanted to pass them by in a quick manner, but seeing them halt completely made him stop, as well. After the normal greetings, Beran asked the young man if they were moving in the direction of Parnvan. Instead of giving them the answer, the young man looked at them suspiciously.

"What business do you have in that country?" he asked.

"We are going there to meet some friends," Beran answered. The rider didn't look convinced and waited for some more details.

"Is it that difficult to answer a straight question?" Hidas asked irately. The young rider felt a little confused and embarrassed.

"Forgive my rudeness, but I can't answer your inquiry until I'm sure that you are really friends," he stammered.

"What do you think? Would we be asking that politely if we were the foes?" Hidas was still stern in his tone. The rider understood what he meant, he smiled and confirmed that they were on the right track, before riding swiftly away from them. "What a person?" Hidas was not happy with the behaviour of the young rider.

"I don't blame him for anything, we ourselves would be jumpy and mistrusting if we met some strangers moving in our direction." Beran gave an argument.

"We were not moving in his direction, he was moving to ours." Hidas corrected.

"I meant moving to his country." Beran explained. He was telling Hidas that he should not forget the stress and strain those people must have been feeling in the face of some imminent attack from some ruthless enemy. After some pondering, Hidas calmed down and agreed to Beran that the young rider had been just correct in his behaviour, but he was still not satisfied as the rider had left them without any sure knowledge about how far they stood from their destination.

"Few days here or there, what does it matter?" Beran was carefree as long as they moved in the right direction. Hidas was not so refined a person when it came to social contact, but he wasn't that difficult to convince as Beran had earlier thought. Hidas was a simple, honest, but a short-tempered person. He was not at all as adamant as he believed himself to be. He was stubborn but not at all closed to all argumentations. Strangely, Hidas was always open to criticism and suggestion, but without a complete conviction he refused to move.

Hidas looked at the sky and looked distressed by seeing the dark clouds above their heads. It seemed it would rain any minute. He had never liked the rain, especially now when there wasn't any shelter around. Hidas was worried about getting wet as he was sure it certainly would make him sick Beran couldn't help asking why he kept looking at the sky.

"Do you expect some help descending from the heavens?" Beran joked. Hidas kept silent.

A few drops of rain fell over them, but Beran didn't care. He looked at Hidas, who looked anxious.

"If there could be a place around, where we could take a shelter and rest." Hidas finally spoke.

"Why! Don't you like rain?" Beran noticed that something was wrong.

"I hate to be wet, and the damn rain seemed to have caught us in the middle of nowhere."

"I promise that you shall not melt down." Beran laughed.

Hidas looked angrily at him before letting his anger come out. "It's not that I am afraid of silly rain. I hate the rainfall as it always makes me sick if I get wet. I have already been ill and don't want to be sick once again."

"When did it happen last time?" Beran asked him, ignoring the raindrops, which were occasionally falling on them.

"What does it matter?" Hidas was reluctant to answer, but Beran insisted.

"I don't remember when it happened the last time, but it's always ending in my getting sick."

"You can confess it, or not, but I can say for sure that the last time you got wet in the rain must have been long, long ago." Beran confronted Hidas.

"Even if your claim is true, it doesn't prove that my assertion is false." Hidas was unmoved.

"Just try to relax; there is nothing we can do to avoid this rain if it's to come. The last time it made you sick doesn't mean that it's going to be the same this time also. You are a strong young man who can withstand some harmless rainwater." Beran told him, without caring if he liked the idea or not.

"It's comfortable for you to say so." Hidas still looked unconvinced. The clouds were getting thicker and thicker, leaving no doubt that the rain was to fall and do it heavily. Lightening flashed across the merciless sky. Beran looked around but saw no shelter, except a few trees standing here and there, but they were not very safe shelters either as they could attract lightning.

"Come we ride that way, who knows; maybe we find some

cave to hide against the thunderstorm, which is gathering its force." Beran was also getting anxious. Hidas wanted to say something but instead they both were galloping towards that direction, Beran had pointed to. But their movement was little too late. In the middle of lightning and thunder, came the cloudburst, without giving them any chance to get mentally prepared. He heard the swearing and cursing of Hidas, whose strong voice was overpowered and subdued into nothingness by the heart piercing sounds of thunder. Hidas was furious by the sudden rainfall and was busy having a battle of sounds, where his angry words were not even audible. It had grown dark, and the wind was furiously strong, and the rainwater was chilling cold, but Beran laughed like he never did.

"What the devil made you that happy?" Hidas screamed at him, trying desperately to be heard.

"What did you say?" shouted Beran at the top of his lungs, but gave up, as the wind had turned into a storm and the thunderclaps were deafening. Visibility was almost non-existent, but Beran and Hidas had no other choice but to continue their search for some shelter. Beran halted and tried to look around, covering his eyes against the battering winds and rain water.

He saw no point in speaking as his words would not have reached the ears of his companion anyway. He signaled Hidas to move into one direction. They both moved, with painful struggle as they were riding against the stormy winds. Even their horses looked both frightened and exhausted from their hopeless but heroic strife to move against the winds. Both beasts and their riders were shivering from the cold. A strange sound of crashing was clearly heard right behind them, making them turn and see. A large tree had just fallen, making a terrible sound. They had no time to stand and appreciate their luck for not at that particular spot at the moment. Hidas looked angry but had stopped shouting in the face of the ferocious storm. He was wondering why Beran did want him to ride against the wind, but there was no time to ask such questions. They were having the most difficult task in the world, fighting against the violent forces of nature, unarmed, unaided and unafraid. They were moving on but only inch by inch, only after severe beatings. The strength of the storm was unabated; they were soaking and shivering but moved with a determination.

It wasn't until they came near to the barn that Hidas took notice of it. Nothing in the world could have made him as happy as he felt right that minute. He couldn't help praising Beran for his hawkish sight. There was no way he could understand how Beran could have spotted the wooden house from such a distance, especially in those terrible circumstances. They immediately came down from the backs of their horses and knocked at the door but got no response. After knocking many times, they could conclude that no one was there, or perhaps the residents could not hear them due to the rumbling sounds of the storm. Hidas pushed the door and found it open. They went in, taking their beasts along. Inside it was dark, but they felt welcoming warmth present there, a thing they appreciated as a gift from heaven. Hidas sat near the hay to get extra heat as he was shuddering from the cold, wet clothes.

"You should change your wet clothes," Beran told him. Hidas didn't answer and looked back as Beran was talking nonsense.

"I know what you mean, but get rid of your wet clothes before you really get sick. I'll try to find something dry if there is anything around." Beran said looking at his violently shaking body.

"This place indicates that there is some life around. The place doesn't seem to be abandoned. When the storm ends, I'll walk around and investigate the area more closely." Beran seemed to be talking to himself as no words were coming out from Hidas. Outside the storm was still raging, though with somewhat less intensity.

"We have deprived the storm its strength," Beran joked, going out to search for some contact with the people who lived nearby.

It took some time before he returned, holding something in his hands. "Take it! Here are some dry clothes I have managed to find for both of us." He said tossing the clothes to Hidas, who was almost hiding in the hay, to cover his naked body. He went to the other side of the building to change his own clothes. When he came back, Hidas was sitting in his dry clothes, looking still sombre but relaxed. Even his body had stopped shaking that terribly as it did a while ago, though it was still twitching from time to time.

"Thank heavens that it wasn't a winter storm. We would have certainly needed big burning fires to get back to our normal selves," Beran said.

"From whom did you borrow the clothes?" Hidas asked.

"No one seems to be around. I have been to the main building, which looks like an inn, but no one is there. If this place has been abandoned, then surely it was done recently. There is even plenty of food in there; we can live for months on that," Beran told him.

"Who is stupid enough to leave food, clothes, and other valuables to get spoiled?" Hidas was astonished.

"I agree that it is strange; nevertheless, I'm telling you that what I have observed."

"Can't it be possible that the residents have been also surprised by the storm and sitting and waiting in some other little building?" Hidas asked.

"It's possible, though I doubt it."

"Why?"

"The kitchen seemed to have not been used for some time," Beran said explaining the reason of his doubt about his premise.

"People or no people, I don't care as long as I have dry clothes and food to eat," Hidas said in an indifferent tone.

"Coming back to clothes, what was that stupidity of hiding in the hay?" Beran pulled his leg.

"What about that?" Hidas was irritated.

"Never ever do that again; there could be some dangerous vermin or serpents in the hay."

"You are right, but I couldn't think clearly at that time. Even now I think that I am getting sick."

"I bet you wouldn't." Beran told him.

"What makes you an expert on the subject? Didn't I tell you that it always happens that way?

"That is the difference between you and me, I don't believe in fate as you do." Hidas was equally firm. "Do you want to put money on it?" Beran provoked him. Hidas was silent.

"What about waging your sword?" Beran continued pushing him.

"No, thanks! There is nothing in the world that can make me such a bet, where I can lose her." Hidas rejected his offer.

"I didn't know that you considered your sword a female? Are you in love with her as well?"

Beran teased him, but he was not in a mood to converse with him on the subject as it ultimately would lead to Beran's questions about princess Danor, a topic that he wanted to avoid.

The whole day it went on raining even though the storm had moved ahead leaving devastation in the shape of fallen trees and other debris. Hidas and Beran had moved to a more comfortable inn, where they had the clean and cosy beds to sleep in, plenty of food to eat, and other comforts that reminded them of home. The whole day had been wasted due to the rain, and there was little they could do about it, except to rest and enjoy the cosy atmosphere. They both believed that the place had been well taken care of. They went to sleep earlier than usual as Beran was dead tired, and Hidas body needed extra rest if he were to recover from the shock of that day. They went sleeping till late next day, forgetting the need to move on to their destination. They might have kept sleeping for another hour or two, but they were awakened up by some unknown sounds. They woke almost simultaneously and looked at each other, wondering what those sounds were. They grabbed their swords and stealthily went downstairs to check as the voices came from there. From a distance, they could see astonished faces of some young men who were sitting and discussing something very intensely. They all turned towards Beran and Hidas as they came nearer. They looked perplexed and waited for them to speak, but no-one spoke.

"Who are you people and what are doing here?" one of the

young men asked politely. Beran explained the circumstances, which had caused them to seek shelter the previous day. They all smiled and looked relaxed as their mystery had been solved. They had been looking around, trying to understand who had been there as they could find the dirty pots and plates and other signs that the place had been visited recently.

"All you needed to do was to come and check the room, where we slept," Beran told them.

Beran expressed his regret that he and his friend had been using their facilities without permission. They all laughed, telling that the place did belong to them as little as it did to Beran and Hidas; the only difference was that they had permission to use the facilities by the owner of the place.

"Where is the owner?" Hidas asked. They shortly explained that the owners of the place were temporarily out of the country, but were kind enough to leave food and other utilities for the wayfarers.

"So, as a matter of fact, it's as much your right to use these things as it is ours," one young man said in a friendly tone. "By the way, where do you proceed?"

"We are on our way to meet some of our friends," Beran explained.

"You mind telling the names of your friends?" the same man asked.

Beran saw no reason to mention the names of Herzod, Shamon and other young men he had travelled along. How did he know all those people, why he was travelling to them, and many such like questions were being asked by many of these young men. They all looked not only curious but also even suspicious as they had never heard what Beran or Hidas has said earlier. Beran smiled and told them that their visit was a surprise and no one knew of his coming.

"I don't think it's a good time to pay a visit to our land," one of them said

"Why not?" Hidas asked.

"We don't have time to entertain friends. Please turn back and come some other time," the young man suggested. Beran smiled and thanked him for his concern but made it clear that they were not to deter from their resolve to visit Shamon.

"You shall make all the trouble for nothing. No one of those whom you mention are there."

"Where can we find them? We are friends who have heard about the distressful situation and have come to help," Beran said.

"What possible help can you offer?" one of the young men jested. Hidas felt insulted, but Beran intervened.

"You don't have a right to tease like that, especially to people who are concerned about your troubles," Beran said softly but firmly. The man who had been speaking looked down as he apologised for the rude behaviour of his companion. He blamed the unhappy and stressful situation for causing the offensive conduct on the part of certain members of his community. He underlined his incapacity to go into details but told them that Herzod and Shamon were in Kildia at the moment and weren't expected to return before many weeks' time.

"But we are coming from that direction. Why didn't we see them?" Hidas inquired.

"It's a big border; one easily can miss each other," he said without thinking.

"Are you people coming from Kildia or going that way?" Beran asked. There wasn't any response, except for a nervous exchange of looks. Beran repeated his question and saw unease sweeping through the whole group of young men, who were about a dozen in number.

"We are heading to Kildia on an important mission." The young spokesperson finally answered, though somewhat reluctantly.

"Alright, we are following you people back to Kildia." Beran said in a decisive tone. He saw the exchange of angry looks taking place and knew that the young man who had been talking to them wasn't very popular that very moment among his group members. Beran and Hidas knew that the group was not happy about two strangers following them, but they couldn't find a polite way to tell them that they weren't welcome to do so.

All day long they spend preparing the food provisions and making other preparations for their journey. It seemed that they had been travelling light as they had counted on the food and water, being available in the inn. They went to sleep early as they were supposed to start early the next day. The group remained polite but reserved, ignoring the two strangers, who had a claim of knowing their folks. They had been causing them anxiety, but there was nothing they could do to have them off their backs.

"Are you from Kildia?" one stranger asked.

"Yes I am," Beran answered.

"Are you also from Kildia?" The same person turned to

Hidas, who either didn't pay attention to his question or chose to ignore the question.

"Why do you ask?" Beran asked.

"I have never been told by any of the people you mentioned that they knew anyone in Kildia."

"How could that be possible?" It was Beran's turn to be astonished. "Are you young people never told the tales from travels? Do none of you ever ask about the important happenings?"

"By the way, how is Jeldris doing?"

"Jeldris, who?"

"The young man, who got bitten by a poisonous snake in Kildia few months back."

"How you know about that?" one tall young man asked. Beran looked at the young face and smiled.

"He is your brother isn't he?" He could see the face of that fellow whom he had been able to save a few months earlier. The boy looked reluctant and astonished for a while but then he smiled and affirmed his guess. He was asking questions about the terrible incident, which no one in his family ever wanted to discuss later on. Beran was careful not to expand the subject too much. He told them that little he knew about the event, but spoke of it just to make it clear that he really knew the people, and they were not playing games with them. He saw them getting more relaxed but still not completely trusting.

"We saw a person riding to your town yesterday. He seemed to be in a hurry. Did you meet him in the way as well?" Beran asked. He noticed that his questions made them anxious, so he decided not to ask any more of them. Both of them avoided bothering their new companions by remaining at the end of the trail, talking to each other as they had done till then.

16

Herzod and Shamon became very happy to see Beran, but seeing him come from the direction of Parnvan made them surprised. They warmly greeted him and asked about Hidas, who he was. Beran thought they had already met him, but they could not recall having been introduced before. Beran laughed, telling them that before them stood the son of the blacksmith, from whom they had bought the swords. Shamon excused himself for not recognising Hidas. "I dealt with your father and had hardly taken notice of you, I hope you didn't mind." Shamon said politely.

"It's no problem, most of the time I'm invisible." Hidas smiled.

Herzod listened carefully about the reason of Beran's visit and appreciated his concern. He apologised for the weird behaviour of his young men, saying that the sensitivity of the situation had forced them all to be more careful. He updated Beran about the state of affairs, which looked direr than they had anticipated. They were receiving intelligence reports, which were gloomy and scary. King Pampicilos was in full preparations to attack their country in the coming weeks. They had evacuated almost all their families and movable possessions from there. They even reviewed their earlier strategy to sit and wait for the enemy armies and engage that force if it was manageable, but were discouraged by knowing that the army consisted of tens of thousands of men. They had decided to evacuate completely, so the enemy met a deserted town, devoid of all its riches, which the enemy could have taken away.

"We could face them if you had a reasonable force," Hidas said with confidence.

"We don't think we have a chance, judging from the formidable force the king of Elbon possesses." Herzod was pessimistic.

They went on discussing the hopeless situation without finding any suitable solution. Their only hope was that the empty town discouraged the army and that ultimately they would go back, seeing no people to whom they could enslave, and no riches to be collected.

"Or they may choose to bring people from Elbon and settle them in your town." Beran mentioned another possibility. Both Herzod and Shamon looked aghast. It seemed the possibility had not struck their minds.

"I really hope not." Herzod said with anguish.

"Why not? Elbon has a little territory and big population to feed while it's the opposite in your case. If I were Pampicilos, it could be a good solution," Beran said, making them more anguished. Shamon had been silent for most of the time as if he was busy solving some riddles of his own. His serious face expressions were some new developments, which Beran had not been aware before. He looked agitated and yet in full control of his feelings.

"I really wonder why we have left our homes. Why don't we take our stand right there in the middle of our own home grounds? What are the wits of running away?" Shamon really was unable to understand the meaning of their whole flight.

"I believe that your father's strategy is wiser than to stand against some terrible force and face an utter obliteration. At times it's clever to make a strategic retreat and wait for the best time and opportunity," Beran said.

"But we are a reasonable force of many thousands who are well equipped and well trained; I believe we are capable to defend our town," Shamon added.

"Yes, most of our fighting men are either too old or too young and inexperienced while we face a professional army, a cunning enemy, and a heartless king." Herzod gave the arguments, which he had been using ever since they received the invitation to surrender their sovereignty.

"How long shall we be on the run? How long are we to live the lives of refugees? Where lies the end?" Shamon was angry.

No-one had any answers to his questions, which were quite logical. Beran agreed to Shamon that the situation was not as simple as they wished it to be. If that was true that the king of Elbon had succeeded in building a terrifying force, then no country in the region was safe any longer. The large armies were ultimately to attack the neighbours one after another if it wasn't feasible to attack simultaneously. King Pampicilos's ambitions could not have been confined only to Elbon. What hindered him from adventuring into Kildia? Why was he to stop at the borders of Furzomia?

"If you young men are that pessimists, then what do you suggest?" Herzod asked. giving up.

"We should stick to our original plan and defend our homes in Parnvan," Shamon said without any hesitation.

Beran was of another opinion; he agreed with Herzod that there was no point in facing the armies of Pampicilos. But it was unwise to stay in Kildia as well as eventually the marching armies were to head towards the Kildian borders. Despite the fact that the kingdom had a strong army, it was too tiny to withstand pressure for a long time and was bound to collapse before some large and persistent force. He suggested that the best solution was to move further west into Furzomia, which under the circumstances was the relatively safe place to dwell.

"Why is that country better equipped than ours and Kildia?" Shamon asked, not agreeing with Beran.

"It is because of its size, preparedness, and most of all its large size population, which has a respectful reputation in the use of arms." Beran defended his hypothesis.

"I must confess that I agree that the Furzomia is going to be the last country that any aggressor would dare to turn to. Everyone is a warrior over there," Hidas said, when asked about his view. Shamon was not happy with a prospect of moving further west, but Herzod decided to take up the matter with other prominent members of his community. The safety of the entire group was the main concern, and they could not afford to live in Kildia if it lay also in a danger zone.

"Why bother? What if Pampicilos was to come even towards Furzomia? Where shall we be moving from there?" Shamon protested.

"Then shall we all fight back, with the combine forces and destroy the evil designs of the Elbonian king." Beran said with confidence.

"Yes, I believe that is the best strategy we can adopt," Hidas said eagerly. "Even the armies of Pampicilos were to spare Furzomia, which is the best ground to fight the aggressor."

Shamon didn't look very convinced but promised to ponder upon the facts, which were brought to his attention. The thing that he hated most was to run from difficulties.

"I believe that the king of Kildia needs a warning as well so that he may get ready for the emergency, in case some attacks is being planned against his country," Beran suggested.

"Not yet!" Herzod spoke. "If we are to tell him now, he shall expect us to stay and fight the enemy. We have to decide first either we are to stay or leave to Furzomia."

They all agreed that it was the most sensible thing to do, without annoying the host country.

The traders and their families were already getting demoralised by the need of living under those wretched circumstances. They simply weren't used to those conditions and wished that it was soon over. They were disheartened by the malaise, misery, and misfortune, which the flight had brought to them. Not even in their wildest imaginations had they ever thought to live that way. All their riches were of no use, and that knowledge was subduing. So when Herzod took up the issue, most of them couldn't help getting annoyed by the mere insinuation that there was even a remote possibility of their moving further away, especially those of the members who had originally opposed the idea of leaving their homes behind were furious. But the deeper they thought, the more they were convinced that the idea was more lucrative than it looked at first sight. They knew that soon summer was to be over and the autumn in those tracts was always short, and the winter was too tough to be spent in that miserable state. So the only reasonable alternative was to move into Kildian towns or to move to Furzomia. In both cases, a movement was required of them, so why not to proceed towards a place, which seemed to be comparatively safer. They almost unanimously decided to head for Furzomia, but they were to move all together, instead of doing it in parts as they had done before. They had neither the required time nor the energies to make the tedious journeys in instalments.

"You all leave, I can stay behind to inform Beran and Hidas about the movement, when they come back from their visit to Beran's parents," Shamon suggested.

"I believe that they would understand when they shall not find us here." Herzod didn't like the idea that he was to stay behind alone.

"I can take care of myself. Go ahead; we shall catch up with you," Shamon insisted.

"It's alright for me, though it shall take much energy to calm down Nori," Herzod said with laughter.

"Where are Tylon and his folks, I haven't seen them for a while?" Shamon asked.

"They are already on their way to Furzomia; they wanted to have some start advantage, remembering their slow pace, which might irritate others."

"I really feel for that the company they are some fighters, I'm impressed by all of them, especially from Aloha. How old is she? She must be at least eighty, isn't it?" Shamon admired tough people.

"I guess her to be more or less of that age," Herzod said with a sigh, feeling empathy for his older folks.

Herzod came forward and hugged Shamon, begging him to be careful and not take unnecessary risks.

"What risks?" He laughed. "It wouldn't be taking long before we are with you."

"Don't try to make business deals. You'll have enough time

to do that in Furzomia," Herzod joked.

To watch them move in a disciplined way moving right after each other in an orderly manner must have been a spectacular scene, but there were few outsiders who could see that impressive movement. There were armed young fellows both in front, in the middle, and on the rear of that procession, vigilantly watching and guarding their community. They all knew that there wasn't any danger, but they couldn't afford to take any chances. Once they came out of Kildia, they moved in a less stressful manner in order to give support to women, children, and elderly. Shamon and other two young men had not come as yet. Herzod was anxious because he feared that time for Elbonian attack against his country was approaching in a speedy way, and he wished for Shamon to be back before that took place. He was worried about Shamon's sentimentality and dreaded the worst. He had placed himself in the rear of the crawling caravan for only one reason that he would know immediately about Shamon's arrival. He kept looking back again and again, hoping to find all three young men come safe and sound. It was now the fourth day since they had left Kildia, and yet there wasn't any sign of those young men. He tried not to worry but couldn't help it. It was the fifth day, and there was still no news from Shamon or the others. He was restless and couldn't bear it anymore.

"I have to go back and see what hinders them from coming." He informed the others before they were about to set off after a night's rest.

"It's not a good idea. You should wait for at least one more day," one of his friends suggested.

"Shamon is a responsible young man, he wouldn't take an hour longer than he needed," reminded the other.

As they sat and discussed this, they saw the rising dust from far behind. "Look they are already here!" cried someone. Herzod jumped on the back of his horse and rode in that direction. He wanted to meet them halfway. They all laughed at his excitement. They were right in their presumption that it was Shamon and his friends. Herzod was already standing at the halfway point, waiting for them to near, and galloped when they got closer. They all came and immediately were encircled by others, who were dying of curiosity to get some fresh news. It was Shamon who was briefing his people about the current situation, informing them that their country had been already attacked. King Pampicilos had attacked Parnvan, not from its own border but had violated the territory of Kildia.

"I feared the clever fox could do something like that!" Herzod said in anguish.

Some cruel general led the army, which was massive. It was such a terrifying force that the Kildian defence forces chose to look the other way when the invaders were making their entry. The mere sight of that gigantic army overwhelmed them and they fled without looking back.

"Hadn't you informed the king about the imminent danger?" Herzod asked.

"Yes, he was well informed through my father, but the king took the whole message very lightly, trusting that his defences were strong enough to withstand any attack," Beran told them.

"Why did you take so long? We were worried."

"The king had requested our help," Shamon said. He said that after seeing the robust force of the enemy, the king of Kildia was forced to reevaluate his strategy. He had come to a bitter realisation that his army fell short of the might, which he confronted. He saw danger looming over the royal heads and therefore requested us to take his whole family out of the country as well. The king himself would flee if the armies of Pampicilos were to venture in his direction, he told them.

"What! Are they not going to defend their fatherland?" someone asked in indignation.

"Why that surprise? Did we defend ours?" Shamon asked without being rude.

A strange silence fell over the company until Herzod asked again.

"I don't see any royal prince or other members of the king around."

Shamon told that they had safely entered in the Furzomia and followed in their own tact. The armed guards were accompanying them, so there wasn't anything to worry about. They started their journey nostalgically, visualising the brutal march of the enemy in their beautiful town. Just the very thought was not inspiring, but what burdened them most at that time was the knowledge that the situation was to last much longer than they had earlier thought if it wasn't going to be a permanent change. They were pensive by the new developments and were happy to have made a right decision to move from Kildia while there was still time. They could see clearly that all their efforts to save life and valuables were to come naught if they had decided to linger there in Kildia. But they faced a big question, which none dared to pronounce. Were they going to find a safe haven in Furzomia or was some other disaster waiting for them even there? Everyone was exhausted from their unending journey and wished that it would come to an end. No-one could tell exactly how long it would take before they arrived at their destination, not even the most frequently travelled and experienced member of their group knew the answer. The slow pace they had been forced to adapt to accommodate the weaker members made the calculation an impossible task. The group that followed behind travelled even slower. They had been stopped many times by the soldiers and asked about the reason for that gigantic migration, but the elder traders satisfied them by telling that they were the traders, who had come and gone that way hundred of times. No one bothered them as the soldiers could see women, children, and elderly in that otherwise armed group.

Hidas was more careful not to face the soldiers as the risk of his being recognised was very real. Most of the soldiers knew him, and his father and the risk to be caught was forcing him to be cautious if the king had issued the orders of his arrest. He wanted to save himself the humiliation of that scene as no one could understand that it was other reasons for which the law sought him and not some criminal act, which he committed. He was approaching the country without having received a green signal as he had been asked to do. The only person, who could understand Hidas's anxiety, was Beran, who kept encouraging him and giving moral support.
"Don't worry! I'm with you," Beran would say, and Hidas would thank him for the support until he had enough of that.

"Your support is of no use to me, so please stop it. Let me work out my problems as they are mine and only I can find a way to come out of them." Beran found his outburst rude but retreated without making it an issue. Hidas was very nervous when the caravan made a camp outside the town. He knew that they couldn't enter the town and seek accommodation for all of them, only because the town wasn't prepared for such an event. Their presence surely would be detected immediately. He was mostly worried about the attitude of the authorities and the king about such a big group, which sought refuge in the country. He knew that the king could be understanding and even helpful, but he could be equally unreasonable and self-occupied. It all depended on his mood, which kept swinging all the time. Hidas wanted to go and visit Shapario but was advised not to do by Shamon and Beran.

"I'll go and visit your father," Beran offered.

"I'm sure he can help us in one or the other way. Both he and Kestarius are very close to the king," Hidas said, taking pride in his words.

Beran left them behind and headed to town on his own. He wasted no time in going to the blacksmith's workshop, but found it closed. He looked around, but there wasn't anyone who could provide any information about why it was closed.

He was about to turn back when he saw two soldiers passing by. They were busy talking to each other, strolling in a relaxed manner. They halted and looked at him in astonishment, when Beran interrupted them in the middle of their conversation They had completely missed his presence over there. Beran inquired about the blacksmiths, and they looked even more surprised.

"Are you a stranger?" asked one of the soldiers. "I thought so," said he again, seeing him nod in affirmation. The soldier told him that the place had been closed for a few weeks. He wouldn't tell the reason for that strange happening. When Beran asked, where he could find the blacksmiths, they laughed.

"I'm sure you wouldn't like to be where they are," the other soldier said looking at his face. Without asking those soldiers too many questions, he could guess that both Shapario and Kestarius were in some serious trouble. He turned, untied his horse and was about to leave, when one the soldiers asked him to stay where he was and wait for him. Getting closer he kept staring at him as if he was trying to recognise him.

"Who are you? Have you been to our country before? How do you know the blacksmiths?" the soldier asked too many questions all at once, making Beran realise that he was suspicious of him. He knew that he could be in trouble if he were to stay and answer all the questions. He had the advantage of sitting on the horse while the soldiers were on foot. Without answering any of their questions, he rode away. He could hear the angry voices of the soldiers, commanding him to halt, but he turned, smiled and rode away, and it was just then that he got sight of another soldier, who came riding that way. A quick exchange of words took place among the soldiers before he found the rider following and chasing him. He easily could ride towards his companions, which were waiting for him outside the town but refrained from doing so. He didn't want to lead the soldier to the place where it would have been too easy to track and arrest him. He was trying hard to get rid of the chasing soldier, but there was no way. He found the stubborn rider on his heels whenever he turned back to see if he had succeeded in brushing him off. The number of soldiers, joining the pursuit was increasing the whole time as if they had no other activity but to hunt a helpless youngster. He felt the pressure mounting and fear getting hold of his heart as the circle around was drastically shrinking. He was encircled, and no escape seemed possible. He finally gave up and halted his horse to a complete halt. He could see triumphant smiles on the faces of soldiers who sat on their horses, still unsure why they chased the youth in the first place. For a while, there was confusion, but then the soldier who had first started the hunt came forward and said that Beran was guilty of not stopping when ordered to.

"Why did you want him to halt?" asked one soldier.

"No, it wasn't me," the soldier said in a nervous tone. The other soldiers looked at him in astonishment but waited patiently for some reasonable explanation on his part, but there wasn't anything he could add, except that he took chase because some foot soldiers had requested him to do so. They all laughed at the mentioning of foot soldiers.

"You took the chase because some foot soldier asked you to?" asked one of the soldiers in a taunting manner. "Those good for nothing soldiers aren't even worth getting a horse to ride." All soldiers were laughing, finding the whole issue funny.

"Go and do something better instead of scaring some youth," one soldier said, patting the back of Beran and signed him to go his way. He dared not look back to see if they had dispersed or still stood there watching him ride away. He was happy to have got out of the hands of those soldiers but still he kept worrying about the fate of the blacksmiths. He looked around before riding in the direction of his friends. He knew that the news he was carrying with was to make Hidas anxious and sentimental, but there was little he could do to comfort his newly made a friend in the hour of his distress.

The scene, which was unfolding at the time of his arrival at the camp, was even worse than the terrible experience he had a few minutes ago. He saw that the camp was full of soldiers, who were busy arresting all the male members of their company. They were not brutal or even offending but were lining them all up after taking their weapons. The way they performed their duties showed that they had no intention of harming the members of that group.

"Why do you treat us like that? Why do you want to arrest us?" cried someone from the gathering.

"No, we aren't arresting you at all. We are only to disarm you until we are sure of your purpose of coming to us. We are sorry, but we have our orders to obey."

"We would like to meet his majesty." Herzod told the soldiers.

"Few of you can come along to the court. We believe that his highness shall be listening to your complaints if you have any," the commander said agreeing to his suggestion. The male members had a quick exchange of views, in order to form a delegation, which would represent them at the king's court. They all agreed upon few names, which were to accompany Herzod, who in his turn wished that Tylon came along. There were few angry comments and murmuring, but no one really made any fuss about that proposition. Tylon on the other hand, was making a strong resistance. He wished to be out of that embarrassing situation. It was years back, when he had seen the king of Furzomia and still remembered the young face of his, shining at the time of his coronation. He was one of the prominent guests at that pompous ceremony, occupying a place of honour and there he stood fearing to enter the same court in degrading and humbling position. He couldn't find it possible to talk about his pain and anguish about that particular association. Herzod kept insisting on his joining the delegation until he reluctantly gave way. None of the young men were allowed to follow them, they were to stay behind and wait for the news.

The group of five was leaving the camp, looking not so positive. One could see their anguished faces and knew that they were shocked from the treatment they had received. They were allowed to ride their own horses instead of walking along the riding soldiers. All the others were worried as well but hoped that the group of wise men would make king change his mind regarding their presence in his country. Beran saw Hidas standing aloof on one side and watching soldiers going away. Beran moved to that direction and put his hand on his shoulder; he turned and smiled seeing him back.

"I didn't know that you are already back. Did you meet my father? What's the message?" Hidas asked.

"Don't you think it's a rough treatment we are getting here?" Beran asked, ignoring his questions.

"Yeah, that's true. But we are talking about king Sarastan and none else, a man full of contradictions, a king most unpredictable." Hidas sighed.

"I hope that princess Danor isn't like that," Beran said looking at him.

"Not even close. She is a most sensitive and wonderful person." Hidas assured him. Beran smiled, without making any further jokes.

"I'm afraid I have some bad news for you."

"What?" Hidas asked with anxiety.

"It's not that anyone told me directly, but I think that your father is in prison." Beran said undramatically.

"What for? What crime had he committed? Did Kestarius suggest that to you?" He could see the surprise in Hidas's eyes.

Beran told him everything he had witnessed and experienced a little while ago, and told about his suspicion that the events couldn't be translated in any other way than that both Shapario and Kestarius were in jail. Hidas got furious and tried to rush to his horse, but Beran stopped him, telling him that he needed to confirm the news and think with a cool head. There was nothing to win from the sentimental outburst. Even if the king had arrested his father without any valid reason, there was little he could accomplish by approaching him.

"Isn't it that he wants to achieve by these arrests? He knows that you shall get mad by the news and would approach him and thereby get arrested. Be prudent! Think what you can do to make him free."

"I'll kill him." Hidas was mad.

"Not without an army greater than his and where are you getting that? And by the way, what shall you achieve even if you succeeded doing so? I don't think Princess shall agree to marry the killer of her father." Beran was calming him down. Hidas did calm down in his outburst but not in his anger towards the king.

"I don't know how, but I'll make Sarastan pay for this." Hidas promised.

"The best way to do that is to marry his daughter," Beran joked.

The group of five entered the court and went near the throne, led by the guards. They went forward and bowed in a traditional manner, without looking in the direction of king Sarastan. It seemed that the king was not in a good mood; he had recently been told about some news, which had made him furious. He was being told that his only clue to the person he sought for some personal grievances had slipped from the hands of the soldiers. The king's terrible mood was a guarantee that he was about to be both rude and perhaps even punitive to the people who had come to seek his pleasure. King Sarastan ignored the greetings of the members of the delegation. He had no intention of listening to their petition, so he turned to their leader and asked what they did in his kingdom. Herzod tried to explain that they had been in his kingdom so many times earlier, but he cut him short by saying that he had no time to listen about the facts he already knew.

"What makes you come to my kingdom with an apparent purpose of settling down here?" The king was not pleased.

"We are facing some stressful situation back home and thought that your highness would be generous enough to grant us permission to live here for some time." Herzod told humbly.

"What reason do I have to do that?" the king asked sternly.

"As your highness is aware that we are wealthy traders, who by no means shall be a burden to your society." Herzod tried once again to soften his attitude.

The king was negative from the very beginning, without giving them any chance to plead their case. He had made up his mind, without even giving them a fair hearing. They all could feel the hopelessness of the situation and feared the worst. Tylon was trying to hide behind others, but there wasn't a big group in which he could melt down. He was cursing the day when he stood there at the mercy of a king who was devoid of all compassion, empathy, and understanding. He was as powerless as his other companions.

"I know that you all had a long journey and need a few days rest before you can take up your drive back out of Furzomia. If it were only men, I would order your immediate expulsion, but as you have your families to think of, I give you two weeks time to get out of my kingdom."

Herzod and others tried to protest about that harsh decision but the unsheathed swords of the guards silenced them. Tylon was standing there with bowed head and trembling like a dry leaf, unable to control his emotions. He was too tired, too weak, and too old to take stand against the will of a monarch, but he looked terribly disturbed.

"You may leave my court now." The king made it clear that there wasn't anything to discuss anymore.

"Where is your compassion that you were so proud of once?" someone shouted from the group of five, making the king more furious than he was.

"Come back all of you. Who uttered those words?" the king demanded. A silence fell; no one was ready to confess his crime of annoying the king.

"Alright, if no one is ready to come forward, then I shall let all of you arrested and order the rest to move out of my kingdom at once." King Sarastan's words were like a cold shower.

"It was I!" Tylon said in a low voice. They all spoke simultaneously; taking the blame, but king Sarastan raised his hand to make them all silent.

"Come nearer to me." He ordered.

"What's your name?" the king asked. Tylon kept silent, reluctant to tell his name. The king repeated his question in an impatient tone. He found no other way than to tell his name, wishing and praying that the king shall not recognise him. He had rather die than to show his degraded position to someone who once looked up to him. King Sarastan was watching the disturbed face of Tylon, trying to remember how he knew the person in front. There was a pin drop silence in the court. Everyone was anticipating some terrible decree to befall the unfortunate stranger, but the absolute silence was inexplicable.

"Tylon, Tylon, where have I heard the name? Do I know you?" the king asked, still distracted by his thoughts.

"I'm a stranger in your country; I don't think your majesty knows me."

"Hmm, but then why does it feel that way?" The king was no longer furious but seemed to be wrestling with his memory. Suddenly, his whole face lit up, and he jumped from his high seat.

"Of course, now I know who you are. Who else would have reminded me of my wild claims of being the most compassionate prince in the world?" The whole court was stunned to see King Sarastan come down from his throne and embrace Tylon.

"You can't imagine how happy I am to find you alive. I had presumed that Razila had killed you." The king was talking in a low tone before turning to his guards and informing them that his decision had been reversed. The people of the group were to enjoy all the facilities and hospitalities of the kingdom without any restrictions or restraints.

"What about their weapons?" the chief guard asked.

"Didn't I say that you should treat them all as royal guests?" the king said before adjourning the court, leaving them all in bewilderment. They were shocked, unable to comprehend what had taken place, what had revolutionised the whole situation. The four members of the group were in utter shock as they had feared some severe penalty for Tylon.

What relation did he have to the king? Why did the king become so happy to recognise him?

How were they to explain the phenomenon to the other members of their community? They were without a doubt very happy for the turning of the events and hoped that it was going to remain that way, knowing from the reputation Sarastan. The same guards who were now treating them with respect and honour. They placed all their weapons on the ground and begged their forgiveness if they had been rude earlier.

"No, you were just doing your duty. We have no complaints about anything," Herzod told them.

"Do you mind telling, who is the man his highness has been so happy to receive," the chief guard asked from Herzod.

"I'm afraid I know so little about that man who is so very kind, so very noble. He is an ordinary man but with a heart larger than the king's." Herzod confessed his ignorance about Tylon. "He never talks about himself or rather they both never did."

"What you mean by both?"

"I mean his wife Haliba." Herzod told the chief guard. They stood talking to each other while the guards were returning the weapons to their owners. The male members were happy that the king had graciously given them permission to stay in his country as long as they wished to do so. There were already rumours regarding Tylon, according to which Tylon was some long lost brother of the Furzomian king, the other placed him as the tutor of King Sarastan. In short there were as many rumours as many were members of that group, even though most of them weren't even involved in spreading such gossips. It didn't take long before the story reached Haliba and her friends, who looked anguished. Haliba was too anxious for her husband. She would have done everything in her power to stop Tylon from following the group as it involved the risk of being recognised. She knew her husband well and could imagine the indignation he went through at that time. Her husband was a man of pride and dignity, who had learned to live a life of distinction and couldn't bear to be looked down by anyone. She was really stunned to see Tylon, when he came to fetch her along with royal guards.

"King Sarastan insists on having us both at his royal palace. He wouldn't accept my refusal as an answer."

"But it's not possible; you know that it will just hurt your pride." Haliba tried, but Tylon seemed not to be caring.

"You know that we can't trust the man. He is a slave of his moods, or at least so the rumours place him." Haliba tried once again.

"I know that, but it is not good to offend the man, especially if he is kind towards all the members of our camp."

The other members of their group were waiting impatiently for him. They were all dying of curiosity and wanted to know the reason of sudden change of king's attitude.

"Look at how I look like? I rather die than to face the royal couple in this beggar like shape." Haliba protested.

"The queen has sent some clothes for you so that you can feel comfortable." Tylon told her, she didn't react but looked more miserable than before.

"What worries you my love?" Tylon felt pain by watching her sad face. He could see that she was trying to hide her tears.

"Here are the clothes!" Tylon tried to hand over the cloths.

"I rather die than to go with these borrowed clothes." Haliba said with a sad smile.

"Why this sudden pride? I have never seen you even half so sad all these years for clothe's sake. Remember how you looked the day I got my freedom." Tylon reminded her of the shabby clothes she wore that day.

"That was different. I was humiliated before you and nobody else. By the way, did you notice such things even in those stressful moments? I thought that vanity was the vice of women alone." Haliba said trying to lighten the mood. Tylon just smiled and watched her go and get ready. The moment she left everybody surrounded him and started asking the questions, which they were so keen to know. Tylon was not telling them anything except that the king was his old friend. They all were not satisfied with his answer but didn't press him for more details.

"Didn't you tell him that you were from Elbon?" one of the traders asked. Tylon nodded positively.

"Then how did you become his friend?" the same person asked.

"It's not easy for me to explain but don't we all travel sometimes and come across people from other countries." Tylon's smart answer made everybody laugh, and the questioner became little embarrassed.

"I believe Tylon has given you all enough explanation. Leave him alone now and take care of other important things."

"What other things? Aren't we to get food and water from the royal quarters?" One of the traders said loudly, showing his happiness and gratitude. They all were still standing there when they saw Haliba coming from the other end, wearing a very simple white dress.

"Come, I am ready!" she said with a broad smile, holding the hand of her husband. Tylon smiled, hiding his surprise that she had chosen the unpretentious of her dresses.

"Why did you choose this dress?" Tylon asked in a whisper.

"To show that a queen remains a queen, regardless of what she wears." Tylon couldn't help feeling proud of her. She was his greatest treasure, which he hadn't realised so clearly before his fall.

17

After dinner, Tylon and Sarastan left the women to talk with each other, he was so very interested in knowing all the details about losing the kingdom, about his survival and other things, which had been covered in some dark clouds of ignorance. There were no survivors from that encounter, who could tell the truth. It was the victor, a very uncertain source, which narrated all the stories regarding that event. Those circulated stories were just pieces of a lie as they were coming from the mighty and prevailing force. Everybody had known that King Tylon had been a victim of some conspiracy, but very few outside Elbon knew exactly how. Where were his armies at the time of the attack? Why did no loyal forces try to defend the country?

Why was Sakuri trusted that much? What happened to his princes? Many such questions were bothering Sarastan.

"If I learned anything from your tragedy, it is not to trust anyone, and to prepare a well trained population, which could face any army of the world." King Sarastan was looking at Tylon with pitiable eyes, a thing which made Tylon very uncomfortable. He turned the other way to avoid those looks. Tylon told him the whole story, about betrayal by the Sakuri, Razila's decision to prolong his miserable life, about his terrible conditions in the dungeon, about his unexpected meeting with Haliba in prison and all the other details. King Sarastan looked amazed at the stunning story of queen Haliba; he failed to find the words, which could describe his admiration for her courage and strength. Tylon noticed that his host was sitting with bent head and was trying to hide his tears, which were streaming down his cheeks. He looked embarrassed for having discovered by Tylon in that emotional state of being.

"Believe me, there is nothing to be embarrassed or to be ashamed of being tearful. For years, these tears had been my only comfort." Tylon was sad but strong.

"How did you manage all those years after you fled the country?"

"Haliba had some of her jewels with her at the time, which has helped us survive. Believe me, it is not the economic conditions, which can make one's life easier or miserable. I was the king, who was brought up to this office as you were, but the worst thing for me wasn't to lose my realm." Tylon was terribly sentimental, and his voice was shaking.

"Tell me, what was the most terrible thing that happened to you?" King Sarastan asked.

There fell a silence as Tylon was trying to recollect his energies and make an effort to be in control of his feelings once again.

"The worst thing for a king is not to lose his crown, but to lose his heirs, as I did. You can't imagine the pain and anguish of my wife and me when we confront the bitter truth of having lost them forever. Sometimes we sit and cry, blaming ourselves for all the tragic happenings."

"But how? It wasn't you who created the circumstances?" Sarastan tried to comfort him.

"Wasn't it my duty to trust only those who are trustable? Didn't I create my own hell when I closed my ears to all voices of reasons? Yes, it was mostly my fault, I had closed my senses, but who paid the price, of course me, but even those who weren't responsible for the crime of misjudgement." Tylon was hard on himself.

"We are but humans we err, don't we?" Sarastan tried to comfort Tylon. "Life isn't an easy task, and to sit in an important position is even more difficult thing. We all have to deal with some imperfection. Look at me, I have all a person can think of, and yet here I am sitting and becoming miserable for not having a son to take over my realm, when I die."

"But you have daughters; can't one of them become your heiress?" Tylon asked.

"Of course, but how many females can run the country without a strong male at their side? A fact, which is attracting all kinds of weed-like men around my daughters, having dreams of taking over that which is not theirs to inherit." The king was a bit sad. His face was turning red because their conversation had brought back the recollection of his getting humiliated by a blacksmith's son. Tylon could see that his host had suddenly become depressed of some unknown reason. He asked him about that sudden change. After some hesitation, he told Tylon about the daring romance of some youngster with his eldest daughter.

"You shouldn't take such a thing that seriously." Tylon smiled. "What you are going through is a common anguish of all parents, regardless of if they are kings like you or some ordinary beings."

"I know that just the very thought that one day my daughters would have to go their way devastate me, but I'm not talking about that. I'm ashamed even to tell that the chap is a simple blacksmith." The king was upset. He was telling Tylon about the escape of that young man and how he had been informed that another youngster, who could lead him to the fugitive, had slipped out of the hands of his guards, a thing, which was the main reason of his bad mood.

"Don't you mean that you want to punish the young man for falling in love with your daughter?" Tylon asked in astonishment. King Sarastan looked little confused but then said.

"Of course not. All I had in my mind was to scare him a little so that he would leave my daughter in peace, but the way the youngster was helped out of my hands has annoyed me, and I feel betrayed." The king explained the real reason of his anger.

"You shouldn't let things go disproportional. Take it easy. You should have looked the other way and even help the person in question to escape." Tylon patted his shoulders.

"I believe you are right but the father of the young man contributed to my fury, by asking the hand of my daughter. You can't even imagine the disgrace I felt at that moment."

"Wouldn't I?" Tylon smiled. "What really is more humiliating to be asked a hand of one's daughter by someone, who is good for nothing, or to lose all one has?" Sarastan understood what he meant.

"Why don't I have wise people like you around?" The king asked with a smile.

"Tell me, what did you do to the father of that young man?" Tylon asked.

"Something terrible. In my fury, I have put him in jail, without even listening to his pleas to get a chance to explain himself." The king was remorseful.

"I believe you should free the man without any hesitation or delay. If you choose to reject his request of asking the hand of the princess, is another thing." Tylon gave his opinion.

"What does the man do? Is he also a blacksmith?"

"Yes, probably one of the best in the world. Nowhere else one could have found the three of a kind collected in one place. How stupid I was to place two of them in prison and forced the third one on the run," King Sarastan said in a regretful way. He promised to release the father of the young man and his colleague the very next day.

"Lucky devil has great luck today. If he can't promise to control his son, then I'll banish them both to their former homeland, Elbon." The king was suddenly in a good mood.

"So he is from Elbon, the daredevil!" Tylon laughed.

"Not only he is from there but even considered me a damn fool by his wild claims of royalty."

The king joined him in his laughter.

"What did he say?" Tylon was curious to know the details.

"I wouldn't listen to that stupid man. I got furious the moment he claimed that his son was a

Prince and that would place him a king, wouldn't it?" he laughed again, but Tylon didn't join him in his laughter.

"What's the name of that man?" Tylon asked eagerly.

"Shapario! Why do you ask?" King Sarastan was astonished at his nervousness. Tylon was sitting in front of him, looking pale, and trembling with shock, unable to bring forth any words from his mouth. The king was worried and believed that his friend was suffering from some disease. It took a few moments until Tylon recollected himself. He was begging the king to bring him to the prisoner at once. Tylon was still shaky when he told the king that Shapario was one of the trustees of his sons, so if all that he had told was true then the young man was none other than his eldest son, Hidas. Both men sat in utter shock, unable to react to the situation.

The royal guards were summoned and were given instructions to bring Shapario from the prison directly to the palace. The guards were stunned by those strange orders and wondered what would be the possible reason that the errand couldn't wait until the morning. The king's orders were obeyed right away, and the man was brought to the palace. Shapario was trembling with fear as he couldn't translate his summons in any other way than that the king was to execute him or that he was to inform him about some terrible news about Hidas. Shapario knew that the stubborn Hidas was not to be away from his princess for a long time and that fear killed him daily. Perhaps he had come back and fallen in the hands of the guards he thought. Nevertheless, he was still confused. If that was the case then why was he taken to the royal palace and those parts of it, where the king and his family lived. The guards took him to the interior of the palace and asked him to sit and wait there. Seeing them disappear, he looked at the majestic room, which was filled with the most expensive things and wondered why he was entrusted to be there, without any guards. He didn't have to be wondering long; he saw King Sarastan entering the large room and he immediately bowed in respect. He could feel that the king wasn't alone but dared not look up.

"How are you, Shapario?" he listened to the voice and raised his head as a reaction to some electric shock and saw Tylon standing there. He rushed towards him and fell before his feet, crying. He had completely forgotten about the King Sarastan's presence there he was so happy to see his old master alive and standing before his very eyes. The shock was slowly giving way, but he was still emotional. Shapario was proud to have done his duty not only saving the prince but also for having raised him into a strong and courageous young man.

"I wouldn't have entrusted you with the task, had I not have a complete trust in you. You have pleased me, and there is no way I can ever pay back." Tylon embraced Shapario. "If only I had the prudence of finding and trusting the people like you!"

Shapario couldn't tell him about the whereabouts of his son, except that Hidas had gone to Kildia along with a young man they came across a few months back. Tylon became worried to know that his son was in the country, which was about to be a target of outside aggression. King Sarastan tried to comfort him by telling him that he would send his soldiers to Kildia, to find and bring Hidas back from there.

"I have heard that the royal family of Kildia is also on the way to your capital. Perhaps they can assist us in the search." Tylon told the king. He looked a bit astonished at the news as if upset that his own intelligence had not informed him of such an important news. But he overcame his feelings and promised to do everything in his power to help Tylon meet his son as quickly as possible.

"The first thing I am going to do in the morning is to remove the head of intelligence from his office; he is not suitable for the job. The royal family of Kildia is seeking a sanctuary in our territory, and we aren't even informed, what a shame!" King Sarastan was upset.

When Tylon came to the camp to take some advice from Herzod, he made no secret that he was going back to Kildia. He couldn't tell him the real reason but said that he was going there to find some fellow, which was of great importance. Herzod asked about the name of the young fellow he was to look for. Tylon told him about the name. Herzod tried to open his mouth but then shut it tightly, without saying a word. He didn't want to tell that the person in question was already there with them. He had a feeling that the youngsters weren't telling him the truth. He suspected that something was going on, a fact, which was getting confirmed by the sudden decision of Tylon to go search for him.

"May I ask, why you want to go and look for him personally? Why these soldiers can't accomplish the task?" Herzod asked. Tylon avoided answering his questions.

"How did you know that he is in Kildia?" Herzod asked once again.

"I'm told by the blacksmith, Shapario."

"You mean his father?" Herzod asked.

"Did you know all the time that I was talking about the same chap? Why didn't you tell that you knew him?" Tylon looked surprised. Herzod felt embarrassed and didn't know how to answer.

"I'm sorry, but I thought the young man was in some trouble," Herzod said without looking into the eyes of Tylon.

"Did you believe that I would hurt the young man?" Tylon asked with a smile. "Look there is the blacksmith, sitting on the horse; he'll be riding by my side in our search for Hidas."

"Then you don't have to go anywhere, we have the man, right here in our camp who can do that. You must have seen him hundreds of times since he has been here from sometimes." Herzod told him and couldn't understand the reason of Tylon getting that emotional. Tylon thanked Herzod for the information, which had saved them much trouble and went to the blacksmith. Both men looked very serious as they discussed something.

Herzod saw that Tylon stood at side, when Shapario was looking for his son, Hidas. His eyes were following the man wherever he moved until he found the young man. They stood and embraced each other and Tylon watched from a distance. Herzod smiled at the warmth of Shapario for his son, thinking that was the most natural thing. Hidas came to the direction of Herzod and informed that he was leaving with his father. He left a message for Beran that he would pay him a visit as soon as possible. "Tell him that things have been sorted out, without my doing anything about them," Hidas said before going to fetch his horse.

"What do you mean by that?" Herzod asked.

"Just tell him that my father came to fetch me, he'll understand," Hidas said and left. Herzod stood where he stood and watched the clouds of emotions taking over the face of otherwise calm Tylon, who didn't even come forward to say hello to the person, for whom, he was ready to make a long, tiresome and dangerous journey. He tried and tried to grasp the situation but found no leads, except that there was something, which remained hidden from his perception. Tylon had requested Shapario, not to disclose the truth about his fatherhood. He didn't want his son to get shocked in front of all strangers. He thought that could wait for another time. Just the knowledge that at least one of the princes had made it, filled him with immense happiness and satisfaction. He was riding behind Shapario and Hidas, feeling very proud to see that his child had grown into a strong, handsome, and tall man. If only he knew that he was of a royal blood, he thought to himself. He noticed that Shapario was turning from time to time and showing regret at that situation, but Tylon was smiling back, assuring him that he could wait one day more for the introduction. The guards were all riding behind Tylon, without being aware that their long journey to

Kildia had been called off. They all were instructed to follow the orders of Tylon, even if he asked them to jump into hell.

The armies of Pampicilos were marching with incredible speed and power, destroying all that tried to offer any resistance. The swarming army wasn't happy to find that the traders of Parnvan had slipped out from their hands, but the knowledge that they had taken refuge in neighbouring Kildia was a comforting thing as they were ordered to attack that country after they had settled down in Parnvan. So not all was lost and soon were they to get hold of all the legendary riches those traders had collected in the process of centuries. Even though the main portion of the booty was to go to the king, still there was a tiny reward to be left for the army, to be divided in between them. Judging from what they had learned, even that tiny part could be far exceeding anything they had ever dreamt of possessing in the life. They were not in a hurry and waited for those, which were to come directly from Elbon. Then and only then were they to consolidate their forces and attack Kildia, not because the conquest of the country demanded such a formidable force but to terrify and paralyse the resistance if there was going to be any. The generals were confident that the whole territory already belonged to them as they had the assessment that no big confrontation was to halt their march. They had well trained soldiers that feared the king and knew that they had left their families behind, which could be in trouble if they displeased the king. The fear, greed, and brainwashing of years had turned those Elbonian soldiers into fighting machines, almost impossible to stop or resist. Pampicilos had vowed to spare the kingdom of his brother Razila, on the condition that he never turned his gaze to Elbon. He was prepared for all eventualities and wished that Razila never ventured that way. Razila was not some stupid person; he understood that Pampicilos was not something to play with, so he accepted the fact of losing Elbon forever. The relationship between those two brothers suffered such a blow that they never recovered and they couldn't trust each other again.

Razila had gotten weak by the constant draughts in his kingdom, resulting in massive deaths and migration of the desperate people, who wanted to live and which saw no such possibility in that cursed kingdom. Razila had been not so popular with his subjects but still no one dared to do anything about that tyrant, especially when his cruel sons, who could kill for even fun, had joined him. The news of Pampicilos marching against Parnvan and conquering it without losing a single soldier reminded Razila of his own conquest of Elbon many years back. He felt melancholy at heart, thinking that it could have been him, conquering the entire territories around, had he not settled down on Elbon. The news that the armies of his brother were on the verge of making a strike against Kildia was awaking the demons of envy in him, but there wasn't anything he could do to hinder him from accomplishing his goals. He wasn't even bordering those countries so that he could try to play some role of his own. He had sent a message to Pampicilos, telling him that out of brotherly love, he was ready to join his hands with him and help him conquer the enemy territories, but the answer he got back was not encouraging. Pampicilos had thanked him no and had made fun of his incompetent soldiers.

"The bunch of ham-fisted ones, you call your soldiers, I have no need of, and you'll have no use either if you needed them some day." The message of Pampicilos was read in the open court, to humiliate him before his courtiers, friends, and advisers. There was an outcry asking for him to punish the insolent brother of his, but he knew more than anyone else that he was no match to the power and cunning of Pampicilos, so it was necessary to have a brave face and blame on the sacred relation he had with his brother.

"I have no intention of getting as low as he has done. I still value that I have shared the same parents and don't want to torture the souls of them by hurting him," Razila told his court.

"If only Pampicilos was to be half as caring as you are." His advisers praised him, knowing that they all were playing a game of toadying and nothing else.

The time of wavering was approaching its end; the green signal to attack Kildia was given by Pampicilos. He was too furious to realize that the traders of Parnvan had fled to Kildia, along with all their riches. He felt bereft of all that was his right as a conqueror of those territories. He had planned not to attack Kildia right away, but now he saw no other choice than to attack the country right away, to secure, that which was his. His orders were loud and clear to the generals; they were to crush all resistance and capture the king and send him to him. He had wanted to execute the deposed king himself, a thing he had wanted to do with the Elbonian ex-king Tylon, the escape of which he could never forget and forgive himself. The marching armies were surprised to meet no one at the borders to hinder them from entering into Kildia. They divided themselves into two groups. One group headed for the royal palace and the other to the direction they believed to find the traders but found none. The palace stood all deserted and without any signs of any army or guards. They went into the town and started beating people, pressing them for details as to where their king had hid himself. The Kildians were as unaware of the facts as were the soldiers. In desperation, they started snatching whatever they found valuable. No one resisted them as they had neither means nor courage to stand against that huge army. The people were not only angry with the king who had deserted them but openly criticised him for that cowardice. They were the natural survivors, who were ready to compromise with their new masters and ready to offer them their allegiance.

"We don't know what we are supposed to do with you? If the

king is to spare your lives, or he is to ordain your heads on the plates is to be seen and known." The army commanders told the people, who were trembling with fear.

The generals were quick to find out that the king of the country had been there until a few days earlier, so the chances were great to arrest him if they entered and chased him in Furzomia.

He had taken all his treasures with him, leaving not a dime for the invading armies. None could understand their outrage for having been robbed twice. First, it was Parnvanian traders and now the double disappointment of having lost the preys, the Kildian king and the traders. Most of the people knew nothing about the coming or going of the traders, giving them the doubts that perhaps they never stayed in Kildia but had just used the land for a transition. There was no time for them to sit and wait for orders of the king, but if they did so then they were surely to lose all possibilities of capturing the local king and his family as they had been ordered, and not to speak of all the riches, which had gone out of their hands.

The dilemma was perplexing and wavering their will to accomplish the given mission. Most of the generals were of the opinion not to move into Furzomia as the country had a reputation of courageous warriors, which were even ever-ready for all eventualities.

"Even if that is true, we are a force impossible to stop by a few soldiers, which might be guarding their territory," One of the commanders argued.

"All we need to do is to enter a few thousands of our soldiers to chase and arrest the king and his family and bring him back along with all his riches. By looking at how the kings and their corteges move, it wouldn't be long before we have them in our iron grip. Our king is going to be happy we all are to be successful in our task, and most of all, the Kildians are going to be happy, seeing that the devil has failed to get out of our hands." The general went on giving arguments. He could see from their faces that they all were confused about the proposition as it was not their orders to enter into Furzomia.

"Why don't you understand, we are not attacking Furzomia, as yet, only entering into it to pursue our enemy. A thing the Furzomian king shall understand, especially when we would have already left his territory behind."

"I believe he is right." The general got his first support and looked content; soon there were others to agree with him.

The army had few generals, which weren't given absolute powers but had to function in coordination, requiring the support of others in important decisions, a precaution, adapted by Pampicilos to have a check and balance in his army. They all were collectively responsible for the success or failure of their task, a thing that forced them to be critical and alert of each other. Though they all had given their consent about entering into Furzomia, none of them wanted to follow the general in the unsure territory.

"All we can do is to give you our blessings, with a sincere hope that you shall succeed in your mission, but we can't come along. We know that the whole army is not required to accomplish the task, so we shall wait for you in Kildia." The other generals made it clear that he had to make the pursuit alone. The general looked towards his colleagues and smiled, sensing that they were still fearful of the king and that they dared not enter Furzomia without his permission. The force which he had at his disposal, was in the thousands, so he felt confident. He saw a golden opportunity unfolding itself before him. He could prove to the king not only his loyalty but also even prudence as general, as a competent commander, who was capable of making decisions on his own. If he succeeded in achieving his goals, the king was not to get angry with his actions, but if he failed, on the other hand.... Which was an impossibility, so why to worry about that, he thought and remained relaxed.

To lead his men into Furzomia was not a difficult task. He had been leading those men from the last many weeks and knew that they would move and react to his slightest signal. He was hoping to find some guards at the border but found no one there. He smiled, thinking that most of the adages had been just the myths, having no anchorage in reality. The wakeful Furzomian soldiers had either gotten used to the frequent large-scale movements or they had grown too confident about their borders to Kildia. Whatever reason, he was pleased to find no one there. His men kept penetrating in the wild territory, confident of catching up with the king of Kildia. But after all day's ride they still didn't see any sign of the royal cortège. Perhaps the king and his men were moving with a faster speed than he had calculated. The night was falling, and he had to decide either to halt or to press ahead. The choice wasn't easy to make as he had been crippled by the collective way of thinking and taking the decisions. The realisation that they were unable to think and act individually came as a shock, and he panicked. The more he thought the more nervous he got as the entire responsibility of the decision was on his shoulders. I should order the soldiers to halt, we can keep up the pursue our search the next day after we have rested and are afresh, he decided in one minute, but the very next minute he was seeing the benefits of surprising the royal company in the middle of the night, when they would be sleeping. He kept being a prisoner of his indecision until he got weary and decided to stay there and wait for the morning. If the commander had hoped to rest and sleep in the night, nothing could be more wrong. All night long they all could hear the terrible sounds of beasts, which were so near to their camp, making it almost impossible for them to sleep. It was a moonless night, and the light of stars was not strong enough to give them any visibility, and therefore, none could dare to sleep and become a prey of the wild beasts, which waited for them to be off-guard, to devour them. They all were still sleepy and tired in the morning but got ready to follow the pursuit. They quickly took their breakfast and rode to the directions they believed the king and his company had moved to.

They rode and rode, without finding any fresh traces of some large movements having taken place. The general seemed to be astonished and was regretting his decision of having a halt during the night, by doing so, he had lost precious time and yet his men had not been able to sleep and looked tired already at noon. He was wavering once again, asking himself if it was a right thing to go deeper and deeper into enemy territory or if it was wiser to go back to his companions in Kildia. The horses and men were getting out of water, and they needed to look for some source of fresh water. He halted at one place and sent a few soldiers in all directions to go and search for water. They came back and reported that they had found a stream by which they all could not only drink sweet water but could take it for their further consumption, as well. The commander asked his men to proceed to that direction. The whole area around stream looked unlike the plains they had been travelling through. There were large trees and bushes, making it difficult for them to move in large numbers. They were trained in dealing with such situations, and decided to move in smaller groups and to spread themselves along the stream bank so that the maximum number of horses and men could appease their thirst. It was that precise moment that they were attacked. There was confusion and a shock as they were not only tired and thirsty, but also completely off guard, not expecting an ambush. They were exposed while the enemy remained invisible. Each time they went forward to drink water, arrows rained on them, killing their comrades and injuring their horses. There was no way of knowing from which direction the enemy attacked them and the knowledge as to how many of them were hiding in the trees, bushes, and other places. The general was quick to realise that the sounds of wild animals the last night were not real, but were made by the same clever enemy that was attacking them right that moment. He was angry for letting enemy make a fool of him and getting him where they had wanted him. He had lost many of his men, but he could lose even more, were he to stand there in indecision. He shouted and gave orders to retreat. The soldiers obeyed his command. The rain of arrows didn't stop, but the soldiers were not looking back to see which of their comrades were falling dead or injured. They were only concerned about their own security.

The commander was leading his tired, thirsty, and hungry men back to Kildia. He had lost many of them, more by the thirst than the arrows. Luckily, they had relocated the stream and quenched their thirst. Had they been not able to, certainly many more men would have been killed in that unfriendly place. The commander felt humiliated by his complete failure and dreaded the ridicule of his colleagues who were to laugh at him both publicly and privately.

He had lost more than a hundred men, not a great loss considering the size of their large army; nevertheless, it was a moral blow to his men and a victory to his enemies. His army unit was tattered, hungry, and humiliated as it came back to Kildia, making the other units wonder what happened to them. No one could stop those soldiers from telling their stories to other soldiers, who shrugged their shoulders in indifference. Didn't they all know that the profession was full of visible and hidden dangers and that their lives were of no value? The general was wrong in his assessment that others would make fun of him. They were more understanding than he could ever imagine. His colleagues requested him never mention the mistake as nothing was to be gained by that; on the other hand, they need to remember the lesson, in order to act more prudent in the future. The commander smiled inside, knowing why his co-generals were so generous in forgiving and forgetting his mistake. They were all scared to death that the mistake was to be collectively punished as they all had been guilty of giving their consent to that unwise enterprise. The generals had already informed the king about the latest developments and awaited his further instructions.

18

The revelation came as an utter shock for Hidas that the man he all his life had considered as his father was nothing but a guardian, a loyal friend of his real father. He felt a rage sweeping in his blood vessels. He was sad, angry, and bitter all at once, not knowing how he was supposed to take the strange news. Was he to be happy for finding his real parents, who were complete strangers? Was he to be proud of his royal heritage? He couldn't remain bitter to Shapario for not having told him of the truth about his background and royal descent. He loved the man who had raised him like his own son. He felt split between two forces and knew that he was to be torn apart if he didn't do something about the matter. He had rushed out, refusing to meet his real father and mother who so desperately wanted to embrace him. He was refusing to understand the circumstance, which necessitated the split of the family. He was robbed of his whole identity, so he wasn't going to forgive any of them. Shapario had tried to reason with him, but he wouldn't listen. Now as he sat alone, feeling very miserable, he tried to ponder upon his reality. His heart was pounding stronger and faster than ever, trying to imagine what his parents looked like as he couldn't recall the face of the man who had been travelling with them. It wasn't any help either to learn that the same was a member of the group, which went to meet the King Sarastan. He was filled with an enormous rage against those people who had destroyed his father's kingdom, torn them apart, and forced them to lives of misery and disgrace. His anger was directed against his parents, against Shapario, against the gods, which decreed such a terrible drama to be enacted. He had made up his mind; he was going to Elbon, to seek revenge. He wanted to reach his homeland and from there to reach further south, to seek Razila, the man who was the guilty one.

"I'll kill the devil with my hands, only then can my anger be quietening down," He thought full of anger.

He was sitting in a very sad mood, looking in front with empty eyes. He had not taken notice of Beran, which was coming from the opposite side. Beran smiled at his unconcentrated looks and wondered if it was still the princess who caused him pain. Hidas wasn't in a mood to joke, so he stared back at Beran and begged to be left alone. Beran wouldn't leave him alone just like that.

"I thought that you had been with your father, but he is going around and looking for you. What's going on? Is he freed by the king or never got arrested?"

Hidas didn't answer his questions but looked disturbed.

"You look not well. I have never seen you in such awful shape. Tell me what bothers you?" Beran was insistent and would not leave Hidas in peace. With a great patience, he listened to the story of Hidas and seemed to be taken aback by it.

"So you are the eldest of the three princes of Elbon? Aren't you happy to have found your parents, the king and the queen of Elbon?"

"No, I'm not!" Hidas said angrily.

"Why not? I would be extremely happy if I were you."

"But you are not. I hate them for abandoning me, for giving me away to some stranger, who put me in the hell of physical labour." Hidas was unreasonable.

"I thought that you were a stubborn, but good hearted person, but I am witnessing that you are even a thankless and headless being too." Beran was provocative. Hidas looked at him with murderous eyes, but he remained unafraid and continued.

"Is that the way you pay back to the unfailing services of a man, who sacrificed his whole life in protecting you, raising you into a strong brave man, giving you an art you could never learn? Is that the way you'll be rewarding the people of great statures in the future? What about your parents? What kind of being you are to blame them for a crime they never committed? Why can't you see them as victims, what they were in reality? I'm really sorry to have known you." Beran said and took a few steps away from him. He was sure that his hard words would have the desired effect on Hidas and that he would wake up to the reality, but he didn't ask him to come back. He was deliberately walking slowly, awaiting his call.

"What the hell you mean by that? He heard the angry reaction of Hidas and smiled without turning back. He waited a few minutes before going back to him and asked,

"What happened to your brothers?"

"I don't know, rather no one knows," Hidas shrugged his shoulders.

It didn't take long for Beran to convince him to go and meet his parents. Hidas was unsure and wanted his moral support to do such a hard task. Beran was so happy, so excited to know that Hidas was one of his brothers and that he was about to see his both parents. He had a great temptation to go and embrace his elder brother, but he refrained as it would have been too much for Hidas, who was finding it hard in absorbing one shock, so he decided to spare him one more. At the time of their reunion Beran was present as an outsider but only in the eyes of other members of his family. He felt the love flow, the presence of some invisible energy, which overwhelmed him. He had difficulty in controlling his own emotions when the king and queen embraced their firstborn. They were sobbing; kissing and caressing Hidas, making him wish that he too could tell them that their second child stood before their very eyes, as well. But he could see that it was going to be too much for their hearts. All three of them were deeply entangled in the moment, and he found it hard to remain there without a need to cry, so silently went out of the room, leaving them alone.

When they emerged from the room, they all looked very happy, their tear-stained faces making it obvious that happiness wasn't without much pain. A pain, which had been unbearable at times for the couple, who had been aware of the loss unlike Hidas, who suffered the pain of missed years, the pain of being ignorant of the truth, the pain of being torn apart from those, who were his own but became strangers by the stormy winds of time.

"Come here, I'll introduce you to my parents." Hidas said holding his hand. Beran smiled warmly towards Tylon and couldn't help embracing Haliba.

"Is it some friend?" Haliba asked, turning to Hidas.

"Hidas is more like a brother than a friend. Consider me also a son." Beran said trying to charm her.

"I can see that you are well bred. I'm happy to note that my son has good friends." Haliba answered. Hidas was looking in astonishment at Beran. He knew that he was a born charmer, but he could never have expected him to call Hidas like his brother.

"The guy is really on a charm offensive," he thought and smiled before going away from there he turned to Tylon and asked.

"Your highness, do you mind if I come and say hello to you both some time?" Beran asked.

"Not at all, young man. We shall be honoured by your visit. By the way don't call me your highness; as a matter of fact no one calls me that any longer." Tylon joked.

"What was that? Why were you trying to steal my newly found parents? Hidas joked. Beran liked that obvious change as the man had never joked with him before.

"I could steal your parents if I wanted , but refrained, because it would be too much for you otherwise." Beran said with laughter.

"What about King Sarastan? Has he changed his mind about you?"

"I have heard that he is no more crossed by my love for his daughter, but I have other things on my mind than Danor right now," Hidas confessed.

"What do you have in your mind?" Beran asked.

"It is much confusion. But I am sure that clarity shall come soon."

Hidas suddenly turned and asked about Shamon, as he had not seen him for a few days. Beran smiled and said, "I thought you would never take notice. He is out of Furzomia on some errand."

"Isn't it dangerous to be in Kildia right now?"

"It depends, but who told you that he went to Kildia?"

"Where else would he go? I'm sure he worries about his own land and went there to get some news about Parnvan." Hidas was confident about his guesswork.

"Have you heard any news about the armies of Pampicilos? Where are they now? Have they occupied the land of Parnvan or have they gone back seeing it empty?" Hidas asked anew, when Beran didn't elaborate his earlier comments and questions.

Beran told him that Shamon had gone to Kildia exactly for that reason. He wanted to know what went on in his country as well as how the Kildians were faring. He told to Hidas that the king of Kildia had also moved into Furzomia along with his small but efficient defence force.

"What's use of that force, which couldn't give any resistance to the on marching armies?"

"Aren't we back to square one? Have we not discussed these matters at enough length? I believe that he did the right thing by giving all his forces in Sarastan's command. At least those units wouldn't be wiped out without getting a chance to prove their worth," Beran said.

"Tell me, are you really men who didn't know a thing about wars, weapons and strategies or you were making fools of us?"

"I never told you that I was completely unaware of the war-games. That was one of the favourite games I used to play with my father," Beran explained.

"What do you think, would the armies of Pampicilos attack Furzomia, when there hadn't been any resistance to his might till now?" Hidas asked.

"There is no doubt about it, especially when they had been robbed twice of all the riches they were expecting from both Parnvan and Kildia. But I think that the attack isn't imminent. It might take another year before the armies of Elbon shall venture this way," Beran said, making it clear that all was his personal opinion and had nothing to do with the reality.

"Do you think that Furzomia is ready for the invasion?" Beran turned the question the other way around. Hidas was thinking seriously before he came with the answer. He was of the opinion that Furzomia, despite its well-trained citizens and augmentation of the Kildian forces, was still too weak a force to give a real match to the enemy. He hoped and wished that they really were given one year's time to prepare the traps and to build a strong fighting force, which could defeat the enemy.

"But all preparations cost a hell of a lot of money, from where shall the Furzomians get that kind of money?" Beran asked

"I don't know. The only thing I can say for sure is that the Furzomians have never been a savings inclined nation." Hidas told.

"Perhaps Parnvanian traders would help?" Beran's eyes shone with hope.

"Why would they do it? Have you not seen how miserly they are?" Hidas laughed.

Beran agreed that it wasn't going to be a simple task, but he wanted to take up the issue with Herzod, who might be able to come up with some solution.

Beran became silent trying to analyse his own words. He

knew that Herzod was a kind hearted and a generous being but he was only one tiny voice, incapable to change the norms of his society, so it wasn't wise to attach too much hope on the help of that person. Hidas was a simple person, so there wasn't any point in discussing the matter in depth with him. On the other hand, he always found it easier to discuss and communicate with Shamon, who was more experienced in the ways of the world and a learned person, fully compatible with him. If there was anyone in the world who could find the solution of the economic problems, it was Shamon, the clever trader, but he was not around.

From time to time, Beran was paying a visit to Tylon and Haliba, which were living at the guest quarters of the royal palace. King Sarastan refused to let them go and live with other Parnvanian traders.

"You are a royal guest and not random traders," King Sarastan would remind them. He had given his other palace, which lay a few hundred miles further west to the royal guests from Kildia. None were aware except Tylon that the king Sarastan was having nightmares at that particular point in time. He could see with clarity that his country was in some big trouble. All his life, the king had been preparing to face some inner or outer danger, but the situation he faced was far more crucial than he could anticipate. His own forces together with the units he got from the king of Kildian and public support was just enough to stop the march of the advancing forces for a period of a few weeks at its most. He kept worrying what was to happen after that.

"We should mobilise and reorganise our army," Tylon suggested.

"We have neither time nor resources to achieve that." King Sarastan was quite pessimistic.

Tylon often wondered what had gone into Sarastan, who was losing all his self-confidence and was encircled by ever more fearfulness. He was afraid to meet the same fate as Tylon, confessing that he and his family could never survive the day. He saw the hopelessness of the situation and was anguished. For the last few days, he was seldom coming out of his chambers. In many ways, he reminded Tylon of his own bygone days. Despite his depression and hopelessness, he refused to seek any sanctuary in some other country.

"No, this is my land, my realm. I was born here and shall die here. None can banish me from here!" He would tell Tylon in an ardent voice and manner.

Tylon was very worried about his moody but good-hearted friend. He knew that the wars were not just fought in the battlefields, where the strength and the weakness of the armies were tested, and fate decided and announced the name of the winner. He was aware that the physical might was only a fraction of the whole, which was required in that trial. He could swear that the wills were the main decisive agents, which were always determining the destinies of nations. Wars were first fought on the mental planes before the physical demons were unleashed. With horror, he could see that King Sarastan was losing the battle without even trying to fight. King Sarastan needed to know that there were great possibilities of losing many battles, but he could win the ultimate war if he involved his will in the fight, but who was to convince him that, at least it could not be Tylon, who had no credibility in the eyes of Sarastan, who looked at him as a loser. With sadness Tylon realised that in the world, there were no weights given to those who had the bad luck of not succeeding in the affairs of the world. He knew that the king was nervous and meant no harm, but it was the third time the king had rejected his advice regarding the defence of the country, each time reminding him that he wouldn't have lost his own realm if he was that clever. Even though it hurt, he had kept smiling, trying to give him moral support, trying to boost his morale, doing his utmost to find some feasible solutions to the given challenges. There was no news from the enemy, or as to what it was planning. One thing was sure that Furzomia wasn't ready for a large-scale invasion, so something drastic was needed if the enemy was to be convinced that Furzomia wasn't any power to be played with. But the question remained who was to accomplish that tremendous task, especially when king Sarastan kept sinking deeper and deeper into the abyss of his imaginary and real fears? Had Pampicilos known Sarastan's state of mind, he wouldn't have wasted an hour in attacking Furzomia, but luckily he was still under the impression that Furzomia was a far more complicated matter than the other two territories he had just conquered. Tylon was worried when Beran came along with Hidas. He could see that his father was anxious and wanted to know what caused him such worry. Tylon told them that he was concerned for the enemy armies, which were ready to invade and consume them. "They wouldn't be able to subjugate us if we fight back with all the might we have." Hidas tried to comfort him. Tylon was not relieved by his soothing words. He told that his real concern was king Sarastan, who was loosing the struggle without even engaging himself in that.

"All we need to do is to convince him that we stand a fair chance of defending his realm. Once confident he too shall fight like a warrior," Beran said.

"And what shall convince him of that?" Tylon asked.

"Can you arrange an audience with his majesty, so that we may try to persuade him of something vital?" Beran asked.

Tylon couldn't promise anything, , but he assured that he was to try his best but before that he wanted to get convinced that they had some viable plan to present to the king. According to Beran's plan they needed to put a complete stop to any designs of attacking Furzomia if there were such intentions. Secondly, it was necessary to realise that such prevention only could win a short respite. While what they needed was a full preparation to get braced for an eventual combat.

"How are we to stop Pampicilos from attacking Furzomia, if the man has an imminent plan to do so?" Tylon asked.

"We need to convince him that he wasn't ready for the task and needed more preparation," Beran said with a smile. Tylon couldn't understand what he was aiming at. When Beran told him about his plan, Tylon couldn't believe his ears. He laughed and laughed, shaking his head in the negative, telling the youth that his plan was not only naive but lacked the touch of reality. The king was not going to agree to such a perilous enterprise of attacking the army of tens of thousands and thereby accelerating the whole process. If the king was anxious about the danger of being invaded, how was he to order an offensive, and even if he did, what could have been gained by that risky move?

"I believe that Beran's plan could work. The enemy doesn't know about our handicaps and considers us a difficult chore; the reluctance to attack us is proving that our assessment is right.

The sudden attack on their forces would be a clear signal that we are neither afraid nor wavering in our resolve to deal with them. Surely that knowledge would force them to prepare for a longer time, thus giving us enough time to get ready for the hard fight ahead." Hidas was more convinced that they could defeat any power on earth, provided they were given a reasonable time to make the necessary preparations. Tylon promised to discuss the subject with the king and see what he thought about it.

The king was horrified to listen to the plan. He would not even discuss it in detail, calling it suicidal. Tylon had quoted the story of Pampicilos's army entering into Furzomia and then being forced to flee in disgrace. He used the same arguments that their courageous bluff might be able to bring the desired results for them.

"What matters if they attack us and subdue us, or we attack them and are defeated? At least we shall have the advantage of surprise. I think you should give the plan a chance."

"And who shall lead such a hazardous plan? Is it going to be some general of my army, who already stress the impossibility of withstanding such a tremendous force? Or is it to be some inexperienced youth, which shall accomplish this impossible mission? Tylon wasn't giving in to his frail will. He was sure that if Furzomia stood any chance it was only to be through convincing Sarastan to agree to some drastic actions, right there and then.

"Alright, I am ready to give my consent. Even if the crazy plan does succeed then what? From where are we to get the resources to build a strong army? From where shall we get the needed soldiers?" King Sarastan was anguished

"Leave the question to the youth; I'm sure they would find some reasonable solution to these problems."

"I know you talk like a father, but don't forget that your son is an inexperienced young man, who needs a lifetime experience if he is to become a commander." King Sarastan tried to reason with Tylon, but he blindly trusted the capability of his son Hidas to accomplish any mission. What really gave him comfort was the fact that Hidas wasn't alone. He had a very clever and intelligent friend at his side: Not only that he liked Beran but even was impressed by his inborn wisdom and knowledge about things. He had never met a youth, which could have matched Beran's insight or in-depth knowledge.

That day, Hidas was not there when Beran came to visit Tylon and Haliba. They were glad to see him and started talking to him about different matters. Tylon started asking him about Elbon.

"I'm told that you and your parents came from Elbon, as well. Why did they leave the country?"

"Most probably for the same reasons as forced you to make the move." Beran said politely.

"You mean the political reasons." Tylon said with a smile. "What did he do there? Was he some prominent person?"

"I never asked. But I presume so."

"Tell me why you left your present country and your parents, who must need your presence by their side now," Tylon said looking at him.

"That is certainly true, but they have enough money to hire someone when they shall grow that old that they can't take care of them." Beran was trying to make it look less serious.

"It's not just the practicalities one thinks of, but the other needs of parents to have their children at their side." Haliba entered the discussion. "Do you have other siblings?" She asked. Beran shook his head, looking at her with a smile.

"Why have you not brought your parents from Kildia?" She asked.

"Because they wouldn't come. They didn't feel the threat to

their lives at the moment, but perhaps they too were forced to change their minds and are already in Furzomia," Beran told them. He could see the question marks on their faces and he explained that there was a possibility that his parents accompanied the king of Kildia in his flight to Furzomia.

"Why don't you find out by going to the palace and asking? The Kildian king lives not that far away." Tylon asked.

"I'll go and visit them, once I have a little time," Beran told them.

"The hearts of parents are constructed differently than the children they conceive," Haliba said with a sigh. Beran just smiled, without even trying to understand what she had wanted to imply.

"Tell me about your other two children. Did you ever try to find them?" Beran asked out of nowhere, making them both look in astonishment at him.

"I'm ashamed to confess that we haven't tried very much," Haliba told him, looking at her feet, wringing her tiny hands.

"Why not?" It was Beran's turn to be astonished. The couple kept silent, an unease engulfing them. Finally, Haliba cleared her throat and spoke regretfully.

"It isn't easy for us to explain the stress of that terrible day, which still torments us even after so many years have passed. My husband had the most dreadful time after he was put in jail. He just remembered having given the princes to the most entrusted and loyal friends, but who they were he had completely forgotten. So you can understand that how are we to search for the other children without even remembering the names of those to whom they were being entrusted to." Beran could hear the trembling of her voice and could feel her pain and anguish.

"So you mean there is no hope of your getting in contact with each other again?" Beran asked.

"Please don't say that. We live only because we have never abandoned the hope of getting all our children back. Look at how gods have been kind enough to reunite us with Hidas." Haliba was tearful.

"Why don't you adopt me as your son?" Beran joked with a smile. Tylon tried to speak, but he could not say a word, he found no words, which could convey his true feelings, but Haliba was more diplomatic.

"You are like a son to us. We believe that your real parents are lucky to have such a brilliant child."

"Who can say, what's real and what's not? Sometimes you consider someone as your own, while the relationship is just a fake, while at other times your real blood stands a meter away, but you treat him like a stranger. Isn't that comically tragic?" Beran laughed, both Haliba and Tylon joined him, without understanding why they did it.

Beran had a great wish to tell his parents that he was one of their long lost sons, but he couldn't do it, feeling that it wasn't the right time. Hidas was still going through an uneven emotional path and had great difficulty in adjusting to his newly evolved reality. He wanted him not to become more confused than he was. He needed to know how he was to react to the possibility of finding his brothers. Hidas was always avoiding answering his hypothetical questions. He was honest in telling that he had not pondered upon the possibility but preferred not the enlargement of the family any further.

"Even after knowing that there are two brothers of yours somewhere in the world you don't long for them?" Beran asked hiding his disappointment in him. Hidas was not an easy person to discuss his feelings. Beran decided not to take up the matter with Hidas anymore as it hurt his own feelings. He was to keep the knowledge for himself and wait for the right time if there was to be any.

When Shamon came back from his mission, he looked somewhat confused and worried, often avoiding the contacts with others. Beran confronted him a few times, pressing him to confide about that thing, which troubled him, but he was denying that there was any such thing. Beran's persistence made him talk one day. He had been to Kildia and seen and known that the enemy forces had the whole area in an iron grip. He had seen hundreds of people moving to the direction of his fatherland, those were the civilians, old, young, male and female. It seemed that the enemy had no intention of leaving their territory as they had hoped but intended to occupy it for good. He was devastated and crushed by the thought of never to be able to move back to his beloved land. He had seen the army of Pampicilos and understood that they had no chance of withstanding them. So the future prospects were bleak.

"All this makes me feel sad, angry and helpless. I find myself in the middle of a dark tunnel, without any ray of hope," Shamon confessed his frustration. Beran tried to encourage him by telling that the situation wasn't that depressing as he deemed it to be. They all were the architects of their own destinies and that the size of the armies wasn't the most important factor in waging the war. Shamon looked amused and smiled, looking at his confidence. He could hardly believe he was talking to the same person, who was completely ignorant of the weapons, wars and the things important in the defence and offence. He wondered what had given him that confidence. Had that confidence enhanced because he could handle the sword to a certain extent, or that he had been too much in Hidas's company? Beran was telling about the plan, he had given to the king. He seemed very excited and positive of its success.

"What do you think of the plan?"

"I don't know. It's quite a risky enterprise. Think if the pre-emptive attack brings the opposite effects, and instead of frightening the enemy we provoke it to attack us even earlier than it had planned. No, I don't think it will be a very clever move." Shamon didn't agree with him.

"Perhaps it is going to be that way, but is it better to sit, wait, and do nothing."

Both Shamon and Beran continued with their arguments without going anywhere. They both agreed on the necessity of reacting quickly. Shamon believed that there only chance to avoid the danger was a peaceful negotiation instead of a direct confrontation.

"How are we to accomplish that?" asked Beran.

"By joining our clever heads, we can pacify the enemy. We need to send a double message that we are ready on one hand, but on the other hand we want friendship on dignified terms."

Shamon was quickly forming his own ideas and a new strategy. When Beran considered his thoughts he got convinced that it could work.

19

Shamon was convinced that Beran was imprisoned by his own contemplation and had strong reasons for behaving in that extraordinary manner but there was little he could squeeze out of him. So he didn't move and tried to press him for any details. He was busy with his own confusion. He had been trying to figure out what really happened to him in Kildia. He could swear that he had been deprived of some understanding, robbed of some consciousness, and confronted with some odd, inexplicable, and bizarre incident. He had never had faith in intangible worlds and yet he had the feeling of coming across one of such. He had been fighting the idea without coming anywhere. He had had lost track of time and couldn't account for two whole days. The keys of his mystery remained lost. He couldn't even discuss the matter with anyone, fearing that that would open the doors of ridicule, disbelief, and doubts about his sanity, which he didn't want to happen. He had the feeling that something of great importance took place during that missing time, but what exactly happened, he couldn't tell. Many times he had considered confiding in Beran, but had dared not. What he knows about such weird things, had he thought and kept silent. But the whole happening was there in the confines of his heart, in the vicinity of his brain, fully recorded, fully perceived but he was still kept out. Shamon was a clever businessman who knew that the mind was a sharp tool, to mint the money, to carve the riches and to trade in an effective manner to get the optimal results. To use that intelligence in some unproductive and unprofitable fashion was a great sin, a thing he absolutely didn't want to do. With a sigh he wrestled with his thoughts for the last time, to find out if there was any hope to find a clue to his mystery. He saw the hopelessness of the matter and decided to leave the issue alone.

Beran on the other hand, was to find out what really had taken place to the third person, to which he had been connected as an integral part of a triangle. He had been dragged to Senklour as he left the tavern. He was excited to see the strange female figure but she remained absent from his sight. Instead, he was met by some other beings, which informed him that he was privileged to choose one tool of uncountable tools, which were there to choose from. He was not to get any information regarding the characteristics and attributes of those unique things. He was confused about what to take and what not to take. In desperation, he tried to seek advice but found none, as it was his call and none else could tell him how to equip himself. He took many of those wonder-waking things in his hands, weighed them, trying to feel if they were the things, which he needed but always placed them back. His heart guiding his choice always informed that it wasn't the thing he looked for. He faced one peculiar thing after the other and admired their rare beauties but it wasn't the beauty he was after. His hosts were watching him from a distance. Their gazes told that they were indifferent as to if he made a wise choice or picked at random. After an initial stress Beran had grown relaxed, leaving his choice to his heart, he moved from one hall to the other without even giving a thought that he was there to choose something. He was moving in a slow pace when he caught sight of an object, which seemed very interesting. He moved near to and looked at it, appreciating its strangeness. It was a stone eye, with such brightness that he couldn't get his sight off that thing. He picked that eye and placed it on the palm of his hand and felt overwhelmed by some strange energy. He could swear that the bright eye followed each and every movement he made. He didn't know what that eye was good for or if he was making the right choice or was just blowing his chances on some toy, but he had made his choice, he was to go for that stone eye. He signalled the beings waiting for him to come near to him. He informed them that he wanted that object to take with him. Beran could hear the wailing sounds, which he remembered from his previous visit to that place. He looked around but found no one there.

"Why this wailing?" He asked the beings.

"Don't worry about them. These sounds are a traditional way of expressing the sorrow of losing the rarities from our world." One of them explained.

"Even knowing that it is only for a while the things depart this world." Beran said in a surprise. Yes, even so, was the answer he got back.

"Congratulations, you have made a good choice." The beings spoke in unison.

"Why is it a wise choice?" Beran asked.

He was told that now that the all three of them had made their choices, he could know the significance of the gifts. Hidas had chosen the sword, which made him the invincible prince of the physical planes, where none could defeat him. He was the victor and lord of the kings. He was to become the most powerful king in the world, who could become the ruler of the world if he chose to.

"What has the third one chosen?" Beran asked spontaneously.

"The third one or the second one as we see it, has chosen for himself the inexhaustible treasures of Senklour. The thing he has chosen, entitles him to get access to all that is precious, valuable, and mouldable. That thing is not money as you know it, but a force so creative, so potent and so huge that no one can comprehend its power and scope in your world." They told him that since the holder of that power was not aware of the real significance of that object, so he was to use it to create the riches alone. He shall be the most powerful of you all three, not in a physical sense or even spiritual sense but in a very peculiar manner. He too shall be a king very powerful, on whose support Hidas would rely as his sword alone shall not be enough to rule his kingdom. Beran was curious to know who this unknown fellow was.

"You had the chance to know the answer when you visited

our world last time. Now you have to wait for another day or two," he was told.

"What about the object I have chosen?"

"The eye you have selected is the symbol of the driving force of our world Senklour, a force, which is necessary to perceive, understand, and provide wisdom. It is knowledge personified, it is the cold light of reason, and this eye is capable to penetrate all depths and heights. It is a watchful eye, which can protect from all evil. It never gets weary or sleepy, armies of millions can't accomplish that what it is capable of performing." They gave Beran good news.

They were quick to add that those gifts were just for the time being and required a close cooperation and collaboration between the three of them. As long as they were unified and used the inherent qualities of those wonderful gifts in a constructive way, they could count on keeping them but if they misused those powers or stopped working as a team, the gifts were to return to their natural abodes, leaving them at the mercy of the forces of decay and disintegration.

They made it plain that Beran's responsibility was the greatest of them all, as it was he alone, who was equipped with the eye of vision, purpose, and the consequences of the disarray.

"It's not that I wish to be, but the prophecy told of me becoming a king as well. Is it true?"

"Without any doubt it'll come true." He was told with conviction.

"Can I meet the female I saw last time?" Beran asked.

"Why? Aren't you afraid to face the biggest mystery of all, the lady destiny? Not always does she smile at one like she smiled at you the last time."

Before Beran was led back to his own world, he was told that he could await a long healthy life, a very harmonic marital life, and beautiful kids, but all was coming to an end one day. Their gifts were to return to Senklour and there to await the new borrowers, which would use them once again in some other times and places with completely different angles.

"Who would be those three?" Beran asked curiously.

"Don't ask the mysteries deep? That's not for you to know, but you have had your chance to know before, though you were not aware what to look: Go in peace and enjoy the life you have at your disposal." One of the beings told him. He opened his mouth to ask another question but found himself riding towards the place, where the king of Furzomia had accommodated Silos.

Silos was really happy to see him there at his door. He was in his nightdress and most probably had gone to sleep when Beran called on him. He was not at all crossed by Beran's failure to pay the visit. Beran told him that he had just been told about his presence in the capital. Silos was telling him about his wife Binti, which had taken Beran's departure very hard. He could understand her feelings as she was more like a mother than his real mother could ever have been.

"Both of us shall become extremely happy if you could come and visit us sometime." Silos requested. Beran promised that both he and his wife were to receive a warm invitation to come and visit him in the capital.

"So you wouldn't come!" Silos smiled. "Alright, you invite, we shall come running, without losing a moment." Beran had a great wish to inform him about his parents and that he had already met one of his brothers, but he couldn't disclose the great news, as it would certainly invoke a surprise on Silos' part that Beran had not disclosed his own identity as yet, neither to his parents nor to his brother.

"Tell me what message you brought to Sarastan" Beran asked. Silos looked shocked at his question but then smiled.

"You remain a prince; even though I could just provide you a humble upbringing. While all I can ever dream of becoming is a simple servant." Silos said with a smile.

"What do you mean by that?" Beran was confused.

"The way you talked about his highness, the king of Furzomia, only a fearless prince can speak. As to the content of the message, what I know? I am just a humble messenger."

335

Beran felt a little embarrassed and asked for his forgiveness.
"By the way do you remember the people, who took my brothers?" Beran asked.
"Let me think." Silos tried hard but couldn't come with any names. He gave up, confessing that he was getting senile.
"Keep thinking and please do tell me if you remember any names." Beran said and leave the place, promising to be contacting him soon.

The whole night Beran couldn't sleep, he kept watching the advancing armies of Pampicilos. It seemed those armies were marching from all sides, moving with the speed of a storm, and they destroyed whatever came their way. The scenes and images were both horrifying and distressing, as they were unfolding themselves in such style and fashion that there was no other interpretation than that the awesome army of Pampicilos was to destroy every single hurdle in its way in a cruel and heartless manner. At morning when he woke up he was drenched in sweat and was so tired as if he had laboured all night. He could swear that all the images he had seen last night were not some dream but taken from some real world and played before his eyes in some peculiar manner. He knew that he couldn't talk about such strange things with anyone, but on the other hand he could not remain still in the wake of imminent danger, which loomed over their heads. He thought of talking to Herzod but rejected the thought as he had seen him smiling at someone who talked about his fears and insecurity in Furzomia. He had told the man that if he didn't feel secure in that country then there wasn't going to be anywhere he would feel safer.
He was conscious that his dream or whatever it was could be just the reflection of his mistrust for Pampicilos and his deceitful nature, according to what he had heard about the man. But the question was if he could afford to brush the whole apparition away as a confused dream or needed to take it as a serious warning, coming from some unknown source.

He decided to talk with Hidas about his vision even it entailed evoking his special smile. He was sure that Hidas would give him a fair chance and hearing without trying to ridicule him. He could have discussed the subject even with Shamon but knew that he would resist calling that anything else than a senseless dream. Hidas listened and didn't even smile, when he confided him the dream, vision, or whatever that was.

"Look, I am a practical person, who doesn't believe in the truthfulness of dreams but I sincerely believe that your intuition is right. The king of Elbon is a deceitful person, who shouldn't be trusted. But the question is what we can do about the thing -- honestly nothing. None pay any attention to our thoughts, considering us inexperienced young men," Hidas said.

"So you believe that we should stand aside and let the matters take their course?" Beran asked. Hidas didn't answer.

"Can't you at least discuss the possibility with your father?" Beran suggested.

"You know it wouldn't help. It's not he, who decides; besides I'm not good in persuading others of anything even though I myself am convinced Why don't you talk to him, he likes you and give value to your ideas." Hidas suggested. They sat, discussed the matter and went their way without knowing exactly what to do if their fears were going to turn into reality.

Tylon listened to the dream of Beran and told him that even though he couldn't trust in his dream and take it as a sign for some new developments; he was of the opinion to take some precautions regarding the defence of the country. He showed the willingness to take up the matter with the King Sarastan. The problem according to Tylon was the long borders of Furzomia and Elbon, which had now expanded even further to Kildia.

"How will these tiny armies of the king to guard and defend these long frontiers?" Tylon looked worried.

"I believe that it can be accomplished, if we allocate our

limited resources wisely," Beran told him.

"What do you mean by that?" Tylon demanded some explanation.

"I don't know right now, but if the king approves a strong and viable defence, I'm sure we can come up with some good strategy." Beran told him. Tylon shook his head with a smile on his face.

"I know that you are young men, with a lot of ideas, but believe me the defence of the country and the war strategies aren't a game. So if you are thinking to play a major role in it, forget about it. We'll check your competence before you two are even allowed to take part in the defence of Furzomia." Tylon wanted to clear up all the misunderstandings of Beran and Hidas, if they had any. The young men looked at each other and tried to protest but Tylon stopped them by raising his hand.

"As I said I'll not deprive you the opportunity if you prove yourself to be worthy of the task."

"What would be your criteria, would you just judge by our physical strength?" Beran asked a little anguished, as he knew that he might fail to impress Tylon in that test, being conscious that he was in Furzomia, the natural habitat of the warriors. Tylon could read his mind and smilingly he told them that the tests might not just be about physical fitness, as the mental readiness was an equally important feature to reckon with.

"I am not sure if your mother would allow you to take part even if you are the most competent warrior. She might not take a risk of losing you again," Tylon said looking at Hidas.

"I'll convince her. Don't you worry about her, she is a brave, remarkable lady," Hidas answered confidently. Tylon just smiled, without challenging the opinion of his son. He retired from the room, telling them that he had an audience with the king the next day. The king wanted to introduce him to someone who had also migrated from Elbon long ago.

"Do you know the person?" Hidas asked.

"Not until I see him!" Tylon said with laughter. "I can't trust on my memory any longer."

Both Hidas and Beran looked at each other and smiled, not knowing who it could be. Beran was anxious, fearing the meeting of two people, who both suffered from loss of memory, one because of old age and the other because of traumatic and tough circumstances, which had erased the certain parts of the memory. What was to happen if none of them was to recognise the other? Beran thought, not liking the idea.

Tylon tried to remember the old man standing before his eyes but couldn't place him anywhere. He had a vague feeling of having seen the man. Silos was standing and looking from time to time at the eminent person in a discrete way, but there was little for him to perceive. Old age was taking its toll and he had already gone almost blind, a fact he had been hiding from his surroundings. If he did that out of vanity or as a denial of the truth, he couldn't tell. King Sarastan had deliberately not mentioned that it was the former king of Elbon. He was to introduce to Silos, but by looking at his behaviour, he was forced to believe that the old man either lied about his being from Elbon, or that he had some grudge against Tylon.

"Didn't you recognise our eminent friend, who is also from Elbon?" King Sarastan couldn't stop himself from asking.

"I'm afraid I have grown too old." Silos spoke bowing his head.

"Aren't we all getting old? The time is the only eternal youth." Tylon said. His words fell like bombs on Silos. He looked stunned. He moved closer to the place from where the sound had come from.

"Who's it? Please say something more. Please continue talking." Silos begged. Tylon was astonished at the reaction of the old stranger.

"Do I know you?" Tylon asked.

"If I am right in my presumption, then your excellency does know this humble servant. O, how happy your voice has

339

made me. How lucky I am to meet you once again?" Silos cried bitterly.

"I'm pleased to know that you are my old friend. Forgive me for not remembering but please do refresh my failing memory." Tylon was embarrassed.

"How can your highnesses forget the servant, who was once entrusted with the most honourable task to accomplish?"

"And what was that task?" Tylon asked with a smile.

"Oh, heavens, you really don't remember." Silos's shocked voice was being felt by all present.

There fell a silence, before they could hear the subdued sobs of Silos.

"Your excellency, I was the lucky fellow who was entrusted with the youngest prince." Silos was telling him, trying to recollect his turbulent emotions. There was a lightening in Tylon's mind, a flashback, he saw the face of Silos and remembered every little detail, even the shaking of his own very hands, while handing his youngest one to the man, who looked so overwhelmed by the responsibility.

Tylon got up from his seat and rushed to Silos. He almost lifted him up from the place, where he was down on his knees.

"Tell me where my son is? How is he? Where is he?" Tylon was very emotional. He was going on repeating the name of his youngest son.

"Your highness, I'm sorry to inform you that for the sake of his security I had changed his name. His name is Beran now," Silos said with bowed head.

"Beran! Which Beran? Is it the same young man I know?" Tylon was confused.

"Does that young man know that you are his Excellency the king of Elbon?" Silos asked.

"Yes, he does," Tylon told him.

"Then he can't be your prince, as your son has the full knowledge of his relation to you," Silos told him. Tylon was so zealous to find and meet his son that he begged Silos to bring his son as quickly as possible to him.

"Does he live with you?" Sarastan asked him, becoming happy for his friend and guest Tylon.

"No, your highness, he lives here in your capital. I met him last night I promise to look for him or I have to ask from his friend Hidas."

"How do you know, Hidas?" Tylon was now convinced that he had already met his youngest son.

"I met the young man already in Kildia, when he came there few months back." Silos was surprised at how and from where Tylon had heard the name of that young fellow. Tylon explained to him about Hidas and the both men rejoiced once again at that great happening.

"Don't worry about introducing us to each other. I'll take care of the matter myself." Tylon said with tearful eyes; he felt overjoyed. He couldn't find enough words to thank Silos for the wonderful job he had accomplished, by not only protecting his precious son but for raising him into a wise, knowledgeable young man. He promised to call for him and his wife to thank them both for having succeeded in the great task and for giving him such a tremendous favour.

That same evening Beran was called by Tylon to come and visit him, he had no idea that Tylon had learned anything about him. He was sure that Tylon wanted to discuss his meeting with the king. Tylon looked little different, when he gazed at him.

"Today I met your father," Tylon spoke.

"Isn't he an amazing man?" Hidas said looking happy that he had met Beran's father. Tylon looked at Hidas and said,

"I didn't know that you two had already met." "He is a remarkable man, isn't he?" Beran agreed with him, without showing much enthusiasm. He was looking sadly at Tylon, disappointed that he had failed to recognise the man, who had been once entrusted with such a tremendous responsibility. He saw the moment come and go, of his getting reunited with each other in a natural manner.

"There is something which puzzles me though," Tylon said

looking directly at Beran, which remained silent.

"What's that?" Haliba asked.

"His father is a strange man; he disclaimed his fatherhood in the meeting, asserting that Beran knew well about his real parents," Tylon said putting stress on his each word. Both Haliba and Hidas looked at him in disbelief.

"Is that really true?" Haliba questioned, but Beran remained sitting with bowed head.

"Who are your parents, my son? Are you ashamed of them? Did they hurt you so you don't want to mention them?" Haliba could remember his jokes, where he asked her to adopt him.

Beran tried to open his mouth but couldn't utter a word.

"He might be ashamed of his parents but we are proud of our wonderful son." Tylon said with a trembling voice and they all turned to each other in shock, not believing what Tylon had just said. Tylon was standing with open arms, ready to embrace Beran, his youngest son. The most shocked was Hidas, who was unable to grasp that the whole scene before his eyes could possibly be true. He had known and liked Beran from some time, but to know that he was even his youngest brother was a fact, too much to digest. Haliba was embracing to Beran and crying, sobbing and caressing him, all at the same time. No one could imagine the joy of Haliba and Tylon. Hidas on the other hand had gone outside the room; he needed some time to grasp, what went on there. Beran had difficulty in explaining that how could he be so cruel and cold not to tell them that he was their long lost son.

"Believe me, that it wasn't an easy task. I did it mostly for the sake of Hidas." He tried to explain his otherwise strange behaviour.

Tylon and Haliba were so happy about getting back their two sons, but somewhere they were still suppressing the loss of their middle child. They had gotten the renewed hope of even getting him back soon. They had complete trust in the mercy of gods, which had been gracious to their other two children.

They knew that it was in their control but only the right time could present them with the opportunity and that time was approaching more speedily than they could ever hope for. Perhaps even more quickly than the armies of Pampicilos, which were entering Furzomia from three directions? King Sarastan had waked up from his slumber like illusion about the deceitful devil, Pampicilos, who had read between the lines and understood the petrified feelings of Sarastan. His intelligence reports were all indicating that Furzomia was not ready for the challenge. Despite all three forces of Kildia, traders and Furzomians together, they were insufficient a force to stand and resist his gigantic armies. He understood that Sarastan wanted little respite, in order to prepare himself for the task, but Pampicilos was not to give him that chance. He had decided to hit the kingdom when she was unprepared and unable to defend itself. King Sarastan was anxious, and asked for advice from Tylon, who was of the opinion that they needed to defend the kingdom, not on the borders but to guard only the larger towns.

"We have just enough manpower to accomplish that," Tylon told him.

"How am I to divide the troops in different groups? To whom should I give the command of these units?"

Tylon was surprised to listen to all his questions, as those were the most obvious choices. Who could be the best person to discuss all those questions with than the commander of the army? Tylon was shocked to hear that the army commander was of the opinion that a combat was out of question, and the only remaining possibility was to surrender like their neighbours did, or to flee out of the country.

"What did you tell him?" Tylon asked.

"The only thing I could do to that coward, I have placed him in prison." King Sarastan told him.

"Do you mind if we ask the young men, how we are to proceed?" Tylon asked.

"You mean Hidas and Beran?" the king looked terror-stricken.

Tylon could understand his anguish and fears about giving the defence of his country in the hands of two inexperienced young men. He tried to convince Sarastan that he had nothing to lose, as the enemy was moving with the speed of a storm towards his capital and he was without any plan of his own, so practically the battle was already lost. Reluctantly and with a heavy heart the king agreed to listen to the ideas of Hidas and Beran.

Hidas kept listening, when Beran was telling about his opinion to divide the defending force into four parts. The lion's share of that force was to remain in the capital and wait for the enemy there. The other three groups were to meet those marching armies in the places, where they were weaker and vulnerable.

"Why not to meet them already at the frontiers?" asked one of the commanders.

"For the reason that these armies are difficult to combat, when they are strong, fresh and well fed. But the long tiresome march would take toll on their bodies and nerves. We would do everything in our power to make them anxious, alert and worried about some ambush, cutting all access to water supplies, and combating them when they would be weak, tired, and suffering from hunger and thirst," Beran suggested. There was a hot discussion, where everyone gave the arguments against or in favour of the suggestions put forward by Beran.

"Why divide the force when there is an apparent danger of getting weaker?" Tylon asked.

Beran said that the enemy was pressing from many sides and that fact required matching moves. The enemy needed to be in the dark about the strength and numbers of the armies at their disposal. Besides that, the diversity of those units required that the people in command to be the ones, who knew them well.

20

The person, who had been second in command was quickly promoted to the post of commander in chief of the royal armies, Herzod was given the command of traders while one portion of the army was entrusted to Shapario and Kestarius. Hidas and Beran were to attach themselves to the Kildian units. The emergency meeting was concluded, and measures were taken to meet the challenges of the day. The Furzomian warriors were quickly formed into organised, combatant units, who were to defend the town in command of Kestarius while another unit was to defend the water supplies few miles away, led by Shapario. The other three bigger units were to engage the enemy, wherever it saw it fit. Despite all the measures taken, the king remained very anxious, he had little confidence and hope of succeeding in defending the country. There was hardly any time to send the spies to get the required information, so the only thing possible for them was to wait patiently. Pampicilos's armies were penetrating into Furzomia from different directions, not only to confuse and intimidate its victims but also with a hope to paralyse the defence of the country. They were aware that the army of the Furzomia was little and demoralised. Its citizens were strong warriors but too disorganised to meet a well-trained and well-organised army. The traders and Kildians they were not even considered as a major threat because the forces, which had earlier fled from the terror of those armies weren't worth even a thought. It was that confidence, which made those armies move fearlessly deep into Furzomia. They were moving from three directions, fully determined to encircle the entire country in an iron grip. The absence of any resistance was not anything to worry about as they were quickly getting used to getting all the achievements without paying any price; the victories were always offered to them on a plate, so there wasn't anything unusual in it. Their only concern was water supplies and their advanced units had secured that a few days earlier. What they were unaware of was the fact that all those advanced units had been either wiped out or were taken prisoner by the Furzomian army. If the advancing armies had counted on a complete surrender from the defending armies of Furzomia, they were to get their biggest surprise as the resistance they were to meet, was not only to be fierce but even the most organised they ever could have imagined. Their army advancing to the capital could never make their way to its destination, as they had to fight for every inch of the way. They were deprived of water, supplies, and sleep, as the enemy was not quiet after the falling of the night, giving them the dread of sudden attack during the night. The strange thing was that those soldiers were avoiding any direct confrontation; they remained invisible, only coming and attacking them when they were vulnerable. The other armies were completely unaware of the fact that their comrades were facing serious problems. They too were facing some opposition but the resistance was not alarming, exactly as they had hoped. The only problem for them was the supply of water, which they had to fight for on each step. They were astonished as to what had happened to the advance units, which were to secure those sources. The only commander, who was worried about the development, was that who had the experience of entering and suffering a defeat earlier in those tracts. He had been pardoned by Pampicilos for his mistake, only because the other commanders gave their assurances that he made that mistake with a good intention. Pampicilos was in the middle of a new expedition and didn't want to demoralise his commanders and that was the real reason of his forgiving the commander. The commander was the only one, who kept blowing the warning signal and asked his colleagues to re-evaluate their decision to advance to the depths from where there was no return. The other commanders were aware of his anxiety and translated that it was a natural psychological consequence of his earlier experienced disaster. The man had almost brought a ruin on them all by his unauthorised entry into Furzomia, and now he wanted to bring a catastrophe by retreating without permission. They did have the permission from Pampicilos to retreat if the calculations they made were proven to be wrong or if there was an apparent danger of losing the war. Pampicilos couldn't afford of a complete destruction of his armies. But there was no such indication, which could confirm that the commander's intuition was genuine, so it was decided to press ahead in the fashion they had earlier planned. They could see that the opposition wasn't persistent or even organised; instead there were pockets of resistance every now and then, which grew stronger the moment they got closer to some important town, where they could get food and water, forcing them to abandon their search for those precious provisions. They were time pressed and had to move on if they were to enclose the circle, to surround the main combatant units, which were supposed to defend the capital.

When these two portions of the army reached the capital, they were exhausted but what really surprised them was the fact that the third army had failed to reach at its given destination, a worrisome development, which they had not calculated before. They decided to camp and wait for their comrades coming from the third direction before they would attack the capital. There was nervousness and even fear as no one could tell, what had happened to the third army. They were afraid to send someone to get the news as it entailed a danger of falling in the hands of the enemy. They all were jumpy and weary as they stood not so far from the main force of their adversaries. They were in a desperate need of water and food and had hoped of finding it from their friends of third army. There was a silence, making them more frightened as they had gotten used to of noise in the nights. The silence made their hearts tremble. Most of them couldn't sleep all night and were almost dying of exhaustion, sleep, thirst and hunger, when they were attacked from all directions. They saw warriors coming from all directions and not only from the direction of the town as they had been expecting them to come from. It was early morning, and they had no idea as to what kind of threat loomed over their heads. There was a war cry from all sides and a fierce fighting broke out. The invaders were fighting not for the dominance as they had initially come there for but were fighting for their lives. The both sides were fighting relentlessly, without showing any signs of giving up. The defenders were fighting bravely despite being outnumbered by the invaders. It was midday, and there was no sign of that struggle coming to an end. Suddenly, a war cry was heard once again and the forces of Furzomia started withdrawing, still facing their enemy armies. They were retreating in an organised manner, still alert and ready to engage themselves in the combat, had the enemy chose to do so. But the armies of Pampicilos were too exhausted to chase their adversaries. They all looked relieved from the end of combat and wished to recover from the initial shock and exhaustion. They could see that Furzomians were going back to the directions they had earlier come from, the fact, which alarmed them greatly. It seemed that they themselves had been surrounded by their enemy, and could face a serious threat if the third army failed to come and join them very soon.

Thrice in four days these forces of Pampicilos were being attacked by the small but daring warriors of Furzomia, which were always taking them by surprise, alternating the timings of their attacks, choosing the weapons of engagement and directions to attack from, always leaving them in dark as to what they should expect the next time. The huge size of these armies was becoming a disadvantage, as it required large quantities of provisions, which at the moment was impossible to secure. There was still no news from the third army, making the forces of Pampicilos get more and more nervous. The time was running out, and they had to act quickly if not all their might was to disintegrate right before their eyes. They

couldn't afford to stay and wait there, exposed to all kinds of dangers and practically starving while the enemy had stopped all ways leading to the sources of supplies. The fifth day, the commanders had decided to move forward, not to the capital but towards the direction their third army was supposed to advance from. If the enemy had engaged that army of theirs, it was wise to add their strength by joining them. What really worried them was their ignorance about the situation and an apparent danger that they were to be chased by the warriors of Furzomia.

The armies of Pampicilos set off in the late night, making as little noise as it was possible to avoid an early detection. The cover of the darkness was to give them some advantages to move without much danger of getting engaged in a battle. By the morning time, they had come to the place, where the third army was camped. It was a hilly area, which required special vigilance. Their soldiers had just come down into the valley, when the arrows started raining over their heads. It wasn't difficult for them to realise what had hindered their third army from reaching the capital as planned. They could see that the narrow passages, poor visibility, and many other factors made the task almost impossible.

"Why did you come this way, instead of attacking the capital if you had succeeded reaching up to there?" The commanders of the third army demanded angrily. The generals from the first and the second army told them about the poor conditions they had earlier faced there near the capital and asked about the conditions of their provisions and felt happy to learn that the position of supplies was more than satisfactory. The units that were engaged with logistic support were successfully providing all the needs from the villages around. Their main headache wasn't food or drink but how to cross that difficult terrain.

"We shall ultimately suppress the tiny resistance. All we need to do is to wait with patience." One of the Generals said hopefully, but it seemed no one else shared his enthusiasm. They all were aware of their limitations. They could endure till the autumn before the snow came to those high altitudes and made their lives miserable. With the coming of the snow and cold, their supplies were to diminish drastically, and they were to die of starvation and cold, even if they were spared from the attacks of the enemy.

"But they are so few. We can easily destroy them now, when we have gotten united with all our units." The general who had remained optimistic told them.

"Not any longer, are they a tiny force. If they are as clever as they have proved until now, certainly they would have consolidated their positions and might in one place as the only danger that can threaten them, is right here." The other commander told to the naïve general and smiled bitterly.

"What are we supposed to do?" one of the commanders asked with anxiety.

"I'm afraid we have not many choices, but to retreat and come some other day."

"If we are still alive after this humiliation."

"Don't worry about your lives, the king shall not kill all of us if he seeks a revenge," said one of the commanders with confidence. The others agreed with his analysis, but still decided to exaggerate the story of their defeat by reporting the number of Furzomian forces to manifold. They had decided to report that the destruction of Furzomia was only possible if they were to prepare cleverly and increase the number of their troops to at least double the size. Half of them were to engage the enemy in combat and the other half to secure the supplies of water and food and of course with an additional lesson to remember was that they were not to cross those hills again. The large army of Pampicilos was retreating without achieving any of its goals. They had lost many of their soldiers, though it wasn't the scarcity of soldiers, which was putting them on the run. They were clever enough to retreat in a secure fashion, leaving behind a substantial number of soldiers to wait and guard the place, to avoid any unpleasant surprise from the rear. No one pursued those armies, which were heading in the direction of Elbon, taking the wounds of humiliation and fears of punishment hanging over their lowered heads.

There was a shock in the air, not only seizing the hearts of the soldiers and commanders of the army of Pampicilos, but even stunning the fighters of Furzomia, who together with the help of their guests from Kildia and Parnvan, had defeated and chased out the army, which was many fold greater than their own. The defending forces were to stand alert and not blow the signal that the danger was over, as yet. They were to wait until the last of the invader had left the territory of Furzomia behind, to be sure that the enemy was really retreating and that it was not some tactical draw back.

No words ever could describe the euphoria, which was to be seen at that time in Furzomia. The warriors of that country were parading on the streets of that joyful town. There were dances, laughter and other expressions of joy. The town was full of locals and foreigners alike, which celebrated the unprecedented victory over such a great army. All taverns and drinking holes were filled to the brim with all kinds of people. There were those which had taken part in those remarkable battles and prevailed, but then there were even those who had not taken part but witnessed the miracle of their times, and watched the armies of Pampicilos running, holding the tails between their legs and felt proud of their country, capable to provide such a scene. But perhaps no one was happier than king Sarastan, who was the least optimistic of them all. He had agreed to fight that formidable force only because there was no other way open to him. Had it not been the obstinate support of Tylon, surely he too had given up the kingdom without a fight. He was standing in his large balcony and watching the parade of all the forces at his disposal, which were returning in a proud manner, saluting their king, the absolute monarch, offering him their full allegiance and loyalty. The glowing face of the king was content, and silently he was thanking the authorities of high above, which had made the victory possible. He had asked Tylon to stand by his side, but he had not accepted the offer. According to him it was the moment of the king and no one else, but he needed to stand and get all the tributes of his people and the armed forces.

Tylon stood with his wife and watched the parade from his own quarters. He smiled seeing his sons pass before him. There wasn't anything in the world than the knowledge that the miracle had been only made possible due to his two sons. His head was high, and his mind was full of pride as he saw them pass and wave at them with a smile. He turned with a smile to Haliba, who was as proud as him. But he couldn't help detecting two glittering tears in her beautiful eyes.

"Isn't this wonderful to watch our kids coming back from the battleground?" Tylon cried.

"Yes milord! My heart is so content with seeing them coming victorious." Haliba said weakly.

"Then why those tears my heart?" Haliba was quite for a moment then she spoke with a painful expression on her face.

"My heart would have ten times happier if only I could find my third child accompanying my other children. It was just the memory of him that has made me sad." Haliba said withdrawing from the large balcony.

"Don't be sad, I am sure that one day we shall get united with him, as well. Then the circle would be complete. He is the only missing link now," Tylon said holding her shaky hand.

"Sometimes I wonder the meaning behind all these happenings." Haliba was tearful.

"No one knows about the meanings of the events but why to waste the energies on the things incomprehensible."

"You are absolutely right," Haliba said with a smile, wiping away her tears. "You go on watching the parade; I go down and see if the food is ready. Soon my kids would come so I want it to be ready by then."

"I'll not take long and join you," Tylon said before going back to the parade.

Hidas and Beran were entering into their portion of the royal palace along with some friends. They all looked very happy and content. The carefree sounds of their laughter were filling the otherwise serene and calm atmosphere with the palace. They all were coming to join them for dinner, which was prepared in the supervision of Aloha and her daughter Davreen, who had become the integral members of Haliba's household.

"How pleased I become to hear the happiness dancing in your home." Aloha said, and Tylon and Haliba both smiled, agreeing with her that their luck had changed.

"Our luck started shining on us again the day I met you Aloha." Haliba said with a smile.

"Don't say that! Didn't I meet you on the worst day of your life?" Aloha reminded.

"You did! But was that not so that the day my luck as a queen was eclipsed, but after meeting you, my luck as a being started shining again." Haliba gave her interpretation, making Aloha laugh. "That is the reason we all love you. You are eternally optimistic, the sunshine of our dark lives."

They were busy talking when the young men entered in the dinning room. They all got quiet finding Tylon and Haliba standing there.

"I believe that you two were invited to the dinner and not the whole army," Tylon joked, making them all laugh in somewhat dampened way.

"Don't mind, he loves making jokes, especially to his loved ones." Haliba said leading them to the dinner table. All together there were five of them. She had seen all the friends of her sons, but there was one she had not seen earlier.

"I haven't had the chance to meet you earlier." Haliba turned and asked the young fellow.

The young man got little embarrassed and introduced himself as a friend of Beran, who had once saved his life.

"That's an interesting story. I would like to hear it some day. I knew that my son is a courageous man," Haliba said patting the back of Beran, who was trying to stop his laughter.

"No mother, you misunderstand. I didn't save his life against some powerful enemies but just took him to a person who could treat him against the snake bite," The others were laughing as well, but Haliba was determined to call him a brave man anyway.

"What? Are you not to join us in the dinner?" Hidas

protested.

"You came late, and we couldn't sit hungry and wait for you. We have eaten." Haliba told.

"Don't say that you have eaten as well?" Beran asked from Aloha, who affirmed by smiling.

"Now have a nice meal, and we can join you for tea later on." Haliba said and left the room along with her husband.

"I am so very happy for you two for having united with your parents. You are the luckiest persons on earth to have such great parents," Shamon told them.

At the tea table, Haliba asked Shamon about his father, how he was as she had not seen him for some time.

"He's fine; didn't you see him in the parade today?" Shamon asked her. She told him that she had not watched the whole parade.

"Herzod isn't his real father." Beran told her. "His real father passed away, when Shamon was a little kid."

"I'm sorry to hear that, but Herzod has never mentioned it." Haliba was really sorry to learn that he was an orphan. She was looking at him with pitiable eyes while he was sipping his tea, unaware of her gaze. All of the sudden she saw something and became frozen. She kept looking for a while before she almost jumped from her seat and went near to Shamon and started touching the locket in his neck.

"Where did you get this?" Haliba asked hysterically.

"Why do you ask?" Shamon was looking at her with big eyes as he watched her trembling body. "This locket and some other jewellery were found beside my dead father's body, he had it in a bag. Those things had been handed over to me by Herzod a couple of weeks ago," Shamon told her.

"Please show me the rest of jewellery and I need to talk to Herzod immediately. Can you do that for me?" Haliba was shaking violently. Tylon came near to her, asking her to calm down and take it easy for what ever it was. She didn't tell him what she suspected; she didn't want to raise the expectations of Tylon and wanted to be certain before even mentioning the possibility of finding her remaining son. Shamon was still confused when he went to bring Herzod.

Haliba was straightforward when she put the questions to Herzod, asking about the conditions, age, and appearance of the child he had found in the desert so many years ago. He told her the entire story as he remembered it and confessed that not knowing the real name, he had given a new name to the child he had found and adopted. He even described the dead man for her, how he looked, what he wore and other details, which could be of any help.

Herzod wondered the reason of all questioning, but she was too eager to know all and seemed to have little time for his questions.

"Would you please mind showing me the rest of the jewellery?" She asked Herzod, who in turn looked at Shamon and signed him to do as she wished. Haliba looked at the jewellery bag, and tears started flowing down her sad face. The shaking of her body was more apparent than before. Tylon and the rest were watching her intensely without understanding what went on. She got up from her seat and went towards Shamon. She was walking as being drunk. She got closer and took him in her embrace.

"My child, my child," she said, kissing, caressing and crying all in one time. "Let the whole world know that I'm extremely happy today. My remaining missing son has come home. Welcome my son. Welcome home my son." Haliba was crying with joy.

"Calm down, my love. Are you sure about the matter?" Tylon asked holding her; he too was shaky by that time. Beran, Hidas, and Herzod were just trying to smile; they all were equally shocked by the declaration of Haliba.

"Let us be sure first, the jewellery could have been stolen by some stranger, who later on couldn't survive the tough conditions of the desert." Tylon was more careful than her as he couldn't remember the man he had entrusted his son to.

"My son had a big birth mark on his back, so big that it could be taken as a shining sun." Haliba told them and waited impatiently for Shamon to take his shirt off. They all waited in anticipation, holding their breath. There was a cry of relief and joy, when they all could see a big birthmark on Shamon's back, which wasn't glowing at all, but perhaps it did in the eyes of a mother.

Now that Tylon and Haliba had gotten all their sons back, they considered themselves the luckiest and most content people in the world. They wished that it would remain that way for the rest of their lives. There wasn't anything in the world, which was worth sacrificing it for. No kingdom, no lust, no compelling need for revenge could make them endanger their happiness, so they tried to convince their princes that they needed to look forward and not behind, but they all were determined to seek justice. Elbon was their home, their cradle and ancestral heritage, which they couldn't promise to relinquish. There was no way that they would forgive the perpetrators of their deplorable crimes. Tylon and Haliba were not worried about anything else than the fear that the struggle to gain back the realm was ultimately to give birth internal rivalries, which could cause the princes to become enemies after some time. Hidas was more agitated than the other two of the princes, but he was less verbal than his brothers. The hearts of Tylon and Haliba were filled with pride, when they saw their kids work and move in unison, they had a wish that it was to remain that way forever and ever. King Sarastan was also happy and had discussed the possibility of marrying his daughter to Hidas. Tylon told him that he would feel honoured, but it needed the decision of Hidas, who had abandoned such plans till he was to destroy the power of Pampicilos and wipe out the kingdom of Razila.

"We all know that there is nothing, which can make Hidas happier than to marry Danor, but unfortunately, we have to wait for that day," Tylon told him, not very convinced that it could come that soon.

"You really believe that these young boys can accomplish such a great task?" King Sarastan was doubtful.

"I don't have any doubt of that, the only worry I have is time. It might take many years."

"But I can't wait for many years to give the hand of my daughter in marriage to him." Sarastan was honest.

"I know." Tylon seemed depressed.

The three princes were not sitting idle for a minute; they seemed to be busy doing something all the time. Hidas had requested Shapario and Kestarius to work fulltime in their workshops, making weapons day and night. All the other blacksmiths in the country were given the task of producing large quantities of weaponry. There was a stress on the quality, and no compromise was allowed when it came to the question of sub-standard weapons. To further enhance the production, special permission was obtained from the king to bring in blacksmiths from the other countries. The preparations were in full swing. Some weapons were even brought by the traders from far away countries. There wasn't any shortage of eager to join warriors, who were offered good wages so that the armies were expanding with an incredible speed. There were many who tried to warn the king that by allowing the three ambitious foreign princes to build the army of their own, he was digging his own grave, but the king was not worried at all. He knew that as long as Tylon lived, none of the princes could harm him and his kingdom. He could trust his royal intuition along with Tylon and Haliba. King Sarastan thought to himself that he was getting old and had no heir of his own, so he had anyway planned to leave the kingdom to Danor and her future husband, which he really wished was Hidas. He even secretly hoped that his other two daughters would be married to the other two princes, but perhaps it was too much a wish to be true. He had noticed that both of the young princes were taking more interest in their war preparation than anything else. How that gigantic enterprise was financed, was the most astonishing thing for everyone , especially the traders, who were not even contacted to give any donations. Shamon had taken the entire responsibility of providing the needed money, how was he to do that he was not even worried about. He was confident that the money was to find its way to him in one way or the other, and it really did in some mysterious way. Sometimes he made a tremendous profit from the goods he sold, at other times he would get unexpected donations from his community, but the biggest resource of his money supply had remained secret even to himself. He just would get it waiting for him to pick, whenever it was drying up. The last time he had found a big treasure, consisting of gold and precious stones, which he had traded in some far away, land, where they were in big demand. Shamon didn't know from where he had earned the right to get unlimited resources, he thought it merely a co-incidence and felt happy for his good luck. Everyone around him envied his ability to attract as much money as he wanted to, more from the community of traders, who hadn't stopped considering him one of their own, and went on loving him despite the envy they feel in their hearts at his tendency to get tremendous amounts of money. Only Beran knew the secret of Shamon's access to the source, which was much greater than to earn money. He had chosen the creative energies of Senklour, which were capable of creating anything in their world, but in order to accomplish that, one needed knowledge, which Shamon lacked completely. He was the master of those wonderful powers, which could change the face of earth, and he was using them in his own primitive way. He was the centre of all economic supremacy. Shamon didn't even remember his choosing that gift from the magical land of Senklour, not to mention the caution and warning, which was attached to his choice.

In his physical mind, he could not retain the words of those beings, which had furnished him with those rays that made it possible to get whatever he wanted and wished. He had been told that those energies were not to be used for selfish purposes but for the general good of the whole, may that whole be a smaller group or the one as large as which covered a nation. He was being told that the selfish uses were not to benefit him at all as it would cause unhappiness and other disasters, as a natural consequence. The beings had given the parable of the body, and its mechanism, they had likened those energies with the bloodstream and its given course. As the heart pumps the blood to supply the needed nutrition for the entire body and to return back to the heart to repeat the process again and again, so was he to use the energy for the whole. He was cautioned, not to allow any stoppage in the flow of that force, which was at his disposal. It was like the flow of the water, which created currents but stank if it got static. Shamon had neither time nor any reason to ponder upon those erased warnings, which went on existing in his mind, though, so deep down that he hardly was aware of them.

21

The kingdom of Furzomia was getting so vibrant, healthy, and strong that people from far and near were attracted to it. It had everything to offer, what their hearts desired. It had an abundance of everything; it had the security and most of all a healthy economic condition. There were plenty of jobs, a lot of opportunities to earn a good living. The wages were not only enough to live a comfortable life, but one could even save. That was without a doubt an unprecedented and unheard thing for people. The soldiers of the newly formed army were already courageous warriors; all they needed was to learn discipline and to work in cooperation with others, a need to learn to obey the orders of their superiors without question. A word had been spread among the citizens of Kildia, and even Elbon that the days of their miseries were approaching an end. All they needed was to endure with patience another few days. That was done to raise the expectancy and to make it difficult for Pampicilos to get a popular support from his subjects. Beran wanted the masses to know that the great change was in making and that the days of the tyrant were coming to an end. Pampicilos was so furious about all those rumours, which were circulating in the width and breadth of his large empire, which he had dreams to expand even further. He was equally busy in expanding his already large army. This time the expansion was based more on compulsions and capricious activities than the voluntary enjoining the army, he sought in the earlier days of his adventure and was proud of. There wasn't enough money to fund the whole venture; the treasuries of the countries had been unable to sustain the huge army, the main cause of Pampicilos's decision to attack Parnvan and Kildia. But he had so far failed to achieve any of his given goals. His all hopes were now to conquer Furzomia, which had grown so rich in the matter of a few months. Pampicilos was certain that it was due to the immense and inexhaustible treasures of the Parnvanian traders, which had made their new country the most attractive place in the whole region. He was aware that his army needed false hopes and promises regarding future if they were to join him in his ambition to conquer Furzomia, the land of absolute riches, as the recent legends placed it. He wasn't worried about the ordinary soldiers, which could be easily recruited from all parts of his country, voluntarily or by compulsion, really mattered little. Pampicilos was a clever king who wouldn't give up his dream of conquest just because there was a shortage of money. He called for his treasurer and asked about the affairs of the state, who told him that the treasuries were almost empty, and there was no hope of filling them again, unless some drastic changes took place.

"Why can't we levy more taxes on people?" Pampicilos asked.

"As your highness knows, taxes that people can't afford to pay are useless. People are already crushed by the burden of existing taxes," the treasurer explained.

"What about the newly conquered lands?" the king asked.

"I dare not say much about the subject as it would require more expert views from someone in authority."

"You mean the chief minister?" the king asked. The treasurer kept silent. The chief minister was called and asked the same question. He told the king that the newly conquered countries were difficult to administer and collect taxes from for one single reason that they required a large number of troops to do the job while every single soldier was needed for the coming task of winning the land of Furzomia.

"As your highness is perfectly aware, the Furzomian armies are getting prepared day and night. They are producing the best possible weapons and have at their disposal the best warriors, so if we are to defeat them, we need every single soldier in the field." The chief minister told.

"But I need to pay these soldiers so that they wouldn't desert the army in the middle of the war." Pampicilos was desperate.

"We can find some short term solution to the problem," the chief minister said smilingly. Pampicilos was told that minting more coins easily could solve the problem. The king liked the idea as it wasn't the gold coins he used to pay to his soldiers, so they were not to notice that the salaries they received were without any real value. The situation was to become normal once they had gotten their hands on the enormous treasures of Furzomia, or at least it was, so the king of Elbon thought. The newly mint coins were to be spread in the whole of the country so that no one could refuse to accept them. They were to replace the older currencies of Parnvan and Kildia, a more natural way of stealing from the people of the conquered areas. All of the sudden, even Pampicilos had a lot of money at his disposal to expand the army and to buy equipments for them.

Hidas went around and inspected every single sword made for his soldiers; he was boiling with anger against his adversaries like Pampicilos and Razila. He was not negligent of the task ahead and kept honing his skills as often as possible. He had noticed that the recent events had given him much confidence even if his skills of weapons had not become any better. Shapario had urged him to forge another sword for himself, but Hidas remained rejective of the idea. He still believed that his sword was best in the world.

"Yeah, it has been the best sword in the world for quite a long time but no more." Even the best sword had the need to be changed according to the requirements and circumstances, he was being told by his old teacher and guardian. He reminded Hidas that he had grown heavier in the body and needed a heavier sword to meet the needs of the day, but he wouldn't give up his sword.

"No, it's perfectly alright for me. Don't worry; I'll change it if I feel it wasn't feeling right in my hands." Hidas insisted.

What Shapario didn't know was the fact that besides its apparent resemblance it wasn't the same sword he once had forged for Hidas, but was the sword Hidas had moulded from the metals brought from the depths of the earth, melted in the burning furnaces of mysterious fires of Senklour. That sword had not only riveted the power of mystifying flames, which had helped form the stars of heaven, but even also absorbed the fury and rage of virtue. The sword until then had remained untested, undetected of its characteristics, and most of all unappreciated, as no one knew about its magic, not even Hidas, who loved it for other reasons.

So jealous was Hidas of his sword that he thought for a long moment before handing his sword to Shapario.

"You are very eccentric person, do you know that?" Beran laughed at his reluctance. He wanted to make a little fun of him. Deep down, he could understand the true reason even more than Hidas himself knew. Shapario took the sword in his hands, weighed it and then waved it in the air and looked puzzled. Beran was watching the expressions of his face and knew what he was thinking at the moment. Shapario's sharp eyes were telling him the truth that the object in his hand was not the same as he had once created.

"Did you by any chance change it?" Shapario asked Hidas.

"What you mean? Of course not, why should I do it?" Hidas was astonished by his question.

Shapario didn't say anything more, but Beran enjoyed seeing his puzzlement.

The sword that was going to change the course of history, the sword, capable to conquer the worlds was in front of their eyes, but they all were blind to that fact, except to him who couldn't reveal the truth to anyone, not even to his brother, the holder of that magic sword. Hidas had to live with his ignorance as Shamon had to live with his regarding the money supply. And there lied their tests and trials. Both of his brothers had chosen to deal with powers of incredible potencies, though different in implication and application. The both of them were to live with the knowledge that they were powerful, without actually knowing the cause of their strength. The power they were to possess could not always be a blessing and not always to be beneficiary as it looked in the first glance. The powers they were to command were to be destructive if they didn't control them with the purity of their hearts, and didn't seek the middle path of balance. The middle path was neither the way of the warrior nor the way of a pacifist, but a road, where one needed to choose from the best available options. Not clinging to one or the other indefinitely. The power was corrupting when it was detached from wisdom, and they both had not even learned how to seek that. Beran was worried for his brothers as they were doomed to remain ignorant about the weighing responsibilities, which were placed on their shoulders. He wished and hoped that his both brothers were to remain noble and sensible, even long after, they had achieved their own kingdoms. He remembered the cautions of the mysterious beings about his own responsibility to make a balance as he was the only conscious cell of the trio. But how was he to safeguard his brothers from faking into arrogance and misuse was a question without any answers.

It didn't take long before they felt ready to proceed to their set target, to face the army of Pampicilos. They had the knowledge that he was at his strongest at his home grounds, and it was deemed wiser to deal with him in the places his forces were weaker, unpopular or both and where could they find a weaker spot than Kildia, where the local population was moaning under the yoke of slavery, economic depression, and other excesses of the occupying force. People remembered the good old days and wished that they had been prepared to face the invaders. They were terribly sorry for not having taken any interest in the defences of their country, but it was too late for any regrets as the evil plight had them in an iron grip. These people were equally angry with their former king who had fled the country without a fight. Hidas had wanted directly to attack the head of the serpent, but both Shamon and Beran wanted to first drive the armies of Pampicilos from the northeastern borders. Accomplishing that could remove their fear of getting attacked from that direction, while they were busy fighting the huge army of Pampicilos in Elbon.

Hidas had insisted that he should lead the expedition against Kildia. Tylon and the king thought that he was too young to bring about such a task and wanted that some more experienced person took charge, but even people like Shapario and Kestarius supported Hidas, telling that the expedition was not that dangerous as everyone believed and could be easily handled by Hidas, who was getting more and more comfortable at the task of commanding the troops. Without any doubt he was a natural leader, with all the inherent qualities , he invoked the respect and trust of his soldiers, who were ready to follow him into the portals of hell if it was that he was to ask of them. Shapario was willing to accompany him as a foot soldier if Hidas wished so, but the king wanted him to stay behind and watch the borders to Elbon, from where the sudden attack could come as a reciprocal reaction. Tylon agreed to Hidas leading his forces but refused that all his sons joined each other in that mission. Shamon and Beran were to stay behind and do other duties and to continue their preparations for the final encounter.

Hidas was taking an insignificant army with him as he was worried about the attack, which might come from Elbon. He was confident that his tiny but effective army could beat the corrupt forces of Pampicilos in the land, where they were without any public support. Sarastan had insisted that he took most of the soldiers from Kildian units, who were equally well trained and well disciplined. He wished Hidas to do so as they not only knew the territory better than anyone else, but also because they all hated the enemy, which had occupied their fatherland. The army he was leading knew each and every inch of their country and intended to use the knowledge as an advantage. They were moving lightly, as access to food and water was not any headache for them, because they knew exactly where to look and get it from. Hidas was eager to proceed towards his first mission ever. His face was glowing of hopefulness, and he looked confident about his success. The only person who shared his conviction was Beran, who came forward and bade him all the best, giving him the happy tidings of a certain victory.

"I am happy for your support and trust in me. But are you really sure that I can manage on my own?" Hidas asked in a whisper.

"Go in peace. May the support of gods be with you. As far as my conviction is concerned, I'm as sure of your success as I'm certain of death, which claims all in due time." Beran was unwavering.

"What gives you this conviction?" Hidas asked.

"It's a secret I can't reveal," Beran said, making Hidas laugh, who took it as a joke.

The news came much quicker than they had hoped; the army

of Pampicilos was aware of the movements of the insignificant force coming from Furzomia to attack them and awaited the arrival of that force at the border. There was a surprise and even contempt at the faces of the commanders, when they learned the number of soldiers, which were coming to fight with them. They were relieved to know that the enemy was overconfident about its ability to overcome such a huge army of theirs. They couldn't stop wondering what made those units of Furzomia that suicidal. The way those units were moving, it looked like as they were heading with an intention of a direct collision with them. The news that a young and inexperienced soldier led those forces was perhaps the answer to all their wonderings. The enemy had camped a few miles away from them, to rest for the night. They were not in any hurry to annihilate that tiny force and decided to wait for them to come into Kildia as they had no authority to go into Furzomia on their own, They were anxious about any surprise attack by the enemy during the cover of the night. The guards were placed everywhere, to inform the slightest movement of the enemy around their own camps.

The night was as calm as they had hoped it to be and at daybreak they re-arrayed themselves for the final countdown. But waiting for the movement was prolonging without any end, making the commanders irritated. They were loosing their patience, wondering what kept the enemy lingering. Could that be that the young foolish commander of the enemy troops was getting cold feet and was reluctant to attack, or could it be that they were waiting for reinforcement? It was too risky to send the spies into Furzomia in the broad daylight to get the fresh news. All day they waited, but nothing happened. At dusk, they were more nervous than ever as it seemed that the enemy was playing some kind of games with them, pushing them to uncertainty, making them nervous and alert, tiring them out without engaging them in combat. They had not expected that from their daring enemy, but still they were sure about the size and strength of the force at their disposal and had no fear in their hearts, which was to creep in their whole beings when the terrible news was broken to the commanders that the enemy force had vanished from the scene, leaving no clues as to which direction they had gone.

"Think, if they have gone behind our lines." One of the commanders was dreaded.

"It's not possible." The other said. There was a hot debate, which followed as to what was possible and what was not. They all agreed that the disappearing of that tiny but robust force was a bad omen. There was little that could be done except to search for that enemy force, but how could they do it without splitting their own force. That was a bad choice, which was to deprive them the clear advantage they had over its enemy. Reluctantly they decided to break their army into three groups. The main part was to stay where they were while the others tried to locate the whereabouts of the enemy and to call forth a reunification of the army before attacking the enemy. They believed that was the only option they had at their disposal. What they remained unaware of was that they were never going to get a chance to reunite. Hidas and his men were not so far away from them, in the rear of that gigantic army they had come to destroy, waiting for the right moment to achieve their goal.

It was midday when the army unit got sight of Hidas and his men, far behind their positions. They were stunned to see that the enemy forces had penetrated deep into the territory they controlled. They wondered how it could be possible without their knowledge. The commander detached few soldiers from the group and ordered them to ride to the main group with the news of finding the enemy, before trying to surround the enemy, which seemed to be not conscious that their presence behind the army positions had been detected.

They had blocked all the ways of escape for Hidas and his men and awaited the fortification.

The help they awaited never arrived. They could see that the enemy was now aware of being surrounded and stood ready to get engaged in a combat, but they had no desire to do so, as long as the reinforcement was not to come. The commanders were not aware that the enemy had already eliminated the soldiers, who were sent to accomplish the task. The nervousness of Pampicilos' army was great when the night was falling, what went on, they wondered. Why the other units were taking so long to come and join them in order to eliminate the tiny force, puzzling them. If they had feared that the enemy was to try to escape at night, they were proven wrong as the enemy chose to engage them in a fierce fight. Hidas and his men had attacked them without any forewarning. They had not expected such a ferocious attack by the enemy. The swords of the enemy were terrorising their hearts, especially the sword of Hidas was like a thunderbolt, sending shock waves in their ranks. The young man was ferocious, fighting with impossible speed and power. That vibrant person was a personification of a storm that was impossible to stop. The darkness was getting thicker, but the enemy soldiers seemed not to be bothered at all. The conditions which were supposed to be disadvantageous to them, they were converting into a benefit. They had not seen a force that potent and effective before. They kept perishing without any hope to face and overcome that tiny enemy. They felt support approaching them from the rear and rejoiced, but it was the other half of the enemy force, which had been out of sight. The attack from the rear made them completely hopeless.

Hidas and his men had destroyed the both parties searching for them and approached the main army in the middle of the day, standing there, eyeball to eyeball, without showing any signs of fear or nerviness. The smiles on their faces were sending waves of terror in the hearts of soldiers standing and looking at those far inferior numbers of the enemy. What made them so confident? Why did they choose to face them in the middle of the day instead of ambushing them, which could have been a more natural way of engagement? The fearlessness of the enemy was the biggest mystery.

"Get ready to die." One of the commanders challenged Hidas and his force.

"We are ready to embrace death, but are you?" Hidas asked with spite. He could see terror on the faces of the soldiers, who were not convinced of the cause they fought for. He had been waiting for the moment when the enemy was to waver.

"If you believe that you are fighting a just war, then the challenge for you is to come forward and kill or be killed, a most natural thing for a warrior to do. But if you don't believe in the tyrant who is paying you nothing for your sacrifices then step aside and we shall spare your lives." Hidas's words were falling at the right place, and there were many, which after a moment's hesitation moved away from the battleground. The threats of the commanders were unable to make them come and take their ranks. They had enough, none of those wanted to die without any valid reason.

"I don't have any intention of harming you, nor have we come to take what's not ours. Here comes the last warning, move away from our way or get ready to die." Those words made few more detach themselves from the others and join the group, which had decided not to take part in the battle. They all were watching the two armies getting ready to attack each other. The tiny force of Furzomia looked so unimpressive, but the way they fought, made them wonder what they were made of. Hidas was leading the attack, sitting on his swift horse, moving from one corner to the other like a storm wind. His sword's sharp edge was cutting all that came its way. The enemy was terrorised by those fierce attacks, which were coming like the never-ending gusts. Their energies were quickly waning, their bodies were getting numb but the forces of Furzomia who looked as fresh as they had been from the beginning of the battle. If they were not wrong Hidas, was getting more ferocious in his attacks, which none could withstand. His one blow could cut the huge horse and its rider into two pieces. The army was diminishing so rapidly that there was little hope of them surviving the day. Many of the soldiers were regretting the decision not to heed the warning, but it was too late for them.

The local population with a great jubilation received the news of the destruction of the Pampicilos's army in Kildia. People were streaming out from their homes to greet the army, which had accomplished the great task. They were unsure about the designs of the new invaders, but when they saw that the soldiers were from their own country, they started dancing with joy. They took it for granted that it was the royal units that had taken the country back from the tyrant of Elbon. Hidas had instructed to the soldiers that they were not to give any information to the people except that their days of miseries had come to an end. The soldiers wanted to proclaim him as the new ruler of Kildia, but Hidas stopped them from doing so. He had no claim on the land and had just liberated it from the clutches of Pampicilos to make him weak. He was not going back before he crushed the next centre of Pampicilos's power, the land of Parnvan. His Kildian troops knew the way very well that could lead him there in the shortest possible time. Hidas wasted no time in taking up his pursuit of Elbonian armies stationed there. When he and his army reached there, they were met with a scared and wretched civilian population, which had been left behind by those units of the army, which had deserted their posts and opted to run away rather than to take a stand. The news of the destruction of the army and their comrades had reached them faster than anyone could have imagined. They knew that the punishment of desertion was death but that death was less sure than the one that was approaching them like a sandstorm. They had taken the route to Kildia, instead of going to their former homeland Elbon, where they would have met a worse retribution. They were hoping to get mixed up with other civilians. Hidas was kind and gentle to the civilians; he was unable to promise anything regarding their future in the country. It was for Parnvanian traders to decide, whether to allow those victims to stay in the country or to send them back. All he could promise to them was that very soon their country was to come out from its slavery, and a better life awaited them there.

Hidas had accomplished his difficult mission and secured the frontiers of the Furzomia at least from the side of Kildia. He left the administration of both the countries in the hands of his soldiers and officers, before turning to Furzomia again.

"Remember the trust I'm leaving in your hands is not to be betrayed. I'll destroy all those who even think of taking some advantage of the situation." He thought that it was a necessary warning. The fate of the territories was to be decided by those whom it belonged. Despite the request of others to stay for a while and the rest, he set on his long journey back to Furzomia. He was happy and content, wondering about the incredible victories, trying to establish his power and skills as a general. He was certain that there was some mysterious reason for the recent developments, but what that could be he was unable to find out. He knew that he had grown more confident, stronger in his already well-trimmed body, and most of all he was shocked by the cut of his sword. No sword in the world could cut that sharply, without even hurting the edge of it. He was certain that something of great importance did take place in the desert that day he was travelling with Beran, but what really was that about, he couldn't tell, and Beran was closed like a seashell. There was something about Beran, which made him uncomfortable, and that was his strange smile, which showed that he was concealing some important information from him, he could swear that Beran knew better about the time in the desert, which he couldn't account for. He was deep in his thoughts when he saw Beran coming from the opposite side. He was riding alone, as well.

"What's up? Where are you heading to?" Hidas asked surprised.

"A little bird told about your grand victory, so I was coming to congratulate you." Beran told him.

"I'm not surprised to learn that the news of my victory is already with you, as it was some time ago, but tell me how you knew that I was on my way to Furzomia." Hidas was mystified.

"The same little bird told me." Beran tried to make a joke.

"Why are you going back to Furzomia?" Beran asked.

"Don't you know? That's strange." Hidas was sarcastic.

"I believe that you should go back and wait for the army units, which are on their way to join you," Beran told him without paying any attention to his sarcasm. He told that the decision had been taken to attack Elbon from all sides. Hidas was to command the army, which was to attack from Kildia; Shamon was to attack from Parnvan.

"Are you chosen to attack from the direction of Furzomia itself?" Hidas didn't look happy to turn back as he had hoped to be the one attacking from Furzomia.

"No, I'm not given any command, though I'm given the choice to choose between two of you" Beran told him that he had already decided to join Shamon.

"My choice wasn't that difficult, remembering that you are capable to work on your own."

"Where is he? Why doesn't he accompany you?" Hidas asked.

"He would be coming with his forces later on. I was sent to inform you of the decision taken by the father and king Sarastan."

"What about Kildia? Who is to rule it, as the Kildians are too bitter from their king, who had deserted them in the hour of their need?"

"I can't answer to these political questions, but surely some solution can be found by the wise. The public memory is not strong, is a known proverb in Kildia." Beran laughed. "It'll not take long before the same people would be swearing the oaths of allegiance and loyalty towards the same very king. All that is needed is to convince people that the king was just tactical and not a coward as they blame him for."

"Why should they believe that?" Hidas asked.

"Wasn't it the Kildian units, which have freed the land?" Hidas could see what he meant and smiled.

The attack was made from three countries simultaneously, led by Hidas, Shamon, and Beran on one hand, and Shapario and Kestarius on the other. After entering into Elbon, they had subdivided themselves into smaller branches and spread like sun rays. Pampicilos had received the terrible news of the complete destruction of his huge army. He was shocked first before getting enraged and had vowed to take revenge. He had ordered a complete mobilisation and preparation for an imminent attack on Furzomia. This time he was to concentrate on his main enemy before dealing with the Kildians and regaining the lost grounds of Parnvan. He was gathering all his forces on the border of Furzomia when he got the surprising news that both sides of Kildia and Parnvan had attacked Elbon. It was too late to deploy major troops to stop the invaders, but the emergent situation had certainly jeopardised his plans to attack Furzomia. He was busy discussing with his generals about, which strategy was best to adopt, when he was informed that even an attack from Furzomia had been initiated.

"I'll not let them return alive. I'll crush these warriors and make an example of them." Pampicilos was furious. He was told that the armies coming from Parnvan and Kildia were not only young and inexperienced, but even consisted of far lesser numbers than they had earlier feared. The most amazing thing was that those unimpressive armies were making the mistake of spreading widely; thinning themselves to the extent that it was endangering their whole mission.

"What can be expected from those puppies? Send a portion of the army to rout them out. Let me deal with the main army of Furzomia first. None can stand my way once I have broken the backbone of this army." Pampicilos knew what he was talking about. He was curious to know about the person who led the Furzomian army. He was told about Shapario and Kestarius, but he had not heard of them before. He looked astonished when he learned that one of the two commanders was not even Furzomian.

"That's interesting, where does he come from?" Pampicilos asked.

"He is believed to be Elbonian." Someone informed him.

His heart grieved to know that despite his terror and immense power he had failed to subdue the whole country. It seemed that the place was still brimming with the ill willed people, which never gave up. He looked resolute to destroy that hand, which had dared to rise against him.

22

The realisation came too late for Shapario and Kestarius that they had made a terrible mistake. According to the plan, they were not supposed to make an entry into Elbon, not that they were aware of the plans of any imminent attack coming from Elbon, but to force Pampicilos to deploy a big portion of his army to meet those forces, which were attacking his country. But now their eagerness had changed the whole situation. Pampicilos had had not enough time to send any substantial part of his army to stop the entrance from Kildia and Parnvan. The untimely entry had made him understand the whole strategy and he had decided to face the Furzomian threat before he turned his gaze to the young and inexperienced army coming from the other direction. The army at his door was equally surprised to find their counterparts standing in array, ready to engage in combat. Seeing the advantage of surprise slipping out of their hands made them anxious. Though their will to fight was undaunted. Most of the soldiers that accompanied Shapario and Kestarius were Furzomian warriors, which looked at the large numbers of their adversaries and laughed in the face of a difficult task of winning a war against them. They weren't afraid of dying, as the life and death for them were the opposite sides of the same coin. They were even unconscious of the fact that some mistake had been made by their commanders.

"We have to meet and fight them, even if we are too early in the country." Kestarius told him, but Shapario just smiled.

"There are no such rules of engagement. We can play little games of rat and mouse with them." Shapario was getting rid of his anxiety and looked relaxed again.

"What's on your mind?" Kestarius asked. Shapario told him about his changed strategy and the both men laughed. The army of Pampicilos was hardly few hundred meters away from them, getting braced to start a battle while Shapario and Kestarius and their officers were busy planning their own scheme.

The commanders of the Elbonian army saw with confusion, when the Furzomian army started retreating to their country. They couldn't understand what was the purpose of that manoeuvre, did the enemy wanted them to chase the fleeing army? And if it did what purpose was to be fulfilled? They were not trained for such like eventualities and stood there, unable to react.

"I think they are fleeing, they are afraid to die. Let us chase them and make an end of the story." One of the commanders cried. None moved as they were paralysed by the fear of the king. One of them was rushed to inform Pampicilos about the new development.

"You fools, who has made you generals? Go and chase those dogs, don't dare to come back until you have destroyed them all." Pampicilos shouted with rage.

"Even if we have to chase them into Furzomia?" the general asked as to how far they were to proceed.

"Even to the gates of hell!" Pampicilos was furious.

Shapario and Kestarius were playing their war games with the army of Pampicilos. They had succeeded in taking them long into Furzomia, where they spread in all directions, making fun of the enemy, laughing at them from a safe distance. They were provoking their pursuers to split and chase them, a very known and effective strategy, which Elbonian army refused to fall a victim of. By now they knew that their strength was in unity and standing as one large body. They were not letting them play that game and awaited a chance to encircle Furzomians, but they were too quick for them.

"We thought that you were warriors, unafraid, honourable and men of principles." One of the commanders of the Elbonian army shouted.

"Yes we are, and we have come that far to fight with you, but we shall do it at the time of our on choosing. Go and wait for us in your own home grounds. We'll not take long" Kestarius shouted back. The army commanders saw the hopelessness of the situation and went back without chasing them around. They were mostly fearful that it might be some trap the Furzomians wanted to drag them into. They were heading back in a careful but swift manner as they wished to be out of Furzomia before dusk.

Hidas and his army had not found any viable opposition in the way, they were closing in the circle they had been trying to form all the time, the main reason of their giving the impression that they moved thinly and had fewer men at their disposal. No one knew that those were the elite soldiers, capable of unleashing the demons of death and destruction. They looked confident and fearless. Most of them were Kildians, but even a large number of them were the young Furzomian warriors, which had come to the verge of perfection, when it came to the art of war. They were all masters of all kinds of weapons and could fight the enemy even with their bare hands. These soldiers knew that the number of the enemy was manifold, but their hearts remained strong; perhaps even stronger was their will to prevail. The army coming from Parnvan had the most difficult task to cross the barren and unfriendly land, but in that group were the Parnvanian traders, who had seen and known every inch of that hostile landscape. The Furzomians that accompanied them were trained to bear such like difficulties. Shamon was happy that Beran had chosen to be at his side as he could take the full benefit of his wisdom. Beran's intuition had saved them many lives and avoided many disasters from taking place. They were sure to have surprised Pampicilos but needed many more accidental occurrences and factors to be benefiting them if they were to get victorious in their mission.

Shamon was not as optimistic as was Beran, but then he knew something, which Shamon didn't. They met an army waiting for them few miles away from the Elbonian capital, and knew that the enemy was aware of their presence in the country and was ready to put an end to their pressing forward. Shamon was eager to get engaged in a battle, but Beran advised him to wait for the enemy to initiate the attack.

The army of Pampicilos made a terrible war cry before attacking them. Both sides were fighting fiercely and refusing to give way. By looking at the large size of the Elbonian army, it seemed that the battle could go on for days before the outcome could be known. Shamon was mostly worried about the danger of getting surrounded by the enemy. Each time the enemy tried to ensnare them, they would make a ferocious attack and break the closing circle against them. They felt that their strength was declining with each passing hour; more and more of their companions were showing signs of fatigue. They all were fighting with all their might and will they held, but that seemed to be not enough in their struggle against a very strong enemy. They had been fighting all day without caring for hunger or thirst. Many of their companions were seriously injured, many were dead, but there was no end in sight. The enemy was conscious that it had driven them to the breaking point and only needed a last push before they could trample them for good. They had no intention of easing up at that crucial moment, so the battle went on raging even after dusk. Beran was fighting with all the might he had but knew that his body couldn't take much more. But suddenly his face lit up and he started fighting with more zeal than before. He was giving courage to his companions and asking them to hold on for a little while longer. He could feel that help was on the way, so he told the soldiers fighting near to him to spread the happy tidings to others. No one saw any reason for that enthusiasm, but they did as they were asked to. For a moment that message filled the fighting men with new vigour, but the hours were ticking away, and no change took place. The tired men were once again gliding back to gloom and hopelessness, seeing the end of their lives. As the hope to survive the day was waning, they heard the tremor of riders coming from some direction. For a while, the fight slowed down. The both armies were confused about the force, which was approaching them with an incredible speed. The army of Pampicilos was sure that fresh units of their army were on the way to help them accomplish their task in a less painful way. The darkness was hiding the faces of the advancing force. When the riders stopped and took their positions beside the army, which had come from Parnvan, the mystery was solved, making the army of Pampicilos lament as they saw the moment of their victory slipping away from their hands, a golden opportunity to extinguish the enemy coming to naught. There was no point for them to continue the battle as they themselves needed rest after such a prolonged and fierce battle. The night wasn't the best time to wage a battle, especially when the enemy had gotten the reinforcement and darkness was making it impossible to distinguish between friends and foes.

Shamon and his soldiers were that tired of their labour that they found it hard even to express their joy over the coming of Hidas to their rescue. They looked at their rescuer with exhausted but thankful eyes and wondered what they were doing in that part of Elbon. Hidas told that he was heading to the capital from the other side, when he met someone, who told them about a fierce fight going on between two armies. He couldn't have translated that other than that it was Shamon and Beran, who were in the middle of a big battle.

"Take all your men and withdraw few miles. You need rest." Hidas told his brothers.

"No way. We shall fight by your side. The enemy is too strong and too many. To overcome it we need all of our combined resources," Shamon said.

"Trust me; their large number is no problem to me. I'll destroy them completely." Hidas was confident.

"We know that you are capable of performing miracles but why to make it harder than it is." Shamon insisted.

"You tell him what I mean." Hidas said turning to Beran.

"Why me!" Beran asked with a smile, getting his hint.

"It's just a feeling, which I feel in my bone marrow that I'm going to prevail. Exactly in the same manner as Beran gets his intuitions and you know, where to turn to in order to get the needed money." Hidas explained

"Alright, but what are we to do about those, which are seriously injured?" Shamon asked advice.

"What else than to leave them behind in some nursing hands. We'll not leave anyone alive of the enemy to harm them. Get ready and concentrate on the final encounter, which awaits near the capital." Beran and Shamon were too shattered to think of the day and just wanted to rest and sleep.

The next morning they didn't stay to watch or to take part in the on-going battle, they were heading to the capital, where they were to wait for Hidas and his army. Most of the soldiers were deliberately moving in a very slow pace, either they were too weary or they were anxious about facing an enemy force, which was tenfold than they had just almost lost against, their Morales weren't at the peak at that very moment. Unlike their commanders, they were not sure that Hidas was to destroy that formidable army of the enemy in a single day. They had their doubts about that presumption as it was different to rout an army, which was so far away from its centre and lacked both the moral support of the people and conviction about the justification. The armies standing at the gates of its capital were strong, large in number and had the moral edge of fighting a war of survival, defending its country against invaders. No one knew the fact better than Beran, who had started growing worried and doubtful about the chances of their success.

"You press ahead but don't get engaged in a new battle until Hidas arrives," Beran told Shamon before he turned back to the battlefield.

"What's going on? Why you have to go back there? If it's your intuition, then we all turn back to aid Hidas?" Shamon looked anxious.

"No, I don't feel any danger for him but I have to talk with Hidas about some things that bother me." Beran told him casually, before returning. Shamon sighed heavily at the strange behaviour of Beran. He stood there in indecision but then started moving to the direction of the capital, thinking how it could be possible to avoid a battle if they were to stand staring in the eyes of their enemy.

Hidas and his men were busy destroying the enemy force; they were doing that job with such ease that Beran couldn't help being stunned. The enemy had been reduced to much smaller size and number. Beran could see the terror stricken faces of the enemy soldiers, which were unable to understand why their opponents were superior to them, why the swords they held were ten times sharper and many times stronger than their own swords? Why the Morales of the combatants were so much higher than their own? In the middle of that battle, Hidas got sight of Beran and looked puzzled. He dropped down his hand, which was holding the sword that was unbeatable and rode towards his youngest brother, without paying any attention to the enemy around. No one tried to take advantage of his apparent off guard attitude. The enemy soldiers looked terror-stricken and watched him move graciously between them to reach Beran. Seeing Hidas make a halt, his men stopped fighting as well, with watchful readiness to resume the fight if the enemy tried to take an advantage of the situation, but the remaining enemy soldiers, who were still at least double than their own numbers were too scared to provoke the resumption of the battle. They were still weary from the previous day's fight, and the renewed battle had consumed all their energies, if the death was the answer, then they wished that it should come to them as quickly as possible, to relieve them from the agony. But the unexpected pause in the fighting was baffling them more than it surprised Hidas's men.

"Why have you come back?" Hidas asked. Beran told him about his thoughts about the forthcoming big moment, about how he feared that their forces fell short in size and number, how he deemed it an impossible mission. He could see from the face of Hidas that he was both angry and irritated.

"Have you come all the way here to share your anxiety with me?"

"No, I'm here to discuss something, which can turn the odds in over favour."

"I'm listening," Hidas said, still irritated. Beran was talking to him while he pondered on the departed words. Hidas's anger was turning into pleasant smile; he patted his brother's back and went towards the battlefield. Hidas made it clear that he intended to say something.

"Before we resume our fight, my younger brother has to say something. Listen to him carefully before you decide to live or die." Beran came near to the enemy positions and waited for them to get completely silent.

"Listen to me, soldiers of Elbon. We have come to your land, not to enslave it as it is already enslaved. We are here to bring back the dignity and freedom you lost long ago. We are none others than the rightful heirs of the throne of Elbon, the princes of this kingdom, who have come to seek justice and redeem the kingdom from those who stole it by deceit and cunning. We are giving you three options; you may choose one of these. You can lay down your arms and walk home, you can become one of us by joining our ranks, or you can choose to go on fighting us and die. If you are to help us in our fight against the tyrant there would be an unfailing reward as you would be showing your loyalties to the rightful king of this country, but if you prefer to serve your evil master, we shall give you the gift of perdition." Beran spoke in a powerful voice, making it clear that he meant each and every word of him. There was a complete silence; the enemy was still shocked at the echo of his words. There were some expressions of doubts; some exchanges of gazes and some reluctance, but there arose a sound, which could make the hearts of even brave tremble. The enemy was rushing towards them, like some uncontrolled natural force. Hidas and his men were not prepared for such a fury, but calmed down, when they realised that the enemy soldiers were expressing their joy after knowing that their former king and his sons had returned to them, to free the country from the hands of Pampicilos. There were emotional scenes, in which the distinctions between the two combatant armies were quickly fading. Suddenly no one wanted to fight back. Some of the soldiers and the commanders had opted to stay neutral by laying their arms while the majority of the soldiers was eagerly joining their struggle against Pampicilos. Beran was a bit worried about his new soldiers. He couldn't help thinking, how were they to react to the fact of facing their own brothers from Elbon, which awaited them in the capital. Were they strong enough to make the distinction between right and wrong and to take a moral stand or were to cause some serious trouble by their wavering attitudes. Only the time could tell, how those soldiers were to act and react, as most of them were young and had no former memories of the bygone days, neither did they have any previous allegiance or loyalties towards the former king and his princes. Beran was certain that those soldiers were not to trust or to rely upon. What he really wanted to achieve was to spread the news that king Tylon and his sons were not only alive but had come to reclaim their rights to that kingdom. He was sure that news was to divide the army and the country into two, and therewith making their task a bit easier. Some of the soldiers of Elbonian army were from the period when Tylon was the king while many had forgotten the name, while most of them had never heard of the man, but even then the news was to bring about the deep divisions among the population of the country and cause anxiety to Pampicilos, who had almost forgotten about the former king and his three sons. The man had been a champion of handling the crises, how he was to face the biggest challenge of his life, was to be seen.

The news of the return of the king Tylon and his princes spread like a jungle fire in width and breadth of the country bringing memories of long gone days back, the bitterness and the pains caused by healed wounds were remembered again. People felt forced to bear in mind the causes of their miserable lives. Many of the people felt happy that their former king was not dead as they had presumed for years and which had come to take the revenge from those, who had deprived him of his kingdom. But still most of Elbonians dared not think aloud as they were scared to death from Pampicilos, who was stronger than any other country in the area. They were not sure if the advancing armies of the former king were capable of re-capturing the land. Judging from what they had learned, the forces of the princes were far smaller in size than the armies of Pampicilos. But they were praying for the success of those smaller but ardent armies, which were coming nearer and nearer to the capital. When Pampicilos was told about the destruction of his huge army he shivered with rage, unable to understand why his well-trained armies were unable to crush a tiny force. He couldn't bear the humiliation of getting the defeat at the hands of some young and inexperienced man but that his troops had surrendered or joined the ranks of the invaders was too much for him to bear. What made him even angrier was the news that the commanders were none else than the former princes of Elbon. His blood boiled with anger, when he thought about the stupidity of his brother Razila, who in fact, was the real cause of his present troubles. Had he taken care of the royal family at the time of invading Elbon, there would be no princes to worry about at that time?

He was worried about the loyalties of his men, which stood cleaved between the two of their kings. He was sure that his soldiers were not to be counted completely, especially when they were not even receiving their proper wages. The minting of the coins had started making people realize that the money had lost its value. Though they were unable to pinpoint the real causes, but the anger against was registered, if not openly then at least in the hearts. Pampicilos had a hope of straitening the affairs, once he had occupied Furzomia, but that hope was fading as he faced the severe problems in his own power centre. He called for his generals and other administrators and reminded them of his kindness and favours he had bestowed on them. He was telling them that he was the best king they ever could think of, a king that had seen to it that Elbon grew richer, stronger and respected. He demanded their unwavering loyalties and promises that they were to fight till death. He was a master of manipulation, capable to conceal his own anxiety and fearfulness from his attendants. He looked as calm and collected as he had always appeared. Some of his friends requested him to make reconciliation with Razila, thereby augmenting his armies with his, but Pampicilos rejected the idea with contempt. He was clever enough to realise that his problems had nothing to do with the size or strength of the army. His army was not only the largest in the whole region but even the well equipped and well trained. The only problem was that not all of them were ready for the eventuality of fighting against their former king. Pampicilos discussed with his commanders and gave them instructions as to how they could approach their soldiers and t poison their minds against the former king and the three impostors, calling themselves the princes of Elbon.

"You are to confront and deny that the king Tylon is alive. All the talk about the king and princes is to confuse and divide the army and people. Once you succeed in accomplishing that task, we have won the war, which waits." Pampicilos was giving them the guidelines. He knew that his position was weakened by the news of royal princes, coming to free their realm from foreign occupiers but he wasn't giving up that easily, he intended to fight back with all the strength and intended to overcome as he had always done till then. No one could win from him in the game of propaganda.

Beran was right in his assessment that it was beneficial to disclose the identity of them before launching the attack. The army of Pampicilos was too big to be encircled and crushed as they had earlier planned in Furzomia. The reality was far discouraging than they could have imagined back home. They felt forced to reevaluate their strategies and finally decided to face the enemy in a traditional battle manner. Both sides were arraying against each other, displaying their weapons and skills to use them. All three brothers and the other two commanders were having a meeting and discussing their tactics of the battle. They had broken the older patterns of the army and had regrouped and reorganised them. Those, which were experts of spears, were to be led by Shapario, who had it as his speciality; the archers were to be commanded by Kestarius while the warriors and soldiers, who were to fight with only swords, were given in the commands of Hidas and Shamon. Beran was little confused about the divisions and wondered if it was necessary to make those divides.

"Don't worry about these tactical matters. You can see for yourself that our warriors are equipped with all kinds of weapons and can use them all according to the need." Kestarius told him dryly, the tall giant like man was always friendly to Beran, even more than he was towards Hidas.

"Which group am I to belong?" Beran asked.

"What more can you do, except wield the sword?" Kestarius asked. Beran understood what he meant by that, but felt embarrassed when the others laughed.

Beran was still anxious about the soldiers, who had recently joined them, but Hidas was more relaxed.

"Don't worry about them, if they tried to be funny, I shall take care of them as they would be fighting in my command." Hidas was confident.

The war signal came, and soldiers from Elbonian army advanced but were pushed back by the powerful warriors, which were holding the piercing sharp spears in their hands while the archers were raining the arrows over the opponents. They were inflicting pain, death, and panic on their enemies. The pressure was mounting, and the desperate attempts to break the lines of these powerful warriors were getting stronger and stronger, but those resolute men were there to resist those pressures as long as they could. The rain of the arrows went on. All of a sudden those warriors with spears gave way, moving quickly to their new positions, exposing the spear holders of the enemy, which had failed to notice that the removal of the warriors from their places was more to expose them to the archers than of any other reason. Many of them were falling victim to the arrow attack, which struck and killed them. The warriors were going on with their given tasks of attacking and retreating as it required, providing the chance for the archers to accomplish their missions. They had caused much harm to the enemy, which were getting furious at their refusal to get engaged in combat. All they had been able to achieve was to push the enemy back a few hundred meters, which wasn't enough, considering the size of their army. All day long Furzomian warriors had been playing with their counterparts, and by doing so had caused much injury and casualty on them. No one had time to count the dead, so Pampicilos's army was forced to sit and re-evaluate its strategies at the end of the day. King Pampicilos was enraged that his enormous army was toyed by a little force of warriors, which were able to hold them back with spears.

"Where are our soldiers who are trained to combat with spears?" Pampicilos demanded.

None had the guts to give the bad news that the most of his soldiers capable to meet the enemy were already dead, pierced by the sharp edges of the arrows. Their archers were not placed in the right positions to inflict any major harm to the enemy, was another truth, they had concealed from the king as it would have caused his outrage.

"I want you to crush the enemy, if you can't accomplish the task, then I'll have no choice but to decapitate you all and lead the army myself." Pampicilos was furious; he made it clear to his commanders that he was not to tolerate any further delay in obeying his orders. The threat of Pampicilos failed to bring the desired effect as it was beyond the power of his generals to crush the enemy, which kept changing its tactics, creating serious problems for them. The more Pampicilos pressured his generals, the more they felt stressed and incompetent. Many of their soldiers were impressed from their counterparts and were deserting their own units to join the forces of the princes or were simply disappearing from their camps, but still the number of Elbonian army was too much, when Hidas and his brothers decided to start the real battle. They had seen the weaknesses and strengths of their opponents and felt ready to have a decisive combat.

23

For five days, both armies made fierce battles against each other, without any side giving way. The army of princes wasn't easy to combat and win over. Those warriors were simply too tough to be defeated. They were fighting so bravely that even larger numbers seemed inadequate to scare them. They were disregardful if they were to live or to die, all they really cared was that they inflicted as much pain and destruction on their opponents as possible. Their fearlessness was sending waves of shock and disbelief in the army of Pampicilos, which was getting not only weary but also even terrified of their strange enemies, which smiled in the face of certain death. The sixth day when these armies arrayed themselves to resume the combat, the generals could not ignore the fact that most of their soldiers had either perished or had forsaken them as their army stood almost matching the size of the enemy force. It was that realisation, which was enough a sign to confirm their doubts about the outcome of the war. If they had been doubtful about their ability to win the battle, it was getting as clear as the noonday that the battle was already lost. Hidas, Shamon and Shapario were standing, giving last minute instructions to their men. The other side was looking gloomy and showed little enthusiasm. Just by looking at their hopeless faces one could guess that they were getting ready for their ends, rather than entering into a combat, which they believed would lead them to victory. The battle was to start, when a rider came from the side of town with some important message to the generals. They were standing and discussing something with each other while the warriors of Furzomia and other soldiers waited impatiently for the battle to start. One of the enemy generals finally rode forward to the direction of Hidas. His lowered sword indicated that he desired a dialogue and not hostility. Coming closer, he started telling Hidas something and then came down from his horse, bowed and threw his sword on the ground, a clear sign that he was surrendering. There was a great uproar and war cries as the enemy generals; one after the other came forward and surrendered before their counterparts. The army of Pampicilos had accepted its defeat as the news was broken to them that Pampicilos had fled from Elbon last night. The soldiers were standing with bowed heads and ignominy covering their faces. They were at the mercy of their enemy, which could make them slaves or kill them, such was the tradition, and they expected nothing else either. The army of the princes' was jubilant; they were dancing, singing and congratulating each other on such a wonderful achievement. They had made a history, they had just achieved something, which none could believe they were capable to attain. They were extremely happy to get the chance to avenge the deaths of their fallen companions by killing the prisoners of war, but they felt robbed as Hidas made it clear that the prisoners were not to be harmed. There was a cry of indignation, declaring the order to be unjust, but Hidas chose to ignore the protest. The anger of his soldiers was many times stronger when he declared that the enemy soldiers were not to be taken as slaves either.

"Those of you, who challenge my decision, let them come forward." Hidas challenged the soldiers, which were dissatisfied with his strange decision. There was a murmur of dissatisfaction, but none dared to come forward. Shamon smiled at Beran. He was a trader, who could understand the desperation of the warriors who had put their lives at stake and wanted some sweet reward for their sacrifices, retribution for all the pains and sufferings that the enemy had inflicted on them, and compensation for all their sacrifices and efforts. Beran could also feel that the soldiers were unhappy and were unable to find any logic to the decree of their commander.

"The reason Hidas asked you to neither kill nor make them slaves is simple, they are our brothers as you all are. How can we make them our slaves or even to kill them? Do you believe that we shall kill you or even enslave you if you stood in their place, repentant and defeated?" The soldiers listened to him in silence, but one could see they were still not satisfied. Shamon looked at his brothers and smiled before going forward and speaking to the soldiers. He told them that being a trader he understood their anger, but saw no other solution and decision than his brothers stood for, except that he intended to compensate them for each and every prisoner of war. They all could get the money equalling to the sum they were losing due to the amnesty given to the enemy soldiers. Every soldier was dancing and singing once again, praising the generosity of the prince who had been blessed with unlimited riches.

Hidas was of the opinion to go after Pampicilos, but his brothers and others were telling him to take it easy as there wasn't any hurry to bring the man to justice. They needed a time to rest and relax and to enjoy the fruits of their hard labour. A message was sent home, and they awaited the arrival of their parents to Elbon, which eagerly wanted to embrace them. The royal palace was decorated like a bride, the streets of the capital were lit with candles and lights of all kinds, the buildings were whitewashed and decorated with fresh flowers, which made the whole town look and smell like a garden. People of Elbon had gathered in thousands to get a glimpse of their former king and his wife who were returning home, they had beaten their enemies and were doing something, which none could have hold possible. Haliba and Tylon entered their capital, sitting in a carriage, which was drawn by ten horses. They both were wearing their crowns and looked far younger than they really were; their faces were glowing of happiness. People could see their broad smiles but couldn't see the tearful eyes. Both of them had not anticipated the day and were silently crying of happiness. They had opposed all such suggestions to make such triumphant entrance to the capital but had to give way to the wishes of their children, who insisted that the couple stepped in as the natural royalties of Elbon.

The festivities were to go on for several days, in which came the kings of Furzomia and Kildia to take part and to give their greetings and best wishes. There were even ambassadors of other far away countries, which extended the best wishes of their monarchs and people. The news had spread that the combined armies of the three kings could conquer any country of the region and that was the main cause of worry, but the princes had no designs to attack any country around, except the land lying to the south of Elbon, where Razila was still the ruler, who had been joined by his brother Pampicilos, the two treacherous people they had not dealt with yet. Hidas' eagerness to turn his face towards the tyrants of the south was finally understood by Tylon, who gave permission to attack that land. Every soldier wanted to join him in his expedition, but Hidas wanted to deal with the men with not so big army as he wanted to give both brothers a fair chance to defend themselves, so he took a few thousand of his warriors along and headed south. He swore to bring the both men dead or alive before his father to get their retribution directly from them. Shamon and Beran wanted to accompany him, but he insisted on going alone.

"The crushing of the snakes isn't that great a task to require the combined efforts of us all." Hidas said with a smile. Tylon and Haliba agreed to their eldest son and felt confident that he was capable to accomplish the mission on his own. A thorough search was ordered to find the whereabouts of Sakuri, the traitor. Aloha and her daughter Davreen were given back all their possessions which they had been deprived of for decades, and they were even given the compensation for their miseries and sufferings. Davreen had married a trader from Parnvan and felt happy. Tylon decided to change all the cruel laws, which had been enforced during his absence. He even abolished all the unjust taxes, to give a chance to his subjects to have reasonable and comfortable lives.

They were impatiently waiting for news from Hidas, but there wasn't any, making them all a bit nervous. They had been anxious and wondered if Hidas had been right in his judgement to face the two of the most treacherous and dangerous men with such a little force. Despite the doubts of others; Beran was the only one, who wasn't nervous at all, he was as confident about the outcome as Hidas had been. The news came that Hidas was on his way back from the south. There were so little details about his mission, so they wondered eagerly what really had taken place. They were sure that he must have accomplished his mission, but were interested to know the details. Hidas and his army were met at the gates of the capital. He was riding with a force, which was half the size he had left with a few weeks ago. Many hearts were anguished fearing personal losses, but the general mood was joyous. Tylon was waiting impatiently for his son Hidas to come and give him the great news himself. Hidas entered the court and announced with a smile that his mission was accomplished. Tylon could see the pride on the face of his son and felt content. On the sign of Hidas, the attendants split and gave way to the soldiers, which pushed the two of the brothers before Tylon. The two prisoners looked down in defeat and humiliation, avoiding the eyes of Tylon. They were tied with strong chains and were bleeding. If the wounds were inflicted in some battle, or were the result of the chains was a difficult task to guess.

"Welcome to my kingdom!" King Tylon said with a sad smile, looking deep in the eyes of Razila. "I'm sure you must be regretting the day when you had the chance to eliminate me you didn't, relying too confidently on the crooked conquest of yours. Tell me how should I punish you for the most hideous crimes that you committed against my family, my people, and me?

"Kill the men, kill the men." Everyone in the court was recommending while Razila and his brother were silent and pale.

"Pampicilos, how does it feel to be deprived of that power and authority, which make you feel untouchable? Do you still advocate the death penalty to the defeated one, as you pleaded the day I stood before your brother as a prisoner?" Tylon was reminding him. Both the prisoners were looking terrified but dared not open their mouths. King Tylon looked at their faces and then spoke.

"You are as much my offenders as you are to my entire family and country, so I leave your fate in the hands of my princes." Tylon's words were met with applaud of the courtiers.

Hidas was too quick to react and saw no other punishment more appropriate for the culprits than the death penalty. Both Shamon and Beran were in deep thoughts, which were overweighing the suitable punishments for the criminals. They quickly counselled with each other, and the Beran spoke on behalf of both.

They both shared the opinion of Hidas that the men deserved death sentence but suggested that they were not only guilty of committing crimes against them and their country, but were equally accountable to the people of the southern country. The best way to punish them was to hand them over to the people of the southern country. Most of the attendants were shocked to hear such a proposition, fearing that it was equal to giving them back their kingdom, but the pale faces of Razila and Pampicilos suddenly looked more terrified than ever. They were pleading and begging for a quick death penalty. To fall into the hands of those people, they had been so cruelly reigning over was too freighting an idea.

"I leave your fate in the hands of your own people if they decide to place you back on the throne or to quench your lives remains with their decision." Tylon told the brothers, who were begging him to change his mind regarding the punishment.

The news came that Sakuri had been found. After fleeing from Elbon, he had settled in some remote part of Kildia, where he had spent calm, anonymous life with his family until he got seriously sick and died a few years back, leaving two sons a miserable life. His widow and two sons still lived in that remote place and were ashamed and regretful about the crime of Sakuri.

"But wasn't I told that the traitor had succeeded in taking all the treasures with him when he fled the country?" Tylon showed his surprise that the sons of Sakuri were leading miserable lives.

"You have heard absolutely right your majesty." He was told. "But the man never entrusted it even to his own family. He had buried the treasures somewhere and had never gotten the opportunity to confine the whereabouts to anyone, even though he desperately tried to tell in the last moments of his life."

"What are we to do with his remaining family? The Kildian representative asked from Tylon.

"Nothing. They aren't guilty of any crime and don't deserve any punishment." Tylon told his guest, and the court praised his prudence.

Tylon and Haliba tried their best to convince their children to free them of their royal responsibilities, but no one was interested. Hidas was deeply in love again and had gone to

Furzomia to be near princess Danor and the man he had
considered his father for his whole life.

Shamon was homesick and couldn't imagine a life anywhere
else than in Parnvan, his beloved town and its broad streets,
with all the luxurious buildings and other comforts he had
grown used to. The only prince who remained was Beran, but
even he was not ready for the task. He believed that the royal
couple was still not too old to perform their duties. He could
think of sharing their burden but only in due course. Right at
that moment he needed to move around in a carefree fashion.
Tylon and Haliba had no other choice but to remain the king
and queen of Elbon, where life was quickly turning to
normal, where people were slowly but surely regaining their
respect and worthiness back along with the economic well
being and political stability. The old trade routes were once
again opened, and law and order were quickly established. A
new era was beginning, and everyone was happy for that.
Beran was heading to Furzomia to meet Hidas, thinking
about the wonderful gift of his, which was providing him
with all the knowledge he desired. No-one knew about his
secret of the magic eye, which could provide him with all the
answers. All he had to do was to look into that stone eye,
which became magnetic and drew him inside. He felt like
being drowned in its bottomless depths, a very
uncomfortable feeling but a mood, which always brought the
knowledge of the things he sought information about. The
eye was like an ocean, where could be found everything. It
was able to pierce the skies, penetrate into the depths of the
earth and yet he found the eye disappearing from his sight. In
a most peculiar way, he had the feeling of loosing his own
self, his identity, his integration. He had the bizarre feeling of
becoming the eye itself until he had gotten the required
answers to his questions. Then the process of getting back to
normality would start, and he would feel the grip of the eye
loosing its magnetic power and he would find his way back to
his own self. Beran knew that the gift was getting over all his

faculties. He was so overwhelmed that he stopped using his own intellect and relied more and more on the eye, a very worrying development, an addiction and reliance, he wanted to break but didn't know how was he to accomplish that? He was deep in his thoughts, when he met Trindras on the way. Beran smiled recognising him, laughing, when Trindras raised his both hands in the air to welcome him in Furzomia.

"What brings you to my way this time?" Beran asked.

"I have come to congratulate you on succeeding in your mission." Trindras told him.

Why so much trouble. Who would fail, when so much power is invested in one's hands? Isn't it all due to the mercy of gods?" Beran asked humbly. Trindras looked amused by his words.

"Sometimes I wonder why you are degraded down to become a prince. You are more a breed like me." Beran laughed at his allegory and added that they both were strange loners, which played with the sharp swords and fought their enemies. Beran asked for advice regarding the gifts they had chosen from Senklour.

"What about them?" Trindras asked.

"I believe that they are more curses than blessings in the hands of uninitiated one's. I fear for my brothers as they can get corrupted by that immense power, which they are not even conscious about." Beran told him. Trindras looked deeply impressed by his fears and thoughts and then smiled, remembering that Beran was not only equipped with the knowledge and insight, but also even possessed the wisdom of the world. He reminded Beran that those gifts were given to them as a favour, as a choice, and it was only they, who could decide how to use them. If they misused them, they were to destroy them and return to Senklour as a consequence; otherwise they could hold them till the end of their lives.

"Is there no third option?" Beran asked. Trindras kept silent as if deciding to speak or not. He spoke finally.

"It seems you are not told about the third possibility!"

"What's that?" Beran was eager.

"If you all lay down your gifts in a certain manner and a certain place, you can get rid of the possibility of misusing them, or even the certainty of them disappearing from your world. If you choose to proceed that way, you can leave behind these gifts for some other people and times a possibility to face some evil, which otherwise would find no opposing force to stop it."

"What do you mean by that? What other times? What other people?" Beran was feeling incited by his mysterious words.

"I am just talking about a possibility for some other individuals, who can get these gifts at their disposal if you opt to leave them behind now, when you are in the prime of your age, and no mistakes have been made."

Beran was pensive he was thinking about the subject, which seemed to be impossible. How could he talk and convince his brothers to abandon some gifts from some mysterious land, which neither they were conscious of nor he was supposed to talk about? Trindras smiled as if he could read his mind and see his dilemma.

"Try to remember: what restrictions were placed on you?" Trindras asked.

"I am not supposed to tell them about the magical qualities that are in their hands," Beran told him.

"Then don't tell them. But still it doesn't stop you from begging them to give those to you."

"You believe that they will agree to that?" Beran was excited.

"I don't doubt for a minute, especially when they remain unconscious about the reasons behind their powers." Trindras told him.

"Where shall I place those gifts when or if I succeed to get hold of them?"

"Just do it I'll come to you myself."

"Tell me Trindras, who are you?" Beran asked.

"It depends from whom you ask, to certain people I'm the hermit that gave the good tidings to your father, Tylon, to others I'm the stranger, who told to Hidas that a battle was raging, in which you needed a desperate help, to you I'm Trindras, the teacher. Isn't your question irrelevant?" Trindras smiled and went his way, leaving Beran to wonder about his words. He was riding in a slow speed, trying to figure out, what he was supposed to do to ask the precious gifts of both his brothers. He wanted to proceed carefully, not to raise any suspicion. He was quite sure that Shamon was not to be hesitant to give him the precious stone, which was fitted in his ring, but to get the sword of Hidas was much harder task, he had to wait for the proper time and place to ask him that. If that time was ever to come, was an open question.

Hidas had decided to marry princess Danor, and wished all his family to come to his wedding. Tylon and Haliba were extremely happy for their eldest son. They both liked the princess who was so very impressed by Hidas that she would fight against the whole world if it were required of her. Her love for Hidas was stronger than anything. She told King Sarastan that she would have married him even if he were a simple blacksmith. They all came to attend the marriage of Hidas and Danor. It was during the marriage ceremony that Beran decided to put Hidas in an embarrassing position. At the time of exchange of presents, Beran gave him the most exclusive sword in the whole world, with the most precious stones engraved on its handle and sheathe. They all couldn't help but to appraise the sword, even King Sarastan took the sword in his hand and praised its beauty.

"Thank you, for bringing the most wonderful present," Hidas thanked him publicly.

"You are welcome." Beran was smiling, watching him happy for the occasion.

"I have something for you as well." Hidas said with a smile and handed him something wrapped in a cloth made of golden threads.

"Do you mind, if I am to ask for something which I have long wished for?" Beran asked loudly.

"Of course, you may, my dear brother, only if it's in my power to satisfy your wish."

"I want your sword," Beran asked in a loud, strong voice so that all present could hear. He could see that pale and shocked face of his brother, who had not expected that request. Hidas was very annoyed at the request but found no way to deny him his request, as he had given him the words before so many people. Beran could see the smile on the face of Shapario, who knew about the passion, Hidas felt for the sword. He looked amused as Hidas was struggling with himself.

"Why this hesitation brother? Is it not in your power to grant my wish?" Beran teased him, making everyone laugh. Hidas was still unmoved.

"Darling, you are embarrassing yourself and me." Danor whispered to Hidas, who struggled hard to smile. His murderous eyes could not conceal the truth of his frustration.

"I didn't know that I'm asking something that's dear to you? If you want to revoke from your promise, it's alright for me." Beran was cunning and knew that wasn't an option.

"Of course not. My words are more holy than anything else in the world." Hidas said giving him the sword with a shaking hand. They all laughed and praised his nobility, but the day had been destroyed for Hidas, no one saw him smile for the rest of the day, not even during the marriage ceremony. He kept looking at the sword, which was his but now belonged to Beran, a thing he was never to forget.

To get the gift of Shamon was a less difficult thing. He didn't have to trick him as he did to Hidas; all he needed to do was to ask Shamon, who without any hesitation or question gave him the ring. Tylon and Haliba though couldn't help getting little hurt at his peculiar behaviour. It wasn't a pleasant thing to note that their youngest son was acting more like a beggar than a worthy prince. But they didn't make an issue out of the whole affair. Beran could know what they thought about him but couldn't explain why he did so. Now he was in possession of all three wonderful things from Senklour. He was very happy and felt the power of those magical things entering his body. He felt incredibly strong and his determination to surrender them grew weaker. He was questioning the need of putting them aside for someone else's possible use. Why should he do it for those people of some other times, to whom he had no obligations for? The more he struggled with his doubts the more strongly they grew. He was on the verge of revoking from his earlier decision to place the gifts of Senklour to the safe place, Trindras had suggested. Suddenly he looked at the eye and saw himself there. He saw himself so very huge, so very powerful that he became scared by it. He saw that it was not he, who was the most powerful being but a prisoner of that immense power. He dragged himself out from the eye and decided to fulfil the promise to himself that he was to leave all three items and lead a normal life.

He saw Trindras coming to him and smiled at him.

"Are you sure that you want to put these things for some future use by someone, who might need these powers to confront some evil prince?"

"Yes, I am sure of that." Beran assured him.

"Even knowing that you can keep all these three gifts in your hands?"

"Yes, even with that knowledge. The more I know the more I shiver, thinking the responsibility of that being, which would be entrusted with these powers." Beran was expressing his awe at such an occasion.

"I can see that you have felt a taste of that overwhelming power." Trindras said with a smile.

"Believe me if anyone would be given a right to use these immense powers, the person or persons must first prove to be worthy. But if he or they failed in their mission, the power shall destroy the world, before returning to their natural abode, Senklour." Trindras said with a smile.

"Why is that?" Beran couldn't understand what he meant.

"I can't explain to you because you wouldn't understand. The qualities of these things are not what you can discover at present. They shall be entirely different in their constructive or destructive uses. The sword of iron shall not exist, except its destructive quality inherent in it, the ring shall not just create the money but the economic power would be the most potent power on the earth, and I don't even want to talk about the power of knowledge as you have already known a little," Trindras said.

"Why worry if this power can stop the evil?" Beran asked.

"Don't you know that everything in the universe has an opposite? So the powers coming from the opposite world of Senklour shall make the world shiver before these gifts shall be even discovered by someone," Trindras explained vaguely.

They both stood there before they decided to move to the place, where they were to hide the three magical gifts of Senklour. For months, they pressed ahead, leaving no trace for anyone to follow, as the sacred mission required all the precautions if they were to accomplish their task successfully.

When Beran came back, Hidas had accepted the fact of losing his best friend, his passion and love, the magical sword, which he never knew was not the same he once got from Shapario. The missing of Beran, without any trace had given him some perspective and bad conscience. He was sorry to have hated his brother for robbing him of his sword. He was happy to know that he was safe and well. Shamon had also found his love in the royal quarters of Kildian palace and was getting married to the princess. King Sarastan had nominated his daughter Danor as his successor, and thereby opening the doors for Hidas to become the king of Furzomia. The traders had agreed to merge their territory with the Kildian king if he promised to make Shamon his successor, which he immediately agreed. He loved Shamon and couldn't find a better alternative to that young, handsome, courageous, rich and generous prince, which was more worthy than him, certainly not from among his own sons, who were all more interested in the luxury lives than the affairs of the state. Beran was nominated as the crown prince of Elbon, where he was loved, respected, and known for his wisdom. Even though he had left his eye of vision at some safe place,

It never failed to give him the answers of the questions he looked for. We are told that all the princes of king Tylon did become kings, not of the same country but of different countries, which all became prosperous, strong and peaceful as none could dare to fight against them, knowing their bravery and unity. As to the magical gifts once they possessed, it is said that the time for their recovery has come, and the world shall soon know the man or the men, who shall be entrusted with those immense powers.

The End.

www.ingramcontent.com/pod-product-compliance
Lightning Source LLC
Chambersburg PA
CBHW031417240626

47154CB00001B/81